BESIDE MYSELF

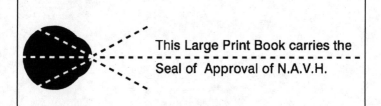

This Large Print Book carries the
Seal of Approval of N.A.V.H.

BESIDE MYSELF

ANN MORGAN

THORNDIKE PRESS
A part of Gale, Cengage Learning

GALE
CENGAGE Learning·

Farmington Hills, Mich • San Francisco • New York • Waterville, Maine
Meriden, Conn • Mason, Ohio • Chicago

GALE
CENGAGE Learning®

LIBRARY OF CONGRESS CATALOGING-IN-PUBLICATION DATA

Names: Morgan, Ann (Ann Beatrice) author.
Title: Beside myself / by Ann Morgan.
Description: Large print edition. | Waterville, Maine : Thorndike Press, 2016. |
    © 2016 | Series: Thorndike Press large print reviewers' choice
Identifiers: LCCN 2016003231 | ISBN 9781410489302 (hardcover) | ISBN 1410489302
    (hardcover)
Subjects: LCSH: Twin sisters—Fiction. | Large type books.
Classification: LCC PR6113.O7375 B47 2016 | DDC 823/.92—dc23
LC record available at http://lccn.loc.gov/2016003231

Published in 2016 by arrangement with Bloomsbury Publishing, Inc.

Printed in Mexico
1 2 3 4 5 6 7 20 19 18 17 16

For Mum

PROLOGUE

Out into the garden, sunlight blaring. Ellie lumbering after. Run along you two and don't get into mischief. The leaves of the apple tree blotching us with shadows.

Away from the dark house with the curtains pulled shut. The cushions huddling. The mumbles and sighs that boil up into yells and sobs at the sight of water rings from the bottom of a glass. A manner missed. Not me — it's always Ellie. Never my fault. I'm the good one because I was born first.

On to the bottom of the garden, behind the blackberry bush. A turn back to watch for eyes, but the coast is empty. Then up with the latch, the gate swings open and the warm sun of the lane spills in. A giggle from Ellie. A jiggle like she needs the toilet.

'Shhh, Ellie,' I say. 'Do you want the world and his wife to hear?'

Ellie's eyes go serious. People say after I came out the cord got twisted around Ellie's neck and because of that she's sometimes not as good as me. But I know she does it on purpose. I see the look she gives down at me when the teacher picks her up because she's tired.

'Do you think we should go out there without Mother knowing?' she says.

'Shut up,' I say and pull her through. 'It's only Mary.'

Mary is where we go when it's time to teach Ellie a lesson. She's older so she's the best at thinking up games. Like, one time when no one came to collect us from school we took Ellie to the park and left her there by herself and ran all the way home. I was laughing so hard I couldn't breathe with how good the lesson was and how much better I liked it than tiptoeing around the missing furniture at home.

And another time we tried to make Ellie eat a yoghurt that we found in a plastic bag on the wall by the bus stop. We did every trick in the box, but it had gone all fizzy and smelly and hard and she wouldn't touch it. Even though we threatened down on her and everything. Even though we told her it was cheese.

Mary's house is up the lane. It's not like our house because it's all on one level, like someone rolled it with a rolling pin. Plus there's all this stuff lying about where the grass and flowerbeds should be. But it is like our house because inside there's only one grown-up — Mary's dad, who does things with hammers and spanners in the garden and sometimes in the bathroom too. Plus there's also Mary's brother who is sort of in-between.

We knock and after a while a shadow comes to fill the swirly circle of glass so it looks like a dragon's eye opening. The door swings back and the sour smell comes out. The brother looks down at us, his face thin and whiskery like a wolf's.

'Hello. Is Mary in?' I say.

'Nah,' says the brother in the flat, hard way Mary says comes from Manchester where they used to live before. 'She's fucked off.'

A tremble comes over me, but I bite it back and stare up into his wolfy eyes.

'Fucked off where?' I say.

The brother smirks. His eyes go between Ellie and me. Behind him in the house, something glints.

'Twins, eh?' he says. 'How old are you girls?'

He reaches out a hand and curls a finger round behind my ear, stroking the hair there.

'You're a pretty one, aren't you?' he says.

The breeze blows.

'Say "fucked" again,' he says.

Suddenly the day comes at me in a rush, all the colours singing. I turn and grab Ellie's hand.

'We've got to go,' I say, and I yank her off down the path, her mouth going 'But, but, but' so it sounds like bubbles bursting all around.

I want to get away and out of there — to unzip my skin and step into another me. But out in the lane here is Mrs Dunkerley from across the way, back from shopping with her cabbage smell that always follows her around.

'Well, girls,' she says. 'Helen and Eleanor, isn't it? But which one is which? I can never tell — you're like two peas in a pod.'

The fidgets are on me, but I stand politely and tell her who is who. Even though I have to do this every time we see her. Even though everyone knows who we are. Even though no one calls Ellie Eleanor.

'Isn't that lovely?' says Mrs Dunkerley, like she always does. 'Well now, won't you girls come in and have some tea and biscuits?'

I know about Mrs Dunkerley's biscuits. They live in a rusty tin on top of her fridge and some of the Garibaldis have fur on them.

'No thank you very much, Mrs Dunkerley,' I say in my best voice. 'We are preoccupied.'

'Preoccupied, are you?' says Mrs Dunkerley. 'Gracious. But are you sure you haven't got time for a quick cup of tea?'

'I'm afraid not, Mrs Dunkerley,' I say. 'We've got to help our mother.'

'Ah well, in that case,' says Mrs Dunkerley,

her voice rising as I take Ellie's hand and drag her off towards the gate. 'But you will come again soon, won't you? And bring your friends!'

The gate bangs behind us. We stand in the brambly shadows.

'What does Mother want us to do?' says Ellie.

'God-uh,' I say, thumping the 'd' so it sounds like a thud on the big bass drum in the music room at school. 'Ellie, what's wrong with you today? You are being stupider than ever. Mother doesn't want us to do anything. I just said it so we didn't have to go to tea at Mrs Dunkerley's.'

'Oh,' says Ellie, and her eyes go quiet. And I know what she is thinking. She is thinking about Mrs Dunkerley's budgie, Bill. She likes to watch Bill twitch and bow in his cage. She sits with her face close to the bars and gets this silly, soft look like Bill is her only friend and maybe one day they are going to run away together. That look makes me want to teach her a lesson really hard.

Ellie scuffs her shoe in the dirt. She looks at me.

'Why did he want you to say "fucked"?' she says.

A tingling feeling comes. I stand and look at Ellie in her shorts and the red T-shirt with the splatter of food where she missed her mouth at lunch. Then I narrow my eyes until all I can see is the dark shadow of her, with her wispy bunches straggling either side of her face and the sun shining behind. And in my head, like Mother's favourite record jumping when Ellie scratched it last year, is Mrs Dunkerley's voice saying 'like two peas in a pod, like two peas in a pod' over and over again.

'Come on, Ellie,' I say. 'We're going to play a game.'

1

Ribbons of sound. The bright streamer of a child's giggle, an ice-cream van's flourish swirling like a sparkler in the gloom, the chatter of a long-finished game. Birdsong spiralling, then stiffening and falling to the earth, congealing into something hard and metallic, measured out in mechanical portions, a harsh trilling. Again. A pause. Again.

Smudge opened her eyes and squinted. A ray of light thrust its way in past the tie-dyed sarong tacked up over the window, to pick out the dead flies, plastic bags, the vodka bottle lying on its side. Morning, was it? No, afternoon — always afternoon when the sun came in at that angle. The day almost spent.

Pens, matches, tampons strewn across the table. A half-smoked cigarette burrowing into the plastic veneer, puckering it like a scar. A toothbrush lying on its side next to an ice-cube tray with magenta and purple paint clogged in its recesses like dried blood.

From the armchair, she stared up at the canvas propped on the shelf above the broken gas fire. Canvas was pushing it: it was really a piece of newspaper pinned to the seat of a chair. Still, it had been enough last night, or the night before — or whenever it was — to get her up and buzzing, charging about the flat in search of anything that would help her create the colours and shapes surging in her brain. She wished she could recapture it now, the inspiration that rolled in like a breaker only to smash against the sea wall of her consciousness and drain away, pulling her with it to drift on a grey ocean, leaving only wreckage behind. The canvas testified to what had happened — the bright squabble of colours in the top-right corner giving way to a thin wash and then nothing. A headline about a pensioner being mugged in the alleyway up the road.

The absorbing idea was gone, but the voices that usually crowded in to fill any blank spaces in her mind — muttering and snarling — were still, for now. Good. That was something. That was something, at least.

She rubbed a hand over her eyes and the ringing started again. The phone, she thought dully. Hadn't they disconnected it yet? There must be more than twenty final warnings in the drift of mail in the hallway.

She listened to the ringing unmoved. No point answering. It would just be one of those recorded messages. That, or the Samaritans phoning to see how she was, unaware that tomorrow she'd be calling another branch with a different story.

Or maybe the ringing was just in her mind. She wouldn't put it past her mashed-up brain to pull some kind of new stunt like that.

She squinted up at the ripped calendar on the wall. What day was it anyway? Hard to keep track. Before you knew it, Thursday had muscled in where Tuesday was supposed to be and you were staring down the barrel of Friday. And meanwhile some bastard like Monday went droning on for weeks. The calendar was giving nothing away. Not Giro day, anyhow. Never that. She drew a deep, snagging breath and her stomach gurgled.

Be good to get some food inside her. She levered herself to her feet and the floor fell away like a trap door on a theme-park ride. Fireworks exploded on the edge of her vision and she gripped the chair. ('Indisputable!' sniped a voice somewhere inside her brain.) Steady.

15

Out into the corridor, ragged nails trailing over the peeling wallpaper, the kitchen doorway belching the smell of sour milk. Inside: the plump plastic bags, tops tied, ranged across the floor and surfaces like barn hens. Rubbish cascading from the bin, the sink piled.

Smudge opened the fridge door and the phone trilled again, making her lose her footing. She put out a hand to save herself and caught it in a wire, dragging something off the wall as she sat down heavily amid the rubbish bags. The ceiling gaped above her, a heavy weight being hoisted the better to fall on her head.

Then she heard another voice, this time seeming to come from somewhere outside her.

'Ellie?' it said in a stern, tinny tone. 'Ellie?'

She looked around. Apart from the dripping of the kitchen tap, the room was still. She clapped her hand over her eyes, feeling the rasp of cracked skin against her face, and shook her head, trying to dislodge the hallucination.

'Ellie?' said the voice again.

She turned and peered through the gap in her fingers. The sound was coming from the phone receiver dangling next to her. Cau-

16

tiously she reached for it and held it to her
ear.

'Ellie,' said the phone, 'it's Mother.' And
then, 'Look, I haven't got time to play silly
buggers. I know this is your number. Nick
gave it to me.'

A silence. Above her, its door still open,
the fridge began to beep.

'All right. If that's the way you want it,'
continued the phone. 'I'm ringing about
Helen.' A sigh. 'Well, there's been an accident and I'm afraid she's in a coma.
There. The others thought I should tell you.
Left to myself, I probably wouldn't have
b— But there we are. At least this way you
won't hear about it first on the news.'

Around the kitchen dark shapes were stirring, unfurling themselves like monstrous,
poisonous blooms. The voices were snickering, getting ready to rush her. She felt numb
and powerless before them.

'Needless to say, we're all pretty cut up
about it this end,' said the phone. 'Horace
is beside himself. Richard's put in for
compassionate leave.'

The shapes were moving towards her, billowing like smoke, curling across the poly-
styrene ceiling tiles as a prickling sensation
worked its way up her arms. She tried to
move but the feeling gripped her tighter, its

17

fidgeting fingers edging their way up towards her neck. Panic beat in the rhythm of the fridge's beep.

'We're all spending every hour we can at the hospital,' continued the phone. 'And of course there's a lot of media attention.'

Another pause and then, angrily, 'Don't you have anything to say?'

The darkness was nearly upon her, stifling, choking, stars prickling on the edge of her vision. She swallowed, took a deep breath and gripped the phone, blinking.

('Whickering,' carped a voice inside her mind. 'Reprehensible.')

Smudge closed her eyes and took a deep breath. 'I'm afraid you've got the wrong number,' she said, laying the words out one by one like coins on the counter of the offie.

Then the receiver dropped as the clamouring rushed in to claim her. She slumped back among the bags. A carton began to leak on to her shoulder, but she did not feel it. There was only the hubbub inside her head and, somewhere beyond it, the light from the fridge playing on her eyelids like sunshine, its beeps mimicking those of a lorry reversing long ago in a suburban street one summer's afternoon.

2

Sunlight spilling between the leaves and the smell of cut grass. A lawnmower buzzing somewhere and a beeping coming from the street in front of the house. We creep back into the lane in our swapped clothes — swapped shoes, swapped socks, swapped hair bobbles, everything. I've even done Ellie's bunches in my hair and raked hers into the plait Mother always does on me so she never has to think about who's who if the fog of a glum day comes. Just the knickers are the same because who is going to look at those? I feel Ellie's orange shorts, rough and crinkly between my legs, and when I look down I see the splatter of food on the red T-shirt. A giggle comes and trying to stop it bursting out and wobbling the world is almost more than I can bear.

I make Ellie go first because she has to be the leader, but she keeps stopping and looking back with that poor-me face she gets when she's learning a hard lesson or she's trying to make the dinner ladies give her sympathy at school.

'Go on, Ellie,' I say. 'You have to be the leader!'

But Ellie just stands there with her fingers at her nose.

'How do I be that?' she says, and I think it's funny how, even now she's wearing my shorts and my green T-shirt with the patterns of birds flying across, the Ellieness is still there. You can see it in the lost look in her eyes and the jiggle of her leg.

'God-uh, Ellie!' I say. 'Just do the things I do. Be me!'

I look down and see Ellie's white sandals and the socks with holes like a snowflake on my feet, standing on the dusty tarmac of the back lane, and the giggle comes at me again. I start to walk in that wonky way Ellie has when she's tired at the end of the day.

Ellie copies.

'No-wuh, Ellie!' I say. 'Not now. Normally. Like, how do I walk when I'm going around the playground with Jessica?'

Ellie thinks for a moment.

'You do this,' she says, and she walks in a straight, marchy way with her hands by her sides like a soldier.

20

'OK,' I say. I'm not sure that's right, but at least Ellie is trying and you've got to be thankful for small mercies. 'And what do I sound like? What sort of things do I say?'

'You say: "God-uh, Ellie! What's wrong with you today!" ' says Ellie. And she looks at me and I look at her, and suddenly we both giggle because it is funny to hear the things I say coming out of her mouth.

'Ellie, I've had it up to here with you!' she says, and we giggle some more.

Then Ellie looks at me and wags her finger. 'You are going to have to learn a very hard lesson,' she says. And this time we really laugh, holding our tummies and bending over like we are going to be sick.

She puts her hand up to the neck of my green T-shirt and tugs at it, looking pleased. It's one of my favourites, the last thing left from millions of years ago when Father bought us something of every colour in the shop in the precinct — the day when we three skipped all the way back from the bus stop, laughing our heads off like we would never stop, until we got home and Mother saw all the plastic bags. I'm afraid Ellie will stretch my T-shirt and make it hang down like an open mouth, the way she does to all her tops, so I go over and pull away her tugging hand.

'That's good, Ellie,' I say, calm and kind, like Mrs Appleby at school when she's explaining number work. 'Now all you have to do is be like that and the rest will take care of itself.'

We do some more walking and talking up and down the lane. But it's boring being Ellie when there's no one there to see. I am beginning to think the game has finished its chips when who should come walking up to the cottage by the postbox carrying a big tin but Chloe, who normally sits in the little room by the hall at school and nods and smiles and writes down everything we say.

'Well hello there, Ellie love,' she says to me, and a surge of pleasedness floods through me that the bunches are doing the trick.

'Hello, Chloe,' I say, and I swivel from side to side and scuff my shoe in the dirt in that way Ellie has. Away by the postbox, I see Ellie putting her hand to her mouth like it is about to spill a giggle, but I ignore her and look up at Chloe, determined to do the game.

'Are you having a nice summer holiday?' says Chloe, taking one hand off the tin to brush her hair back from her face. Today Chloe's nails are pink and glittery and she is wearing a big silver butterfly ring.

I nod and try to think about what Ellie would say next but Chloe doesn't wait like she normally does in the little room at school. Today it's like she's doing my side of the talking as well.

'I'm just off to see my mum,' she says, nodding at the cottage. 'She's not been well, so I'm taking her a cake.'

'Oh,' I say, and I put my fingers to my nose the way that Ellie would. A chuckle comes, but I swallow it down and stare sadly at the cracks in the tarmac.

'And what about you, Helen?' says Chloe, looking over at Ellie. 'Are you enjoying the summer? I'm sure you're taking good care of your sister, aren't you?'

I expect that Ellie will be silly and laugh right away or else go serious and quiet, but instead she looks at me and does a big swallow. A flash of fun glimmers from her eyes to mine and she goes, 'Yes, thank you very much. The weather has really been marvellous.'

She does it in a funny, pinched old-lady voice and I'm sure that Chloe will know it's really her. But Chloe does not notice a thing. She shifts the tin from one hand to the other and yawns.

'Great. That's wonderful,' she says. Then she looks at the cottage. 'Well, I'd better get going otherwise Mum'll wonder where I've got to. You two take care, won't you? I'll see you next year.'

And with that she bustles up to the front door, puts a key in the lock and disappears.

Ellie and I look at each other as the quiet settles back into the lane. Then the laughs explode and it is like our tummies have turned into trampolines, bouncing giggle after giggle up our throats. I stagger over to Ellie and put my arms around her shoulders, gasping with the effort of the laughs.

'We tricked her good and proper,' I say.

'She thought you were the one who needed looking after,' giggles Ellie. 'She thought I was the leader.'

'She didn't smell a rat at all,' I say.

'She thought I was the leader,' says Ellie again.

I think she doesn't need to say it twice, but I still laugh along because it was very funny how well the game went and really I am very pleased.

'You did well, Ellie, you did well,' I say, stroking the wispy bit of hair that snakes out of her me-plait. 'If only you could be as good as that all the time, I wouldn't need to threaten down on you nearly as hard. We could always have the sort of fun we used to have back before.'

Because, when I think about it, tricking Chloe is the most fun there has been for a very long time. Even more than the day when the actors came to school and did a show about a dog who got lost and all the while he was hiding in the cupboard and kept popping out to say 'HELLO!' in a funny voice when they weren't looking. Even more than being included in the lessons with Mary. The truth is that this game today is the best fun there's been since the days back before the Unfortunate Decision when we'd do things like go on the merry-go-round until they locked the park and throw paint in the air just to watch it splatter — and sometimes even Mother would laugh.

Thinking about Mother makes another idea put its hand up for attention. Because what if this is the sort of fun that could jump her out of herself and make the house sunny again? What if we could surprise her into smiles with our cleverness? As soon as I think it, I know what we are going to do.

'Come on,' I say, taking Ellie's hand and pulling her over to our garden gate. 'We're going to do the game to Mother.'

'What?' says Ellie. 'We're going to tell about tricking Chloe?'

'No-wuh!' I say, and a bit of the impatience comes and I am afraid she is going back to her silly ways. 'We're going to play the swap and then, when Mother thinks she knows what's what, we're going to take her unawares and shout "Surprise" and make her know it was all a game.'

Ellie puts her fingers to her nose. 'Do you think Mother will like that?'

'Yes!' I say, pushing her inside the garden and shutting the gate with a crash. 'She'll think it's the best fun ever.'

And now I hear myself say it, I know it's really true. I can see Mother laughing and putting her arms round us. I can see the days of the shut bedroom door and wonky-cut bread and margarine for supper going away for good.

Ellie leans her head on one side. 'Will it be better than the Christmas when we all played at being astronauts?'

I think carefully. 'At least as good as that,' I say. 'But we have to do the game properly otherwise it won't work. No forgetting and being you by mistake. Otherwise it will be worse than useless.'

I hold up a finger to show it's not a joke. Ellie looks at me with a solemn face and gives a nod.

We walk up the garden, over the tufty lawn, Ellie carefully being me and me following behind. When she gets to the edge of the patio, she stops and looks up at the glass doors that stand open to the dining room.

'Come on, H-Elle-n,' I say, keeping my voice strict so Ellie knows there is no way out of the game. 'Let's go in.'

We step up on to the patio. From inside the house comes the sound of banging and heavy footsteps like there is a really good bit of cleaning going on somewhere in there. I think of Mother's face when she sees us and how she won't know what's hit her, and suddenly the excitedness is back again, sending giggles bubbling up my throat and bringing a needing-the-toilet feeling that makes me press my legs together tight.

Ellie looks back and sees me and she starts to smile too, so I frown to show that now is not a laughing matter.

We go up the steps to the inside. In the dining room, facing us, there is a big, fat chest that wasn't there before. It looks funny behind the thin legs of the chairs and the table, like a toad, and I know that if I opened it there would be questions inside. But there isn't time for that right now this minute because me and Ellie have to do the game.

Outside in the hall I hear a cough, and the needing-the-toilet feeling floods in more. I push Ellie forward to the edge of the doorway.

'Look round,' I say.

So Ellie puts her head out, over the little gold line that marks the change from the swirly, brown carpet of the dining room to the Angel Delight-coloured carpet of the hall. She looks back at me.

'There's a man,' she says.

'What sort of a man?' I say. Ellie looks again.

'A big man,' she says, 'with glasses like a teacher.' Then she jerks back into the room. 'He's coming!'

We hear footsteps and a voice booms out.

'Hello there!' says the voice. 'Now is that Nellie or Ellen?'

A shadow comes over the doorway and the man's head peers round. It is a big head, pinkish and blobbing out of its shirt collar like it is made of Plasticine and someone had to squash it hard to get it in there.

'Well hello, girls,' says the man in a voice like Father Christmas's. 'Which one's Nellie and which one's Ellen?' And the way he says it makes me want to laugh because Nellie and Ellen are names from a story book where everyone is about to have a picnic and drink ginger beer, and they are not our names at all. I am about to tell him which one's which when I notice something strange about his face, so instead I close my mouth and stand looking up at his round nose and his little raisin eyes behind his glasses and try to make my brain think.

A click-clacking sound comes across the kitchen floor and Mother stares down at us. But this is not the normal Mother. This is like Mother times ten plus three. Her hair is all fluffed in curls and her mouth is small and red like a rosebud. The flannel dressing gown is nowhere to be seen and instead there is a smart jacket like a doctor's receptionist.

'Come on, girls,' she says. 'Come out of there and say hello.'

So we go out into the hall, which is the proper place for hellos and goodbyes. Mother brushes past us and goes to stand next to the man, with her hand on his arm. Behind her wafts a sharp, lemony smell.

'This is Mr Greene,' she says with a smile, all the while looking at the side of the man's big, pink head. I watch carefully but there is no sign of what-in-God's-name-do-you-want-now and the mopey why-mes. It is like all the glum days have been shoved into the cupboard under the stairs and the door locked tight.

'Horace,' says the man.

'Mr Greene,' says Mother again firmly, with a little squeeze of Mr Greene's arm.

And this is the first lie, because now the light from the kitchen window is shining on his face, I can tell who it is: it is Akela from the Scouts who does games of quick-cricket in the park. There is no woggle today but it's him all right — Akela, trying to pretend to be Mr Greene.

'This is Helen, and this is Ellie,' says Mother, glancing at the plait on the top of Ellie's head and getting us the wrong way round like the plan says she's supposed to. Only now I am not pleased because, out of the corner of my eye, through the doorway into the lounge, I can see lots of new things and they are saying 'look at us and give us attention', so there is no time to be happy about the plan. There are cardboard boxes and things wrapped in plastic and over by the electric fire there is a fat, shiny armchair with cushions as bulgy as Akela's head. The room that has been thin and empty since Father made his Unfortunate Decision is now full and bustling, and there is no space to breathe.

'Mr Greene is going to come and live with us,' says Mother in a strange, breezy voice, smiling and craning her neck back to give her eyes a chance to look at all of Akela's head in one go. 'Won't that be fun?'

Next to me, Ellie's leg starts to jiggle.

'But —' she says. 'But doesn't Mr Greene have his own house?'

Akela and Mother look at each other and give a chuckle.

'I think yours is much nicer,' says Akela, reaching a hand around Mother's waist and squeezing it with his sausage fingers. The wee inside me gives a surge and I squash my legs together tight.

'Why?' says Ellie.

But another question is brimming up in me because I am thinking about our room and Mother's room and the box room at the front full of bric-a-brac and things from back before, and no matter which way round I think it, I can't see a space for Akela. Suddenly I am worried that he will have to come and sleep in our room, stretched out on the floor between Ellie and my beds.

'But where will Ak— Mr Greene sleep?' I say.

At that, Mother purses her lips. 'Never you mind,' she says. And then with a flash of spikiness: 'Honestly Ellie, why do you always have to go lowering the tone?'

For a minute I am confused until I remember that I am wearing Ellie's clothes and bunches and she is dressed like me. I stare up at them while my brain sorts the muddle out and see Mother mouthing words at Akela and doing the eye-rolling look that comes out when Ellie lets the side down. It is strange to think it's me that's caused it — me, Helen, the one who's always good.

Akela is fussing at Mother, patting and stroking her face and her arms in a way that you'd think would be annoying but actually seems to be making her smile. Then he turns and looks at us. I give a twitch as the wee inside me gives a rush, trying to come out.

'Oh, I nearly forgot,' he says in his Father Christmas voice, and he fumbles in his trouser pocket. 'Here,' he says, and hands over two chocolate bars — a Marathon for Ellie and a Wispa for me.

'Thank you,' says Ellie, and without waiting to see if she's allowed, she rips open the wrapper and begins to stuff her face.

I expect there will be hell to pay because it can't be long til supper, but instead when I look up Mother is staring at me.

'What's the matter, Ellie?' she says. 'Aren't you grateful to Mr Greene for bringing you a treat?'

'Yes,' I say. 'Thank you.'

And even though the Wispa is warm and soft from Akela's pocket, and even though the wee inside me has started to tug and jiggle so that I have to cross my legs to keep it in, I tear open the bar, being careful not to drop the spare bit of wrapper on the carpet, and begin to eat. The chocolate sticks all around the inside of my mouth.

Suddenly the front door swings back and a monster comes in.

'Where do you want this?' he grunts, and then I see it's not a monster but a man with bits of metal stuck in his face and blue drawings up his arms.

'Just put it in the second bedroom for now,' says Mother with a wave of her arm, and the man starts off up the stairs, scuffing at the walls as he goes.

'Well, then,' says Akela, rubbing his hands in a pleased way. 'What do you girls say we give Mummy a break for the evening and order a Chinese takeaway to celebrate?'

'Yay!' shouts Ellie, jumping up and down. 'Sweet and sour chicken!'

Chinese takeaway is my favourite too but I don't bounce around. I just stand where I am, gripping the doorframe. Because as the man climbs past me up the stairs, my body gives a jerk and the wee that has been struggling to get out comes in a hot flood, running down my legs to soak into Ellie's socks and leaving a dark patch on the front of the silly orange shorts.

Everyone looks at me and I crouch away against the wall, trying to hide the stain.

'Oh Ellie,' says Mother in a small, disappointed voice. 'I thought we'd got past the accident stage.'

'Too much lemonade at lunch!' Ellie pipes up. Even though nobody asked her.

'Horace, I'm so sorry,' says Mother. 'As I explained, there have been —' And here she stretches her lips as though the word needs a mouth bigger than hers to say it: 'PROB-LEMS.'

I stand, feeling the hot go cold on my bottom half and the cold go hot on my face.

Mother gives a sigh as the monster-man clumps down the stairs and out the door again. Her shoulders slump and I worry a glum day might be hovering. Then she gives a little twitch and shakes her head.

'Helen,' she says to Ellie in her bright, breezy voice once more. 'Would you take your sister upstairs to the bathroom and get her some clean clothes so we can all have a nice evening together?'

Ellie takes my hand and leads me off up the stairs and pushes me into the bathroom. I peel off the wet shorts and knickers and do my best to wash the wee away. When I have finished, Ellie comes back with a little heap of her clothes: a blue T-shirt with a rip at the neck where she has tugged too hard, shorts with orange stripes, socks and a pair of her Tinker Bell pants.

'You can give me my own knickers,' I say. 'No one will know about those.'

Ellie stares at me.

'Come on, Ellie,' I say. 'It's not like anyone's going to make us show our pants.'

But Ellie just stands there. In her eyes I can see the reflection of the bobbly bathroom window, where the sun is starting to sink down to get ready for the end of the day.

'Actually, I think it's time we stopped,' I say. 'We've played a good trick, but it's different now Mr Greene is here. Let's go back to normal.'

Ellie puts a finger to her lips. 'Shhh, Ellie,' she says. 'Mother will come and you'll make her sad if you're difficult.'

'Ellie,' I say, 'the game's not being played between us. Give me my pants.'

I reach out to do the pinch that always makes her do what I say. But she steps out on to the landing. I hear the thuds of the man coming up again and fear fizzes in my tummy. I don't want him to see me with no clothes on, looking down at me with his monster face.

'All right,' I say in a hurry. 'Give them to me. But this is just for today, do you hear me, Ellie? After that everything goes back to the way it was.'

And I take the clothes and start to get dressed.

3

Nothing under the bare mattress in the bedroom. Nothing in the hall, apart from the drift of letters banked up about the front door. The fag packet on the table in the living room: empty. Shit.

The sight of the chair made her pause for a moment. A faint memory of metallic trilling, sunlight and a child's giggle tugged at the sleeve of her mind. Hadn't there been something? Hadn't something happened? Something to do with before. Something significant. Then anxiety burst in and set up its festival, amps blaring, chasing away the thought.

She needed a smoke. Rummaging through the rubbish on the table, her fingernails crescent moons of dirt. Keys, tissues, Rizlas. Ah, here it was, the pouch — empty except for a few wisps at the bottom. Not enough to go on. She'd have to go out to the shop.

On to the mantelpiece, sweeping the painting to the floor. Something hard went with it too and smashed on the lino. She glanced down and saw the fragments of the windmill mug from Amsterdam. The last thing she had from back then. A pang tried to get her, but she flinched it away. All that was over a long time ago. It was not like the mug was keeping anything alive. Fuck it.

Here it was. She snatched up the money on the shelf: a tenner and some shrapnel; £11.13 in all. Irritation crackled along her nerves. There should have been more than that. Why wasn't there more than that? Her fingers drummed out a nervous tattoo on the shelf.

She tried to think. Had she been out and spent it during one of her times? But her brain would only turn up useless images: a leaf dangling from a spider's web; the pudding face of the woman in the dole office; a baby's bootie stamped in the mud.

The craving for fags was bringing the nausea with it now, the shakes. If she didn't leave soon, she'd have to start going through the rubbish in the kitchen, looking for butts. She hurried out into the hall, jammed her feet into her slippers and threw on her anorak. The scarf was hanging on the banister at the foot of the blind staircase that led up to the ceiling they'd stuck in when they carved the house up into flats. She hesitated over it. She hadn't been spotted in ages. What with the way her cheeks and mouth had greyed and sunk in, there was really very little similarity between them now. You no longer needed the scar and the tattoo to tell them apart. When she caught her reflection in shop windows these days, she barely recognised herself. Still, the scarf made her feel safe. And it would be a help against the bastard February cold that these days bit at her bones as never before. She wrapped the black wool round her head, leaving just the upper part of her face visible.

('Edifying,' announced a rather camp voice approvingly. 'À la mode.')

The wind rushed in, bringing with it the roar of the traffic on the Old Kent Road, as she walked round the house, past the stairs to the flat above, and down the steps to the pavement. It was fucking freezing and everywhere was as grey as her mind. The entrance to the estate loomed ahead of her, yawning to reveal its grey blocks rising to different heights like rotten, broken teeth. She walked quickly, head bowed against the gusts, keeping her eyes to herself. A gaggle of teenage girls appeared out of an alleyway and sidled past her. One of them spat and the gobbet landed next to her slipper, but she didn't turn round, leaving them to their squawks and laughter coming in waves on the breeze.

The shop was set into a concrete wall underneath the walkway leading to the tallest block. It was the only one still open, its windows fractured into spiders' webs that sent out shards of light to glint on the cans and crisp packets blowing across the concourse.

She pushed the door open and stepped in, past a bucket of bright plastic children's umbrellas. The shopkeeper looked up and his expression darkened as he registered her, taking in the stains on her jacket, the tattoo poking out from the scarf over her left eyebrow. He turned his attention back to the small television showing Al Jazeera on the corner of the counter, but she could feel his mind on her, just waiting for her to make a false move. She walked between the shelves and picked up a loaf of sliced white and some peanut butter. Then she went to the counter and put them on the pile of newspapers beside the till.

'And a bottle of value vodka and a small pack of Amber Leaf and some Rizlas, please,' she said.

The shopkeeper pursed his lips and reached into the cabinet behind him for the tobacco and booze. He plugged the figures into the till.

'Twelve pounds fifty-six,' he said.

She dug out the money from her pocket, looked at it, then at him.

'Don't suppose —' she began.

'No,' he said firmly, holding up a hand. 'I am not a charity.'

She shrugged. Inside her head, a voice was launching into a fraught monologue about pedestrianised zones.

'Well then, I suppose I'll have to put the peanut butter back,' she said hurriedly.

He watched as she took it over to the shelf.

'Ten pounds and nine pence,' he said when she got back to the counter.

She handed over the money and waited as he put the items into a blue plastic bag. When he moved the bread, she was startled to find her face — the correct, whole version, the way it used to look but shinier — staring up at her from the front page of the newspaper. *Daytime star Sallis in car crash coma,* read the headline.

Like a blast from the heater above the shop entrance, it came back to her: the phone call, Mother's voice. She gasped. Her body jerked as if shunted by a car. The voice

41

in her head went mute.

'Can I get this too?' she said, pointing to the paper.

The shopkeeper frowned at her. His eyes strayed to the door, wary in case this was a diversion.

'All right,' he said, as though granting a favour.

She handed over the coin, snatched up the bag and the paper and was gone, hurrying from the shop, her heart pounding, her hand clutched over Hellie's smug face. Outside, the laughter of the teenage girls echoed in her wake across the concourse from a place she couldn't see.

4

The next morning I am up before everyone else. While Ellie is still sleeping in my bed by the window under my *Rainbow Brite* duvet that Mother tucked round her last night, I creep to my drawer and put on my Helen clothes, including my Alice the Camel T-shirt with the bit of soft fur on the hump. Just stroking it makes me feel Helenish again. I smile and do my hair in Helen's plait the way Mother would. It's fiddly because I can't see what my hands are doing behind my head and when I look in the mirror it's sticking out to one side rather than straight down the back, but that doesn't matter: anyone would know it was me. I go and sit by the bookcase to wait, grinning to myself, and all the time Ellie is dreaming away, not knowing that the game is being tidied away right under her nose.

When Mother comes in, I beam up at her with my best Helen smile. But here's the odd thing: Mother isn't wearing her normal buttoned-up-to-the-neck dressing gown. She's in a silly, floaty pink thing that shows the bumps and curves of her underneath. There is a strange smell about her, like salt and earth and flowers all at once, and when you look in her eyes you can just tell they are switched off from their normal seeing.

'Oh Ellie,' she says. 'What are you lurking down there for? And what have you done to your hair? I've never seen such a bird's nest.'

She takes my hand and pulls me up. 'And wearing Helen's clothes too. How many times do we have to go through this? Yours is the left drawer and Helen's is the one on the right. Left is where you can look at your hand and see the "L" in your fingers.' She takes a deep breath and closes her eyes. 'Still, good girl for trying to get ready by yourself, I suppose. Even if you have done it all wrong.'

'But —' I say.

But Mother doesn't listen. Instead she has started to hum: a bright, trumpety tune that sounds like it's going a little too fast. I have never heard Mother hum before so I am too surprised to argue when she pulls the Alice T-shirt up over my head and puts Ellie's stupid Pigeon Street top on me instead over my head. But when she scrapes my hair into two sections and starts doing the Ellie bunches, I squirm away and slap at her hands.

'No!' I shout. 'That's not right! That's not how my hair's supposed to be!'

Mother stops humming and leans down to bring her face close to mine. Behind her, I see Ellie sitting up in my bed, blinking.

'Oh, Ellie-bellie,' sighs Mother, frowning as though she is trying hard to see through a thick fog. 'Not today, please. Mr Greene has organised a nice surprise and we're going to have a lovely day out. Don't ruin it.'

'But I'm not Ellie-bellie,' I say, my voice wobbling with crossness because Ellie has got out of bed and is wriggling into my clothes, pulling the Alice T-shirt this way and that so the neck stretches over her silly head.

Mother puts a hand to her face. 'Oh, not this again,' she says. 'How many times?'

And now I am surprised because when did Ellie ever say that she was me before? We have always been us just as we were and no exceptions. Changing places was never one of the Mary lessons.

'But —' I say.

'And as for you, Helen,' says Mother, dreamily straightening up and going over to do my Helen plait in Ellie's hair, 'I'm rely-

45

ing on you to be the grown-up, sensible one. Understand?'

'Yes, Mother,' says Ellie, with a little nod like a secretary in a TV drama who has been given important work to do. She stares up at the Beatrix Potter clock above the door, far away from where my eyes are trying to scream all her wrongness at her.

We go downstairs. All through breakfast, my fingers itch to take the bunches out, but when I see Mother shaking her head sadly at me over her steaming cup of coffee, my hands go still. Instead, another plan comes: I make up my mind to do everything I can to be my best possible Helen so that even with the rubbish Ellie hair and clothes, the real Helenness will shine through and Mother will have no choice but to know that it's me.

For the rest of the meal, I mind my Ps and Qs and sit up straight keeping my elbows in. Except it's hard work because Ellie is Helening for all she's worth too, smiling and talking politely and passing the sugar before anyone's even asked. When she neatly mops up a spill from Akela's mug and rinses the cloth out in the sink, I stare at her with my mouth open until Mother tells me to close it. Ellie purses her lips and peers off into the distance, like I am not even there. To look at her you would have no idea about all the wrongness underneath. You wouldn't know she slurps from her cup at breaktime or that the PE teacher has to help her up on the climbing frame in the gym because she's scared.

It turns out the special treat Akela has in store for us is that he is taking us to Thorpe Park. We both nod and smile and say how exciting it sounds, and I look up at Mother especially hard, making my eyes big and blinking like those children you see on the adverts that ask you to give a pound, in case something in her brain goes 'ping' and she suddenly knows who I am. But she just says, 'Oh Ellie, for goodness' sake,' and goes to take the rubbish out. It makes me worried that my Helening looks like Ellie nonsense to her, but then I take a breath and give myself a good talking to, moving my lips silently and jiggling my feet under the table, while Akela smiles at us with his eggy breakfast mouth. If I just keep being Helen, I tell myself, then sooner or later the truth will be there for everyone to see. Besides, Ellie is too stupid to keep the game up. Before long she'll be dragging her feet and whinging and moaning in that way she has, and then it will all go back the way it was. I am better than Ellie at things like this. I am cleverer and everyone says so. I just have to wait.

The car journey to get to Thorpe Park takes three years. First there is our road, then the high street, then the road that leads to the swimming pool, then another road with shops on it, then a roundabout, then a big road with cars whizzing past, then an even bigger road. Then it turns out that Mother's been looking at the map the wrong way and we should have been on a different big road all along. But instead of getting cross about it, Akela just gives a laugh and pulls into a petrol station where he buys us all Feast lollies before turning back and going the other way.

I sit and eat my Feast as the cars flash by. Feast is my favourite ice-cream, because I like how the outside layer of chocolate and ice-cream crumbles around the slab of chocolate in the middle. Always when I eat it, I want to save the middle bit and then take it off the stick and put it in my mouth so it pokes out like a tongue, but I never manage it because the chocolate is so tasty that you just have to bite right in.

The road carries on rolling. I tuck the stick from the Feast into the wrapper and put it carefully by my feet so that I don't get chocolate mess on Akela's car. Ellie has already finished hers and dropped off to sleep. I can hear her snuffling and I am pleased about this because I hope it means Mother will spot who she is. But Mother is busy looking at the map and saying things to impress Akela in a bright, giddy voice that is even worse than the crystal-chandelier talking she used to bring out when well-wishers came to the door after the Unfortunate Decision, which was pol-ished and hard and sounded like it might crack. Plus there is noise coming from the radio that drowns out the snuffling. Soon after that a drowsy feeling comes over the car, and I lean my head on one side and go to sleep.

Thorpe Park is more than just a park. It is a big place with rides and rollercoasters and people dressed up as cuddly elephants. When we get there, there are so many cars lined up that I say it is more like it should be called Thorpe Car Park. Everybody gives a laugh at that and I watch them carefully to see if anyone realises it's actually clever me.

When we get inside, Akela says, 'Now what do you want to do?' and Ellie, who always gets excited by silly things, shouts that she wants to go on the whirling teacup ride. So we go and sit in one of the cups and soon we are whirling in and out and round and round. It's fun and we all go 'Whee!' but it also makes you feel a little bit sick. It's not just me because when I look at Ellie I see that she has gone quiet and the sides of her nose are white and when we get off she walks slowly with her hand to her head in a slightly staggery way. Mother and Akela are striding ahead because they want to find somewhere we can have lunch, but I stay behind with Ellie because I think now might be my chance to talk to her properly about putting a stop to the game.

In a minute we are passing the toilet block and there is a big high hedge where you go in, so I reach out and grab Ellie's wrist in a pinch and pull her behind it.

'Listen Ellie,' I say into her swaying white face. 'Enough's enough. We've had our fun but now it's time to tell the truth. You have to swap back to being you and I have to swap back to being me.'

She looks at me with dull, wandering eyes and her lips do that trembly thing that makes me want to get the hard lessons going again really quickly.

'Besides Ellie,' I say, 'they already know what you're up to. I heard them talking about it last night after you were asleep. They're just waiting until you've done enough naughtiness so that they can punish down on you really hard. That's all they're waiting for. So you might as well own up now and save yourself some of the punishing.'

Ellie slumps forward with her eyes closed and gives a slow, saggy nod. I put my arm up round the back of her neck.

'That's a good Ellie,' I say. 'I knew you'd see sense in the end. Some people just aren't meant to be the leader.'

Ellie opens her mouth to say how sorry she is and that she'll never disobey again, but instead what comes out is a long stream of chocolate-coloured sick that spatters all down my front and on to my feet in Ellie's white, holey socks and sandals. I stand blinking in the sour smell as a shadow falls over us.

'There you are! You mustn't wander off like that!' says Mother. Then she looks at me. 'Oh God, what have you done now?'

'Ellie's been sick all down herself,' says Ellie quickly, wiping her mouth with the back of her hand and pointing at me. 'It really smells.'

'Oh, Ellie!' shouts Mother, reaching down and snatching up my hand. 'You couldn't manage to keep things nice for even one day, could you?' She drags me out from behind the hedge to where Akela is waiting, holding two cuddly tigers.

'I'm so sorry, Horace,' she says, loudly and brightly so that all the families walking past can hear. 'We've had a little accident. She's been sick everywhere. You couldn't be a dear, could you, and go and find something we can dress her in? One of those big T-shirts from that stall by the fountain will do fine. I'll take her in here and try and get her cleaned up.'

Akela trots off and Mother turns and starts to pull me back towards the toilets. But my feet don't want to move. Suddenly all the things of the last two days — the game and the monster-man carrying the boxes and 'fucked' and the smell of the eaten Feast lolly — build up and build up and start fizzing in my head until there is nowhere left for them to go and they have to come spilling out, like mind sick, all over everywhere.

'No!' I scream and I pull back on Mother's arm. 'No! It wasn't me! It was her! She was the one! She was sick, not me! No one's being fair!'

Mother rounds on me and there is a look in her eyes I have never seen before. It is like all the mumblings and spikiness and clouds of glum have hardened into a sharp, black point.

'Ellie,' she hisses. 'You are not going to have a tantrum here. This is going to be a nice day out and you are not going to spoil it. You are not going to take this away.'

But the tantrum is coming thick and fast now, and with it sobs flood up my throat like backwards gulps.

'I'm not Ellie!' I yell. 'I'm not Ellie! It's her! She's the one! I'm Helen! I'm the one who does everything right! I'm Helen!'

But the sobs are making it difficult to speak and the words come out all broken up as a rollercoaster swoops over our heads and all the people put their hands up in the air and shout with glee.

Mother glances at Ellie. A frown comes over her face. Something glimmers in her eyes.

'What's this all about?' she says.

I do my most Helen of all faces. Surely she must see. Surely the me-ness in me will shine through.

'What's going on?' says Mother, wrinkling her nose like someone has done a windypop and no one is owning up.

Ellie takes a deep breath. She looks at me, then back at Mother. For a minute the world tips and sways like the magic carpet ride wavering in the distance.

'Oh, it's just Ellie,' she says in a pinched little voice. 'You know how she's always making things up and saying she isn't her? Well, now she's made up a story that she's really me and I'm really her. She won't stop going on about it. I've had it up to here.'

I stand looking at her with an open mouth, because none of that is true. The real Ellie was far too boring to make up stories. This is a new Ellie — an Ellie that she is making to fit me.

Mother rolls her eyes. 'I might have known!' she sighs and starts to pull my arm again.

'No!' I shout, tugging and stamping. 'She's lying! She's lying! It wasn't me!'

The smack sounds like a gunshot. I clutch my bottom. A big boy in a baseball cap gives a laugh as he walks past. He points at me and his friends turn to look. Tears flood into my eyes.

'Ellie,' says Mother, her mouth narrow and tight, 'I will not stand for this. You are going to behave. This is too important to be ruined by silly games. Do you understand?'

I sniff, nodding up at the blurry Mother in front of me. 'Yes,' I say.

'Right,' says Mother. 'Come along then, like a good girl.'

I follow her into the toilet, the sick

squelching round my feet. At the door, I turn and look back. Ellie is standing by the hedge. Her face is still pale from feeling ill, but on her mouth there is a small twist of a smile.

5

She spread the photograph of Hellie, smiling at the camera with a glint in her grey-blue eyes, on the living-room table and pegged it down with drawing pins. She stood back and stared at it. The face looked up at her, nervousness in the eyes now — some of the old Ellieness still peeking through. After three hours of sitting reading the words about the crash over and over again, smoking her way through the tobacco, she finally knew what she had to do. Her nerves zinged with it. Her head voices were in agreement. ('Yes!' they all shouted. 'Yes!') She was glad of their support.

'Don't worry, Hellie,' Smudge whispered softly. 'It's not what you think.'

And it wasn't. It wasn't nasty. It wasn't vengeful or mean. It was brilliant. Something new and entirely different. It would make sense of everything at last. She didn't know why she hadn't thought of it before.

She arranged her materials: the dregs of the paint, water, toothpaste in place of white, the brushes, the mirror. She also laid out some old make-up — foundation and eyeshadows in garish colours. She didn't know how they'd mix up, but she liked the idea of using them. No doubt critics would have something to say about her choice of materials — a comment on the superficiality of the modern age.

('Estimable,' said an authoritative, woman's voice somewhere inside her ear.)

She let fly a laugh. Critics! Ha! She could see it now: the crowds, the awards, the interviews with the national press. There'd be exhibitions and books published on the subject. They'd probably even name a new school of art after her — Hellenism, perhaps? Or hadn't there been that before? Oh well, she'd leave it to others to hash it out. She had enough to be getting on with. She was too busy being a genius. Because who else in the history of everything had ever come up with such an idea? A self-portrait painted over someone else's face. It was fucking inspired.

Thinking about it, it could be the start of a whole series. *Marilyn and Me, The Queen and I* — there was no end to the possibilities. She was on a roll. This could be, like, a whole new art form.

She bit her fist and jiggled with the excitement of it all. The doors of her mind blew open and she saw suddenly how it all aligned, how everything had been leading to this point. Everything made sense. The world linked up; shining threads running through the passages of her brain, turning the dusty, dark places into chambers of light. There had been a purpose to it all; through all the suffering, all the shit, she had been bringing herself steadily to this moment, shaping and refining her being until she was pure and lithe and alert to the rhythms of the higher plane with nothing but creativity, energy and will. And now it was here: her opportunity, her moment, her time to shine. And the best thing about it was that this was not her having one of her up times. This was not her being delusional. This was actually, properly real.

('Real as strawberry jam,' agreed the woman's voice.)

Hellie watched her, warily.

'There, Hellie, there,' said Smudge, stroking her sister's dewy-looking cheek.

Poor Hellie. She felt sorry for her now, fixed in all her daytime perkiness. She thought she might cry for a moment, but then the impulse passed.

She rubbed a hand over her face. What now? Oh, yes, music. She needed music. She flew over to the CD-cassette combi-player in the corner and rummaged through the cases lying around it. Joni Mitchell? Nah, too ephemeral. Radiohead? Too down-beat. Nirvana? Fuck off. The Beatles, Oasis, Carole King . . . She swept them all aside: she needed something uplifting and sub-stantial, something to urge her on to bril-liance. Mozart's *The Magic Flute*? That would have been good but it wasn't in its case. Beethoven's *Ninth*? Nah — too mili-tant. Besides, it wasn't even the proper ver-sion. It was one for a xylophone orchestra that she'd picked up in some car boot sale and only realised when she got it home. Rachmaninov's *Piano Concerto No 2*? Now we were talking. She slipped the CD into the machine and turned it up as loud as it would go. The music shivered the speakers in gusts — sinister, moody, clouds gather-ing before the weather broke to let the late-summer evening at the piece's heart shine through.

She walked back to the table in time to it, nodding to herself. This would carry her. Borne on Rachmaninov's great surges of sound she'd crest over the mountains of self-doubt and on into the stratosphere. She could feel the universe shifting and reordering itself, the stars thrumming. She was ready, she was open, she would channel it all.

As the music swelled and then scattered into rivulets of running notes, she twisted the top off the concealer and blobbed it on to the page. The beige liquid collected in drops, streaks of clear liquid running through them where the mixture had separated in the weeks lying out in the hallway. She reached out and smoothed it across the paper, feeling it spread like silk beneath her fingers, until the full wonky oval of Hellie's face was covered in a uniform, neutral shade. That done, she used the eye pencil to shade in some of the shape of her face. She traced back the features that loomed through the mist of the make-up, lending a leaner slant to her cheekbones and the hollows beneath and narrowing the eyes that Hellie's make-up team had widened so artfully for the camera.

The music shimmered, sending bright streams trickling through the whorls and crevasses of her brain as she set to work on the tattoo. This was the most technically complicated part and she spent some moments studying the letters on her temple in the last shard of the bathroom mirror. The trick was to get the angle correct. It was tempting to bend the rules and print the word on so it could be read backwards by anyone looking at the picture. But that would be a lie. From front on, only the 'M' and the 'O' were visible. That was what she had to capture if she wanted to present the picture as it really was. And this was what it was all about: truth.

She selected the indigo tube of paint and squeezed a worm's head of it out into the ice-cube tray. The music seethed around her, throwing up shapes only to topple them like so many houses of cards as she painted on: harnessed, focused, absorbed.

At first she thought the banging was the timps thundering in the furious climax of the third movement, but when the noise of the orchestra ebbed away, leaving the piano alone on the shore of melody, the thuds continued, insistent and brutally out of time. She frowned. What now? The family with the Rottweiler next door? Someone new moving in upstairs? The orchestra flooded in again carrying the piano with it to the penultimate crest of the piece and seeming to sweep the banging away. She shrugged and turned her attention back to the picture: 'A Selfish Portrait', she was beginning to think she would call it. It was a good sign, the title beginning to crystallise like that — it meant the work was sound.

'Ellie?' called a man's voice from the hall-way.

She stiffened. Fear gripped her, sending thoughts ricocheting through her brain: social services? Dom come to huff and puff and scratch his arse about her rent? The police? The kids from the estate setting off bangers outside? Bailiffs? No, they wouldn't call her Ellie like that. Then who?

The banging resumed, accompanied by the rattle of the letterbox. As the music surged to its finale, she edged to the thresh-old of the living room and peered out into the gloom of the hall. A dark shape stood behind the frosted glass of the front door, its outline shifting and changing like pat-terns in a kaleidoscope.

Then it disappeared. The letterbox flipped up.

'Ellie?' said the mouth it revealed: a man's mouth set in a smooth, clean-shaven face.

The mouth slid away and a pair of big brown eyes swooped in to take its place. She jumped back into the living room as the music tumbled to its final chords.

'Ellie?' said the mouth again. 'Look, I know you're in there. I can hear the music. I can see your shadow. Can you just open the door?'

Smudge looked down and saw her black outline spilling away from the bare bulb above the table and out into the hall. She shifted too late and sank down against the wall to minimise it, wincing as the paper rasped at her descent. She crouched, hugging her knees, feeling naked as the applause after the music ebbed away, leaving her exposed. Even her breathing seemed crude and loud in the silence.

('Irrefutable,' pronounced the woman.)

'Shhh,' said Smudge.

She heard a sigh come through the letterbox. 'Look, Ellie, you don't know me, but it's Helen's husband, Nick,' continued the mouth. 'I know this is difficult, but there are some things I need to talk to you about. It could be important. Would you please just open the door?'

He talked on, but she couldn't hear him. For, from the ceiling to the lino on the floor with its burnt patches gaping over scarred boards, everything was starting to reverberate with the notes of the Rachmaninov, giving back the waves of music absorbed over the preceding half hour in a swelling gush until the air itself quavered and pulsed with noise and the screech of a million violin strings seemed to come from the taut wires of her nerves. She stood up suddenly, sticking her head into exploding stars as the sound closed in, crushing her and forcing out one high, ringing scream that seemed to rebound off the walls and the window panes and come back stronger to torture her again.

She rushed to the table. There was the picture. Clumsy, demonic, skewed, it seemed now; laughing at her. She had thought she was in control when she made it — she had thought this time she was the one. But it was just like before. The Hellie bitch was still after her. Even now, at death's door, she wouldn't leave her in peace. She had tracked her down somehow. She had sent them after her. She would never be free.

Smudge picked up the black pencil and scored and scored and scored across the face. She scratched on to the point where the eyes of the face became blind and the mouth had no more smile in it and the paper ripped and gaped like a wound. She scratched on until her hand ached and her palm bled from where her nails had dug into it, and there was no longer anything to see.

6

As September comes closer, I start to get excited. My excited is a sharp, jagged thing that I hold inside me, ready to rip and tear at everything and change it all round. It is an excited that comes from still being stuck being Ellie. Plus ages sitting outside Chloe's mum's house in the lane in case she comes by and I can tell her the matter and she can make the truth come real. Plus trying to find Mary in the park and still there is no sign and I am worried that the house with the dragon's eye has eaten her up. Plus the silly looks that are still going on between Mother and Akela like there is no tomorrow and Mother floating about the house like she is a lady in a film and not in real life at all. Plus the times in the night when the tears come and shadows crawl on to the ceiling to laugh at me.

On the third of September I am the most excited I can be. It is a day I would not normally be excited because it is the end of the holidays, which means the first day of school, but this time it's different because the mistake is going to be discovered. The mistake is going to be discovered for three reasons. Firstly it's going to be discovered because Jessica and Charlotte and that lot will see me and know who I am. Next, it's going to be discovered because I am much cleverer than Ellie and anyone seeing her doing work that tries to pretend it's by me will say, 'Ellie, you stupid silly. What are you doing? Get back in the colouring in corner where you belong.' And last of all it's going to be discovered because we get to see Chloe again and that will really cook Ellie's goose.

When I think about the mistake being discovered, I am so pleased, I can hardly breathe. The way it will happen is one of the teachers will come and clap a big hand down on Ellie's shoulder while she is spelling things wrong in my storybook — like writing 'people' when everyone knows it has no 'o' anywhere at all. Then we will all have to go off to Miss Marshall's office, where it smells of cigarettes, and we will sit by the fern in a pot and the shelf with a trophy from the county under-tens long jump championship 1986 on it and we will have to tell the whole story like it really is. And Ellie will have to submit how she has been lying her head off and then everyone will go 'Ummm' at her. Next they will make Mother come in and Miss Marshall will put on her glasses and say 'I'm afraid there has been a serious incident', like she did when Thomas Jones was knocked down by a car and we all had to spend time driving go-karts around a little racing track to learn about road safety. After that they might put Ellie in prison, or if not they will make her clean out the games cupboard, and mean-while everyone will feel sorry for me and give me sympathy and it will be like I've broken my arm, except without the plaster cast or having to fall over.

When we come in the school gates, I can see Jessica and Charlotte and that lot stand-ing over by the broomstick trees and my heart gives a little skip like it can't wait for my body to get over there and be amongst its friends. But before I can get to them, El-lie speeds up beside me and powers across the grass doing my strong, striding run and swinging arms, and because of the blouse and the skirt Mother dressed her in and how confident Ellie is being, they all gather round to hug her. From a distance, she looks taller somehow, like a famous person.

They look over their shoulders at me as I come up in Ellie's tunic. 'Oh, hello, Ellie,' says Jessica.

Jessica's face looks longer and she is all golden from spending the summer at her uncle's house in Sicily, where there is a swimming pool and a tennis court and a little donkey you can ride.

I shake my head.

'It's me: Helen,' I said. 'Ellie's trying to play a trick.'

Jessica looks between Ellie and me. The moment wobbles. I see them all narrowing their eyes and staring and it makes me wish I had some of the Cola bottles Akela gave us left, to bring out and offer round. That would prove that I am Helen because Ellie is always greedy and finishes her sweets without offering any to anyone else. It's one of the worst things about her and everybody knows it and always says about it in secret chats. I think maybe I will buy some and bring them in tomorrow. That will show what a genuine Helen I am.

Then Ellie puts her hand on her hip, standing proudly, and says: 'God-uh, Ellie. I've had it up to here with you. Haven't you had enough of Let's Pretend? We're in Class 3 now, you know.'

Charlotte and that lot all burst out laughing, bending over like it hurts with how funny it is. I wait for them to finish, watching Jessica's smile curl into a sneer, like a piece of paper burning on a bonfire, but just as I open my mouth to say how it really is, the whistle blows and they all run away, screaming and giggling, to go and line up.

Ellie might have got everybody on her side at the start, but I am determined to have the last laugh, so when we go in I run quickly to get a place at the popular table, right next to Jessica. As we take our chairs down Nadia rolls her eyes and Seema waves her hand in front of her nose and says 'Does it smell in here?', which is what they always used to say about Ellie, but I smile because I know the truth. When Ellie finally comes in with her arm around Katy, there isn't any room left at the table so she has to go and sit with Ruth and Hannah C, who bites her fingers and smells of Quavers. I am pleased that things are getting back to the way they should be.

The new teacher is called Miss Inchbald. She is young and shiny, with corners on the collar of her jacket that look like they have been put through a pencil sharpener to make them point. When she comes in, the first thing she says after 'Good morning' and writing her name on the board is: 'Now,

Class Three, see how smooth my forehead is? There are no lines on it. I don't want there to be any lines by the end of the year, so you'd better make sure you behave.'

Next, there is the register. The names go in the normal order except for the new boy, Pascal, who comes from France. He looks worried when he hears his name and looks round to see what he should do. Then he realises everyone had been saying 'Yes' and he says it too in a funny French way and makes us all laugh. He puts his hands in the air like a footballer scoring a goal and suddenly, just like that, he is not new any more. He is one of us.

Then it gets to Ellie's name.

'Eleanor Sallis,' says Miss Inchbald. Nobody says anything. Everybody looks around.

Miss Inchbald taps her pen on the page with all the blank squares on it, two for each person for every day in the term. She looks up.

'Eleanor Sallis?' she says again.

I see the movement beside me before I hear the words.

'She's here, Miss,' says Jessica, pointing, and the others join in: 'She's here! She's here!'

Miss Inchbald looks at me through the

forest of their hands. 'Hmmn,' she says, and she marks Ellie's cross with thoughtful eyes.

Then it's Helen on the list and I lurch to put my hand up, only Jessica grabs it and holds it firm under the table so I have to watch while Ellie nods and takes my name with a pinched little smile.

After the register, we get ready to write all about what we did in the holidays. A new year means new exercise books and I am looking forward to getting mine and writing my name on it once and for all. And I am especially looking forward to telling the story of Ellie's naughtiness and how she is lying at everybody left, right and centre. But instead, Miss Inchbald comes over and takes my hand and leads me to the special corner where there is Ellie's old workbook that she didn't finish last year. The workbook has pictures that you have to match up with words and then copy out the spelling so your hand learns how to do it properly and I have to sit between James, who always wets himself, and Parvez, whose family moved here from Bangladesh last year and who still thinks 'hellohowareyou' is one big long word. When I look up from the book, I see Ellie swaggering to the space next to Jessica, hugging her new exercise book and my pencil case like they are teddy bears, and a black feeling comes over me that makes me pick up my pencil and scrawl all over the pictures of the dog and the cat and the family car that I am supposed to be matching up. I am so busy scribbling, wanting to make every last bit of the page grey, that I don't notice anyone is there until a hand comes to rest on the edge of the table. It is a hand I know: a soft hand, with purple, sparkly nails and rings on all the middle fingers.

I look up. 'Chloe!' I shout. And quick as Count Duckula's teleporting, I am out from behind the desk and into her arms, pressing my face against her soft, furry pink jumper and breathing in her flowery smell.

'There,' says Chloe, stroking my hair pulled into Ellie's bunches. 'There. Nice to see you too, Ellie.'

And even though she says Ellie, I don't mind, because I know now that Chloe is here everything will be OK.

We go to the little room beside the hall, the one with carpet on the walls where they keep the TV on wheels. Chloe gets out her notes and I am surprised to see a big wodge of papers because when I was in here last year there was just one form and at the bit called Progress it said: 'Very good'. I know because I saw Chloe writing it. Even though it was far away and upside down, I managed to read the words.

'Now then, Ellie,' says Chloe, turning on her bright smile like the light on the overhead projector in the hall. Either side of her face, the gold hoops of her earrings gleam. 'Why don't you tell me what you got up to on your summer holiday?'

And suddenly it all rushes at me: Jessica forcing down my hand, and Charlotte and that lot laughing, and Ellie's bunches pulling at my head and Mother keeping on putting them back in no matter how many times I pull them out, and the stupid, scratchy tunic dress, and Akela, and Thorpe Park. And there in the little TV room with the carpet smell from the walls, I feel all the things boiling around in my tummy until it comes bubbling up in sobs that spill out through my nose and mouth with big, wet tears.

Chloe bends down to get some tissues from her bag.

'There, there,' she says. 'Poor chicken.'

And I nod because I am a poor chicken and for ages now no one has known it but me. I blow my nose into the tissues, which have little pink pictures of butterflies on them, and cry some more. Then Chloe comes and puts her arms round me and we stay like that for hours.

'I'm sorry to see you're still so sad,' she says. 'You seemed much better when I ran into you that day I was popping to see my mum.'

With a lurch I remember about the lane and the game and tricking Chloe.

'That's it!' I try to say. 'That's when it all went wrong!'

But the words get sogged up in the sadness and for a while all I can do are bubbling, burbling sounds.

At last, when Chloe is back on her side of the table and the sobs have quietened down, I open my mouth and start to tell. I tell it all: about the game when we saw her and the knickers and about Mr Greene who is really Akela and Ellie making me stay as her. About halfway through Chloe gets out a piece of paper and starts making notes. This makes me feel pleased because I know it means she is taking it seriously and soon everyone will know, so I talk on and on, telling everything I can think of, even when it's not really to do with the main problem. Like, I tell about Mrs Dunkerley and her budgie Bill. And I tell about how we haven't seen Mary for ages and the monster moving the boxes in the hall. The only thing I do not tell about is Mary's brother and the 'fucked' because I suspect it wouldn't fit nicely in the room.

When I have finished telling, I am quite thirsty and my head is starting to ache from all the tears it has cried, but I wait because Chloe is still writing and I want her to get it all down with no mistakes. Chloe's pen twirls and twitches over the paper, like an elegant lady whirling and swaying across a ballroom. Then it gets to the end, does a jump and stops.

'Goodness,' she says. 'That is quite a story, isn't it?' Then she gets a bit of hair and twirls it round her finger like she's trying to make it curl more. 'And what about your daddy?' she says. 'Have you done any more thinking about him?'

I think it's a strange question to ask because Father made his Unfortunate Decision a long time ago, way before Ellie and me swapped places, and do we really still have to talk about all that? Plus, I can't really remember what he looks like any more. My memories of him are like a sweet that you have sucked too long until all the flavour is gone. Now there is just a smoky smell and the picture in my head of the day in the precinct when he bought all the colours in the shop and we skipped and laughed all the way home. But it is a story I

75

have told myself so many times, I'm not even sure if it's true. Even the favourite green T-shirt is going a mustardy yellow now and there are rips in the neck from where Ellie has pulled it out of shape in the days of being me. I know he was a real man because there are still the Pointless Creations in the little room upstairs at the front of our house — I go in and see them sometimes and run my fingers over the rough paint and see how the colours are like exploding stars — but I don't feel his realness any more. That part of him has vanished into thin air.

At the funeral, Mother's friend Susan read out a thing that said Father had just gone away into another room. Me and Ellie spent a long time looking for the door to that room. We looked all along the hallway and in every corner in the living room and I even made Ellie crawl all the way to the back of the cupboard under the stairs where the spiders are, but we never found it. So I am pretty sure that Father won't be coming back from the other room now, which means talking about him is what Mother would call 'an irrelevant question'. But I get the feeling this is not the answer Chloe wants to hear, so instead I screw up my eyes and try to imagine Father coming bursting through from a door to the other room and making Ellie behave.

'I think he'd be furious if he knew what was going on now,' I say. 'I think he'd come punishing down hard on Ellie and not let her watch television for a week. I think he'd say: "Bad Ellie. Naughty Ellie. Go outside and stand in the corner and never darken my door again." '

Chloe takes a deep breath and taps her fingernails on the table. Her earrings jiggle.

'Do you know what I think, Ellie?' she says. 'I think it would be a good idea if you drew all this out like we talked about before. Here's a bit of paper. Just sit and let the pictures come out of your head and when you've finished we can put it in the file with all your other picture stories from last year.'

And now I am surprised because when I look again at the wodge of papers, I see it is not forms with Chloe's neat writing but stacks of graph paper covered in spidery drawings. There is one with a spaceship and another one with a witch zapping someone with a spell, and poking out the top I see a picture of a girl in bunches with tears flying out of her eyes and a long, dangly string. And now I am thinking of what Ellie said to Mother about Ellie always telling stories and suddenly here they all are, lined up, and I didn't even know. And even though the pictures are rubbish, it is strange to think that everything here came out of Ellie's brain. Ellie, who smells her fingers and stares at Bill the budgie for years and years.

I am so surprised that I don't notice that Chloe has used the wrong name until she reaches out across the table and says it again.

'OK, Ellie love?' she says.

'But, but, but . . .' I say, so it sounds like bubbles bursting all around. 'But I'm not Ellie.'

'I know, chicken,' says Chloe, standing up and walking to the door. 'We all feel like that sometimes. It's part of being human. But do the drawing and you'll feel better, I promise.'

And with that, she goes out, leaving me staring at the graph paper. The little squares zoom towards me, getting bigger and bigger. They fill my view until, if I squint, I can almost believe they are doors that I could open and step through into another room.

7

Over the days that followed, he kept coming back. At first he stood at the front door, a dark shape against the panel of frosted glass, bending now and then to peer and call through the letterbox. As time went on, however, he got bolder, wandering away from the front door to peer in between the throws and scarves tacked across the living-room window into the gloom beyond.

Sometimes she didn't know if it was the head voices or him calling her. They cottoned on quickly and took to catching her at odd moments, mimicking his voice with a cruel edge, sniggering when she jumped. They'd been getting worse since Nick arrived — nastier, more insistent.

On the third morning he found the path round the side of the maisonette and made his way into the scrubby back garden, with its burnt patch and empty bottles of White Lightning and Buckfast left by the local kids. He peered in through the kitchen windows and banged on the back door. Smudge crouched amid the bags of rubbish behind one of the kitchen units as he did so, hoping against hope that she'd remembered to lock the back door the last time she'd stumbled in. Luckily he didn't try it — not that time — but he did bang and call, his voice getting ever sharper, louder.

'Go away,' she moaned quietly, rocking back and forth with her head in her hands. 'Go a-fucking-way!'

On the fifth morning, after he'd been banging for what felt like several hours, wandering back and forth around the place, she picked up the phone.

'Hello, Samaritans?'

('Hello, Smarty Pants,' sneered a head voice.)

'He's at it again,' said Smudge. 'He's trying to get in. I'm here on my own and he won't go away.'

'Take your time,' said the woman.

('Put your back into it,' insisted the voice. 'Give it to her with both barrels.')

Smudge took a deep breath and tried to focus. She was young, the volunteer. A teacher, maybe, in a primary school. Or a librarian. Soft, like Ange at the unit all those years ago used to be; eager to be kind.

'It's just,' she said, trembling, 'I think I've had about as much as I can take.'

('You've had about as much as you're getting,' said the voice. 'You selfish bitch.')

There was a pause.

('Animal, that's what you are,' muttered the voice. 'Shouldn't be allowed.')

'When you say you've had as much as you can take, what do you mean?' said the woman, Ange.

Smudge swallowed. The silence stood before her like an open door, waiting.

('Do you think we're made of money?' said the voice.)

'He beats me,' she said hurriedly. 'He abuses me. He won't leave me alone. I'm covered in bruises — all up my arms. I can't tell anyone. It's a nightmare, it never ends.'

'That must be awful,' said Ange.

('Windscreen wipers!' shouted the voice.)

Smudge nodded. It was awful. It was a nightmare. It was more than she could bear. She broke down and, against the heckling of the voice and the shouts from outside, she talked through juddering sobs about the abusive relationship she'd been in for three years. About how he kept coming back every time she threw him out. About how he was out there now, thudding and hammering like there was no tomorrow. About how he wouldn't — wouldn't — leave her alone. No, she wasn't suicidal, she told Ange impatiently — she knew they had to ask it, that it was in their rules, but it still pissed her off every call — just tired and sad and lonely. So lonely. She'd been on her own with this for such a long time. They all wanted to hurt her. That was the thing. Every last one of them. Even the people she should be able to trust. Especially those. They were all out to do her harm.

After a while, the banging subsided. She heard the letterbox flap shut for the last time and the soft slap of something dropping into the hall. Then the silence washed in. She felt peaceful sitting there amid the rubbish sacks with the sunlight slanting in through the bent slats of the blinds, serene.

There was a hush on the line. They'd been sitting together saying nothing for some minutes. Even the voices were quiet.

'And how are you feeling now?' said Ange.

Smudge started. She'd forgotten there was anyone there. She had forgotten who she was supposed to be.

Impatience surged through her. She hated herself for her stupidity and felt disgusted at this soft-voiced stranger whispering sympathy for her lies.

'Oh, all right,' she said. 'He's gone now. I

don't expect he'll be back today.'

'And will you manage OK this evening?' said Ange. She no longer sounded kind. She sounded pathetic. A mug. Smudge couldn't wait to get off the phone.

'Oh yes,' she said. 'Thank you. Yes, I will. You've been very helpful.'

She put the receiver up on the side and sat hugging her knees. The golden light of the day was shifting and beginning to grey. A dog barked and she heard the family next door arrive home, kids bounding up the path, voices piping. A great sense of numbness washed in. ('Mouldy old swizz,' observed the voice.) Maybe suicide wasn't such a stupid idea after all.

8

Autumn brings colours in reds, golds and browns and when you are in the upside-down tree in the park you get to be inside them all. What the upside-down tree is like is a big skirt of a lady's dress from the olden days and it sweeps right down to the ground so that when you go under it no one can see you from outside, except in winter when the lady gets undressed and it is shivering-cold.

Today, we are out by ourselves in the upside-down tree because Mother needs space to get organised for the dinner party that she and Akela are giving in the evening, where there will be people from Akela's work and Mother's friend Susan, whose laugh is hard and bright like a telephone. Space to get organised means space away from us and our nonsense. Even the nonsense we do when we are trying to help. We know this from the time when Mother cooked a roast lunch and the gravy went on the floor and I tried to help with a tea towel like Helen would always do, only it turned out it was the wrong one and Mother's especial favourite — even though she'd never said about it before. And then it was like the day got scrunched up and thrown away like the spoilt pages in Ellie's workbook and lunch turned into Akela pushing us out the door with five-pounds-to-spend-at-the-shops pressed into Ellie's hand. Ellie spent it on a Tiny Tears doll and we sat in the upside-down tree watching it to see if it would come alive but it just stayed in its box and didn't move even when it got dark and you'd think it would be scared.

This Saturday has been a day of sorting things out. In the morning we went to the shopping centre. Mother was in a shiny mood and smiled at all the people, walking fast in her cloppy shoes so we had to run to keep up. First we went to the make-up place, where Mother had a long talk with an orange lady about what colours were right for her face. Mother's credit card went zip-zip in the machine where it presses down on the paper and you have to sign your name. Next it was the nail bar, where the colours go on with a little brush that licks each fingernail like a tongue.

Ellie got excited watching and her leg started to jiggle.

'Can I have colour on my nails too?' she said.

Mother smiled and patted her head even though Ellie wasn't minding her Ps and Qs.

'Maybe when you're a bit older, sweetheart,' she said.

'Can I?' I said so that I could be a sweetheart too.

Mother shot me a sharp look. 'For God's sake, Ellie,' she said. 'Didn't I just say no?'

Then it was time to do our clothes because we've been growing like Topsy and we just don't know where the time goes. Before, I always liked buying clothes when Mother was in one of her shiny moods. She would whirl around the shop with a basket, throwing in all the things she thought would be nice and choosing extra-special things for me because I am the daintiest. But today Mother's special things were for the Helen she thinks Ellie is and I was left with the practical top and the skirt that looks like it belongs to someone who is five. I put them on quietly, but when Ellie came out of the changing room in the princess dress with the shiny pink bow and everyone clapped their hands together and gasped like she was Cinderella, I couldn't stop my hand from reaching out and pinching and grabbing at the bow till it tore off.

Mother was coming back with another basketful of clothes and when she saw the bow flopping in my fingers with threads dangling like spiders' legs the white, spiky look came about her mouth and suddenly it was time to go and no arguments and don't you dare say a word I'm warning you. She paid for everything, even the stuff that didn't fit, and we drove home with the car charging and growling and the shiny mood all gone.

Now in the upside-down tree, Ellie is talking in that way she always does when it's just us two, like if she keeps speaking there won't be any room for anything else. She is spinning around to see the swish of her new skirt, which has buttons down the back like someone getting married in a film, and she is saying how soon she's going to ask Mother if she can have Magic Step shoes like Charlotte and that lot because she wants to see if it's true that the key in the bottom can magic you into another world.

I know it's not true because last year Nadia spent all lunch break trying to get whooshed away and nothing happened. Even when we made her spin round three times and click her heels she just stayed

right where she was. But I don't say anything because I am too busy standing there
in nobody's clothes, watching the skirt that
should be mine twirl and whip over the
leaves and the cigarette packets and the old
popped balloon that looks like the skin of a
pink slug filled with slug slime. And suddenly it seems like the saddest thing of all.

'Of course, you won't be allowed the same
shoes as me,' says Ellie, sweeping round and
making her arms go over her head like a
ballerina. 'You'll have to have something
else so everyone will know the difference. I
expect Mother will make you get some of
those Start-rite ones with the bar across or
maybe —'

She stops and looks at me.

'You're crying,' she says.

I nod and sniff. She comes and looks at
me like she is on a school trip to the zoo
and I am a lizard in a tank with diamond
patterns round its eyes.

'Why are you crying?' she says, and
reaches out to touch my tears with her
finger.

I open my mouth to say it all, but the
words get impatient and tumble over each
other and all that comes is a big waily
sound.

She gives a sigh. 'If you really want Magic

88

Step shoes all that much I suppose I could ask Mother to get them for you,' she says like she is talking to a baby.

I shake my head. 'No, it's not the shoes,' I make my mouth say even though it comes out in big, Ellie-ish gulps. 'It's everything. Me being you all the time. I don't like it any more. I want things to go back to how they were. Before Akela. Before the game. That day.'

The blank look comes over Ellie's face like she is a television and someone has turned her off. She spins round and tries to go back to her ballet twirling but I grab her hand.

'Please, Ellie,' I say. 'It's not a joke any more. It's making me really sad. Please.'

Ellie looks at me. Her eyes flicker. A wisp of hair that can't be disguised by the plait no matter how hard she tries wriggles loose and blows across her face.

'Please, Ellie,' I say again to make the moment last and get bigger instead of shrinking away. 'Please. You're the only one who can make it better.'

Ellie's eyes go quiet. She reaches out and curls a finger round my eye. I feel her nail skimming over the skin.

'What do you want me to do?' she says.

Something in my chest lurches awake like Akela snorting and saying he wasn't sleeping on the sofa. I clench my fingers into fists to stop the glad feeling from fidgeting them into silliness. I take a deep breath.

'Promise me the next person we see we'll tell the truth to about you being me and me being you,' I say.

Ellie puts her head on one side like Mrs Dunkerley's Bill.

'All right,' she says in a strange, faraway voice. 'The next person we see, we'll tell.'

And now I am excited. If I had it my way, we'd go tearing out, spit-spot, to find someone in the park and end the game right there and then. But I know I mustn't show Ellie how pleased I am, so all I let myself do is a jump and a small shuffle ball change among the leaves. Then I sit on the branch that runs along the ground and watch Ellie spinning and jumping and a bubbly feeling goes all round my body.

When it is time to go, we wriggle out from under the upside-down tree and then more excitement comes because who should we see sitting in the playground but Mary? It's all I can do not to give a squeak because now I know the goose is really cooking.

'It's Mary,' I say, and I see a worried look come over Ellie's face. Then she gives herself a little shake like a bird ruffling its feathers. A promise is a promise and even

Ellie knows that.

'OK,' she says. 'Come on.'

We go over. Mary is sitting on one of the swings, dragging her feet over the tarmac and staring at the trees far away. She doesn't seem to see us arrive. It's been ages since we last saw her, but I know she'll be just as ready as me for the punishing down and the lesson teaching, particularly when she hears about the naughtiness Ellie has done.

'Hi Mary,' I go. 'How are you?'

There is a pause then Mary turns her head towards us. 'Oh, hullo,' she says, looking somewhere between us, like we are really standing over the other side of the park down by the pond.

'We've been looking for you,' I say. 'Where did you go? Did you go to your uncle's in Manchester?'

Mary shrugs. 'Holiday,' she says. But here's the strange thing: the way Mary says 'holiday' makes it sound like the greyest, saddest word you could think of. Plus September isn't the time for holidays and why is Mary only wearing shorts and a T-shirt when already the winter winds are starting to whisper in the trees?

Still, I don't talk about all this because I am too excited and my brain is mostly taken up with the most important thing. I open my mouth to tell about the game and all its secrets, but before I can say anything, Ellie says: 'What happened to your legs?'

And then I notice that there are purply-blue patches all up Mary's legs and around her wrists, like bracelets pressed into the skin. There is also a big scab across Mary's knee like maybe she fell over when she was running for a bus to the big school.

Mary looks at Ellie and doesn't say anything. Then her eyes disappear back to looking at the trees. Behind her a Coke can rattles its way across the playground, chuckling to itself like it is busy and has lots of places to go.

It feels like the telling of the game is slipping away, so I give a jiggle and shout, 'Mary, Mary, we've got a secret to tell!'

Then I look at Ellie, because it has to be her too and not me on my own. 'Go on,' I say. 'Do the promise.'

Ellie gives a cough and makes her eyes go round in her head.

'God-uh,' she says. 'O-*K*.' She points at me. 'This is H-elle-n. I'm El-lie. We've been swapped round the wrong way but now H-elle-n has been crying and made me promise to tell the truth.'

I don't like the way Ellie says my name like it's got another 'l' stuck in it and I'd rather she left the crying out — it is Mary after all — but I am so pleased to have the truth said that all I can do is stand there with a big grin. Mary looks at us both. Then a glimmer comes into her eye.

'Oh, I see,' she says, stretching like a cat and bringing the old Mary back after all. She turns to me. 'Well, then, H-elle-n,' she says, 'since you're the leader, why don't you suggest a game we can all play?'

My heart is thumping now and my head is clambering with all the lessons I've been wanting to give, and there is a feeling like a balloon rising up through me to fill the space between my ears.

My mouth flips open. 'Teaching Ellie to fly over the big ditch,' I say. And as soon as it comes out, I know it is the wrong choice, because actually that is quite an old game that we used to play a lot last year and how old are we now? Still, there's nothing I can do about it now: the game is said and that's what we must play.

Mary gives a nod like it is actually a good decision and stands up.

'All right,' she says, with a smile unfolding like a note passed under the desk. 'You do the demonstration and I'll wait here with the pupil.'

And now the pleased feeling is playing like

a disco in my head, drowning out the whisper of worry that comes from the smile going back and forth between Mary and Ellie, because Mary has said the game exactly how it used to be and now I know everything is going back to normal again. I am so pleased that I don't even go to the proper starting line for the lesson. I just take off across the grass then and there, galloping as fast as I can. To make myself go faster, I even go 'yah-yah' and thump my bottom like somebody riding a horse, and the evening comes at me, the air whistling past my ears.

When I get to the edge of the trees, I do the trick that always fools Ellie. I give a massive jump just before the ditch so it looks like I have gone over and just me and Mary know the truth. Then I stand to the side, giggling. I am thinking about what will happen when Ellie comes lolloping down the slope and lands in the ditch like always. I wonder if there'll be a little bit of blood this time and if me and Mary will have to give Ellie the talk about trying harder and maybe one day she'll be good enough and how it's all her own fault because if she believed in the flying properly she would have gone over the ditch and we wouldn't be having this conversation. I especially want to give that talk.

I stand aside and peer through the bushes, waiting to see Ellie come puffing over the grass. A minute ticks by, then another. Somewhere up in the branches above a big black bird gives a squawk and a flap, like someone has given it a surprise it didn't want. The breeze comes and tickles my ears.

I give a call. 'Ready!' I shout. 'Ready for the lesson!'

But there is no reply.

I peer round the edge of the bush. The park is quiet and empty with the shadows creeping in towards me across the grass. There is no Mary by the swings and no Ellie lurching across the grass. Only if I listen carefully there is maybe a laugh floating on the wind. Or it could be a car alarm blaring in the next street. I narrow my eyes until the tree trunks look like people standing round. And inside, like the flame jumping into life on the gas cooker, something sparks and catches and begins to burn.

9

The woman — Chantelle according to her name badge — said she should be proud of herself for making it to the ESA interview only half an hour late. It was, she said, a marked improvement on the two missed previously, a sign that things were moving in the right direction. Smudge thought about making some joke about the chance to escape from Nick making the appointment a welcome distraction, but she couldn't think of a way to say it that would make sense. It would require too many words to bring it into focus. Keep it simple. That was the best policy.

She sat in the dingy little room and watched the woman's mouth move up and down like something on a mechanical doll. A realisation dawned on her that there was something untrustworthy about the set up. It seemed fake; the woman was trying too hard to be convincing. After a minute or two, Smudge was glad she hadn't said that thing about Nick: she was pretty certain this was being filmed.

They went through all the usual suspects. Was she getting enough to eat?

She thought of the empty fridge, the tub of marge. 'Yes,' she said, and as Chantelle wrote the answer down in a slow, sloping hand, Smudge glanced into the corners of the room trying to spot the red eye of a camera. There was nothing that she could see: only a spider's web and the discarded wrapper of a Starburst. All the same . . .

And the drinking? Was she keeping that under control?

She crossed her legs and winced as the cut she'd got from treading on the broken vodka bottle the day before throbbed. 'Yes, it's all much better,' she said firmly.

Chantelle sat forward chummily in her chair, her pen poised. And what did she do when she got an urge to hit the bottle?

This was how they got you: pretending to be your friend, pretending to be the same as you. Textbook stuff. She definitely wasn't being paranoid.

She thought for a moment. 'I go to the park and feed the ducks,' she said.

It was so stupid, she almost laughed, but Chantelle nodded and smiled and wrote it down busily as though it was just what she'd hoped.

That was when Smudge noticed that Chantelle's suit jacket was too small for her. The top button was about to give. An obvious disguise. It clearly wasn't even hers.

What about the voices? Was she still hearing those?

'Oh no,' she said steadily. 'Not for a long time.'

(She listened for the inevitable retort, but this morning they were staying quiet.)

And the paranoid thoughts?

Smudge shrugged and pulled an exaggeratedly happy face (good for the camera). 'Nup.'

'Excellent,' said Chantelle, threading her fingers through the handle of a 'You Don't Have to Be Mad to Work Here — But It Helps' mug. 'Really, really good.'

They'd talked for five minutes about Smudge's volunteer work at the community garden. Smudge hadn't been for six weeks, but she wasn't about to reveal that. Instead she waxed lyrical about how lovely it was to get fresh air and see things grow. She got a bit carried away and started to worry she might have overdone it, but when she looked at Chantelle, it was clear there was no issue: the woman's eyes were fixed on the picture of the group of volunteers that had appeared in the *South London Press* five months back, showing Smudge, with the 'M' of her tattoo just poking out from her hair, looking wide-eyed next to a bunch of runner beans under the headline 'Green Shoots in Community Care'. The photograph had been cut out and pinned on the noticeboard by the door and Chantelle was very pleased with it. It had won the staff at the centre a commendation from their higher ups and for a long time now it had covered a multitude of sins. Chantelle wasn't the only one missing things, it seemed, because Fat Sandra, who was supposed to supervise the project but instead sat in the back office eating crisps, had produced a glowing report stating what an 'exemplary' volunteer Smudge had been. It was there in black and white: 'exemplary', or rather 'exempulry', circled with a ring from a coffee mug. It wasn't even true but Smudge got quite emotional looking at it, stupid Smudge that she was.

Chantelle smiled and handed her a box of thin, pastel-coloured tissues. It was only natural she should feel like that, she said. It was a big achievement. She knew exactly how she felt.

The worst bit was at the end of the session, when Chantelle, dotting her final sentence with a flourish, launched into a speech about how proud she and everyone else at the centre was of her: how she was just what the Employment and Support Allowance scheme was about. How, reading over the file, she couldn't believe the difference between the anxious, depressed, alcoholic person who'd sat in that chair a year ago and the confident, positive woman facing her now. How she was a lesson to everybody. How there was no doubt in her mind that come the imminent termination of her allowance, she would be fit to work and ready to contribute fully to society once again. A momentary panic seized Smudge, hearing this version of herself trotted out, but she bit it back and smiled enigmatically. She was not about to let them snare her with a bluff.

Outside the centre, she hawked and spat on the pavement. Thank fuck that was over. Thank fuck she'd got out of there without giving anything away — nothing they could use against her further down the line. She dug out the roll-up she'd saved for the occasion and took a grateful puff.

There was no money for the bus, so she had to walk back. By the time she turned on to her street, the day was fading. Her feet were throbbing, the cut oozing and causing her to limp. She kept her eyes on them, focusing all her attention on each faltering step. Anyone who saw her would think she was drunk. Hopefully she soon would be.

She didn't notice the man sitting on the wall until he stood up and blocked her path. She made to step round him, but he put out an arm to stop her.

'Ellie,' he said in the voice that had come through the letterbox. 'It is you, isn't it? Even after all these years, you look just like her, even —'

He paused to fumble for a tactful way of describing her dishevelled state. She didn't wait to hear his solution. Spinning round, she sped off up the road, painful feet forgotten, panic pumping in her ears.

'Wait,' called Nick behind her. 'Ellie! Please! I just want to talk to you! Ellie!'

She heard his footsteps thumping after her, beating against the thuds of her heartbeat. He was gaining on her. She could almost feel the heat of him behind her, closing in.

'Please, Ellie,' he shouted again, his words exploding close to the back of her neck. 'You owe her that much at least! Please!'

She owed nothing; she was no one, she

wanted to shout, but her lungs were aching and there was a plug of pain in her throat.

She stumbled on. If only the bastard would leave her alone. But he kept edging closer. Then she felt him make a grab for her arm.

With a gasp, she ducked between two parked cars and out on to the road. The next thing was two lights flying at her, a screech, a bang and the world somersaulting into space.

10

The cologist's office is up a flight of stairs. What you do is, you go in and say your name and then they tell you to wait and then, after some people come and go and it feels like you are never going to get out of there, they tell you you can go in. I don't mind the waiting though, because I get to miss school, which means today I don't even mind about having to be Ellie, or at least not while I'm walking up the path to the gate in Ellie's coat and scarf and all the eyes from the classrooms are watching me, feeling jealous.

Mother looks at pages in magazines while I do the waiting. I kick my feet back against the board on the front of the sofa we are sitting on until Mother looks at me with her one-more-peep-out-of-you eyes. So then I have to think of another game to make the time go and I look all about the room at the other people there and decide about who they are. Opposite, there is a fat girl eating crisps, and her mother who is also fat. The girl has eaten so many crisps that she has almost turned into a potato and if we don't look out there will soon be a vegetable sitting there in her school uniform and maybe we will have to cook her for supper. It makes me laugh to imagine the top of a big potato poking out the neck of her blue jumper with the yellow line round the edge, but I only do it quietly in case Mother gets annoyed.

Round by the fish tanks there is a little boy with a big head, sitting next to his mother. The mother is in a soft dress that is the same colour as inside the Roses strawberry chocolate and every minute or two she smiles at the little boy and strokes his big head, like every part of him is precious. Her name is Mrs Honeysuckle. (It isn't really.)

Then there are two grumpy boys who sit chomping and sucking like they are trying to eat up the inside of their own heads. I say about it to Mother, but she says it's rude to point and anyway it's just chewing gum. So for the rest of the time I sit and chew my gums just like them, moving my mouth up and down and making a golloping sound like a cow on a farm until Mother hisses, 'For God's sake, Eleanor, stop letting the side down.'

And then I know it's serious because 'Eleanor' only comes out on Sunday-best occasions and sometimes not even then. I pipe down and sit with my finger over my mouth for the rest of the wait.

For the first part of going in, the waiting mostly continues. There is an old man in a suit with lots of questions to ask Mother and a big form to fill in and he writes carefully like he wants to get everything right because soon a teacher will come and make an example of him if he gets it wrong. I look around the room and mostly what I see is toys. There are toys sitting on all the shelves in front of books, and toys in boxes on the floor. Normally this would make me happy, but there is a sad feeling about these toys that makes me wish they weren't there. Like, the Barbie on the shelf by Mother is missing an arm and someone has scribbled blue biro on the Mr Potato Head and you can tell just by looking at the box that hardly any of the Hungry Hippo balls are still there. It is like the toys have had all the good fun played out of them and now there is no one left to put them away nicely and make sure they sleep well at night.

I am about to ask if I can get down and go and look at the *Where's Wally?* book in the corner, when the conversation changes colour and it is like we are in a television and someone has twiddled the knob to make it go orange and fuzzy.

'So,' says the man, who it turns out is called Dr Palin, clapping his hands on his knees and leaning towards me, 'what seems to be the problem?'

'We've been having a lot of tantrums,' says Mother. 'And her schoolwork has deteriorated dramatically since the start of the year. I mean, she's always lagged behind her sister in just about everything, but over the past few months she seems to have taken a giant step backwards.'

'Uh-huh,' says Dr Palin, and he begins to write on another pad.

'There's also been some erratic behaviour,' says Mother, as the Barbie behind her head gives me a big wink.

'Umm?' says Dr Palin, making his voice go up and glancing sideways at me.

'Well, for example, the other week she hid in the park and wouldn't come home,' says Mother. 'We had friends coming round that evening and you can imagine the disruption it caused. Horace spent the whole night looking for her.'

'Horace?' says Dr Palin.

'My, er, gentleman friend,' says Mother.

'I see,' says Dr Palin. 'And is Horace — ?'

'We're cohabiting, yes,' says Mother, talking in the pointed voice she uses for words like 'lavatory', so that for a moment it feels like someone has sprayed a puff of Country Fresh in the room.

The Barbie shakes her head and does a poo-ey face.

'I see,' says Dr Palin, not looking up from his writing. 'For how long?'

Mother's cheeks get red and she tosses her head. For a minute I think she is going to tell Dr Palin to mind his business and not to lower the tone, but instead she says, 'Since August, I think. Yes, August.'

'Uh-huh,' says Dr Palin and goes on with his writing. 'And the problems began — ?'

'Just before the start of the school year,' says Mother. 'But I'm quite convinced that couldn't have had anything to do with it. Horace is gentle. He's kind and he's reliable. He's quite simply the best thing that could have happened to us, given the circumstances.'

'Mmmn,' says Dr Palin, flicking through some sheets of paper. 'How long is it since your husband — ?'

'Committed suicide?' says Mother, with a wrinkle of her nose. 'Three years this spring.'

I look up at the Barbie again but now she is sitting still.

'I see,' says Dr Palin. 'And does Eleanor talk about him much?'

'Not really,' says Mother, her red finger-nails picking at a thread coming loose on her skirt. 'Neither of them do. To be honest, it all feels a very long time ago. That day and everything around it are pretty much a blank in my mind and I'm sure even less of it remains for the girls. They were only four when it happened and he'd hardly been a model parent before that, so . . .'

'Mmmn,' says Dr Palin and his pen pauses, hovering in the air.

'She's been making up stories too,' says Mother, hurrying on.

'Oh?' says Dr Palin, and his pen starts writing again.

'All sorts of wild things, but she does keep going on about swapping places with her twin sister. Quite honestly, we're sick to the back teeth of it.'

'Mmmn,' says Dr Palin, looking at me. 'And her sister is — ?'

'Thriving,' says Mother. 'Good as gold. If anything, she's made even more progress with her schoolwork this year.'

'Uh-huh,' says Dr Palin. 'And what about bedwetting?'

'Oh, yes,' says Mother. 'We've had a few incidents.'

And now it is my turn for my cheeks to go red, because it is like Mother has pulled up my skirt and showed Dr Palin my knickers, all without asking me. Plus, it was only a couple of times and Ellie used to do it a lot more. I cross my arms and scowl at Dr Palin, and inside, the angry feeling starts to sizzle.

'Uh-huh,' says Dr Palin. 'Faeces too?'

'No,' says Mother.

And they carry on talking like nothing has happened. Like there has been no rudeness here and nothing for anyone to feel ashamed about, while waves of hotness run up and down my body.

Then Dr Palin leans towards me and puts his hands on his legs again, and this time he nods and smiles like he really wants to hear me speak and not just Mother saying it.

'So, now, Eleanor,' he says, making his voice go all sing-song like a character on children's TV. 'What's it all about?'

I stare up at him, at his glasses and his nose that has been wiffling into my toilet business. And all the words I have been wanting to say about Ellie and Akela and Mother and Mary and Chloe and the sick come rolling up in a big unsayable ball that clogs up my throat. Behind it more words are rushing to speak, swarming up like wasps that cluster on and sting whatever they can get at, and all I can do is sit and stare at Dr Palin's toilet mouth and his eyes that have looked into everything and think they know it all.

'Come on, Eleanor,' says Mother. 'Tell the doctor what the matter is.'

Behind her head, the Barbie's expression has changed from friendly to superior, as though she is thinking: I might be broken, but at least I'm not her.

I open my mouth but there is nothing there, only the silence of the words all fighting, wrapped up in the hotness of Dr Palin's toilet questions. I close my mouth again.

'Mmmn,' says Dr Palin. He runs his pen down the writing on his pad. 'This story about swapping places,' he says. 'I don't suppose there's any possibility it might be true?'

Mother goes red and sits up at that so that the Barbie disappears behind her forehead. And inside me all the angry, unsaid words are blowing up and up like a balloon.

'Are you suggesting that I don't know the difference between my own children?' she says in her most get-me-the-manager-this-instant voice. 'After seven years of caring for them single-handedly, throughout their father's . . . illness? After sacrificing my own interests and happiness to make sure they are washed and clothed and fed, without any outside help? What sort of a mother would that make me?'

The air in the room quivers like a twanged elastic band. Dr Palin holds up his hands as a thrumming sound starts in my ears and the fidgets come in my hands.

'Not at all, not at all, Mrs Sallis,' he says. 'It's just important that we explore all the options . . .'

'Well, you can start by exploring more realistic ones,' says Mother in a loud voice that still sounds far away behind all the rumpus happening in my head.

'Such as?' says Dr Palin.

'Well, this business with the umbilical cord for a start,' says Mother. 'I mean, no one's ever truly got to the bottom of any damage that might have caused. And then there's —'

But whatever Mother was going to say next gets lost because all of a sudden the balloon of words that have been trying to get said has popped into a roar, which bursts from my mouth and goes all round the room. And I am up and powering over to the bookshelf where the broken toys whisper, and I am sweeping and hurling and scudding them and the books behind on to the floor, as if, if I can just get all their wrongness away, it will be much better. Again and again. Handfuls and handfuls. The Barbie and the scribbled-on Mr Potato Head and the building blocks that are sticky from too many children's hands. And even when fingers come and try and pull me back, I slap them away, shouting and stamping how I won't stop and I won't give up and I won't be quiet and sit back down. Nothing is ever going to make me be quiet. Nothing is ever going to make me behave. I won't. I won't. I won't.

11

There was a tray in front of her and a pair of chocolate-coloured hands manoeuvring it into position. A smell of disinfectant.

'There,' said the nurse in a sing-song Nigerian accent, her face lit by light from the window on the other side of the bed. 'Good to see you're awake. I expect you're hungry.'

She bustled around, her shoes squeaking. Beeping. The hum of fluorescent lights.

'Your brother chose it,' continued the nurse. 'Cottage pie and raspberry flan.'

'My brother?' said Smudge, shaking her head to try to dislodge the cotton wool that seemed to have packed itself round her brain.

'Oh, he's been so good,' said the nurse. 'He was here all night waiting out in the corridor. He brought you a change of clothes and chocolates. Nothing was too much trouble. He's gone home now for a quick shower and change but I don't expect it will be long before he's back here again.' The nurse smiled. 'You must be a very close family.'

Struggling into an upright position with pain jabbing her right side, Smudge wondered vaguely if she had woken up in another life. She touched her forehead and found that thin strips of material had been stuck slantwise above her left eyebrow, right through the tattoo. Shit. She looked around for a mirror, but there was nothing to hand — nothing to show her what she was dealing with or how bad the damage was likely to be.

'Mind you, I'm not surprised he was worried,' continued the nurse, fiddling with a contraption set up next to the bed. 'That was a nasty accident you had there. You were lucky to get away with just that bang on the head and those two broken ribs, especially with you so rundown and dehydrated. You really should take better care of yourself.'

A handful of images were coming back to her now: clattering along a road, headlights, that man — who was he again? Something sinister, something unpleasant. Bailiff? No, worse. Something to do with Hellie.

She shuddered. 'I don't want to see him,'

she said.

'Nonsense,' said the nurse, batting her protest away. 'You don't know how lucky you are. If everyone had relatives like that, the beds here would be empty, let me tell you. He even spoke to the police and asked them to come back later when you were better able to talk.'

Smudge gave a start. 'Police?' she said.

'Oh yes,' said the nurse. 'The driver reported the accident. He said it was your fault. He said you ran out without looking. The police just want to talk to you to check that you agree, that you don't want to press charges.'

Smudge slumped back on the pillows. 'Oh yeah, sure,' she said. 'Whatever.'

The nurse tutted and launched into a speech about the importance of taking care when crossing the road but Smudge wasn't listening. A familiar craving was beginning to trickle through her. She glanced around for her coat but couldn't see it. The rollies were in the pocket — she was sure she'd left a spare for when she got home. If she could just find it and get a few drags in she'd be able to think straight.

'Sorry,' she said to the nurse. 'Do you know where my coat is? Only I really want a fag and —'

'Oh no,' said the nurse, wagging a finger. 'You are not going anywhere. You are staying right there until we can be sure that bump on your head hasn't done anything serious. We are not taking any chances.'

Smudge gaped as the zinging in her nerves intensified.

'But —' she said. 'But surely you must do something for people who need to smoke?'

'Like what?' said the nurse, placing a hand on her hip.

This was getting to her now. 'Smoking rooms? Nicotine patches?'

'Ha!' The nurse slapped her thigh and laughed loudly. 'Nicotine patches? Where do you think you are? This is the NHS. We are not made of money. Excuse me.'

And with that, she turned on her heel and bustled away up the ward, her shoes squeaking like basketball players dodging around a court.

Smudge clawed at the bed sheets, feeling the rough stiffness of them underneath her fingers. Any minute, she knew, the fizzing would start and then she wouldn't be able to think straight. She had to make a plan.

She looked around the ward: five elderly people slumped in beds, and her; a television above the window playing a news report about a campaign to stop some aggressive new building in London, the Hairpin. Nothing promising.

She pulled up the sheets and eased her legs out of the bed. Perhaps if she stood up, she'd be able to sneak out and bum a smoke from someone out in the car park. But the floor lurched alarmingly when she put her feet down and there was a painful tug in the back of her hand from a tube that seemed to be hooked up to the device beside the bed — some sort of drip by the looks of it. Pain gouged her side once more.

Fuck. Something else then, quickly. Something else. Her brain scrabbled like a dog trying to dig its way through a door. Smoke was flooding her thoughts, fogging her synapses and bringing the same useless ideas looming again and again through the mist: getting up, going outside, bumming a smoke from someone in the car park.

A man in a dark leather jacket, with flecks of grey at his temples and shadows under his big, brown eyes, appeared at the end of the bed. She stared at him with a wild, hopeful expression.

'Thank God,' she said. 'Do you have a fag?'

The man frowned, confused.

'Uh, I think so —'

He glanced at the contraption beside the bed.

'Are you sure you should be smoking while you're —'

'Oh spare me the lecture,' she groaned. 'I'm gasping. I can't think straight. Seriously, if I don't get a fag in a minute, I'm going to crack up.'

The man nodded uneasily. Glancing up the ward, he pulled the curtain round the cubicle. Then he took a box of Marlboro Lights from inside his jacket. 'Here.'

She reached out and took one, fighting the old habit of taking another for later on — for Ron, as someone in the unit once told her. Her fingers thrilled to the feel of the tight roll of paper and the urge to smoke came on stronger than ever.

'Right,' she said. 'Now just help me pull the bed and that drip thing over towards the window so I can lean out.'

The man shook his head. 'Oh no,' he said. 'There's definitely no smoking in here. There's a sign.'

'For fuck's sake,' said Smudge, rolling her eyes. 'Either you help me or I rip this thing out of my hand.'

The man lurched forward, hands outstretched. 'Oh no, don't do that,' he said. 'It's just — well, can't you wheel it outside?'

'Nah,' she said in a low voice. 'They won't let me. They say I've got to stay put because I hit my head. If that nurse sees me trying to get out, she'll kill me.'

The man nodded. 'Oh *that* nurse. Yeah, you don't want to get on the wrong side of her. She saw me adding sugar to my machine coffee last night and I didn't hear the end of it. For about three hours.'

'Mmmn,' said Smudge. She drummed her fingers on the rail of the bed and started to gnaw at her lip.

'Maybe it wouldn't be an issue,' he said. 'The fire alarms in this place are only old spot-type detectors. If you lean far enough out, no one will be any the wiser.'

'What are you? A health and safety inspector?' she said. She looked at him with narrowed eyes and saw how clean-cut he was, how straight. His shirt was pressed and tucked into his jeans.

('Red alert!' shrieked a voice.)

'Who are you?' she said.

He ducked her gaze and went over to the window. After a moment's fumbling there was a click and the plastic casement swung outwards by about three inches, allowing a puff of cold morning air into the room. The faint hiss of drizzle came with it. Spring was still a long way off.

119

'Now,' he said, coming back round the bed, flushed with his own daring, 'if I can just push this over there —'

She fidgeted with impatience as the window came closer, broadening the view out across the car park towards the grey block opposite. When the bed was flush with the sill, he handed her a lighter and she lit up, leaning forward, trying not to tug the drip in her hand.

'God, that's so much better,' she said, feeling her head start to clear after the first few drags. Turning round, she saw him watching her with such intensity that she felt obliged to offer him a puff.

He waved it away.

'No,' he said. 'I'm supposed to be trying to give up. H— the family don't like it.'

She stared at him, feeling the good effects of the cigarette halt and freeze in her veins.

'Fuck. You're him, aren't you?' she said flatly. 'John, Dave — whatever your name is. Her husband.'

'Nick,' he said. 'Yeah. Afraid so.'

She turned back to the window and finished the cigarette in quick, rough drags, before flicking the glowing butt away.

'You shouldn't do that,' said Nick weakly. 'The cars. What if there are people —'

She turned back to look at him, scorn on

her face. An urge rippled through her to do something extreme — something freaky to send him running out of there. She thought about ripping the drip out of her hand and shaking blood all over the floor.

'Look, I'm sorry, OK?' he said, starting back at her expression. 'I'm so sorry. I never meant for this to happen. I just wanted to talk to you. I had to talk to you. There are things —'

She screwed up her eyes and shook her head violently. Voices clamoured inside her mind, trying to drown him out ('Buffoon! Curmudgeon! Cleft-footed weasel!'). She would not hear him.

She felt a tug on her arm and opened her eyes to find him standing beside her, his eyes filled with tears.

'Please!' his mouth mimed through the hubbub in her head. 'Please!'

'Fuck off!' she shouted with all her strength, blasting the clamour into silence.

Then a loud voice rang out across the ward: 'Do I smell smoke?'

The sound of a team of basketball players ducking and feinting its way across the court came towards the cubicle. Smudge and Nick looked at each other and then at the lighter and fag packet on the bed.

As the curtain was swept aside, Nick

stepped in front of them.

The nurse advanced, lips pursed.

'Has someone been smoking in here?' she said.

They shook their heads.

'Then why is the bed pushed to the window?'

'I wanted to look at the view,' she said, gesturing to the car park as Nick groped behind him and transferred the packet and lighter into his back pocket. 'And to get some fresh air. I was feeling faint.'

'Hmmn,' said the nurse. 'Then you should have called for me, not started rearranging the furniture. Besides it's too cold for open windows. The lady in the next bed is ninety-six. How would you feel if she catches pneumonia and dies and it's all because of you?'

The nurse bustled over and reached between them to yank the window shut. Her nose wrinkled.

'There is definitely a smell of smoke in here,' she said.

Smudge opened her mouth to explain, but the ready story was not there. Her mind was blank and she felt tired. She caught sight of Hellie's face flashing up on the television over the window and looked hurriedly down at her hands. It could be in her head, for all she knew, but she didn't want Nick seeing it and launching into pleading mode again.

'Well?' said the nurse, tapping her foot. 'I'm waiting.'

'It's my fault,' said Nick, a blush spreading up from his throat. 'I had a cigarette before I came in.'

'You?' said the nurse, folding her arms and sucking her teeth. 'So you do sugar in your coffee and you smoke? Boy, you are setting yourself up for a miserable old age, let me tell you right now. If you are lucky enough to live that long.' And with that she turned round and bustled out of the cubicle, shaking her head and muttering.

After she'd gone, they burst into sniggers. They looked at each other, shaking their heads. Smudge's expression hardened.

'You have to go,' she said.

'Helen needs you,' he blurted. 'We all need you. It's been a month now and there's still no change . . . Every day, it's the same. They say the hearing is the thing that lingers longest and sometimes that can be the thing that brings them back. There are stories of people hearing conversations while they're under . . . I don't know. We've all been trying but nothing seems to make any difference. But I can't help thinking that perhaps if you came —'

He stopped to fumble a tissue from his pocket and dabbed at his eyes, sniffing.

She regarded him coldly. 'You're wasting your time,' she said. 'Anyway, they all hate me. Mother, Horace, H-ellen. Richard probably too. They all hate me for what I did. For what they think I did.'

'But all that's in the past — way in the past,' said Nick, holding out his hands. 'Time heals. Maybe it could here. You're twins after all. You share the same DNA. You lived for nine months in the same womb.'

A wave of nausea engulfed her. The walls were starting to throb. She was getting sick of his face, of the wheedling tone in his voice.

She swallowed hard. 'You need to leave me alone,' she said. 'This is not going to work. You don't know what you're dealing with. We can't be in the same room as each other, me and her. You have to fuck off.'

He winced like she'd slapped him.

'Fuck off,' she said again, relishing its impact.

Above them, the fluorescent strip light flickered. Nick's mouth trembled. With his big, brown eyes, he looked like a scolded little boy.

'If that's what you really think,' he sniffed,

and turned to go. Then he paused.

'But —' he said, looking back. 'Just answer me this: if you can't be in the same room as each other, how were you going to speak to her that afternoon?'

Smudge narrowed her eyes until he was just a shadow across from her, dark against the cubicle curtain.

'How do you mean?' she said.

'The day of the crash,' said Nick. 'It happened just coming off the roundabout at Elephant and Castle on to the A201 — leading down to the Old Kent Road.'

'So?'

'Well, there was no other reason for her to be driving on that road that afternoon,' he said. 'Even if she hadn't left the piece of paper with your details on by the front door, it would have been obvious: Helen was coming to see you.'

12

I am thinking about ideas for tempting a murderer to get Ellie today while we are on the seesaw in the park. The seesaw is an old clanking thing next to the swings. It lurches up and down when you push off with your legs and, if you are not careful, it can bump you when you land so you have to hold on tight. Underneath there is tarmac with lots of cracks spreading all over it like a spider's web. Mrs C, who is the mother of Hannah C at school, who bites her fingers and smells of Quavers, has been trying to get it changed for, like, three years. She's even been going around with a petition about getting a new soft, squidgy material to spread across the ground. She comes and talks at you with her bossy face and in the end all the parents are so tired and bored that they sign it just to make her be quiet.

I push off with my legs and soar up into the air as I think about what might get a murderer's attention. Like, in most of the programmes, it's usually because someone wants to kiss someone they're not supposed to. Or sometimes it's because of money. I can't imagine anyone wanting to do a murder that involves kissing Ellie so it will have to be money that gets the murderer going. And this is where there is a stroke of luck because there is actually millions of money in the pottery owl piggy bank that Mrs Dunkerley bought for me. Last time I pulled the plastic stopper out of the bottom and played the counting game, where you line up all the coins that match the same size, there were two five-pound notes and one ten, plus a lot of shiny pound coins. It is much better than what's in Ellie's pottery elephant, which has almost nothing except for two pees because every time there was a programme about children with no clothes on and covered in flies, Ellie used to put all her money in an envelope addressed to Africa and drop it in the postbox on the way to school, even though I told her it wouldn't work in their shops. And even though Ellie has stolen all the other bits of Helen, she has forgotten the pottery owl, which is good news for me.

It is lucky that I never did anything stupid like that with my money, because now it turns out that all the pound coins that come from Aunt Bessie every Christmas, Sellotaped inside cards with cats and flowers on the front, will do a very useful thing indeed. And that useful thing will be to lure a murderer into doing Ellie a mischief and getting me back where I belong.

I give the ground a shove of glee, so hard that the seesaw lurches Ellie down and bumps her and we both have to scrabble to hold the handle and stay on.

'Play nicely,' says Ellie crossly, and she tries to shove back so I'll bump too, but even though she is being Helen with all her might these days, her legs are still clumsy and Ellie-ish and all she can manage is a gentle push that sends my end of the seesaw drifting lazily back to earth. I narrow my eyes at her and think of all the murderer traps I could set. Like, maybe I could dangle the money in a bag from a branch and get Ellie to show off her ballet skills underneath. Or maybe I could put the money in Ellie's clothes when we go for our swimming lesson so that the murderer will come and surprise her when she tries to get dressed.

I especially like that idea and I give another pleased shove as I think of Ellie being all shocked and surprised as she comes out of the footbath to find a murderer standing over what should be my clothes.

'God-uh, Ellie,' shouts Ellie. 'I nearly fell off that time. What's wrong with you today? Play nicely!'

I look back at her, at her Ellie-ish face all outraged and smug gliding up past me in the air, and suddenly the fire that has been smouldering inside me flames into life. A hard feeling comes over my arms and legs and it's like they take over and do everything by themselves. When I land back down on the ground, I don't push off again. Instead I throw all my weight into keeping my end low, so that the seesaw hovers with Ellie up high in the air. She looks down at me, shuffling to try and stay on the seat, her fingers white with gripping the handle in front of her. I let her hang there for a moment, watching the breeze lick the wisps of hair free from the Helen plait. Then, gathering all my strength into a fiery ball, I hurl my end hard at the ground so that the seesaw clanks and judders and up at the far end Ellie shrieks and flails and bounces free, tumbling on to the tarmac at my feet.

For a second, nothing happens. I stare down at Ellie, and all there is is the breeze and the sound of a car alarm screeching in the next street. Then Ellie moves and starts to wail and a voice is shouting: 'I'm com-

129

ing! I'm coming! Don't worry, girls, I'm almost there.'

I turn and it's Mrs C, galumphing across the grass and snorting like a horse.

'I saw it all! I saw it all! Oh, you poor darlings,' she bellows, running on to the playground. 'Don't worry, sweethearts, it wasn't your fault. It's this wretched tarmac. This is a prime example of why we've got to get this changed. Wet-pour rubber would be so much safer.'

She plonks herself down next to Ellie, who is sniffling now, and pulls her on to her lap.

'There, my darling. Are you hurt? Are you?' she says, squeezing Ellie all over like she's a mango she is thinking of buying at the supermarket. 'Oh, your poor knee. We'll get that cleaned up for you. What a horrid thing to happen. Here,' she says, delving into her bag. 'Let me see if I've got anything that can help make sore knees better. I know.' She pulls out a packet of Opal Fruits. 'Here. And I expect your sister would like one too, wouldn't she, for such a nasty shock?'

We unwrap our sweets in silence and pop them in our mouths. I suck at the fruity square, feeling its hardness turn to soft mush. Then I look up. Ellie is watching me over Mrs C's arm. Our eyes meet. And in that moment, we both know.

13

The back door swung inwards when she tried to insert her key. She must have left it ajar. She'd have to stop doing that. Anyone could have got in. She glanced round to check that Nick wasn't watching and was relieved to see he'd already gone back round the side of the house. Evidently her stone-walling throughout the cursory questioning by the police and the ride back from the hospital had finally done the trick. Perhaps now he would leave her alone. Good.

She stepped inside and the sour smell hit her. Christ! Had it really been this bad? She held her breath and felt pain scissor through the cracks in her ribs. Fuck!

Daylight spilled over the rubbish bags strewn across the floor, belching plastic wrappers and rotting takeaways. She stared around at the walls smeared with grease, the cobwebs looped down with dust like ghastly Christmas decorations, the clutter spilling off every surface.

She'd only been away for a few days, but the place felt different, smaller somehow and dead, like a museum of someone else's life. She could imagine groups of tourists shuffling from room to room in hushed disbelief, the way she'd done during a visit to the Anne Frank House in Amsterdam way back in that brief, anomalous time when she was happy.

Her eye fell on the yellowed bra slung from the banisters on the blind staircase in the hall. Just as well she'd refused to let Nick come in. For all that he had been kind to her — writing down his phone number on a scrap of paper, pressing it into her coat pocket, telling her she could call him any time — he'd never have coped with this. Kindness had its limits.

('Kind, who said it was kind?' carped a voice. 'He wanted something and he felt guilty for causing the accident. That was all it came down to. You stupid, worthless piece of nothing. Why would anyone want to be kind to you?')

'Shut up,' she said, smacking the side of her head so that the gash on her temple burned.

She winced. It was true. He had been kind. She was going to hold on to that.

Because it had felt nice. Because it had felt halfway normal. And because it was a long time since she remembered feeling that way. Probably that had been Amsterdam too.

('Oh, you're a classic case, aren't you?' retorted the voice. 'I'd wager sex is all it comes down to. Rutting. I bet you just want to jump on his cock. Your own sister's husband! You disgusting piece of shit. I'd like to put you over my knee.')

She shook her head to dislodge the voice and walked into the hallway, feeling the dirt and grit crunch between her plimsolls and the bare concrete. God, what a dump! She saw the flat suddenly as a visitor would — as Hellie might have done if she had made it that day — and the chaos of it rushed her, assaulting her with its filth and un-lovedness. She felt ashamed and her mind turned tail in the face of it, rooting through its trash heap of associations in search of something that would comfort and obscure. She wondered about having a drink, but her stomach heaved and she had to take deep breaths to calm it. Then her thoughts fled to the telephone and the Samaritans. But the idea felt hollow and she knew the voices would crowd around whatever scenario she concocted today, scoffing at her and the poor fool expressing sympathy at the other end.

She reached into her jacket pocket and extracted a fag from the packet Nick had left with her. At least she still had this. She sighed as she lit up and took a deep breath. Perhaps she should just dedicate herself to this: keep smoking, fag after fag, until she puffed her way to death. The world's longest-ever suicide. Who knows? If she got it properly adjudicated, it might even make *The Guinness Book of Records*.

She croaked a laugh and caught sight of the letters piled up in drifts around the door. More chaos — this time from the outside, seeping in. She walked over and stared down at them, cradling the elbow of her smoking arm. Bills, blushing red. Circulars. A note from Nick asking her to please call him. Something from the doctor's surgery — nagging for a smear test no doubt, as if avoiding death was something that everyone by default would want to do. She kicked at the pile of paper with the toe of her plimsoll and a letter promising cheaper car insurance flipped over to reveal a handwritten envelope lying underneath. The address was written in Hellie's rounded, schoolgirl hand, but that wasn't what made her freeze where she crouched, her cigarette sprouting ash. She put a hand out to steady herself against the wall and checked the envelope again. No, there was no doubt: it was there in black on brown. Disbelief exploded in her brain, sending squibs of joy, fear and amazement whooshing and squealing through her. The letter was addressed to Helen Sallis.

14

Sometimes I think I have made it up. Days come where it feels like the whole thing is a story in my head and there was never any swap and any game and it is really me who has been the Ellie all along.

Sometimes it lives in the place in my head where the other stories that don't fit in the world hide — that day skipping along the pavement clutching the bags from the shop in the precinct containing the things in all different colours, Mother in her dressing gown slumped behind the closed curtains on a sunny afternoon, the day they laid a big doll out in a man-sized box and told us it was Father and that we were being very brave even though all we were doing was just standing there. These things feel like broken-up pieces — bits of a puzzle lost behind the sofa, waiting for the day the Hoover will come and suck them up and they'll be gone.

Then there are days when nothing can be trusted any more. Words run away and hide and, by the time I have come chasing after, they have wriggled off somewhere else to be another thing. 'Mother', 'Father', 'sister', 'Akela', 'twin' — nothing does what it means any more. They all just sit in a black lump, whispering together and making up games to trick me. When they tell us to write stories in school, all I can do is sit and look at the lines on the page and think about how words are liars, while next to me Hannah C bends her head down with her tongue poking out, watching her hand make the words of her boring stories about going to see her father in Milton Keynes and getting the tarmac under the seesaw changed in the park.

When Miss Inchbald comes to collect our work, she just looks at my blank page and shakes her head.

'Oh dear, Ellie,' she says. 'Having another bad day, are we?'

But I think the blank page is the best I can do. Because it is a lot better than the mess that would come out from inside my head if I really got to work.

Other times, it all just makes me sad. Everyone seems a long, long way away and it is like I am inside a tunnel looking out through a tiny hole. If I held up my finger and covered the place, the world would be gone and there would be nothing but blackness all around. All I can do is sit on the bench at lunchtime with my arms around myself and my hood up and pulled tight with the string.

When the tears start, people sometimes come to see if I'm OK. Like, there are these girls in the year above who try to look after me because one of them wants to be a childminder when she grows up. Other days, Katrina the dinner lady comes and sits next to me. Katrina is originally from another country, which means her accent is sour like a Cola bottle, and she says things like 'the loser weeps, the finder keeps' when people come to complain about older boys stealing their ball.

Usually what people ask when they come to sit next to me on the bench is if I am sad about Father. Sometimes I nod and say yes and let them give me sympathy and share their sweets if they have any, even though all there is left of Father now in my head is a dark shape with a blur where the face should be and the stack of Pointless Creations in the little box room. If it's Katrina, I shake my head and say nothing, and then she tells me about how her parents lost their house and everything they worked for in her country and really we don't know we're born.

But after a while, I get bored of taking sympathy because of Father, so instead, when someone comes to ask me what's wrong, I do another story. Like, sometimes I'm sad because my uncle lost his job or another day it's because my baby brother had to go into hospital. Telling these stories makes me feel better, but it also makes me sad in another way because I get jealous of the me inside the new problem and I want it to be my problem too. I see me standing at the incubator of the baby brother, with Mother and Akela's hands on my shoulders giving me loving support, and I think how busy and important I would be if I had to stand by the incubator all the time, mopping the baby brother's brow. Or I imagine me sitting up at the grown-ups' dinner table giving advice to my uncle on how to get a new job and everyone being impressed.

Sometimes, the stories get so exciting that they wriggle out of control and I have to watch out, like when Gemma the going-to-be-child-minder screws up her eyes and says they don't put old babies in incubators, only new ones that have just got born. That made me have to swallow hard, but I nodded and said how normally that was true but my baby brother's illness was so serious that the doctors were at their wits' end and were trying everything they could think of. That made all the older girls look wise and nod, like they heard about this sort of thing all the time, and a pleased feeling sprung up in my stomach and grew like a creeper to wrap around my heart.

When the outside gets too much, I go in and slink up the corridor to Mrs Courtney's room that says 'Welfare' on the door. I put my hand to my head and screw up my eyes and say how I am feeling dizzy and there is a pain going round inside my skull. And when I say it, often the headache comes to back me up and then I lie on the bed that smells of swimming pools and medicines and stare up at the orange light and the nits poster at the end of the bed. It has a giant nit on it that looks like a woodlouse with fangs. The nit has an evil glint in its eyes and I stare up at it from the bed and think how much I would like it to come and eat Ellie up. Because even if the story is all made-up-in-my-head it would make me feel much better not to have to see her gallivanting around with Jessica and Charlotte and that lot while I sit on my own on the bench. But sometimes I look at Ellie and I can see the truth. Her eyes flinch and her mouth twists like she is tugging it from inside to stop it trying to talk. She turns her head away and puts her nose in the air like she is too good for the likes of me but I know that deep down there is a worm of worry wriggling through her insides. And then I know that I didn't make it up, that the story is real because it is in her head too. There is a copy of it lodged in there and it makes no difference how good she tries to be or how much she dances around with my name and the inside bit from behind the name that she has stolen and won't let me have back: what happened will always be there, like a rock from the olden days slammed into the grass. She will always be Ellie, trying to be me.

Those are the times that the calm thoughts come and it feels like the sea is lapping on a beach and a hand is steady and warm on my back and someone is laughing a river of notes that flows upwards on the breeze. For those little moments, it is peaceful.

Then the clouds roll in and everything is lost again in the fog.

15

She sat up most of the night, staring at the envelope lying on the scarred living-room table. She reached for it over and over, but always, just as her finger found the gap at the corner of the flap, she would drop it again. She wasn't ready, she felt. She wasn't prepared. Her mind was too cluttered, too disordered for whatever the letter might contain. She needed to get command of herself, to find some equilibrium before she felt equal to reading it. She had to be her best self and she wasn't there right now. Just a little longer, just a moment more. A cup of tea (she went to the kitchen). No tea. Hot water then. Next, a cigarette. Perhaps if she went for a walk? The hours ran on, but the readiness never came. It was always hovering there, on the other side of the next minute, just out of reach.

When the voices woke her up first thing and she saw the brightness of the spring day glimmering through the dirty living-room window, she knew what she had to do. Of course: she would clean. She would get the flat straight and chuck out all the crap. And then, with her mind finally quiet and calmness as far as the eye could see, she would sit down in her neat, orderly domain and read the letter. Then she would have the mental space to take it all in.

The voices were in agreement. ('Washing day!' they'd crooned in the manner of Mr Humphries in *Are You Being Served?* 'Time to rise and shine!')

Oh yes! Today was the day. She was up from the chair, she was out, she was buzzing. Seething with energy, she donned a pair of rubber gloves from under the sink and took all the rubbish bags out to the bin. After that, she whisked through the living room, sweeping everything into a black sack and carrying armloads of junk outside. When the wheelie bin was full, she used the one from upstairs. And when that was gaping, she dumped the rubbish in the spaces between — anywhere, so long as it was out and away. She shifted all the furniture in the bedroom — oblivious to the thumping on the walls from the family with the Rottweiler next door — and snatched up the shards and scraps and dustballs underneath.

In the kitchen, she threw wide the doors of the cupboards and turfed out the mouldering contents: the paints and brushes stuffed in among the rusting tins and packets of dried-up pulses, supergrains and desiccated leaves from the Chinese supermarket she'd bought on one of her sprees. And in the bathroom she sluiced water around, creating white streaks and then white expanses in the layer of grime coating every surface until it was all gone and there were only the essentials left, along with the envelope tucked down the side of the armchair in the living room for safekeeping.

Now she was off out to the shops. The ESA money would have come in on Wednesday and with that she was going to buy cleaning products to get the place new and shining, ready for a fresh start. And once that was done, she would sit down in the armchair facing the window. And then, finally, in her clean home, she knew she'd feel ready — feel fit — to read Hellie's words.

She cackled as she crossed the road, every nerve zinging. Fuck, it felt good to be alive! It felt good to be living in this way, to have a purpose, to have a plan. She pitied the poor sods lying asleep now behind their curtained windows, drained and dulled by the grind of the working week. What sort of life was that when you could be up and out at seven in the morning to see the world in all its fresh colours? To taste possibility on the tip of your tongue? To laugh? Ha! ('Ha!' the voices chorused. 'Hoo-hoo!')

The cash machine was on the corner by the Seven Eleven, next to a newspaper stand full of copies of the *South London Press*. Its front page was taken up with a computer-generated image of the controversial building proposed for central London: the Hairpin, so-called because of its pair of sloping towers that seemed to meet in the middle. She stood for a moment, staring at it. There was something alarming about the way the two towers twisted together, as though locked in a nightmare embrace. She glanced away towards the heart of the city, where the dagger point of the Shard sliced its way above the other buildings, and tried to imagine the cruel slant of the Hairpin there. The image made her shudder.

('Oh go soak your head,' grumbled a voice.)

She fumbled her cash card out of her pocket and plugged in her pin. The screen took her through the motions. Fifty pounds should do it, she thought — not that she had any idea how much cleaning products cost these days. Well, fuck it, if it ended up being too much, she could always treat herself to breakfast out. She hadn't done that in, like, never. A coffee and a bacon roll — her stomach growled at the thought. Really, she deserved it after all she'd been through and for what she was doing now — turning a corner, rebuilding her life. Wasn't that what they'd always been on about at the unit? Looking after yourself? Cutting yourself some slack. Putting yourself first. Well, that could be her slack. That could be her mark of putting herself first: four pounds for a slap-up breakfast in the caff up the road and not a sip of vodka in sight (well, maybe she'd pick up a bottle for later on, for Ron, but definitely not until the cleaning was done and dusted). Ha! Fifty pounds, yes. That would still leave her with half the money to see out the rest of the week. And it was already Saturday. She was on a roll.

The machine whirred and beeped and then the screen flashed up the message: 'Insufficient Funds'. She rolled her eyes and retrieved her card from the slot. Typical. They clearly hadn't got round to topping it up yet after everyone had been on the lash on Friday night. What a shitter. She had stuff to be doing. She had an itinerary. This was holding her up. She looked around.

Should she wait here until they came with the van? The road was empty, but for a pensioner wheeling her trolley across at the lights. It could be hours.

('Rattlesnakes,' griped a voice. 'Big hairy baboons.')

Sod it. She walked on up the street, eyes raking the frontages for the familiar blue and red Link sign. There was one — set into the wall of the HSBC. She darted across the road, causing a car to slam on its brakes, and stuffed her card into the slot. She followed the sequence of screens and waited impatiently, hand held out to receive the cash. The message flashed up: 'Insufficient Funds'.

For fuck's sake! People must have been out on one hell of a bender here last night. What was it? The end of the month? Payday? A memory of Friday-night euphoria flared in her mind. Everyone leaving the studio early and heading down the Cock and Hen. Vodka tonic with a slice of lime. That feeling of work done and rest earned and the weekend stretching away in front of you like an eternity. She tamped the sensation down and pressed on up the road.

It was the same story at the next machine and the next. She lost track of the time she spent wandering, jamming her card into one cash point after another, until at last she stood, hands gripping the plastic casing of a dispenser, forehead pressed against the rim, staring at the screen. Behind her, the road was starting to get busy. Someone coughed.

'It's telling you you haven't got any money,' said a matter-of-fact voice.

She turned round, bristling, and the man stepped back.

'It's just, you know, you were taking rather a long time,' he said, gesturing at the queue forming behind him.

'What do you mean, it's telling me I haven't got any money?' she said. 'It's the fucking machine!'

He coughed again. 'Well, if that's the case,' he said, 'how is it the woman before you got it to work?'

She followed his gaze up the street to where a fair-haired woman was paying for a bag of groceries from a market stall with a crisp ten-pound note.

Smudge opened her mouth. 'But . . .' she said. 'But . . . But the money's there! It went in on Wednesday.'

The man shrugged. 'Sounds like you'll have to take that one up with the bank. Excuse me.'

And he pushed past her and inserted his card. The people in the queue behind him shifted awkwardly, not meeting her eye. One of them gawped at the gashed tattoo on her forehead, still oozing through the steri-strips. She stepped away from them and stood in a doorway, her mind a blur. The money should have been there on Wednesday. It went in every Wednesday — £100.15 exactly. There were times when she'd been driven to going into the bank and taking out the fifteen pee over the counter. So why wasn't it there?

Her thoughts were interrupted by the door behind her opening and a woman with shopping bustling past. Glancing back, she saw it was the door to the bank in which the cash machine was set. Her bank.

Smudge stumbled in and stood twitching in the queue, feeling the need for a smoke beginning to nibble at her nerves. She drummed her fingers on the plastic surface of the barrier that separated the queue from the space in front of the counters. There was no other sound in the room except for the hum of voices and rustling paper.

When the cashier beckoned her forward, she took a deep breath. She closed her eyes and tried to breathe steadily, summoning the image of the sun glinting on shingle to calm herself as they'd talked about doing during sessions at the community centre, but it eluded her, slipping out of her grasp. She walked to the counter, swallowing hard.

'Er,' she said. 'Well, it's my account. There was supposed to be some money going in on Wednesday. Only it's not there and I need to know where it is. Please.'

The girl — 'Shannon' according to her name badge — nodded, making her dyed-blonde ponytail jiggle.

'Just pop your card into the machine there for me,' she said.

Shannon tapped at her keyboard and stared at the screen above. She was young — around twenty — with heavy make-up and hooped earrings that swung and glittered in the light.

'And what was the money you were expecting?' she said.

Smudge leant forward towards the holes punched in the shatter-proof screen, conscious of the queue behind her in the hushed room. 'It was my ESA money,' she said. 'A hundred pounds and fifteen pence.'

The girl frowned. 'Your — ?'

'ESA money,' she said again. 'Employment Support Allowance . . . you know.'

The girl's eyes narrowed. 'Oh right. Well, there's nothing here. Nothing's come in.'

('Grace and favour!' a voice piped up.)

Smudge gripped the counter to hold the

world steady.

'Well,' she said, 'could you find out what's happened to it? Please?'

The girl clacked a couple of keys and looked at the screen.

'Just says the direct debit's been stopped,' she says.

('Grace and favour!' the voice repeated.)

Smudge swallowed hard against the rush of feeling that threatened to surge up her throat and spill out across the counter there and then.

'Why?' she croaked.

The girl shrugged. 'Doesn't say. You'll have to take it up with them.'

('GRACE AND FAVOUR!' roared the voice, furious now, before subsiding into an ominous muttering.)

Smudge raked her fingers through her hair in alarm. The girl stared at her for a moment. Recognition bloomed in her eyes and Smudge remembered too late that she had forgotten to put on the scarf in her hurry to get out of the flat and embrace the breezy day.

'Are you — ?' the girl began.

'No! I'm not,' Smudge shouted. The people at the other counters turned to look, the girl shrank back, and a man in a jacket and tie popped his head round the corner behind her.

'Everything OK?' he said.

The girl eyed Smudge and nodded. 'It's all right,' she said. 'Customer's just had some bad news.'

'Mmn,' said the man, glancing at Smudge's tattoo and the stains on her anorak, before disappearing again.

'Is there anything else I can do for you today?' said the girl, her eyes straying hopefully to the next woman in the queue.

'No,' said Smudge. 'I mean, yes. I mean, wait — there must be something!'

The girl looked back at her. 'Like what?'

('Poke 'em in the eye! Kick 'em up the arse! Get 'em in a half nelson!')

Smudge clenched her fists with the effort to think.

'Well . . .' She stared around the room, her mind switching back and forth between different tracks like points gone berserk on a railway line. 'I mean, can't you call them up or something? I don't have a mobile, you see and —'

('Work 'em! Aim for the legs!' 'Call that an aubergine?')

The girl shook her head. 'Office won't be open until Monday,' she said. 'Anyway, I can't discuss your benefits with a third party. It's confidential. I wouldn't be insured.'

('Down it! Down it! Down it!')

'But . . .' said Smudge, spitting now in her anxiety, spattering the glass with her fear. 'But what am I going to do now? I haven't got any money. Like, literally no money. And I was in the middle of, like, a project. And I haven't had anything to eat since yesterday and —'

The enormity of it rained down on her: a galaxy imploding and raining molten matter down upon her head.

('Please sir, can I have some more?' whined a voice.)

'Shut up!' yelled Smudge, hitting the side of her head, sending pain sizzling through the gash and into her brain.

The girl rolled her eyes. 'Is there anything else I can do for you today?'

Smudge gripped the counter and stared at the streaked image of the girl. 'So what am I supposed to do now?'

Behind her, someone muttered something. She spun round and faced the queue.

'What?' she said. 'What was that?'

They stood there in their overcoats and jackets — all durable fabric and value for money — and glowered at her. The man at the front coughed.

'I said, I think you should get a job,' he

said, and jutted his chin forward.

She gaped at him.

'A job?' she said. 'A job? But I'm ill! I need that money! Do you think I'd be here —'

A fat woman in an anorak piped up. 'Well, you were well enough to find your way here and have an argument, now weren't you? You had money enough to get whatever that thing on your face is done.' She sniffed. 'Honestly, some people don't know they're born.'

Smudge stared at them and saw they were a million miles away. Between their world and hers was a surging gulf of silence across which no meaning could travel without being wrecked. There was no talking to them.

Without a word, she turned and blundered out through the wooden doors into the morning. She stumbled up the street, oblivious to where she was going, her mind churning. Shock tingled along her arms and legs. Again and again, like goldfish swimming round and round a bowl, her thoughts returned to the cleaning and the letter and how she hadn't eaten and how she needed to get some money out and how there wasn't any money to be had. The faces of the people in the bank loomed at her from shop fronts and post-boxes: closed and shuttered.

She walked on. Schools, community centres, fences, ranks of flats, townhouses and mansion blocks, which eyed her stonily as she walked past. Life organised, laid out, neatly arranged. Life insurance and pensions and saving for a rainy day. Don't spend it all at once and mind how you go. A stitch in time is worth the candle. A bird in the hand is worth nine. When the road split and the pavement gave out, she walked on the tarmac. Up on to the flyover where the wind whipped and the trees nodded far beneath her feet. Soon the cars were rushing towards her in a stream and she weaved between them, watching the white line appear and disappear like stitching fixing the tarmac to the ground. Horns blared but she ignored them, waving her arms at the blurred faces scudding by to show she didn't care. A lorry rumbled past and, when it was gone, she looked through the swirling air to the far side. And there, fixed to the concrete, she saw it: Hellie's picture, the one from the newspaper, beneath a sign that read 'In our thoughts and prayers'. There were bunches of flowers tied to the barrier, trembling in the rush of wind from the cars, and from this angle, as the paper flapped, Hellie seemed to be winking, sending out a message just for her. She stood and stared at the face that was nearly hers, trying to read it as it bucked and swayed. She stood there as the cars streaked by, grazing the air with reds and blues and greens. She stood there until the clouds thickened and drops of rain began to fall and the sound of the horns curdled into a siren's wail.

16

A Saturday afternoon and Mother and Akela have gone off to buy furniture for the little room upstairs at the front of our house. Ellie is playing at Jessica's house but I wasn't asked, so instead I have been brought round to Mrs Dunkerley's since it seems I am not to be trusted on my own.

'Yes, dear. Don't you worry. You take your time,' says Mrs Dunkerley to Mother, clasping her hands up under her chin like a woman sending a soldier off to war in an old film. 'We'll be just fine, won't we?'

I scowl up at the adults. There is a starry look about Mother's eyes and Akela is standing with his arm round her like she is a prize turnip he is exhibiting at the church harvest fete. It seems a lot of fuss about a trip to boring old John Lewis.

'There now,' says Mrs Dunkerley as we wave Mother and Akela off. 'I expect you're very excited about your Mummy and Mr

Greene going to buy all that new furniture, aren't you? What a wonderful time it must be for the whole family.'

I don't say anything. First, because Mother has never been Mummy and that is obviously not her name. And second because what kind of a stupid thing to say is that? It's not like the furniture is going to come alive and do a dance or perform magic tricks. It is going to be furniture like everyone else has in every other house ever: a chest of drawers and a wardrobe that stands there saying nothing. Personally, I don't know why there has to be anything in there at all. I like it clear and empty like it was when Mother boxed up all the things from before Father's suicide; when the Pointless Creations got carried down the stairs and out to the garden, the bright streaks of colours on their canvases winking as they disappeared through the French doors, one by one.

Suicide. That's what we call the Unfortunate Decision now in the interests of Getting Things Out in the Open like the doctors suggest — except that no one tells you whether it's the same as dying or something else. Suicide. It sounds like something you might order in the French bistro Akela takes us to when it's Mother's birthday. 'I'll have the suicide with extra sauce,' I can imagine Mother saying in that tight voice she uses with waiters. 'And could you make sure the meat is well done?'

After the little room was emptied, I went in and stood there while Mother, Ellie and Akela watched *Jim'll Fix It* downstairs. It was peaceful and I liked the way the sun threw a wash of gold over the walls, blurring the lines left by years of propping up the Pointless Creations, which in the end Mother burnt in a big colourful bonfire at the bottom of the garden. There were no belongings to nag at my brain in there, nothing to try to hem me into Ellieness. I could just stand in the golden space and look out over the street, with the bottom of the net curtain flicking in front of me, like a cat's tail. I decided that room would be my place and it made me calm to think about going there when the rest of the world got too loud. Then one day I got back from school and there was a man in there up a ladder, whistling and painting away. Soon after that, the little bed with the bars up the sides came and the room went from calm and peaceful to tight and anxious, and I didn't go in there any more.

Mrs Dunkerley opens her back door and the smell of feet comes out. We push through the beaded curtain and I hold my hand up to stop the strands from whipping at my face.

'There now,' says Mrs Dunkerley with a big smile, like we have climbed a mountain. 'Why don't you go and have a sit-down in the living room and I'll bring you a nice cup of tea?'

It sounds like a question, but really I know it isn't, so I give a nod and walk through to the living room and go to sit on the brown armchair next to Bill's cage. On the television there is an ice rink and a man and a lady in sparkly purple clothes sliding around doing a dance. The lady's skirt is very short and the man keeps picking her up and flipping her round to show her knickers and everyone claps each time he does.

'Isn't it lovely?' says Mrs Dunkerley, coming through with a clinking tray. 'Not as good as Torvill and Dean of course.'

I think lovely isn't the right word and I think if I was the lady I would be telling the man off and making him behave, but everyone else on the television seems to agree what a jolly good show it is so I give a smile and accept Mrs Dunkerley's tea cup with good grace.

'Biscuit?' she says, jiggling the tin.

I peer in and do a calculation. The ginger

snaps have definitely been here since last year because I remember at Christmas when me and Ellie came to give Mrs Dunkerley her smellies they were here then. I can't be sure about the Garibaldis because I suspect Mrs Dunkerley eats them when no one's looking, but the currants in them make me think of squashed flies so I prefer to leave them alone. That leaves the digestives, which are anybody's guess. I am about to pick out one of those when I see a glint of silver underneath and my heart does a leap. I rootle my fingers in and, even though it wouldn't be allowed at home, I do a bit of digging around until I manage to pull out a Kit-Kat.

'Thank you very much,' I say, pleased now that Ellie isn't here and at least this is one thing that I am getting that she won't have this afternoon.

Mrs Dunkerley sits down with a groan in the armchair by the gas fire, which is off because it's summer. 'There,' she says.

She looks at me. Behind her, the clock on the mantelpiece gives a whir. Soon it will chime.

'So,' she says. 'Helen, isn't it?'

A thrill floods through me. 'Yes,' I say.

'Ah yes, Helen of course,' says Mrs Dunkerley. 'What a mercy to get it right for a change. You and your sister are like two peas in a pod.'

And even though it is just Mrs Dunkerley, I am so pleased to hear someone calling me my name, someone recognising me, that I sit very still holding the Kit-Kat like the happy feeling is a very hot cup of tea and I might spill it if I say a word.

On the television another couple of ice dancers are coming out from the crowd. You can tell that the man is itching to get up to the knicker-showing tricks, but this lady looks fiercer and whizzes around making spiky shapes with her hands. I am hopeful that she might do some kicking and hitting if the man tries to get too rude.

'So, Helen,' says Mrs Dunkerley after another click and whir from the clock. 'What do you think of my new Bill?'

I turn and look at the cage and inside up on a bar I see that Bill has changed from blue to green. A tinkle of notes comes from the clock and the new Bill bobs and bows like he is taking the credit.

'What happened to the old Bill?' I say.

'I'm afraid he passed on, sweetheart,' says Mrs Dunkerley, slurping at her tea.

'You mean he died?' I say.

'Yes,' says Mrs Dunkerley. 'He did. He died.'

I watch the new Bill hooking his beak on to the bars and hoicking himself round the cage.

'Was it suicide?' I say.

Mrs Dunkerley looks at me hard for a moment.

'Do you know what?' she says. 'I've just remembered. You'll never guess what I found in Oxfam. Now where did I put it?'

And she levers herself up and starts thumping around the living room, opening cupboards and drawers to show all sorts of higgledy-piggledy business inside — much worse than the little front bedroom in the very most unfortunate moments after the Unfortunate Decision, back when the hours went topsy-turvy and Mother slept all day and got up and wandered about at night.

'Aha!' goes Mrs Dunkerley, holding out a cardboard box. It is a game of Connect 4 that someone has had to Sellotape round the sides of to make the lid stay on. 'You children always love this, don't you?'

I want to say that we used to love it when we were, like, six, but now we are seven-nearly-eight it is a bit babyish. But I remember my manners like Helen would and instead I say 'Oh yes, my favourite' and try to look pleased.

While Mrs Dunkerley sets up the game

on the little table between our chairs, I open the Kit-Kat to give myself a reward. I slice down the foil and make the snap like they do in the adverts, but when I take a bite, instead of smooth sweetness and then a crunch, I get soggy grittiness in my mouth, and when I look down, I see green fur where the chocolate should be.

My throat seizes up and my stomach gives a jerk, but Helen would not sick it up, so I close my eyes and make myself swallow it down, fighting back the tears that come a bit from feeling ill and a bit from the shock of nastiness where a nice thing should be. I put the rest of the Kit-Kat on the arm of the chair and play the game, giving polite 'oohs' and 'ahs' when the boring counters go in and Helening as hard as I can. A picture comes of the fun Ellie and Jessica will be having in Jessica's playroom, above the garage and away from the adults, where you can climb up a ladder and tell as many secrets as you like, but I push it aside and carry on with the game. If I can Helen it for all I'm worth, I think, maybe, even now, after all this time, it will still be possible for the truth to get recognised. Mrs Dunkerley will be so impressed with me that she'll tell Mother how good Helen was, and maybe Mother and Akela will be so busy thinking about their new furniture that they'll forget who is supposed to be who, and by the time Ellie gets back from Jessica's clutching her make-your-own-fashion-design or whatever fun they've been up to today, it will be straight back to the old Ellie ways for her.

I'm so keen to make the plan work that when Mrs Dunkerley points at the Kit-Kat and says there are children in Africa who would be glad of that food, I pick it up and gulp it down, not caring how it sticks to my teeth or sludges round my stomach so long as it works the magic and makes me Helen again. I play on, game after game, as much as Mrs Dunkerley wants, pleasing and thankyou-ing for all I'm worth. On the television, the ice skating has changed into *Alice in Wonderland,* and even though we've got it at home and can watch it any time we want, I keep half a polite eye on it to stop the game from boring my head off.

At last, just after the Mad Hatter's tea party and the unbirthday song, Mrs Dunkerley gets up with a groan.

'Well, I'll tell you something: that tea has gone right through me,' she says. 'Whatever you do, young Ellie, don't get old.'

And with that she stumps off out into the hall and up the stairs to the bathroom. I sit in the armchair with the stink of the 'Ellie' settling on me like the drops from a toilet freshener spray. On the television, Alice is wandering away from the Mad Hatter's tea party into the Tulgey Wood and the trees are closing in. A fiddling feeling comes over me and I don't want to sit on my own. I turn and unhook the little door that opens Bill 2's cage. Inside, Bill 2 is huddling on his swing. I reach in and wrap my fingers round his feathery body. Bill 2 jerks his head and puts his beak down to give me a nip, but I am bigger than him and he has to come with me.

We sit, Bill 2 and me, and watch the cartoon, my fingers round him, making him behave. Every so often he gives a cheep and I feel his claws sharp against the palm of my hand and his little heart throbbing. When the dog with the brushes on its beard and its tail comes and sweeps the path up from around Alice's feet, I laugh like I always do. Only this time it isn't funny: the woods are very dark and the singing seems to swell with sadness and there is nowhere to go. The world becomes a tight place and every door is closed up tight, no matter how hard you scrunch your fists and bang on the wood.

After the Cheshire Cat helps Alice back into the light, I look down at Bill 2. He has gone very still, like he is asleep except his eyes are open. I lay him down gently on the floor of his cage and sprinkle sawdust on top to keep him warm. Then I get up.

'Goodbye, Mrs Dunkerley,' I call up the stairs.

'Oh, you're going, are you, dear?' calls Mrs Dunkerley's voice. 'Is your mother here?'

'Yes,' I shout.

'All right then, sweetheart,' calls Mrs Dunkerley. 'Come again any time — and bring your friends.'

I nod and let myself out of the back door. A streetlamp blinks on and somewhere up the road an engine is sputtering into life.

17

They pulled out of the car park in silence. She watched in the wing mirror as the police station shrugged when they went over the speed bump and slipped away behind them, like a butler backing out of a room. The radio whispered an easy-listening track, almost too quiet to hear.

'You could just take me home,' she said.

Nick kept his eyes on the road.

'After you nearly get killed wandering into traffic because of some infection from an accident I caused?' he said, flicking down the indicator to pull off a roundabout. There was a quiver in his voice and a flush spreading on his cheeks. 'You must be joking. You're coming home with me. And you're going to stay with us until you're well.'

She opened her mouth to say something else, but the words failed her. Her head felt heavy. Keeping it balanced on her shoulders was effort enough. The last few hours —

the form-filling, the antibiotics they'd given her for the infected gash, the faces talking at her, uttering streams of calm, reasonable words — had taken their toll. Too prolonged an exposure to common sense nearly always had this effect on her and today her tolerance was especially low. The only bonus was the voices seemed to be equally whacked. She hadn't heard a peep out of them in hours.

Once they were on the dual carriageway, he said: 'So what actually happened? Why did you go to that road?'

She puffed out her cheeks. 'Oh, I just freaked out, I guess,' she said. 'I don't really know. The last thing I can remember, I was standing in the bank —'

'The bank?'

'Yeah, I went in there to try and get my ESA money — Employment Support Allowance. Only there was a problem and when I went in they told me it'd been stopped. I don't really know what happened after that. I sort of stopped thinking.'

'Oh,' said Nick, pulling out to overtake a lorry. 'So it wasn't Helen then?'

Smudge blinked. 'Helen?'

'You weren't looking for Helen?' he said. 'I thought, you know, being on that road, in that particular spot, maybe it had something to do with her. With the accident. With you maybe wanting to see her.'

Smudge batted the words away. 'Oh no, that had nothing to do with it,' she said. She looked at him. 'Sorry.'

They pulled back into the middle lane behind a coach carrying a load of school children on some trip. Those on the back seat turned round and began to gurn at them through the window. One boy with a tie knotted round his head pressed his nose against the glass in imitation of a pig.

'How is she anyway,' said Smudge. 'Helen?'

The word felt unfamiliar and forced in her mouth — a stopper jerking loose from a bottle.

Nick flinched. 'Oh, you know, much the same,' he said. 'There's been no change for a while now. In the early days they thought she was improving, but she's been stuck at the same level for ages. Weeks. She mumbles and jerks around from time to time. Her face pulls some of the old expressions. Sometimes, if you glance at her and look away quickly you can fool yourself into thinking she's back. But she's not there. Not really.'

He turned to meet her eye and saw her look away.

'But anyway,' he said, clearing his throat, 'you. That money issue. ESA, was it? That must be . . . quite a thing.'

She shrugged.

'Yeah, it did fuck me over somewhat.'

A car cut in between them and the school bus, forcing Nick to jam on his brakes.

'Idiot!' he exclaimed. The mildness of the word shocked her.

'Sorry,' he muttered, and applied himself once more to the matter at hand. 'But they can't just do that, can they?'

'What?'

'Stop the money? They can't turn it off, just like that.'

She snorted. 'Seems like they just did.'

'But surely, when you contact them and explain the situation —'

'Oh yeah,' said Smudge, nodding. 'Sure. They'll be very understanding. If I'm lucky they might sort it out in about six weeks.'

'Six weeks!' said Nick. 'But that's outrageous. What will you do for money in the meantime?'

She shrugged. 'Guess I'll have to fall back on my extensive savings.'

But he didn't get the joke.

'Six weeks,' he said again, shaking his head. 'That must be really difficult for some people. I mean, what do you do if you've got kids?'

She shifted in her seat and kicked something. Looking down, she saw it was a Barbie doll. She bent down and picked it up.

'Oh sorry, that's Heloise's,' said Nick. 'We've been looking for that.'

'So you've got kids then?' said Smudge, staring at the Barbie's rigidly perfect features. 'You and Helen.'

Panic gripped her: the image of two little girls running across the grass, plaits and bunches flying. She dug her fingers into the armrest of the door and tried to breathe.

'Yes,' said Nick. He paused. 'Just one. Heloise. She's six. Margaret's been very helpful about looking after her while all this has been going on.'

Relief flooded through Smudge, thrumming against her eardrums, so that for a while she didn't register the final sentence, didn't realise that Margaret meant Mother.

When at last she did, she opened and closed her mouth like a fish. The thought of Mother being helpful, playing the grandmother role, was unsettling. She couldn't make it stick. In her mind, Mother was poised for ever as she had been the last time she'd seen her: standing on the doorstep in her evening wear, her hair teased into a brittle cloud, watching the police car drive away.

18

After Bill 2, things change. People look at me in a narrow way and there are muttered conversations behind the kitchen door with the light shining through the cracks like a warning. When Baby Richard comes — in a bluster of footsteps on the stairs and Akela's car garrumphing into life and Hannah C's mother coming and making us play Ludo because Mrs Dunkerley doesn't like to see us any more — I am not allowed to touch him.

Part of me is pleased because Baby Richard is fat and bald with a big head like Akela's and playing with him would be boring. But another part of me is sad when I see Mother sitting with her arm round Ellie, showing her how to hold him properly and everything. Sometimes I stand in the dark of the hallway and peer in at them sitting in the glow of the gas fire: Mother, Ellie, Baby Richard and Akela, with the television twinkling behind. They are like a family in a story that has nothing to do with me. They don't even know I'm there. And when I creep to the front door and slink out to go and sit in the upside-down tree in the park nobody says a word.

The years go round like the cars on the old Scalextric track the boys play with during wet breaktimes. We are the third-oldest class, then the second-oldest, and then all of a sudden it's the last year and soon we will have to say our goodbyes and go off to different big schools. On the last day, there's a show in the main hall and all the popular girls do their party pieces to show everyone how talented they are. Jessica wiggles three hula hoops at a time and Charlotte and that lot do a dance they made up by themselves to Michael Jackson's 'Heal the World'. Then Ellie steps forward and recites a funny poem about a lady running a tombola at a church bazaar. She does voices and everything and when she finishes, everyone cheers and says how talented she must be. I sit, small and not-clapping, at the end of a row, thinking how the old Helen would never have said a poem and done funny voices — how Ellie has taken Helen and pulled her out of shape and added bits, so that now there is a person you would never recognise in the place where the old Helen should be. It is a Hellie now, not a Helen at all. Helen is gone. And I begin to think maybe she won't come back again.

In September, when we start at the big school, I hope things might be different. Most of the other people we know have gone to St Stephen's down by the shopping centre and Jessica and Charlotte are off to the Guild of Our Lady, a school where parents pay so you can wear a nicer uniform and have a swimming pool. I hope the fact that we are going to Bridge Oak means that there can be a fresh start so that I will stop being pushed into the Ellie corner that seems to get smaller and smaller every day. If I have to be Ellie, at least I can try to be the best Ellie possible, I think, and maybe Bridge Oak will be the chance I need, away from all the people who think they know what Ellie is before she opens her mouth.

Except that when we get there on the first day in our navy blue jumpers, white blouses and ties, it turns out that people have been sending letters about us and before the register has even finished, someone has come to tap me on the shoulder and lead me off to another room with carpet on the walls where there is a fat woman in a spangly jumper who wants me to match up animal pictures with the words that represent them. Anger blows through me like a gale and all I can do is sit there, gripping the table, trying not to let tears bubble up out of my eyes. When the woman goes out to the toilet, I get the pencil and slash all over the page until the elephant, the rhinoceros and the giraffe are just bits of eyes and legs and tails, and then I sob and cry until they have to take me to the headmaster, leading me down the corridor past the gym, where Ellie is twirling around in her new leotard, spiralling a red ribbon over her head. And that makes me scream even louder because I know it's all starting worse than ever and now there will never be a way out.

That evening when we get home Richard runs up all bright and smiley wanting to show a picture he has been drawing. Ellie takes it and makes all the right cooey noises so that Richard laughs and slaps his hands on his thighs like she has made the best-ever joke.

No one is looking at me, so I slip out and away to the park where the upside-down tree waits like a cascade of glistening hair. The September sun is starting to sink behind the houses at the far side of the park, poking their shadows out towards me like tongues as I make my way across the grass. A rook cackles as I reach in and push the branches aside. And then I stop, because where there is usually empty space and the tree trunk to sit on, there are bags and legs and faces. Teenagers.

'What the fuck do you want?' says a lad with spots, staring up at me.

A girl holding a plastic bag turns and peers blearily at me.

'Give it a rest, Baz,' she says. 'She's only little. What's your name, sweetheart?'

I looked round at them, sitting hunched around a pack of beer cans, their hands tucked into their sleeves.

'El-lie,' I say slowly.

The boy, Baz, narrows his eyes at me. 'What school do you go to?' he asks.

'Bridge Oak,' I say. 'But I only started today and —' And suddenly the room with the carpet walls and the animal drawings is rushing at me and it's all I can do to stop the tears spilling out of my eyes.

'Ah, poor love,' says the girl. 'Did they give you a rough time? Well, you come and sit next to me, sweetheart. I'll look after you.'

So I go and sit next to the girl, who smells of smoke and chewing gum and Impulse vanilla body spray. The others stare at me.

There are six of them: four boys and two girls. On the floor between them, next to the slab of cans, there's a tube of glue like the stuff Akela uses to fix the parts of his miniature planes. I look around for the model they are making, but I can't see anything among the twigs and leaves.

Baz cracks open a can of beer and thrusts it at me. 'Here,' he says, not meeting my eye.

I shake my head. I've seen what drink does: Mother giddy in the kitchen and the bedroom door not quite closed while Akela's pawing at her. 'No thanks,' I say.

He rolls his eyes. 'Just trying to be friendly,' he mutters.

'Don't mind him,' says the girl sitting next to me. 'He's a grumpy fucker. You stick with me.'

Baz jiggles his legs so his feet tap fast on the ground. He looks around.

'Here, Shaz,' he says, tilting his head in my direction. 'Give her some of the . . . you know.'

'Baz . . .' says the girl next to me.

'Ah, come on, Gina man. It'll be funny,' he says.

Gina turns to me. 'You don't have to do anything you don't want to, Ellie,' she says.

She is all softness. And when she says

180

'Ellie' it sounds all right — just a name that might belong to anyone. Nothing more terrible than that. I would like to show her how mature I am so that then we can be friends. I look at the Tesco bag Shaz is holding. How bad can its contents be? I think. Whatever it is, I can always just pretend to take a bit and then chuck it away when no one's looking.

'Yeah, OK,' I say. 'I'll give it a try.'

'Classic!' says Baz, clapping his hands together.

They pass the bag over. But when I look inside, there's nothing to eat in there, only a sort of clear, sticky substance at the bottom.

I go to dip my finger into it, but Baz laughs and says, 'Nah, you don't eat it. You've got to sniff it.'

So I put my nose close to the bag and sniff. There is a faint, petrolly smell.

'Nah,' says Baz again. 'You've got to do it properly. Put the bag round your nose and take a proper huff, you know.'

So I press the edges of the bag to my cheeks, close my eyes and breathe in as hard as I can. A sour wind rushes up through my head and the ground falls away. I am pedalling my arms and legs in deep water and all around me stars are pricking through. I look at the others, but they have all tilted off at an angle, their heads bent and stretched like faces in a mirror at the fair.

Then the water starts to ebb and I am sitting back on the log with a headache and a sick feeling bubbling inside me.

'Fuck me,' says Baz. 'I told you to sniff it, not honk the whole bag!'

'Are you OK, love?' says Gina, putting her arm around me. 'Takes you out of yourself a bit, doesn't it?'

But when I look at her, her eyes are huge and I shuffle away in alarm.

'I think I need to go home now,' I say, standing up as the floor jerks sideways.

'Are you sure?' says Gina. 'Why don't you sit here and wait for it to go off a bit?'

But I can't look at her any more. I shake my head.

'I've got to go,' I say again, and I turn and push out through the branches into the park that has become one big shadow. I run across the grass, which someone seems to be shaking out in great waves, like a tablecloth ready to lay a meal on, until I am at the gate where the streetlamp lights the way to the road beyond. Then a figure peels off from the dark bushes and stands across the path.

'Oh hello,' it says in a flat, wolfish voice.

'Where do you think you're going in such a rush?'

I look up but all I can see with the street-lamp behind is the orange dot of a burning cigarette hovering about his face.

'Please,' I say, as my stomach lurches. 'I've got to go home. I'm feeling sick.'

'Wait,' says the voice, and a hand reaches out to grab my wrist. 'Aren't you one of the little girls who used to come round to play with Mary? The twins.'

I nod, gulping back a mouthful of vomit.

'Well, isn't that a fucking stroke of luck?' says the voice. 'I've been thinking about you twins a lot, you know. Especially you. I've been wondering how you are. Why don't you just come with me and —'

But my stomach is heaving now and any minute it's going to go everywhere. I yank my hand away and push past him, stumbling up the path. I run along one street that lurches and tips like a seesaw, then another, until at last there is the front door. I put my key in and burst through, and there, in the warm, yellow light, with Akela's model Spitfire zooming down towards me on its stand, I throw up all over the carpet.

19

It was dark by the time they pulled up outside the house. The wrought-iron street-lamps glowed orange, throwing splashes of light up at the underside of sycamore trees coming into leaf and wisteria buds dangling like mini bunches of grapes. Nick got out to unlatch the gate and they swung on to the rectangle of drive, crunching gravel under the wheels.

The house loomed over them, ghostly white with exposed brickwork on the upper storeys. Early Victorian, she supposed, or maybe older, built back in the days when this part of Islington was still a village and there seemed to be plenty of space.

'This is where you live?' Smudge said as they got out of the car.

Nick made a shushing gesture as he let them in, but when they got into the hall they found themselves caught in the glow of light spilling from the living room, where a familiar figure sat on a large cream sofa. A bolt of fear shot through Smudge and she shrank back, pulling her hair over her face, but it was too late: Akela looked up with a start. The years had coarsened him, thinning the hairs on his head and speckling his cheeks with purple. He was fatter too and his clothes had not kept up, so that he had the appearance of an over-stuffed soft toy, bulging at the seams.

'Hullo,' he said. A table stood in front of him, level with his knees, bearing a half-finished jigsaw puzzle on a board. The rest of the pieces were in a box beside him on the floor, a bright picture painted in the ruddy colours of a *Boys' Own* annual showing what appeared to be a Boeing 747 taking off.

'Horace,' said Nick, stepping forward. 'You remember Ellie. Of course you do. She's been . . . unwell and needs some TLC so she's going to be staying here for a few days.'

'I see,' said Akela dubiously. 'Does Margaret — ?'

'I'll speak to Margaret about it,' said Nick. He swallowed. 'Is she . . . ?'

'She's gone to bed,' said Akela, keeping his eyes fixed on Smudge. 'Early night.'

'Excellent,' said Nick with evident relief.

He looked between them.

'Have a seat, Ellie,' he said, gesturing to two other cream sofas arranged around the coffee table. 'Would you like a drink?'

'Tea, please,' she said. It was the last thing she wanted: the caffeine would make her angsty. Still, it was something to say. It was stupid, but she actually thought she might wet herself, faint or be sick. Standing here under Akela's reproachful gaze, it was as though no time had passed since that evening fifteen years ago — as though any minute they would come, static crackling through their radios, and manhandle her into the car.

'Great,' said Nick. 'Horace?'

'Hmmn,' said Akela.

Nick bustled out to get the drinks and Smudge perched on the farthest sofa and looked around the room. It was tastefully done, with lots of ingenious little touches — hideaway stools that slotted into the wood of the table and a deconstructed chandelier overhead, all bare bulbs and slivers of metal. Hellie must be doing very well, she thought dully.

She picked at some dried blood clotted along one of her cuticles and gnawed the inside of her cheeks. Her muscles felt tight. The silence stretched.

At length Akela coughed and fixed her with a benevolent grimace.

'So,' he said. 'How's life in . . . Where is it now? Sidcup? Slough?'

'Walworth,' she said.

He pointed at her with all the scout leader's forced jollity. 'That's the badger,' he said.

She shrugged. 'It's —' Shitty? Grim? Hopeless? 'OK,' she said.

'Recession hit there much, has it?'

She frowned, swallowing a plug of vomit. 'Umm. Not to my knowledge.'

He shook his head and picked up a piece from the box on the floor beside him. 'It's taken its toll where we are,' he said. 'Shops closing left, right and centre. Queues outside the job centre. And they've knocked down the library to build another Tesco. I don't expect you'd recognise the place if you saw it now.'

He looked at her then quickly back at the piece, holding it out for comparison against a wooded area in the top left corner of the picture emerging in front of him. After turning it from side to side for a moment, he laid it down outside the frame and bent to rootle through the box once more.

'I don't do the models nowadays,' he said, seeing her watching him. 'Margaret — we thought it caused unnecessary clutter. These are a pretty good replacement. And the great thing with the board is you can tidy it away and cover it over any time you like. Once it's done I'm thinking about gluing it together in a frame and hanging it on the wall. At home, obviously. Not here.'

He coughed again. 'So, er, what are you up to now?'

Smudge stared at him, at his pink, balding head. What did he think about when he was by himself? she wondered. What did he tell himself when he looked in the mirror? Did he ever think about what happened and whether maybe — just maybe — he could have intervened to make it all fall out another way?

She opened her mouth. 'Well —' Visions passed before her eyes of the grey wash of days, the afternoons spent watching a sun ray move across the ripped lino and bare concrete of the living-room floor, the evenings where everything seemed to sag and slosh as though the world were underwater, and then the flashes of lightning and pits of darkness that sucked in everything and crunched you to the bone. 'Actually, I'm working part-time in the post office,' she said.

Akela pursed his lips and widened his eyes

as he slotted a piece of runway into place.

'The post office,' he said. 'I see. What? Cashier work, is it?'

'Mostly,' she said. 'And a bit of low-level managerial stuff. I think they're training me up.'

She talked on about her responsibilities, hearing her voice sound smooth and capable. In her mind, the post office took shape and it soothed her. The shelves filled with stock — useful things like post-it notes and jiffy bags, ballpoint pens. She saw herself pricing them up, helping old ladies send packages to their grandchildren in Australia, stopping to exchange a word with Sam, the visually impaired man who came in every week to deposit his pension into his post office account because the people there were friendlier than at the bank. It was a busy and tiring job, but it was rewarding too. You felt like you were really doing something in the community, making a difference — particularly in this day and age when local services were closing everywhere you looked. In fact, she was wondering about going full-time. Everyone wanted her to. The customers all asked for her when she wasn't there. Her line manager had even offered to increase her hours, but she had to think carefully about it. She didn't want to overdo it, and besides, she needed to leave enough time for her art.

Akela raised his eyebrows. Then: 'What are you doing out of bed?' he said.

Smudge looked at him, her eyes bright with all her success at the post office. But his eyes were on the doorway. A small figure in SpongeBob SquarePants pyjamas slunk into the room.

'I want to show Daddy my picture I drew to make Mummy well,' said the little girl, her hand scrunching the bottom of her pyjama top so that SpongeBob developed a menacing frown.

Akela laid down the piece he was considering and turned to her.

'I know you do, Heloise sweetheart,' he said, 'but the picture will still be there tomorrow. You can show it to him then.'

He reached out a hand to pat her arm but she skipped out of his reach and turned to face Smudge.

'Who's that?' she said.

Akela coughed. 'That's a friend,' he said. 'That's Ellie. Stay over here, sweetheart,' he added. But Heloise was already walking over, her fingers trailing along the wooden surface of the coffee table.

'She looks like Mummy,' she observed. 'Only her face is narrower and she's got writing over one eye with plasters on it.' She turned round and looked at Akela, hand pressed to her head. 'Did she get born with writing on her forehead?'

'Well, now, gosh,' said Akela, puffing out his cheeks. 'I don't —'

The little girl continued to advance, until she was near enough to reach out and touch Smudge's face. She ran her fingers over the tattoo, tracing the shapes intently.

At close range, you could see the Ellieness in her: a vagueness deep in the grey-blue eyes, although in her it was backed by something steelier. She was darker than Ellie too — than either of them — and determined with it. If there'd been two of them, she'd have been the confident one, Smudge decided, the one for whom the cards always fell the right way. The lucky twin.

'You don't sleep much, do you?' observed Heloise, running her fingers over the dark shadows under Smudge's eyes.

'I suppose you're right,' she said.

'You can sleep here. We've got big comfortable beds. And a trampoline in the garden.'

She stepped back and put her finger in her mouth.

'Are you in our family?' she said.

Akela leapt up, sending the puzzle board

jerking to the floor and scattering the pieces.

'That's enough now, sweetheart,' he said, holding out a hand to Heloise as though beckoning her back from the edge of a cliff. 'The lady — Ellie — is tired. We don't want to give her a headache with all our questions, do we? You come along with me and I'll tuck you back into bed.'

Heloise stared at him. For a moment, the look of someone older flashed into her eyes — as though she didn't buy his fawning for a second and was weighing up the pros and cons of making a scene. Then the little girl was back.

' 'K,' she said, skipping across the room and taking Akela's hand.

'Sleep tight. Don't let the bed bugs bite,' she said, looking back over her shoulder at Smudge as they disappeared round the door.

A moment later, Nick appeared carrying a trembling tray of mugs.

'Everything all right?' he said.

20

Today we are in the car going to Grandma's house in Hastings, me, Mother and Ellie. Richard is staying with Akela at home. We normally don't go and see Grandma because she and Mother have their differences but we're making an exception today because Aunt Bessie has decided it's time to pack Grandma up and send her to a home and she can't do it all on her own.

When we get to the house, Auntie Bessie is already there in a horrible floral housecoat with her hair going everywhere.

'Honestly, Margaret,' she says. 'You were supposed to have been here two hours ago. The taxi's coming at four.'

Auntie Bessie is what Mother would be if someone melted her and spread her with a butter knife. She is wider and bigger in all directions and there is a softness to the edges of her, but her eyes are just as strict. She stands with her hands on her hips like she is waiting for the magic word, but instead Mother purses her lips and strides into the house. If you stand them side by side, even with them being so different, there is no doubt they are twins.

Inside there are open boxes with stuff spilling out — a frying pan, a china dog with sad eyes, a pack of knitting patterns — all around the hall. Grandma sits hunched in an armchair in the corner of the living room, rocking back and forth like a child. She looks up when we come in.

'Are you the people from the council, dear?' she says.

'No, Mum,' says Mother in a pointed voice. 'We're here to help you pack.'

'Oh, I see,' says Grandma and turns away. She starts to cough and her face goes wonky. Then she spits and a semi-circle of teeth slides out of her mouth and lands in her lap. Ellie gives a frightened laugh, like a bird chirruping.

'Oh Mum!' says Mother, snatching up the teeth and looking around fiercely. She catches sight of me.

'Ellie, go into the kitchen and get a glass of water,' she says.

I hurry through, almost tripping over a box of records on my way. The kitchen looks like one of those bring-and-buy sales they ask you to do on *Blue Peter*. Everything is out of the cupboards and half the mugs are wrapped in bits of newspaper ready to get packed. On the side is the kettle that got Grandma into this mess in the first place, all bent and warped with its plastic bottom licked like ice-cream from where she put it on the hob and nearly started a fire. Because 'kettle' in her day meant something different.

I look around for a glass, but all I can see are small ornamental ones in blue, green and pink. I pick up the biggest one I can find and fill it at the tap. When I get back into the living room, Mother rolls her eyes at me. She takes the silly glass and dips the teeth in the water.

'Here, Mum,' she says. 'Try to slot them back in.'

Grandma takes the teeth like a good child and fits them back into her mouth. 'There,' she says, giving a crooked smile. 'Fit to meet the King.'

'Give me strength,' mutters Mother.

She looks at us both.

'Right,' she says. 'Helen, you come and help Bessie and me. Ellie, you stay here and keep an eye on Grandma. Don't touch anything.'

They go out of the room and up the stairs.

I stare at Grandma.

'Well,' she says brightly. 'My little Helen. I knew you'd come eventually.'

I shift from one foot to the other, pressing my shoes into the brown swirls of the carpet.

'Don't you mean Ellie?' I say.

Grandma frowns.

'Are you telling me I don't know my own granddaughters?' she says in Mother's that's-quite-enough-of-your-nonsense voice. 'I may not have seen you in a little while, but I've looked at you every day.'

And she waves a hand at the mantelpiece, where there is a picture in a frame decorated with shells that says 'Love and friendship' in rope letters at the top. Inside is a photograph of me and Ellie before the swap, standing on a cliff top in red and yellow raincoats with the wind blowing our hair. I am wearing a big smile and Ellie is standing a bit behind with that doubtful look she used to get and you can see us as we really are.

I walk towards Grandma and give her a kiss on her powdery cheek, scrunching my eyes against a rush of tears.

'There,' says Grandma, pleased.

Then she looks at me and the weather changes in her eyes.

'But what is it? You've got . . .' and her

fingers open and close as they try to scrabble the word from the air '. . . empty, haven't you?'

It's not the right word, not in an English-teacher-marking-your-work way, but in another sense it is. Amid all the cracked words that no longer do what they say, it clangs like a deep, resonant bell.

I sit down next to Grandma and take her hand. And while Auntie Bessie, Mother and Ellie rustle packaging upstairs and bang things around, boxing up Grandma's life, I tell her about the game and being locked out of Helen and everything that's happened since.

Grandma sits and listens. Sometimes she puts her other hand to her eyes and says 'Oh dear, oh dear,' and shakes her head like she can't believe what's she's hearing. And sometimes she rocks back and forth.

When I get to the bit about the big boys and girls in the park and the stuff in the bag and Mary's brother, she turns and looks at me.

'Tell me, dear,' she says, 'is Margaret all right? She never mentions anything about Uncle Albert, does she? I always suspected, but in those days, what could you do? You didn't say anything, you just got on with it. It wasn't all . . . fish and chips like it is now.

You just had to get on with it. You kept quiet. You did. You did.'

I pat her hand as she rocks and tell her that Mother's fine. And then I go on saying about the lonely feeling that comes when I see Ellie with the popular girls at school and how everyone looks at me like I am a monster in a cage that belongs in the zoo. And how if everyone could see inside my head — except for the burning angry times — they'd know I was all right, but they can't because all the Ellieness is stacked up round me like a high hedge and every year it grows thicker and taller with big spines so that now there is no way out. And how Ellie has taken Helen and stretched her out of shape like she used to do with her T-shirts. How Helen is now a girl who does drama and likes standing up on stage instead of getting prizes for reading, and not even someone I could be any more. She is a Hellie good and proper. And that is the loneliest thing of all.

After a while, Grandma takes her hand away from her face and looks at me.

'Tell me, dear,' she says with a smile that is like the sun breaking through watery clouds, 'are you Cousin Elizabeth's girl?'

I stare at Grandma and she blinks. I open my mouth to speak, but at that moment there is a toot from the road outside and footsteps come thumping down the stairs.

'Mum,' says Aunt Bessie, hurrying into the room, 'your car is here. It's time to go.'

Grandma blinks again.

'Go?' she says. 'But we've only just arrived. This friend has been keeping me company.'

'I know, Mum,' says Aunt Bessie, brushing back a wisp of stray hair. 'But it's time to say goodbye now. Be a love.'

Shadows appear on the threshold and Mother and Ellie enter the room.

'Come on, Mum,' says Mother sharply, striding over to take Grandma's arm and pull her out of the chair. 'We haven't got all day.'

Grandma's face crumples.

'No,' she wails. 'I won't stand for it. You can't make me go!'

'There isn't any choice, Mum,' says Mother, steering Grandma across the room. 'It's all been arranged.'

At the threshold, Grandma stands firm and looks around furiously at us.

'You ought to be ashamed!' she shouts. 'Call yourselves gynaecologists! If it were up to me, I'd have you all bang to rights!'

Then something cracks in her face and she starts to cry. 'Oh dear,' she says. 'Do excuse me. I think I'm not quite myself.'

Mother leads her down the garden path with Ellie following behind, carrying Grandma's suitcase. When they get to the taxi, Mother opens the door and presses her hand on Grandma's head to stop it bumping when she gets in. I hurry after with the photograph from the mantelpiece, the one of Ellie and me.

'Here, Grandma,' I say, handing it into the car, while Mother gives me an impatient look. 'You might like this to remind you.'

'Thenk yew,' says Grandma in a small, pinched, posh voice like the Queen's.

Auntie Bessie gives the instructions and then we stand back to watch the taxi drive away. Grandma sits staring forward and doesn't look back at us once. All you can see when the car rounds the bend is a little white cloud of hair poking out above the top of the back seat. From here it looks like cotton wool.

21

She woke up to find the blankness had come back. The fizz and spin of the preceding days was nowhere to be found and instead there was only flatness, as though the whole world had gone stale. She looked around, dully. Grey light slanted in through a Velux window revealing a little attic room furnished with a bed, chest of drawers, wardrobe and a bookcase tucked under the sloping ceiling. The walls were painted primrose yellow and the carpet worn through in patches. She groaned as the weight of the previous day landed on her — the people in the bank, the streams of cars, Hellie's face blown up and stuck to a road sign, surrounded by withering flowers, Nick, Heloise, Akela.

The gash on her head throbbed and was hot when she touched it. She ought to get up, she knew. She ought to creep downstairs and get out of there, before Nick had a chance to stop her. She ought to find a way to get across London and back home to the flat, and then she should start making a series of assertive calls to Jobcentre Plus, demanding that her ESA payments be reinstated. She buried her head in her pillow and groaned. The idea was inconceivable. It was like suggesting a person with no legs jump across a ravine.

The hours drifted past. Now and then sounds floated up from the house below: scampering feet; a door banging; muttered conversations; hissed arguments; once, unmistakably, the sharp edge of Mother's voice. A couple of times there was a quiet knock — once she heard a giggle — but she always ignored it, turned over and closed her eyes again. Sleep cocooned her. Reality went out like the tide, until it was nothing but a grey sliver at the end of miles of gravelly beach.

When she went to use the little bathroom at the end of the corridor, she found a tray bearing a plate of fish pie waiting for her. She left it where it lay, congealing and going hard round the edges. She did the same with the pile of clothes left there too: jeans, woolly jumpers, T-shirts, thick socks, some sensible knickers and a handful of bras. Hellie's things. As if she was going to buy into the cruel joke of putting those on.

In the late afternoon she found she was sick of lying in the bed, so she got up and paced around the room. The furniture was battered and mismatched — a world away from the subtle pieces composed just so in the living room downstairs. Glancing at the bookshelf next to the heavy chest of drawers, she saw with a jolt that it was the one that had been in her and Hellie's room back in Mother's house. There was the chip on the shelf from when she'd hurled the glass of water and there the deep scratch from her boot as she'd clung on when they'd tried to drag her away that final night. She lay down on the floor next to it and ran her finger along the mark. More than fifteen years later, the cheap wood still showed up pale and vulnerable against the dark veneer.

She found a lighter and a pack of elderly Marlboro Lights on top of a pile of clutter in the bedside table and smoked one out of the skylight, peering over the ledge into the garden: a rectangle bounded by a brick wall and trees backing on to a park. She could see the glass roof of the kitchen extension jutting out below her. The room inside was airy and light, and dominated by a large, spiky vase of irises plonked in the centre of the table. The flowers seemed to watch her resentfully, like a crowd of little Mothers, as she took each drag.

At the other end of the lawn sat a building with a roof jutting up at a sharp angle at one end. There was a porthole next to the door and a glazed section at the lower end and the whole thing had the feel of a boat crashed into a conservatory. It took her aback — so edgy did it seem, so un-Hellie — and stare at it as she might, she couldn't work out its purpose.

She was just sliding another cigarette from the packet when the door of the room juddered and a piece of paper slipped underneath it. She picked it up to find a message printed in an uneven hand:

Dear Mummies Friend
How are you? I am fine.
We went to the park but then we came home. The end.

Love Heloise.

She turned the paper over but there was nothing more to it, apart from a shopping list scribbled and ticked off in Mother's spiky handwriting.

A few minutes later there was a scratching sound at the door and another bit of paper slipped underneath:

Dear Mummies Friend
You can right back if you like. The end
again.

Love Heloise.

She laid the paper to one side, intending
to ignore it, but five minutes later another
slid through:

I am waiting for your ansa.

Frustration flared. Smudge went to the
door and opened it.

'Look,' she said to the little figure standing there. 'I'm not going to write back, OK?
Just . . . go and play somewhere else.'

A pair of grey-blue eyes stared up at her
above a trembling bottom lip. Smudge
sighed and ran a hand over her face.

'Look, I'm sorry,' she said. 'I didn't mean
to be angry. I just . . . don't like writing
letters.'

Heloise stared at her.

'Why?' she said.

She blinked. 'Well,' she said. 'I suppose
I'm not very good at it.'

'Why?'

(A voice cleared its throat in her head.
Shit, that was all she needed.)

'Jesus,' she muttered, rolling her eyes.

'Look, I'm just not, OK? For fuck's sake!'

The eyes creased and the mouth blossomed, shaping a wail.

Fearful of who might come if Heloise started to cry, Smudge took her arm and pulled her into the room.

'Shhh!' she hissed. 'Sorry. I didn't mean to be nasty. I'm just not very good at controlling myself sometimes.'

Heloise regarded her solemnly. 'Like your insides are too close to the surface?' she said.

Smudge looked at her, surprised. 'Yes,' she said. 'I suppose. Something like that.'

Heloise looked at the bed and the coat on the floor beside it.

'You don't have a lot of things, do you?' she said.

Smudge twitched and reached up to drum her fingers on the frame of the skylight. 'No, I suppose not,' she said.

'Is that 'cos you're poor?'

'I —' In Smudge's mind, black fireworks started to explode, coating her thoughts with dark glitter.

Heloise went to the window and bounced up, gripping the sill to look at the view until her arms gave out. 'What's it like being poor?' she grunted. 'Is it like the chimney sweeps in *Mary Poppins* dancing on the rooftops?'

Smudge ran a hand over her eyes. A guitar struck up inside her mind, thrumming out the introduction to Nirvana's 'Smells Like Teen Spirit' with ominous intensity. 'Not exactly,' she said.

Heloise bounced again. 'Or like *My Fair Lady* with the people selling flowers and hats that you strap on your head?'

The panic was beginning to grip her now, making the walls of the room loom in at her as though they were speakers shuddered by an impossibly loud sound. The effort of the conversation, of following its looping thread, was too much.

'Look, I think it might be better if —'

'Lucky you could stay in Mummy's place while she's not using it,' said Heloise.

Smudge gave a start. She looked behind her as though suddenly Hellie might be there. 'What do you mean, Mummy's place?'

'This is where Mummy always comes when she needs quiet time away from everyone else,' said Heloise. 'Away from us.'

'Oh,' said Smudge, blinking. 'I see.'

'She comes up here most afternoons,' said Heloise, going over to the bookshelf and running her fingers along the shelves. 'Before, I mean. Not now she's sleeping all the time. Sometimes in the night she comes here too. It is like her room. Except if I was a grown-up lady and I had a room, I'd make it more exciting than this.'

'But —' said Smudge.

'Heloise?' came a voice up the stairs. 'Heloise?'

Heloise froze. Fear mingled with guilt trickled over her features.

'I'm not supposed to be in here,' she whispered.

Smudge frowned. 'What do you mean, you're not supposed to be in here?'

'Granny said,' said Heloise, shifting from foot to foot. 'Because of you.'

'Because of me?' said Smudge.

'Because you're sick. And you might make us all sick. And then we might all be like Mummy lying down in beds all day. And then we might die.'

'Heloise!' came Mother's voice again, accompanied by the sound of footsteps starting the climb from the entrance hall. 'Where are you?'

'And she said you tell lies,' said Heloise hurriedly. 'And that you're not a nice lady. Even though you look nice to me, apart from the writing on your head and the wonky bit next to your eye.'

'Heloise!' called Mother again from the landing below, her voice cracking. 'Come with me this instant. We're making cupcakes.'

'Coming!' shouted Heloise, and she scuttled out of the room and thumped down the stairs.

'What were you doing up there?' came Mother's voice.

'Just seeing,' said Heloise.

'You didn't go into the visitor's room, did you?' said Mother as the pair of them started off down the lower flight.

'No,' said Heloise.

'Because I've told you about that,' drifted up Mother's voice. 'Curiosity killed the cat.'

Smudge shut the door and went to sit on the bed, breathing hard. Panic fizzed within her, the gash on her temple seared and burned. To think she'd nearly come face to face with the old witch! Trembling, she jerked open the drawer in the bedside table and fumbled for the fag packet. But it was not there: instead, her fingers met something hard and smooth and cold. She drew it out: a photograph frame, decorated with shells, some of which had dropped off leaving yellow blobs of glue to mark their places. 'Love and friendship' it read in rope letters along the top. And there they were, in the picture: two little girls in coloured raincoats, faded yellow with time, standing on a blustery cliff top with the sea behind. Horror hoofed her in the heart and she flung the frame away, sending it clattering to the floor. She glanced around Hellie's room — her place — taking in the ceiling, the skylight, the bookshelf, the door. There was nothing for it: she had to get out.

22

Christmas Day: Richard running around draped in sheets of wrapping paper, Hellie listening to the Walkman she got for having a good report from school, Akela starting a new model with 1,500 separate parts that will need to go on two bits of cardboard spread over the dining-room table and makes Mother purse her lips and tap her fingers on her arm. After lunch, she goes upstairs to lie down and I let myself out of the front door.

It is a green day and not that cold. The wind gusts down the street frisking up leaves and crisp packets now and then, but for the most part everything is still. The garden gate groans when I open it. I know how it feels. I've only walked down the path and already my feet are hurting from the new Start-rite shoes that were my Christmas present, along with a red top and a tartan skirt. 'Kilt,' said Mother, frowning like she is cross

I didn't know that before. And like somehow the kilt is spoilt by my not knowing, and no longer as good. She made me put them on and said they were very elegant and made me look older and not like a schoolgirl at all, but I know that now she is also pleased that she won't have to take me shopping for more school shoes after I dropped paint on my old ones when the angry feeling came one day.

The street is quiet. All the houses shut up tight with Merry Christmas inside. You can see the blue light from the televisions flickering in the windows: the Queen and then *Noel's Christmas Presents.* No one is out and about, which means the world belongs to me, and my feelings soar like a balloon tugging me along on a string at the thought of all the hours and hours that lie ahead of not having to be polite and mind my Ps and Qs and be pleased at Richard driving his tricycle into my legs.

When I get to the park there is a woman there walking a brown dog, which ruins things a bit. I stand by the swings, kicking at the metal frame, until she goes, taking the dog with her. Then it is like the sky yawns and the park swells and everything is mine alone.

I stand for a while, breathing in the

Christmas air, seeing how much of the day I can suck in in one go. Then with a hop and a skip I barrel across the grass to my place: the upside-down tree. I push through the branches, putting my hands up to stop the twigs scratching my face.

It is gloomy inside the tree, so I don't see him at first, sitting on the log. Then he looks up and his face is white in the half-light, the whiskers shadowy: Mary's brother.

'Oh, hello,' he says in his flat, Manchester voice. 'Fancy seeing you here.'

I take a step back.

'Nah,' he says. 'Don't go. Stay and enjoy the Christmas cheer. I brought you a drink 'specially.' He waves a hand at a bag by his feet where a bottle glints.

I look over my shoulder at the park, but the thought of going back up the road to the house and Hellie and Akela makes me tired. I give a shrug.

'All right,' I say.

'Good girl,' he says. 'Come and sit down here with me.'

He pats the log beside him and I go over, tucking my kilt round me so the bark doesn't dig into my thighs. He hands me the bottle.

'Get that down you,' he says. 'Pure magic.'

The liquid in the bottle is brown and

smells sour. I tip it and take a sip. Burning seeps down my throat and I cough.

'Not like that. Take a proper pull,' he says, and he tilts the bottle against my lips so a flood of it pours into my mouth and out down my neck over the new top and kilt. I swallow and gasp.

'There she goes,' he says, and he puts a hand on my knee to steady me. It stays there after the bottle comes away.

'So,' he says. 'Have a good Christmas?'

I shrug. 'All right,' I say in the husky, don't-care voice teenagers use on the bus. 'You?'

He shakes his head.

'Nah, it was shit,' he says. He locks his gaze on mine and I have to swallow a gasp at the deadness in his eyes. I look away to the far side of the upside-down tree where the dry leaves are swirling around in the breeze.

'How's Mary?' I say quickly.

Then it's his turn to shrug. 'Dunno,' he says. 'Probably off somewhere getting fucked, the little slut.'

He looks down and we both watch as his hand slips up under the folds of the kilt.

'The little slut,' he says again, slowly this time, so that the 's' gets all messy and frayed and tangles with the letters coming after. In my head, it makes a picture of an ice-cream dropped on the pavement, sweetness mixing with dirt.

'I haven't seen Mary for ages,' I say in the bright voice Mother uses when Akela's farted and no one's allowed to say.

He looks at me again and his eyes feel greedy, running down over the new red top.

'How old are you?' he says.

'I'm eleven-twelve-in-April,' I say.

'Eleven, eh?' he says and his hand creeps higher. 'A big girl then. A really big girl.'

His other hand starts to fiddle with something in his lap and there is a click and the rasp of a zip, but I don't look down. I just keep looking at his face, at the pasty skin between his eyes where his tufty eyebrows start, and I think if I can only keep talking about normal things everything will be OK.

'I'm in Class 7B at school and art is my favourite subject,' I say, even though it isn't really; it's just the one where there is no special work that I have to sit separately to do and everyone is too busy messing around to pay any attention to me.

'Uh-huh,' he says, his voice taking on a breathy tone. 'Are there lots of boys in your class?'

'It's about half-half,' I say.

Under the kilt, his hand reaches the top

of my thigh, making me jump, but I keep looking at him.

'This term we did a still-life of fruit and vegetables arranged to look like a face,' I say.

'Uhuh,' he says again. 'I bet they fucking love you, don't they, the boys? You and your sister. I bet they queue up at breaktime to take turns. First one, then the other.'

His thumb starts to slide round the elastic at the top of my leg and I shuffle backwards.

'I —' I say.

'And you love it too, don't you?' he says, sliding closer, his breath hot on my face. 'I mean, you say you don't, but secretly, underneath, you're gagging for it.'

His hand plunges in under the fabric and I jump up.

'I think I'd better go home now,' I say.

'Oh, no you don't,' he says, leaping up and grabbing my shoulder. 'You're not going anywhere before you finish what you've started. This is your fault. I was here minding my own business and you just barged in, getting me all excited, remember? Now it's up to you to make it right. You can't just have it all your own way.'

I look up at the black shape of him topped by his wolfish face, pale in the gathering dusk. And in my mind I see Mother's face, grim with disappointment, and Hellie wagging her finger.

'I'm sorry, but I don't know what you want,' I say.

He laughs and a rook joins in.

'Oh, don't you worry about that,' he says. 'I'll show you. You just lie down quietly like a good girl. It won't take long. Trust me, the way you've got me, it won't take long at all.'

His hand presses on my shoulder and I sink down into the dirt and leaves until he is above me, fumbling. Then a sharp pain comes and he is plunging and jerking above me, his face twisted with fury.

And that is when I learn the secret: that you don't have to be anyone. You don't have to be Helen or Ellie. You don't have to be any kind of person. You can just float up through the branches into the sky like a balloon, until you are far away looking down on the people scurrying about their Christmases like ants and no one can touch you at all.

23

She waited until the middle of the night, sitting hunched on Hellie's bed long after the last thud of footsteps on the staircase and the final closing click of a door. Then, shrugging on her stained coat with the pocket hanging off one side, she let herself out of the room. Her body protested as she walked down the corridor and she moved slowly, as if wading through water, past a doorway on the right to the head of the stairs.

At the top, she paused to listen: nothing, only the sound of a siren in a nearby street. She walked down the stairs, her knees aching with each step. On the landing below, she heard the gentle sound of breathing emanating from one of the rooms and the snort and whistle of Akela's snore. She hugged her coat round her and hurried on down, grateful for the thick carpets.

In the hall, she went to the front door and

pulled down the handle of the snib, but the door refused to budge when she tried to pull it, held fast by some sort of heavy-duty lock further down. She looked around. Where would they keep the keys?

The rest of the house yawned behind her, stretching into blackness. There was the doorway to the living room where she'd sat with Akela that awkward first night. Beyond it was another, giving on to darkness, and then there were more stairs leading down and round a corner. There were no coat hooks or stands that she could see for jackets that might have keys in the pockets and the bookshelf with the telephone on it was otherwise bare.

She tiptoed across the wooden floor and peered into the other doorway. Dim, orange light spilled in through a tall, French window that looked out on to a patio above the garden. The light picked out silver in a cabinet, a long, gleaming table and the cellophane over a collection of presentation sets spread across its surface. She went over to one — a basket of fruit, garnished with exotic flowers and tied with a bow — and squinted at the tag attached to it. *To Helen,* she made out, *from all the team at ITV.*

There were no jackets hanging on the backs of the chairs around the table, but a

219

long, low sideboard caught her eye. The first door she opened proved to be a non-starter — just revealing plates and cups. But behind the second she discovered ranks of bottle and decanters, jostling and winking up at her. Her brain's clamour for the keys muffled itself as a new urge took hold. She reached in and selected a bottle of vodka. The label was for a brand she didn't recognise, but when she unscrewed the top and breathed in it smelled rich and smooth. None of the rough edges of the value range here. This was the good stuff.

She closed her eyes and put the bottle to her lips, anticipating the feeling of it spreading through her — peace, deadening the machinations of her mind. Just a nip or two to help get her across London. Just a taste to take the edge off the miserable creaking of her bones. She readied her arm to tilt the bottle, took a deep breath and —

'I knew I didn't dream it,' said a voice.

Smudge spun around. Heloise was standing in the doorway in her SpongeBob SquarePants pyjamas, rubbing her eyes. 'Oh,' she said. 'I thought you were Mummy coming back.'

She blinked, looking small and young all of a sudden.

'Sorry,' said Smudge.

'What are you doing?' said Heloise.

Smudge looked at the bottle. 'I'm just . . . checking this.'

'You weren't,' said Heloise, advancing into the room. 'You were going to drink it. I saw you.'

'Shhh,' said Smudge, waving her arms in an effort to tamp down the little girl's indignation. 'You'll wake everyone up.'

'It's naughty to drink out of the bottle,' continued Heloise. 'It spoils it for everyone else.' She turned and pulled out a tea cup from the first door in the sideboard. 'Here,' she said, holding it out, pleased.

Smudge looked at the tea cup in Heloise's tiny hand. The handle was the perfect size for her fingers. 'No, thank you,' she said firmly. 'I'm not thirsty any more.'

She put the bottle back in the cupboard.

Heloise scuffed at the Persian carpet with the toe of her Shaun the Sheep slipper. 'What are we going to do now then?'

'Now?' said Smudge. 'Go back to bed. It's the middle of the night.'

Heloise looked at her with narrowed eyes. 'You're not going back to bed. You're just saying that to make me go.'

'I'm not.'

'Are too.'

'Am not.'

'Are too. You're even wearing your coat.'

They stood staring at each other for a moment. Then Heloise shifted abruptly and whirled around in a pirouette. 'Why don't you come and see Emily instead?' she said.

Smudge frowned. 'Emily?'

'My sister,' said Heloise.

'But —' said Smudge. The horrible thought resurfaced of another girl living in the shadow of this precocious child, following half a step behind. Surely Nick had told her there was only one? She cast her mind back. The memory of the conversation hovered, just out of reach. What if she was wrong? What if she'd misheard? Or what if a voice had said it and tricked her into thinking it was the truth?

She shook her head. 'I don't think that's a good idea,' she said. 'Not tonight. Anyway, it would wake everyone up.'

'It won't,' said Heloise, coming over and taking her hand. 'We'll do it quietly and nicely and it won't wake anyone at all.'

The little girl led her out into the hall, but instead of making for the staircase, she turned and started down the steps to the basement. Smudge followed her, as if in a dream, mesmerised at the thought of the other little girl, Emily, cowering somewhere in the bowels of the house as part of a cruel game.

The steps rounded a corner and gave on to the generous kitchen. At the far end, she saw the dim lines of the table with the massive bowl of irises throwing out sharp shadows in the light coming through the glass ceiling. In between, a stainless-steel island glimmered beneath a hoard of implements hanging from a rack. Everywhere was clean and minimalist. When she turned and looked behind her, she saw a doorway to a utility room containing a large washing machine with a red light blinking like a malevolent eye.

She peered through the gloom, searching for the hunched figure, her ears primed for the sound of snuffling, the dying whimpers of a storm of sobs, but there was nothing: the stools at the island sheltered empty air beneath them, the table covered vacancy.

'So where's Emily?' she said at last, unable to bear the thought of the other child hidden in some miserable corner any longer.

Heloise giggled. 'Emily in the kitchen?' she said, shaking her head. 'What would she be doing in here, you silly?'

She went to a cupboard tucked under the stairs and opened it to reveal a rack of keys fixed inside the door. After groping among

them, she pulled out a set on a silver fob
with a triumphant squawk. Then she scampered across the room to the glass doors at
the far end of the dome.

She turned back and looked across the
room. 'Come on,' she said, beckoning.

Dizziness billowing up around her like
mist, Smudge crossed the floor, drawn on
in spite of herself, as though the very
shadows were sucking her back to the time
before. Of course, she should have known
the child would be outside. Where else did
you go when you were on the fringes of
things like that? Where had she gone? The
inevitability of it all was sickening. She
could not escape.

Heloise got the door open and together
they stepped out onto the lawn. The walls
of the garden rose up around them, cutting
off the trees nearby so that there was only
the blind sky. Flowers nodded in the breeze,
releasing night perfume to the air, and
somewhere a bird, thrown by London's
perpetual dusk, warbled on.

Heloise stumped to the edge of the lawn,
where a hydrangea bush huddled close to a
rhododendron, their outermost branches
touching as though clasped in a conspira-
tors' handshake. 'There she is,' she said,
pointing at the space in between.

Smudge peered into the hollow — straining to make out the sorry little shape, the sheen of nut-brown hair — but could see nothing. There was only the earth and a bit of rock stuck in the middle. She crouched down and looked to left and right but still there was nothing — only the leaves of the bushes and an old plastic ball that must have got left there when it rained and was slowly being absorbed into the earth.

'Where?' she said.

'There,' said Heloise, pointing at the centre of the space.

Smudge looked again and found that the rock transformed itself before her eyes into a little marble stone with some sort of pot set into it and inlaid with silver letters. *Emily Margaret Davidson,* read the inscription. *20 August 2012 — 29 October 2012. Briefly known, but for ever loved.*

'Oh,' she said.

'She got born for a while,' said Heloise, her fingers curling the bottom of her pyjama top. 'But then her body wouldn't work very well and she couldn't live with us any more. Mummy comes to see her every day but now she's asleep all the time I have to do it.' She stood on one leg and held her arms out to keep her balance. She looked up at Smudge. 'When do you think Mummy will wake up?'

'I don't know,' began Smudge. 'I think the doctors say . . .'

'Oh yes the doctors!' said Heloise, losing her balance and stamping her foot down. 'But doctors are silly poos!'

'Mmn,' said Smudge.

Heloise closed one eye and squinted up at her. 'Do you think one day my body will stop working properly and then they'll make me a stone in the ground?'

A breeze skipped over the lawn and tousled her hair.

'That's a big question,' said Smudge uncertainly.

'Anyway, you're not going anywhere, are you?' said Heloise, sneaking her little fingers into Smudge's hand. 'You're not planning on doing something stupid like dying or going away without saying goodbye?'

'I —' began Smudge.

But suddenly Heloise was bouncing. 'Come on,' she cried. 'Let's go and play *Dora the Explorer* behind the hut!' And she scampered off across the lawn, the light from the lamps in the park twinkling on the soles of her feet.

24

Not being you has its advantages. You can do what you like, when you like, whether you like it or not. You can stay out all night, bunk off school, steal lip balms in Boots. You can rip up your homework, laugh in teachers' faces, smoke in the living room. You can swear whenever you want to, eat honey out of the jar with a spoon, write on the walls. You can rip up Hellie's awards and certificates, scrawl faces in lipstick on the bathroom mirror, guzzle from Akela's drinks cupboard until you throw up. You can rake patterns in your arm with a compass, stamp on Richard's toys, scream until it sounds like the voice is coming from somewhere far away outside your head.

And when they come at you with their sour faces and sensible words, when they blame and cajole and bribe, when they threaten you with the consequences of what you've done, you can just shrug and look away. Because the truth is, it's not you who did those things and it's not you they're talking to. You're far away, floating in the sky, looking down on them all, laughing until you want to die.

Sometimes when you go to the park, you find the others in the upside-down tree. Baz and Gina and all of them. They're a bit wary of you at first because of what happened the time before but you soon break them down. Now you can drink deeper and huff harder than all the rest of them because you just don't care. You enjoy it, the rush, the buzz, but behind it all, you know there's nothing there. Getting high is like the bright backdrop they put up for the school production of *Kiss Me, Kate,* the one with Hellie dancing centre-stage: it looks impressive, but when you crash through it, yelling and shouting swearwords, there's nothing but the breeze-block wall and the steps that take you down to the bins.

It's an amazing secret to discover: the power of not caring, of having nothing to lose. It opens doors, it wins respect. It means people don't mess with you because they know that if push comes to shove and then to rolling, biting and kicking on the playground tarmac, they'll be worrying about how they're going to explain this to their mums while you will be thinking of nothing at all. You don't care if you hurt them and you don't care if they hurt you and — weird, isn't it? — that means you hardly ever get hurt. And even if you do, it doesn't matter, because you're not really there. They can't touch you.

But sometimes you want to feel something. And when you do, there's only one place to go: you let yourself out and go down the back lane to the house where Mary used to live. And there, with the music thumping and the cigarette smoke curling up from the ashtray next to your head, amid the piles of fake IDs he cobbles together with sticky-back plastic to sell to the school kids up the precinct, you let him do it to you as hard as he likes. Now and then when you go there are women there: peroxide blondes in tight jeans teetering on little heels, drinking miniatures and flipping through his CD collection. He makes you wait round the corner while he gets rid of them, mouthing excuses about work. Then he comes and snatches your wrist, dragging you inside with all the strength of his anger at how you have power over him, at how he can't resist. You get a flicker of triumph from that, at the way you control him. But it's towards the end, in the final moments when the thrusting quickens and his face twists into a snarl, that the string of the balloon of who you used to be dangles near and you feel you could reach out and clutch it if only your arms weren't pinned by your sides with his writhing.

You don't think ahead. That's the key. Pregnancy, injury, expulsion, death — none of these are things that could happen, right now, to you. As if falling in with the plan, your body stays childish and compact, a tightly shut bud. The consequences are somebody else's problems, another girl's, far down the line, broken shards for someone else to sweep up. Shards like the fragments of glass from the tumbler you smash in the kitchen — the ones you think about lacing Hellie's plate with before carrying it through.

When you float out of your head above the world, none of this means anything. It is like events in a dull soap opera: an episodic script that does not hang together well. You watch with occasional interest, mostly boredom. Around you, people press on as though everything matters so much. You wonder where they find it in them to be so committed to the lie that every moment links to the next in a coherent manner. It is as though, at the gateway to existence, they

230

were handed a script for being them and yours got lost in the post. Sometimes it makes you cry: standing in line in the canteen, hanging on to the bar on the bus, in the newsagent's. You wear your tears angrily, glaring at people, defying them to ask you what's going on.

It works. No one does. They don't because they're scared of you. Because you're the girl who throws things in corridors. Because you're the bitch who elbows her way through the lunch queue, sending people flying. Because when they look at you closely, they see there is nothing behind your eyes.

In the park, they're scared of you too. Even being that much older. It's the un-predictability that gets them. You never know with you. One day you might walk up to one of the boys, bold as brass, and shove your tongue down his throat then and there. You don't even care if he's got a girlfriend. Another day it might be sizzling a cigarette into the back of your hand for a bet. And then there's the swing-frame incident.

That day you're all bored. The highs feel small and nobody's got any beer left. Even Shaz and Jon, who normally go off to have sex in the bushes, can't be arsed doing it today. So it's down to you to think of something to do.

'How about we walk along the bar over the top of the swings?' you say.

They all look at you. You can see that jerk of alarm that tells you you've got them.

'Come on,' you say. 'What are you? Scared?'

A few of the boys bridle at that.

'Nah,' they mutter, rolling their shoulders like boxers before a fight. 'We could do that. What's the big deal?'

You go to the playground. The frame looms above you: two As linked by a pole in between. It's very high — higher than you remember — but you don't care. You look around the group.

'Who wants to go first?' you say.

They all look at each other, shift from foot to foot.

'Pussies,' you say, enjoying the way the word lands among them. You heard someone say it up the precinct not that long ago and the way it made everyone look the other way told you all you needed to know about its power. 'Guess I'll have to do it myself then. Someone help me up.'

Baz steps forward. He holds up his hands. 'Nah, Ellie man,' he says. 'You don't have to do that. We believe you.'

You don't back down. That's essential.

You've learnt this. Once you commit to a thing, you see it through to the bloody, gritty end.

'Someone help me up,' you say again, looking around.

No one moves.

'Fine,' you say, cheeks flushing hot. 'I'll do it myself.'

And even though it's too high for you and it hurts your knees and hands, you go and scramble up on the cross bar. Then it's about pulling yourself up to stand on top. A flash of fear streaks through you as you glimpse the tarmac slanting way below, but you squash it 'til it burns out. It's nothing you haven't felt before. Chances are, it won't kill you. Not that you mind much either way.

When you get up to the top and balance there, feet angled on the bar, you look down at them. They stand with their heads tilted up like children staring at a giant. They can see up your skirt from where they are, but nobody's laughing and you don't care. Let them get a good eyeful if it gives them any pleasure. Something for their wet dreams. Perverts.

You turn to face the end of the bar. Left to your own devices, you'd shuffle your way along, but you know you need to look confident with them all watching, so you take a step, slanting your foot so it splays diagonally across the bar. Then you take another and another. The end of the bar wobbles closer, jiggling with the treetops behind. But suddenly it's all going too fast, your feet have to run to catch up, and before you know it, you are teetering and your arms are flapping like the wings of a flight-less bird. The tarmac shifts and leans below you, arranging itself at a crazy angle that surges up suddenly to come and meet your face.

The next thing you know, you're in the hospital. Gina's there and Akela in his wind-cheater, and it's the middle of the night. An Indian doctor comes in.

'Oh dear, oh dear,' he says, shaking his head. 'Got ourselves in quite a little state, didn't we?'

He peers at the side of your face.

'Still,' he says. 'We've patched you up, although I'm afraid there will be a scar. A lesson learnt, isn't it?'

They don't want you to see, but you make them give you a mirror: Gina's compact, the glass dusted with powder. They are wor-ried that you will be upset. But when you peer in at the Frankenstein stitches running up the side of your head, wriggling round your eye like the tracks of Richard's train-set, you feel a warm sensation flooding through you. You are pleased. Now no one will mix the two of you up ever again.

The following Saturday you're lying on your bed, watching the afternoon sunlight shift across the ceiling and down the scratches in the yellow wallpaper covered in rosebuds where you carved FUCK! with the kitchen paring knife. Hellie's out somewhere — a party, the cinema, some girly thing with kids from school. You weren't invited, of course — why would you be? You'd just screw it up — have everyone backing away nervously from your idea of fun. Fuck them anyway. You don't need them. They're boring. They're children. They don't know life like you do. Besides, your head still hurts from where you whacked it on the tarmac. The stitches itch and the kids all call you Frank-enstein when they think you can't hear them at school. You don't need that kind of ag-gravation.

A click and the door opens. You look up to see Mother's face peering into the room.

'She's not here,' you say.

'I know,' she says. 'It's you I've come to see.'

You shrug and look at the wall. Then you

glance back and see her coming in, shaking her head.

'What?' you say, even though you know what — she's annoyed about all the stuff flung about the room. Your clothes and make-up tumbled everywhere and cluttering up Hellie's neat half. You don't talk about it any more, the two of you. When Hellie gets home, she just gathers everything together and shunts it towards your bed, over the invisible line.

'Well,' says Mother, reaching a hand up to pat her rigid curls, as though checking they're still there, 'it is rather a mess in here, don't you think?'

You look around the room and shrug again. You know your nonchalance infuriates her and that makes you glad. You like to see her tensed up, angry words poised, but holding back from letting rip for fear of what you'll do. It feels like an achievement, like all of Hellie's LAMDA certificates rolled up into one gold-leaf scroll and delivered to you at a public ceremony, in front of photographers clicking pictures as fast as a typewriter's keys.

Mother sighs, picks a dirty bra off the edge of Hellie's bed and sits down. She clears her throat.

'How's your head?' she says.

You reach your hand up, touch the rail-track stitches.

'All right,' you say.

She nods, coughs again, turns to the side and looks at you through one eye.

'They told Horace at the hospital that you'd been taking drugs that night and that was why you did it,' she says. 'Is that true?'

You frown for a moment. Then it all falls into place, like letters through the front door.

'Oh, you mean the glue,' you say. 'Yeah, I suppose — if that's what you want to call it.'

Mother shuts her eyes.

'Drugs,' she says with a moan, like a character on *EastEnders*. 'Why on earth would you want to go and do a stupid thing like that?'

Anger prickles at the back of your neck.

'I don't know,' you say, quickly. 'Because I'm bored? Because I'm lonely? Because I hate my stupid, fucking life?'

Mother winces.

'Don't swear, please, Eleanor,' she says.

'It's Helen,' you say, tracing the contours of the 'K' carved into the wall.

Mother sighs. 'Oh dear. Haven't you grown out of that yet?' she says.

You curl your fingers in under the paper

sliced open by the 'K' and rip it from the wall. The pink plaster below looks like an open wound.

'You don't grow out of the truth,' you mutter.

'What's that?' says Mother, leaning in. Then she sees the wall. 'Oh, for crying out loud,' she says. 'Can't you be trusted with anything nice? You're almost fourteen years old. You really should —'

She stops herself, sits down on your bed.

'What I'm trying to say,' she adds, after a deep breath, 'is that this can't go on. We're worried about you. I'm . . . worried about you.'

She reaches out a hand and taps your arm. You lie there, feeling the thump of her fingers, and wonder if they practised this, her and Akela, muttering between themselves this morning in the kitchen while you were still asleep.

'This situation is not good for anyone,' Mother continues, her voice assuming a newsreaderly tone. 'These episodes have got to stop. Richard's only small still and —'

You give a snort. 'Oh yes, precious Richard,' you say. 'We mustn't upset him.'

She pulls her hand away. 'So that's what this is about, is it?' she says. 'You're jealous of Richard. Of things moving on. You don't want me to be happy. Is that it?'

You give another snort and turn more resolutely to the wall. The paper gapes at you and you itch to grab another piece of it and rip as hard as you can.

There's silence for a while. Then Mother swallows and puts her hand back on your shoulder. You feel her lacquered nails through the cotton of the bleeding skull T-shirt you know she hates.

'Look,' she says. 'I understand things haven't been easy. Perhaps I haven't always been . . . perfect. But, you see, your father made life difficult for all of us when he did what he did, and —'

'Killed himself, you mean,' you say, leaping in. 'Topped himself? Looped a tie around the banister and choked himself to death?'

It's all in the papers in the local archive. You spent an hour going through them one afternoon when you should have been in geography. You drank in every detail there was with a sort of grim satisfaction. An artist, they'd called him. A family man.

You hear a sharp intake of breath. The nails tighten on your shoulder, digging in like claws.

'That's enough,' she says. 'I will not have you talking like that. Whatever you may feel, whatever you may know, you have to keep it to yourself and find a way to carry on with things. Because that's what decent people do. No matter how much it hurts. We all have to do our best.'

You carry on staring at the wall, tracing the rip along the edge of the primrose-yellow paper with your eyes. The tinkle of an ice-cream van playing 'Pop Goes the Weasel' drifts in through the window.

Mother shifts on the bed, jolting you. 'You don't see Helen missing school and running around snorting glue,' she says. 'She's not out God knows where every night. She's home at a sensible time, doing her home-work, helping with Richard.'

'Oh yes,' you say in a pinched voice, imitating her for the amusement of the wall. 'The golden child. Miss Perfect-Pants.'

'Eleanor, don't talk about your sister like that,' says Mother. 'All I'm saying is that maybe if you took a leaf out of her book things might be different. I can't understand why you'd want to ruin everything now life is finally getting back on track.'

The nails relinquish their grip on your shoulder and scuttle up to tuck a stray hair behind your ear. 'You could be such a nice girl,' she whispers softly.

Throughout this speech, you narrow your

eyes more and more so that the rosebuds on the wall become flies caught in the amber of the fury that boils up out of you to coat the room. You flip round on the bed and she gives a start.

'This isn't about Richard,' you say in a hard, robot voice that seems to be speaking through you from somewhere else. 'Or Dad. Or having my life stolen. Or even fucking Scoutmaster Twatface downstairs.'

You look up at her. The eyeshadow has collected in the creases around her eyelids and there is a clot of powder stuck in the line at the side of her nose. Her nostrils quiver.

'I was raped, Mother,' you shout. 'Does that make sense of it all for you? I was raped.'

Mother blinks and touches a hand to her face.

'Raped?' she says uncertainly. 'What do you mean, raped?'

'I mean raped,' you roar. 'I mean a man took his penis and forced it inside me and —'

'Shhhh,' says Mother, flapping her hands. 'Richard might hear!'

But you don't care and you can't stop and now it's all pouring out of you in one big stinking gush, as tears flood down your face.

'It was on Christmas Day two years ago,' you say, gasping. 'I went to the park. I didn't know anyone else would be there. But he was. I didn't understand what was happening and he made it feel like it was all my fault. Like I'd asked for it.'

You look at her. Mother is sitting with her hands clasped round herself, shaking her head in odd little jerks, as if trying to shift a headache.

'It hurt so much,' you say, your voice a whimper. 'I didn't know what to do. I —'

Mother looks at you. 'Oh,' she says, and this time there is no false stiffness in her voice. When her hand reaches for you it is soft. 'My poor little girl,' she says, enfolding you in a hug. 'My poor, poor little thing.'

You lean against her and she rocks you gently as you sob, shuddering cracks in the loneliness and sadness and pain that have for so long walled you in.

'I didn't think you'd understand,' you say after a while, wonderingly.

You sit back and look at Mother's face and see a sorrow deep in her eyes that you've never spotted before. A dam breaks in your brain, sending realisation flooding through you. Images surge to the surface of your thoughts: a sad little living room, a line of false teeth.

'That day at Grandma's house,' you say. 'That thing she said . . . Uncle Albert —'

Mother's arms drop away and she sits back, staring into the distance. Down the road, the ice-cream van starts playing 'Yankee Doodle'. Mother gives a sour laugh.

'Oh, yes,' she says in a strange, hard little voice. 'I see what you're trying to do. You nearly had me fooled too. Mug that I am, I nearly fell for it. I might have known.'

You open your mouth to say something but Mother stands up and rounds on you, her face ablaze.

'You little bitch!' she spits. 'You filthy, lying little toad. Making up stories as a small child is one thing, but this is disgusting. Manipulating, lying, because of whatever you might have heard — whatever rubbish you picked out of that old woman's ramblings. You won't get me that way. I won't have it. Not after I've worked so hard to build a decent life. I won't have it, do you understand? Disgusting! I won't have this in my house.'

You're so shocked, you forget to be angry. You've never heard Mother swear before. 'But,' you say, your voice breaking like a small child's, 'but, Mother, it's true.'

'No,' she says, backing away. 'It's not true. I won't have it. We won't discuss this. I will

243

not have you raking up the past. I'm putting my foot down.'

'But it is!' you plead. 'I really was raped. And it keeps happening. And I don't know how to —'

Mother shakes her head, puts her hand out and opens the door. 'No,' she says again. 'Absolutely not. This didn't happen. Understand? This pollution ends today. It ends right now.' She pauses, turns back, and looks across the room at you.

'You'd better sort yourself out, Eleanor or whoever you are,' she says. 'You'd better learn to keep this under control. I will not have a monster for a daughter.' And then she is gone, shutting the door behind her with a sharp click.

You stare at the space where she was, through a wash of tears: the yellow rosebud wallpaper and the cream door. For a second, the world stands still. Then the black eagle of rage flaps down on to your shoulders and sinks its talons in, enfolding you in its wings. You want to hit, to hurt, to kill. You want to take what is going on inside you and smash it and spread it all over the world. You grope blindly and your fingers close round the glass on the bedside table. This you hurl, stagnant water and all, at the place where Mother stood. Only you can't even do this

right: the glass veers off-course and crashes
into the bookshelf at the foot of your bed,
gouging the wood and showering the books
there with droplets and glittering shards.
You grip yourself, biting your knees, as the
world folds in and the house crumbles and
you are left completely alone.

25

A knock on the door in the hazy hours of the afternoon. Heloise standing there. 'It's OK,' she whispered, contorting her mouth into improbable shapes. 'Granny and Peeps are out. Come on!'

Bleary from just waking up, Smudge stumbled after her, past the closed door in the attic corridor and down the stairs to a playroom filled with toys. A child laughed hysterically in her head as Heloise thrust gadget after gadget at her: dolls that blinked and moved their arms, little handheld video games, spinning tops carved out of wood to look like the playthings of yesteryear. As Heloise scurried from cupboard to cupboard in her blue pinafore dress and white hole-patterned socks, Smudge found she had to remind herself that this little girl was not Hellie and that the pair of them had not been sent up to amuse themselves in the bedroom of a rich friend's house while

Mother drank tea and crumbled biscuits in the sitting room below.

Heloise stood and regarded Smudge holding the toys limply on her lap.

'Bored now!' she announced after a moment. 'Come on!'

She led her aunt through the house.

'That's Mummy and Daddy's room. It goes up a spiral staircase,' she said, pointing along the playroom corridor. Smudge stared at the shut door with a shiver, imagining Hellie, all made-up and pristine, standing on the other side.

They passed a hall table bearing a photograph of Hellie shaking hands with Tony Blair and another of her cutting the ribbon to open a children's ward, and on through the kitchen to the garden.

('Well, this is a turn up for the books,' snickered a voice. 'A real big horrible surprise!')

'Get in,' instructed Heloise, pointing at a big rhododendron bush.

'What? In there?' said Smudge.

Heloise folded her arms. 'I won't tell you twice.'

('Move your ass, you lazy scum,' agreed another voice.)

So Smudge sighed, crouched down and wriggled her way into the foliage to a hollow space inside. Heloise crawled in after her.

'You see?' she says. 'It's a secret place where you can be and no one knows. You can be in here for hours if you like and no one will find you. Safe.' She turned and picked something out of the shadows. 'And there's this.'

It was a bird's nest with fragments of blue shell and three wisps of feathers still clinging to the twigs inside.

'Don't break it,' said Heloise. 'I think it might have magic powers, but I haven't worked out how to use it yet.'

She looked up at Smudge and then snatched the nest away and tucked it behind her.

'But the best thing about this place is how you can be in here when guests come and shout things out to give them a surprise,' said Heloise. 'Like you can shout "BOOO!" and "I CAN SEE YOU!" and then they'll be surprised and maybe they'll drop their drink and splash the red wine all down themselves.'

There was the sound of a door opening.

'Is everything all right?' called Nick.

'Oh fuck,' muttered Smudge.

She crawled to the edge of the rhododendron and looked out. Nick was standing at the doorway to the wacky hut at the end of the garden. She sighed and wriggled out on to the lawn.

'Yes,' she said, stumbling to her feet and brushing the soil off her knees. 'I'm sorry. I hope we're not disturbing you. Heloise was just showing me —' she caught sight of Heloise scowling and shaking her head as she wriggled out of the bush '— something. I didn't realise it would be so loud.'

'Oh no,' he said, waving a hand vaguely behind him. 'It's just work. It's not important.'

There was a pause while they stared at each other. Then both of them tried to talk at once.

'Sorry,' she said again. 'You go.'

He smiled and shook his head. 'No, please. You.'

'Well,' she said. 'I just wanted to say sorry about what happened and thanks for putting me up. For everything really. I know it's a difficult time and the last thing you needed was to come and bail me out. Particularly with Mother and, er, Horace here. To be honest the last few days are a bit of a blur.'

She stopped. It felt weird to hear herself trying to conduct a grown-up conversation: stilted and unnatural. For a moment, she had the unnerving feeling that the two of them were actors on the set of a bad, old-fashioned play, performing for an invisible audience. She shook her head to dismiss the thought.

('You little toerag-chewing worm,' sneered a voice.)

'Anyway,' she said, 'I can go any time. I can leave this afternoon if you need the room.'

He held up his hands. 'Nonsense,' he said. 'You're not going anywhere until you're fully recovered — and until we get that benefits nonsense sorted out. It was all my fault in the first place — the head injury, at least.'

She stared at him. The breeze blew a whisper into her head that there was some-thing wrong here, that it didn't make sense that he was being so nice. She shrugged the paranoid thought away and winced a smile.

He reflected it back at her. 'How are you anyway?' he said. 'Are the pills helping?'

She thought of the unopened packet lying on the bookshelf.

'Fine,' she said. 'Much better.'

He looked doubtfully at her forehead. 'Hmmn,' he said. 'It still looks quite inflamed.'

'It's fine,' she said loudly, through the

anxiety starting to rise up around her like mist from the grass. ('Imbecile! Lech!' heckled a voice.)

'Why are you being cross?' said Heloise, sidling up.

'I'm not being cross,' said Smudge. 'I'm being firm. There's a difference.'

Heloise stared at her. 'Oh fuck,' she said.

For a moment, time lurched and Smudge was back in the garden with her old self all those years ago, about to creep into the house and shoehorn herself unwittingly into another life. She put a hand to her mouth and took a faltering step backwards.

'Heloise!' said Nick.

'What?' said Heloise. 'She taught me it!' And she broke away to zoom about the garden making a 'nee-naw' sound.

'It was an accident,' said Smudge. 'It slipped out. I didn't mean —'

Nick waved her explanations away. 'She likes you,' he said.

'Does she?' said Smudge, embarrassed suddenly, shifting from foot to foot.

'Oh yes,' he said. 'You should have seen how she behaved when Margaret and Horace arrived — she hid in her bedroom for three days. Poor Horace couldn't even climb the stairs without her starting to scream.'

Smudge swallowed a smile. 'Well,' she

said. 'It was a difficult time. It *is* a difficult time.'

The breeze sent a leaf whirling down on to his shoulder. He twitched it away with an awkward gesture.

Smudge coughed. 'How is — ?'

Nick puffed out his cheeks. 'Oh, much the same,' he said. 'Bit of a chest infection, I think. Apparently that's normal for coma patients — something to do with the fluid on the lungs building up because of lying still.' He watched her for a moment. 'Actually, they're thinking of moving her. To some specialist neurological hospital in Putney. They're waiting for a bed.'

Smudge nodded. 'Well, that's good, isn't it? Specialist care and all that?'

Nick sighed and shook his head. 'Do you know what the original name of that hospital was? The Hospital for Incurables. They've got patients there who've been in comas for years. Vegetables. They're giving up on her, Ellie. They don't think she's going to get better.'

Something opened up inside her. What was it? Hope? Joy? A strange kind of pain? She didn't have time to examine it — he was watching her too closely.

'Oh,' she said. 'That must be —'

He scratched his ear. 'Look, I don't suppose —'

The anxiety started back into life and began to rev angrily. She held up her hands, backing away.

'Please don't ask me to go and see her,' she said, her voice tight. 'You don't understand.'

He shook his head. 'Actually it wasn't that,' he said. 'Not today anyway. It's just, well, I wouldn't normally ask this, but I've got to go out. It's a work thing — some crisis with this big project we've got on — and Margaret and Horace aren't here. Would you mind keeping an eye on Heloise until I get back?'

She felt almost high with relief. ('Silly sausage,' crooned a voice.)

'Sure,' she said. 'Why not?'

'Thanks so much,' he said, and hurried into the house.

She turned back and found Heloise standing in front of her. They stared at each other for a while until the front door slammed and Nick's footsteps receded down the path.

An awkward feeling settled on Smudge. She walked into the kitchen with Heloise trailing after her.

'What shall we do now?' said the child with a hint of a whine.

'Ummn,' said Smudge, looking around for

inspiration. She thought of the stack of boxed games in the corner of the playroom, some of them still in their cellophane wrappers. 'What about a game of Hungry Hippos?'

'Hungry Hippos is boring!' said Heloise in a rising wail. 'I want to do something better!'

Smudge massaged her temples against the fizzing and popping beginning in her brain.

('Rambunctious!' shouted a voice. 'On the razzle!')

Heloise tugged at her sleeve.

'I want to do something better!' she moaned again.

Smudge rounded on her with a snarl. 'FUCK OFF!' she screamed. 'Just fuck right off! There isn't anything better! There's fuck all! All right?'

She collapsed, panting, into one of the chairs at the kitchen table as Heloise scampered off up the stairs in a blur of blue and green. Smudge's brain raced and her gaze flitted about the room. On the table in front of her was a big pad of creamy-white paper and a pack of coloured pencils. She pulled them towards her and began to draw absently: the long, sharp profile of a crooked nose and a protruding chin. She sketched on. As the minutes ticked by on the kitchen clock, she forgot the house and Nick and Heloise and Mother and Akela, and Hellie lying somewhere in her hospital bed. Her breathing slowed and she became absorbed in watching the figure emerge from the page in front of her, as though the image had lain just below the surface and she was merely uncovering it piece by piece. The old confidence began to take over.

'Is it a witch?' said a voice at her elbow.

She turned to find Heloise huddled there, staring up at her with curious, half-fearful eyes.

Smudge looked back at the crone on the page.

'I suppose it must be,' she said. And then, as the memory of her outburst hit, bringing with it a surge of guilt: 'Here, why don't you come and help me?'

Heloise dragged up a chair. 'Give her a hat then,' she instructed. 'And a cauldron.'

They worked on, creating the witch's world, shadowing in a broomstick and cobwebs looped from a rusty chandelier.

At one stage Heloise looked up at Smudge with narrowed eyes.

'You're very good at drawing,' she said suspiciously. 'Why are you so good?'

Smudge shrugged, brushing back a strand of hair from her eye. 'I used to be an illustrator,' she said, leaning in again to work a sense of movement into the witch's cat's tail.

'What?' said Heloise. 'Someone paid you just to do pictures? What kind of silly were they?'

The witch's magic room grew in size and stature. Shelves bearing books and bottles lined the walls and bundles of mysterious leaves lay heaped across the rough floor.

'Now you start the colouring in,' said Smudge. And she showed Heloise how to trace round the object first to avoid going over the lines and to darken the shading to suggest shadows and depth. Heloise worked with the tip of her tongue poking out of the corner of her mouth, intent.

They were both so absorbed that they didn't hear the front door. It was only when the footsteps came clattering down the basement steps that they became aware that someone else was in the house. Smudge looked up, flushed with achievement as the figure rounded the bottom of the stairs, anticipating Nick's pleasure at their work.

The witch stepped out of the shadows, her face every bit as sharp and angular as her picture on the page.

'What on earth is going on?' said Mother. She stalked forward until the light from the glass roof fell on her face. 'Where's Nick?'

'Daddy went out and left me and Smudge to play by ourselves,' announced Heloise. 'And look what we made!'

She proudly tilted the drawing in Mother's direction.

Mother's face turned pale and she put her hand to her throat.

'How dare you!' she exploded. 'How dare you come here and try to poison this house too? How dare you try to turn my family against me?' She held out a trembling hand to Heloise. 'Come away, darling,' she called in a brittle voice. 'Come away this instant. Let's go upstairs and watch *Dora the Adventurer.* This Splodge or whatever nonsense she's calling herself is not a nice person. Mummy wouldn't like it if she knew you were talking to her.'

Heloise regarded Mother with a thoughtful frown.

'Fuck off,' she said at length.

'Right, that's it!' said Mother, clattering across the room, snatching Heloise's hand and yanking her off her chair. 'Upstairs this instant or you're in for a smack.'

Heloise stumbled across the room and up the stairs.

'Anyway it's *Dora the Explorer,*' she

257

shouted when she was safely out of reach. 'Not *Dora the Adventurer,* you big poo!'

Mother turned to Smudge, a wild look in her eyes.

'Right, that's it,' she said again, through clenched teeth. 'This nonsense ends here. I don't know what kind of spell you've cast over Nick but I won't have it. For the good of everyone, I'm telling you to leave. Right now.'

Smudge stared at the grain of the wood on the table, a hum building in her ears.

'This isn't your house,' she said quietly.

'What's that?' said Mother.

'This isn't your house,' said Smudge, erupting from the table to stand and face her. 'This is Nick's house and he's asked me to stay. You don't have the right to tell me to leave.'

'Wrong!' said Mother. 'This is Helen's house too and in her absence I speak for her. Nick's a man. He's weak. He doesn't know what he needs. But I see. I see how things are. I see the problems between them — how this is a . . . delicate time. And the last thing they need is you here spreading your filth around, disrupting things. I will not have it. And I especially will not have you corrupting the innocence of a little girl.'

Smudge barked a laugh. 'Oh yes,' she said.

'You'd know all about that, wouldn't you? Protecting innocence?'

The slap came out of nowhere. Smudge winced as the gash on her forehead ripped into flame once more.

'How dare you!' shouted Mother. 'Dear God, how I wish Richard were here. There's no way he'd stand by and let you abuse me like this.'

'So why isn't he then?' said Smudge, holding the side of her head. 'What could be so important that he wouldn't make time for precious Helen in her hour of need?'

'If you must know, he's in Afghanistan,' said Mother, drawing herself up. 'He's on a tour of duty and they couldn't spare him. Unlike some people I could name, Richard is making something of his life.'

'Getting as far away as possible, more like,' muttered Smudge.

Mother glared. She snatched up the witch drawing and strode to the foot of the stairs.

'I'm not discussing this any further,' she said. 'I'm taking this and I'm showing it to Nick and explaining everything. By tomorrow morning, you'll be out on your ear.'

26

Blackness. Pain. Not caring. It's all non-sense, and only you know. No consequences, no structure to anything. It's only lies that keep everyone in place, playing at being who they're told they are. Fools. You find a mixer tape of music by a band called Nirvana on a Walkman you snatch from another kid, and you listen to that over and over again. You like the crunch of the chords, the way each intro seems to open a tunnel of despair and suck you down to wander labyrinths of dark chambers, insulated from the banal chatter of the everyday world. You think this is what being in a coma must be like. You also think this is what's underneath every-thing else if only people would stop to listen, but most people, you realise, are too scared. Most people have to drown it out with irrelevancies — with daytime television and long phone conversations where they say hundreds of words that add up to nothing at all. You're not scared, though. You've looked into the emptiness beneath the cracks in the floorboards of life and you know the truth. And now it turns out that, with the music you hear crackling through the headphones, you're not alone. Other people have seen it too.

You listen to that music day and night, Kurt Cobain's voice like a coyote call in a desert of pain. You listen to it on the bus and in bed and in the lessons you go to, with the earphones threaded down your sleeves to your hands so the teachers can't see the wires. You listen to it in the sessions the school organises for you, with a series of well-meaning, pastel-wearing people who nod earnestly, ask you questions with apologetic expressions, and then disappear after a few weeks. Sometimes you don't even need the earphones: your head DJ takes care of it, playing the music on and on inside your mind.

There are days when the pain gets too bad, when even Kurt seems far away. On those days you stay in bed. Or you get up and grab Akela's car keys off the hall table and sit in the driver's seat, revving the engine until it screams. Or you go and raid the drinks cabinet, pouring sherry, whisky, eggnog, Tia Maria down your throat, until the dizziness and the vomiting overtake what's going on in your head and banish it for a while. Change, you learn, can be a sort of release, even if it's for the worse.

Sometimes, Akela comes and talks at you in his blathering, scoutmaster way. If you close your eyes and just listen to the tone of his voice, you can imagine he is giving some lecture to his troop — something about tying knots or lighting fires in the woods. You let him talk until he runs out of words and slips away back to his model planes out in the garden shed, feeling justified.

Mother has nothing to do with you. Hellie keeps out of your way too. When she sees you coming down the corridor at school, she turns her back and faces into her group of friends. But in the night, when you can't sleep, you sometimes get up and stare down at her, lying in the space where your little bed used to be. The moon shines through the gap in the curtains on to her pillow, picking up the fronds of her once-wispy hair that has now turned thick and luscious, plumped by an array of sprays and mousses on the bathroom windowsill. You look down at her, dreaming peacefully in her perfect life, the life you should have had — full of prizes and performances and invitations to the cinema and sleepovers and parties —

and it makes you burn. You reach out and trace the shape of her downy cheek and imagine what it would be like if a razor cut it in a clean line and blood oozed out. Other times your fingers tingle with the urge to clutch her throat and squeeze. You picture it: the second she awakens and the mingling of surprise and knowledge in her eyes before her features freeze like a picture paused for ever on a TV screen. You don't think beyond the moment of it happening: the pure release. White energy, like magnesium spitting in the Bunsen burner's flame.

After a while, the thoughts start to come in the daytime too. When you pass her on the stairs, you imagine sticking your foot out to trip her, sending her tumbling in a flurry of light-brown hair, and on the school trip into town to the Natural History Museum it's all you can do to restrain yourself from lunging at her as the tube train approaches the platform. You find you are watching, waiting, hesitating on thresholds and round corners, in case she is coming and an opportunity presents itself. You are starting to plan.

Then they discover the head in the park. Unusually for you, you are sitting at the breakfast table with the others when there is a knock at the front door. Akela rolls his eyes and goes to answer and from where you're sitting you see the black and white of police uniforms and a hand and a notebook scribbling things down. For a moment, you think they've come for you. Akela thinks so too, because he glances back and meets your eye, but it's quickly clear it's something else. It turns out some local woman, a dogwalker, has discovered a severed head in the undergrowth across the grass from the upside-down tree. The police are going house to house to find out if anyone saw anything.

The neighbourhood goes into crisis mode. All through that day and the week after people stand in huddles whispering what they know. Police tape flutters at the entrance to the park. People swap grisly details like top-trump cards in the playground. The headmaster gives a solemn assembly.

It freaks you out too, if you're honest. But unlike the others, you're not worried about a vicious murderer walking the streets or lurking in the precinct to lure his next victim. For you, it's something different. Because you know how the head got there. Not the details, not the individual story, but how it came together in someone's mind to end another person's life. You know the recipe, the ingredients it would take to cook something like that up. And that scares you.

It scares you so much that for a few days, you are the picture of goodness. You help with dinner, you go to lessons, you even hand some homework in. Teachers smile at you, bewildered, pleased. The other students give you wary, curious looks. You ignore them, keep your head down, hope that if you pretend it long enough normalness will seep back inside you and occupy your whole being. At night when you close your eyes you picture the dog sniffing round the sightless eyes, its tongue licking. You play Kurt on the Walkman to blot it out, but it's always there at the back of your mind, rooting around.

Still, you persevere. And as the days pass and turn into weeks, little by little, it gets easier. People stop acting surprised that you've got a brain, that you can work out sums, and start expecting it from you. You begin an art project, drawing a heap of trainers from lost property, and the teacher gives you a B+, then an A. Josie, a fat girl with not many friends, invites you to go to her house to watch a film.

You start to believe that it's possible for things to work out after all, that perhaps all this has been a bad dream. Even living the wrong existence — if the swap and the game really did happen (and there are times when you doubt this now) — maybe you could have a chance at a normal life. You spend time in Boots, looking at lipglosses and eye shadows in subtle, shimmering colours, like the kind the popular girls at school wear.

Sometimes you catch yourself laughing with the excitement of it all. How right everything is, how much you can do. You shut yourself in the dining room after Sunday lunch and draw and draw, producing picture after picture. These you take in to show the art teacher, Miss Hogan, on Monday mornings, taut with anticipation of her reaction, like an elastic band stretched on the braces of the kids who stare at you in the canteen. Miss Hogan smiles at you vaguely and puts a hand to her head. 'Did I set all this work?' she says breezily. 'I suppose I must have. Well done. Very good.'

Sometimes, when you walk home from the bus stop, you see energy fizzing out of the corners of your eyes. You are in love with life. You're amazed by the colours in everything — the trees, the houses, the flowers on the roundabout spelling out HONDA. The sky, you discover, is the most extraordinary light show, putting on display after display as people scurry about beneath it, minds elsewhere. It's awesome, in the fullest sense of the word. You could watch it for hours, lying on your back on the hill in the park, exclaiming as people wander by.

You can't believe that all this exists freely, unbidden. The generosity of nature astounds you and fills you with gratitude. You want to embrace the world, to thank it and whatever life-force lies behind it, for being so bountiful, so extraordinary, so good. You feel duty bound to share what you've discovered, to usher others to this window on to the essence of reality that has been vouchsafed to you. When people get close to you in this mood — in the playground, in the precinct, on the bus — you talk and talk to them about the beauty of the world. They look at you distantly — sometimes they move to get away — but you don't mind. You are an ocean trying to pour through a tap and all you can do is open your mouth and let the words run. You are on fire with the brilliance of being, burning in a clean, white light. Life astonishes you.

But it can't last, and you ought to know that by now. One day, walking past the newsagent's at the entrance to the precinct, you see a pair of black-rimmed eyes staring out from under shaggy, blond locks on the cover of the *NME. Kurt Cobain (1967–1994)*, reads the caption. He killed himself, you discover. A gunshot wound to the head.

They didn't find him for several days, not until an electrician came to fit a security system at his house. It looked like he was asleep at first. There was very little blood.

When you look up from the copy, the world is dulled. The sky is white and blind as a milked-over eye. And a chilly breeze is blowing, probing your neck with cold fingers, fingers that at any minute will clutch you and start to draw you back to chaos and darkness once again.

27

She sat on the bed in the little room, in her coat, waiting for the knock on the door. In the rest of the house she heard footsteps, muttering voices, doors banging and the sounds of things being dragged and moved. A couple of times someone came up the staircase to the attic floor and she braced herself, ready for the polite rat-a-tat and Nick's grave face, but it didn't come: instead, whoever it was walked up the corridor and seemed to go into the other room where further thumping and scraping ensued.

She was on the point of shrugging off the coat when the knock came. She swallowed and stood up. The room lurched, but stayed the right way up. She opened the door.

Nick was standing there. He looked tired. There were pouches under his eyes and the lines on his forehead seemed deeper, as though, overnight, someone had chiselled him into a more severe version of himself.

'I'm sorry,' she said quickly. 'I didn't mean
—'

'What for?' said Nick.

'Giving grief,' she said. She reached for
one of Mother's old phrases: 'Making a
scene.'

He stared at the hinges of the door and
frowned.

'What? Margaret and Horace?' he said.
'Oh, don't worry about that. It's not your
fault. It's been a long time coming. I should
have handled it better. I mean, it was good
of them to be here to help with Heloise and
everything, but it's been three months now.
It's time we started getting back to normal
and working out how to cope on our own.'
He grimaced. 'Anyway, it's not as though
we had much to do with them before the
accident.'

Smudge twirled her finger in a strand of
her hair. 'You didn't?' she said.

'No,' he said. 'Helen has a rather difficult
relationship with Margaret. To say the least.'

He shifted and put one hand on the doorframe, leaning there rather awkwardly.

'So, I saw the drawing you did with
Heloise,' he said. 'It was really good. More
than good.'

She blushed. 'It's nothing. I worked as an

illustrator, or a sort of graphic designer really, for a few years. That's all.'

Nick nodded. 'Heloise said "drawrer". I thought it must have been something like that. Funny, Helen never told me.'

Smudge shrugged. 'I don't think she knew,' she said. 'We weren't in touch at the time. Designer's probably not even the right term anyway. More like corporate artist.'

'Interesting,' said Nick. 'Who did you work for?'

She fiddled with a frayed bit on her sleeve. The corridor behind Nick was developing an unnerving habit of swinging alternately closer to and farther from her, as though the house were expanding and contracting, like a breathing lung.

'Just this company called Edgewise,' she mumbled.

'Up in Manchester,' said Nick. 'I know. Aren't they the ones that did the Old Masters tablet campaign for that company out in Amsterdam?'

Smudge nodded. 'That was me. And one other colleague.'

Nick raised his eyebrows and whistled.

'Wow,' he said. 'Well, it's only right that an artist of that calibre should have her own studio.'

Smudge narrowed her eyes and touched a

hand to the hot side of her face where the gash burned. 'What do you mean?' she said.

'Come on,' said Nick, and he led her to the threshold of the adjacent room. She followed, sparks dancing on the edge of her vision, dryness in her mouth.

'Ready?' he said.

She mustered a smile, fighting the hectic feeling crowding its way up her throat.

He thrust open the door and ushered her into the room. An easel had been set up by a big window looking out towards the park. Beside it stood a table bearing all manner of pencils, paints, pastels, oils and charcoals. Good brands too: Derwent and Faber-Castell. There was even a radio on the windowsill, just like they used to have in the studio all those years ago.

She started forward and picked up some of the pencils. The words loomed at her, seeming to throb.

'Wow. Nothing but the best,' she said. She looked up at him and a faint note of alarm sounded way inside the muffled corridors of her mind. She narrowed her eyes. 'Why are you being so nice to me?'

He dodged her stare and drummed his fingers on the doorframe.

'Oh, it's nothing really,' he said. 'Just stuff I get through work. Freebies, really. I'm an architect, so —'

She blinked.

'What kind of architect?'

'Oh, you know. Buildings,' he laughed, then saw her expression. 'Sorry. I'm working on this big project at the moment, actually. This tall pair of towers in central London. It's causing quite a bit of controversy. That's why I had to leave you with Heloise yesterday.'

'Not —' She snapped her fingers, trying to pick the word out of the air.

'The Hairpin?' said Nick. 'Yes.'

She looked at him, eyes widening as somewhere inside her brain a connection sparked. She remembered the cruel twisting of the towers, the two structures locked in a monstrous embrace.

'I've seen that,' she said. 'Pictures, I mean. Computer-generated things. It's really . . . something.'

'Thanks,' said Nick, pursing his lips against a smile. 'Who knows? It might not happen if all these Nimby campaigners get their way. Still, we had the same trouble with the Barnacle and that went ahead.'

Smudge put a hand to her throat. 'The Barnacle!' she said. 'Up in Manchester?'

Nick looked pleased.

'Yes. Do you know it?'

273

She shrugged. 'I went shopping there once or twice,' she mumbled. 'Years ago.'

Then she fell silent as the memories of the other things that had happened there — that dreadful day — swarmed into her mind.

'Well, anyway,' said Nick. He stretched out an arm towards the easel. 'What do you make of this? Will it do? Do you think you might spend a few hours in here while you get back to full strength?'

She fought to stay in the room.

'It's —' she said. 'It's —'

But the voices and the faces crowding round her were too insistent. She felt the bubbling and the soaking and the beginnings of agony.

Then the sparks that had been spiralling and fizzing on the extremities began to burn the room away and the floor tipped and gaped, swallowing her into the blackness beneath.

28

Time ceases to mean much. When the others are getting up, you're going to bed. When they're in, you're out. You rarely see them.

Days, hours and minutes, you realise, are arbitrary things, created to make people feel guilty. To stamp a sense of duty on their hearts, so that they are always running late or up against it or behind. You haven't got the patience for such things. Life is such a random, brittle thing — gone at the touch of a trigger and only discovered some days later by a lighting engineer — and you are not going to let anyone dictate yours to you. Fuck everybody else.

Sometimes that's precisely what you do. You go to pubs and stare at groups of men until one of them can't take it any more and leads you off into the toilets or out back behind the bins. It amuses you that that's all you need to do — give them the look

275

that Mother would call insolent — to make them abandon the social graces for grunting and puffing with a stranger in an alley instead. It also amuses you how two people can take such different things from the same act: shallow, short-lived pleasure on one side, and a holiday from your head for you as the jerking, clutching and thrusting crowds out all thoughts. You use them and they don't even know it. And that's the biggest kick of all.

You can't predict how you're going to react to things. You keep yourself guessing. Personality, you discover, is a lie. There's always the freedom to laugh in a policeman's face, splatter a white wall with Coke and lie screaming on the floor. You don't conform to a set pattern. There's no recipe for who you are. You're free. Dizzyingly, exhilaratingly free. You never know how you're going to happen next.

Like the day you find yourself standing outside the tattoo parlour. You don't know until you do it that you're going to go in. The place is at the far end of the precinct, set back behind a half-barrel containing some bedraggled pansies and an evergreen fir. You've passed it for years on your way to Boots without noticing — the colours and swirls of the designs in the windows registering hazily, on the edge of your consciousness. If you've thought of it at all, you've assumed that it must be some artist's studio or an unsuccessful colour photocopy shop.

But one day — because of boredom probably — you stop to look at it. Your eyes travel over the faded photographs in the window: the dragons inked on beefy shoulders, the mystic, Celtic symbols, the Chinese characters that probably say something obscene or nothing at all. And suddenly that flame that spurs you into action — the same one that makes you shout without warning until the top deck of the bus is clear or swipe a child's ice-cream into the gutter — ignites.

You push the door and a bell clanks, rusty with disuse. The small salon lies before you, table and implements swathed in gloom. The place smells of dust and for a moment you think it's empty until something stirs and a figure detaches itself from the shadows of the back room. The man comes forward: large and speckled with pictures, a spike through the middle of his nose.

'Yes?' he says.

'I want to get a tattoo,' you say.

He scratches his nose. 'How old are you?' he says.

'Nineteen,' you say, thrusting your chin

forward to ward off any doubt. Nineteen, you've learned, is a more effective answer than eighteen: people don't expect you to lie more than you have to.

The man regards you a moment longer. His eyes stray to the precinct beyond, calculating probabilities.

'All right,' he says.

He heaves out a ringbinder and shoves it at you. 'Find what you want in there,' he says.

Then he turns and shambles off into the shadows. The lights click on and you hear water running and the clink of implements being prepared.

You turn the pages of the binder. The photos inside have a dated look: Mohicans and aggressive eye shadow hinting at decades past. Where are these people now? you wonder. Are they still rocking out at underground punk-scene revivals or have they turned respectable, hiding their wrinkling body art under long sleeves and office skirts? What if you see them out and about all the time and don't realise? What if you know some of them? An image of Akela with a Celtic sun around his bulging belly button pops into your head and makes you cringe.

There is nothing in the book that you like.

But on the last page, you see some samples of writing and they make you think. There are names in copperplate and mottoes that walk the line between naff and wise.

When the man comes back into the room, you snap the binder closed.

'How much to do a word?' you say.

The man shrugs. 'Depends what you want to say,' he says. 'I charge by the letter.'

You look around, your eyes questing for inspiration. Suddenly a memory flashes up in your mind — Mother's face, taut and shouting — and a word swims up to meet it. You know without a shadow of a doubt that it's what you've been searching for.

'Monster,' you say.

The man raises his eyebrows. 'OK,' he says. 'Probably be about thirty quid. Where do you want it?'

You point at the centre of your forehead. 'Here.'

He takes a step back and coughs, raising a fist that has H-A-T-E stamped on the knuckles to cover his mouth.

'Are you sure?' he says. 'I mean, that's a pretty prominent place.'

'Yes,' you say. You're sure. You've decided.

But the man still isn't convinced. For all his piercings and aggressive tattoos, he looks a bit intimidated.

'How about I do it round the side instead?' he says. 'That way you can cover it up with your hair if you want to.'

Anger flashes through you.

'I don't want to cover it up with my hair,' you say. 'I want the world to see it. Otherwise what's the point of getting a tattoo?'

It's a solid point and he knows it. Still, he hesitates. There's a silence. You scuff the sole of your Palladium back and forth on the greasy floor.

'I really think —' he begins after a moment.

Suddenly, you're bored of the argument. You want the tattoo to be done and you to be out of there, on to the next thing. This is already taking too long.

'Fine,' you say. 'Do it round the side. I don't care.'

He nods, relieved, and motions you over to the big dentist-style chair in the middle of the room. It's too big for you and he has to pump the base with his foot to get it so that you can lean back against the headrest. When you're in place, he trundles a trolley over and plugs something in.

'Try to keep still,' he says.

Your body tingles with the anticipation of feeling something new. It's been a while. You think of the compass point you used to rake over the back of your arm in lessons and wonder if it will feel like that. Your left temple thrills with the promise of the pain.

The machine buzzes into life. The man leans over you. You can smell cheese and onion crisps and fags on his breath. A split second, then the point starts to bite. The nib whirs over the thin skin above the edge of your eyebrow, stamping you with fire. It hurts, but the sensation is good, clarifying, giving a focus for your dispersed, rambling thoughts. You use it as you've done before, converting the pain into pictures, so that a big purple flower seems to open above you, drawing you into its centre. You become oblivious to the man's face hovering above you, his tongue poking between his lips in concentration. There is only you and the flower that seems to be drawing you to another world.

You don't know how long you sit there, but sooner than you expect the man sits back and flicks a switch. Quiet floods the room.

'There you go,' he says. 'All done.'

You touch a hand to the side of your face and feel the letters raised, like a scar.

'The swelling will go down after a few days,' he says, handing you a dusty mirror with a crack running through it.

You look and see the letters: small, crooked and fringed with redness, stalking like spiders off the edge of your eyebrow and away towards your hairline. The first feeling is disappointment. You'd expected it would be slicker, more impressive than that. You'd pictured the characters as thick and Gothic-looking with pointed ends — the sort of writing you'd see on the titles to the horror films you smuggle out of the precinct under your jacket to watch in the living room at night. Instead, this looks clumsy and homemade, like something you could have done yourself with a needle and a ballpoint pen. After a minute or two, however, the initial feeling subsides and you start to be pleased. You like the rough-and-ready feel of it, the ugliness. You like that it looks as though someone has come at you in the school toilets with a permanent marker. It feels powerful somehow to embrace that side of life, to make it your badge. It feels an honest statement about who you are.

'Yeah,' you say, nodding as a smile spreads over your face. 'I like it.'

You hand over the money you took from Mother's handbag yesterday and leave the shop. The daylight rushes at you. You blink and shake your head. People push past on their way to Boots. No one gives your tattoo a second glance.

A feeling bursts open inside you. You were planning to stay out tonight, head up to the pubs by the mill pond — it is Saturday, after all, and there's bound to be someone you can tap for a drink or three — but now you've got a different idea. You glance up at the clock set in the wall above the fountain that stopped running three years ago for want of public funds (a notice explains it all to anyone who cares). It is six o'clock. They'll just be sitting down to dinner. Perfect.

You stride out of the precinct. The bus comes quickly and you board it, holding the rail and swaying amid the gaggles of teeny-boppers and school kids off to the cinema for a Saturday treat. You bite your lip and have to work on keeping your fingers still as excitement bubbles up through you. The thought of Mother's face when she sees it, as the force of the message hits home. You can't imagine what she'll do — you've no idea what you want — but you know it will be big and you know it will change things. This is not something she can ignore. Wild, vicious hope bobs in your heart like a kite on a string, jerking in a gale-force wind.

You get off the bus by the postbox and

stand for a few minutes with your hands on its cool, curved surface, taking deep breaths. You must not fuck this up by being overexcited, by saying something outrageous that sends things off on another track. You have to be cool and collected, let the tattoo do its work. Oh God! It all makes sense now. It's all been building to this day! Everything you've been through — it all adds up, it was all so you could be ready for this. When you look around, everything agrees: the bus shelter gleams encouragingly, the trees nod their approval, the postbox gives you a grin. Even the registration numbers of the cars driving past seem spread in happy smiles. *HI 2,* reads a personalised plate on a black Jaguar gliding by. See? The world knows! The universe has got your back.

You take another shuddering breath and set off up the road, digging your fingernails into your palms as you go. There is so much inside you that you are amazed your body holds together, containing all that feeling in one space. The house stands among its sisters, waiting for you. Akela's car is parked outside. Everything is prepared.

You let yourself in at the front door and the buzz of conversation in the dining room stills. The smell of fish pie hangs in the air. You shut the door and walk past the living room to the threshold. There they all are, sitting round the table: Akela, Hellie, Mother and Richard, swinging his legs on a grown-up chair.

'Hello,' says Akela in the tone of a scout-master trying to jolly his troop through a wet weekend in the woods. 'Fancy seeing you here.'

You don't say anything. You don't trust your voice. Instead, slowly, trying to keep your hand from shaking, you reach up and brush your hair back from your temple. You turn your head so they can get a good look. You stand still, letting the force of the message hit home in all its raw, shaming power. You imagine the feelings rising in Mother as she sees her word turned back against her, engraved on your head. Confiscated.

When you look back, it is as though someone has cast a spell over the room. You feel like the White Witch in that BBC adaptation of *Narnia* you and Hellie used to watch years ago. Akela, Richard and Hellie are all frozen, mouths agape. Only Mother, in the midst of them, continues to eat her food.

Her eyes drift up to meet yours and she sniffs and turns her head away. Her silence pricks the balloon inside you, dispersing your hope and excitement and anger to the air, until you are nothing but a shrivelled, empty rag. She eats on regardless. And she doesn't say a word.

29

Muttering, voices, hands on her face and neck, a light shone in her eyes. At one point someone lifted her up, popped a pill into her mouth and made her drink. She swallowed obediently, wondering where in time she was. She heard the chatter of Heloise's voice but then other voices muscled in too so that she couldn't be sure what was real and what was part of the chorus in her head. Day, then night, then day again.

Then a hissing voice: 'Listen, please, just go and snap her out of it. I can't take much more of this.'

Her eyes flipped open and Nick was sitting there.

'Quite a scare you gave us, not taking those pills,' he said cheerfully. 'Temperature up to a hundred and two — a severe fever from the infection. No wonder you weren't all there.'

('You were a complete fruitcake,' whispered a voice. 'You were off in La La Land. We all saw you. We've been monitoring you for quite some time now.' So they were back then, she thought dully.)

She stared at him. He had a scar, she noticed, on the underside of his chin.

'Sorry,' she said. 'I didn't mean to.'

'But surely you knew you had to take them. I don't get why you didn't.'

She opened her mouth, but the words to explain the great vast sea of not-caring, that ocean of indifference on which she spent her days drifting, buffeted now and then by squalls of rage and pain, simply weren't there. She shut her eyes against him.

When she opened them again, Heloise was sitting there in an apron and a white pudding bowl that had a red cross Sellotaped on it for a hat.

'I'm going to be your nurse,' she announced. 'And you *will* get better.'

She held up a book she had taken off the shelf across the room: *Frankenstein* by Mary Shelley.

('Get the onions, put the kettle on and make us all a nice brew,' instructed a voice.)

'Today, it's reading medicine,' said Heloise. 'Except not the hard words because they might frighten your mind back inside your brain like a snail into a shell, and then where would we be?'

She opened the book and began to read. As it turned out, there were a lot of hard words. But Heloise did not let these faze her, simply missing them out altogether or swapping in alternatives she thought would do instead:

'Number one . . . Letter one . . . To Mrs So-vile, England. You . . . will . . . read . . . to . . . hear . . . that . . . no . . . daughter . . . has . . . the . . . comma . . . of . . . end-surprise . . . which . . . you . . . have . . . mmmn . . . with . . . such . . . eel . . . four-bodies.'

The voice piped on and Smudge lay back and let the tide of words wash over her. Heloise was right: it was therapeutic. She particularly liked the way the near-senseless string filled the echo-chamber of her head, crowding out the whispers from within.

When she looked again, Heloise was gone but the book was still there. She picked it up, feeling the vertical ridges in the spine and the thick edges of the brown-spotted pages against her thumb. But when she opened it, the spine cracked, sending pages cascading over the bed. As she gathered them up, she saw that some of them were annotated with underlinings and little notes in the margins, written in a cramped, jagged hand. 'Feeling isolated — on the outside of society,' said one. 'Cruelty of people to those who don't fit in,' observed another.

'Ha!' said Smudge.

('Ha!' seconded a voice.)

'What would Hellie know about that?'

('What would Smellie nose in the vat?')

She looked around the room, and the bookshelf, chest of drawers and bedside table looked back, waiting. So she picked up the book, put the pages in order, and began to read.

30

A cloudy day. The sky sulking. You're sitting in Akela's car, the old Vauxhall Cavalier, looking up at it through the shaded glass at the top of the windscreen. You've got the cassette in your hand: a mixer tape you've recorded off the radio. Stiltskin's 'Inside', Radiohead's 'Creep' (the annoying version where 'fucking' is changed to 'very'), a bit of Metallica — all the best stuff. It took you ages to get it together, finding versions where the DJ didn't come crashing in over too much of the outros, and now you're going to play it through for the very first time.

You like listening to things in the car instead of on your Walkman because that way you can be inside the noise. You can feel it on your skin. Even though Akela's speakers are rubbish and there's no mega-bass on the car stereo, they can pack a punch if you turn them up loud enough, until the beat thuds in your heart.

You should be excited about this one, about hearing your creation for the first time — it's all you've been thinking about for weeks — but instead you're feeling a bit disconnected. You put the key in the ignition and just sit there, staring out to where the first few leaves of autumn scutter around the pavement in an endless game of 'It'.

Everything feels like an effort this afternoon. Even breathing feels hard — so much so that you decide to stop for a while and sit in the stillness, feeling the pulse in your neck throb until your lungs heave open and the tide of air rushes in once more. Strange to think that one day there won't be any more breath, that this body — so solid, so together — will break up and dissolve. You stare at your hands — the scabbed fingers and bitten nails, the inked-on doodles — and try to imagine them rotting in the earth or crackling in a furnace, but it doesn't seem feasible. You're locked into this life; your body is like a straitjacket, binding you to the world.

Suddenly, there's a knock at the window. You look up. Hellie is standing there in one of her teenybopper outfits: pink miniskirt and a fluffy jumper stretched over the bra she's padded with wads of loo roll. The sixth Spice Girl.

She frowns and makes a spiralling gesture with her arm. Cautiously, you wind the window down an inch. The early-evening air rushes in: casseroles cooking and the six o'clock news.

'You're going to have to get out of there,' says Hellie.

You stare up at her. She's taken extra care over her hair today, you can see — torturing it with straightening irons until the wispy bits lie flat — and there's sparkly make-up smeared around her eyes.

'Why?' you say.

She puts her hands on her hips. 'Dad is giving me a lift in, like, five minutes.'

'Where are you going?' you say.

'What's it to you? You're not invited.'

A party then. One of those Saturday evening things in people's houses she's started going to recently. You know because you've heard her gossiping about them on the phone, sitting on Mother and Akela's bed talking into the extension where she thinks no one can hear. Plus you've been reading her diary.

The diary is a pink, obvious thing which appeared in Hellie's underwear drawer a few months ago. You couldn't believe it the first time you saw it — rummaging through in case a few of your Alice Cooper T-shirts had got mixed in with her stuff by mistake — it was so blatant. But then, that's always been Hellie all over — that wide-eyedness, that inability to see how transparent she is to the rest of the world. Even with all the youness she's barricaded around herself she can't shake that. Every so often she'll do something that proves her Ellieness through and through. Like the time she fell for that prank call from her best friend Alia, pretending that Simon Pritchard in the year above wanted to ask her out. She got all extra dressed up for school that day — lipgloss, purple body peeking from under her unbuttoned school blouse — and then she had to spend the day pretending it was just a new look she was trying out.

At first, it doesn't occur to you to read Hellie's diary. You know you'd be bored by its plastic secrets. But one day when the batteries have run down on your Walkman and there's nothing else to do, you dig it out and have a look. Turns out, you're sort of right. The diary is mostly boring. It's all about Alia and Charlene and which of the Heathfield boys they fancy. Worse than anything, apart from the round handwriting with the circular dots over the 'i's, it's not even written the way Hellie writes. It reads like something off one of those American teen sitcoms she watches obsessively in the school holidays — like Hellie is trying to be in *Blossom* or *Clarissa Explains It All*. And when it gets to the bit about the parties, it gets even worse. Because it turns out that Hellie's idea of a party is going round to someone's house on a Saturday night when their parents are out, drinking two Hooches and waiting to see if Peter Damrosch from Science will look at her. She's never even spoken to him. That's how sad she is. Even her taste in music is pathetic. Like, she thinks when one of the boys puts on Oasis it's heavy metal. She actually wrote that.

You stare up at her standing by the car, all pretty and sure of herself in her teenybopper gear, all locked into a version of the world that you can never have, and the burning feeling flames up once more. It's not that you even want to get angry or hurt her or anything like that — to be honest, right now, you couldn't give a shit about any of it, about any of them — but it sort of happens through you. It's like you're a channel through which all this energy has to pass. You couldn't stop it if you tried.

'For fuck's sake,' you say. 'Don't wet yourself. It's not like anyone's going to care whether you're there or not. Peter Damrosch is never going to finger you anyway.'

You watch as realisation dawns. Her eyes go wide. Then the fury erupts.

'You fucking bitch!' she yells. 'You've been reading my diary. You fucking bitch!'

She grabs the door handle and begins to yank it, but you're too quick and you push the knob down so it locks.

You stare up at her flushed face, her mouth gaping as she tries to dredge up more things to call you — words she's never needed before in her perfect life. Is this what you look like when those men do it to you? you wonder. Your face all red and your eyes watering? It's amazing really that they want to see it through — you're so ugly.

'Calm down, Hellie. Nobody cares,' you say when the yanking subsides.

Then she really gets angry.

'Don't call me that, you fucking weirdo,' she screams. 'Don't put all your weird fantasies on me. You should know by now that nobody believes you. It's just some rubbish you made up because you're broken. Do you understand? You're sick. That's what everyone says about you: you're sick. Even Mum and Dad. They think you should be locked up. They're frightened about what you'll do to Richard.'

A pause. The breeze blows in through the crack in the window. The Indian family across the street is cooking curry tonight. You can smell the spices on the air.

'He's not our dad,' you say slowly.

She frowns. 'What?' she says. You stare up at her for a moment. Then, like a truck, it hits you: she doesn't know. She's separated it off in her mind and blocked it out. Her reality is even more twisted than yours.

'Akela,' you say. 'Horace. Mr Green. He's not our dad.'

She rolls her eyes and opens her mouth to unleash another tide of invective. But something in you knows the cold steel of what you're saying can cut through her bluster.

'Our father's dead,' you say. 'He died when we were four. That man in there is not our father.'

Hellie blinks. Her gaze flits here and there, weighing things up. Then it hardens.

'You fucking liar,' she whispers. 'You fucking, shitting liar.'

'It's true,' you say. 'It's in the newspapers in the local archive. You can deny it all you want, Hellie. You can keep on living your perfect life, but that doesn't stop it being real.'

But Hellie won't hear it. 'You filth!' she continues, her voice rising. 'You disgusting, disgusting girl! You should be a-fucking-shamed of yourself for coming up with such shit. Mother's right. You're poison. Do you know that? That's what she says about you. You're toxic fucking waste!'

You stare up at her mouth as it goes on flaring and contorting, a wisp of mouse-coloured hair stuck in one corner. It seems bizarre, almost hilarious — a grotesque exhibit in the zoo. And yet Hellie is the one they all think is normal. Oh fuck it. You're sick of them all and their edited lives, their rosy world where anything unpleasant simply doesn't exist. They're fucking insane. You don't want to listen to it any more. You've had enough. You need your music to drown them out.

You turn the key in the ignition to start the mixer tape as Hellie comes round the front of the car, arms flailing. But something's wrong, the gear-stick's not in the usual position, and instead of starting smoothly like it always does, the car lurches forward, butting Hellie off her feet.

It all happens in an instant: one minute she's standing there, face red and streaked with No. 7 mascara, and the next she's disappeared. You wait for her to stagger to her feet, angrier than ever, but the moments stretch and nothing happens so you open the door and peer round the side. Hellie is lying on her back on the tarmac, her head against the tyre of the car in front. She is still. Nothing is moving. Nothing except a thin line of blood trickling from her mouth, down her cheek and past her ear, to pool on the road.

31

She'd expected a horror story. From the little she knew of it, gleaned mostly from adverts and an abortive attempt to show the Kenneth Branagh film version in the unit, she'd assumed it would be all flashes of thunder and vast laboratories packed with a range of weird and unnatural devices. She'd expected cackles of laughter and a wild-eyed mad scientist in the midst of it all, unleashing his creation to wreak havoc on the world.

But it didn't come, the horror. Instead what she got was sadness — lots of it — and the blundering of the poor misshapen monster as he ripped the world around him apart in his eagerness to enter it and be recognised for what he was. It gripped her, drawing her on through the glaciers and the streets of Geneva and Ingolstadt, in the wake of the unlucky student and his bastard creation. And when it came to the account of the nameless creature (who was not called Frankenstein, it turned out, despite what they'd muttered about her scar in school) living in an outhouse, peering through a crack at the family life he would never be part of, she could not help but cry. As the fever ebbed in her brain, the story flooded in to replace it, filling the empty hours with urgency and sensation, stifling the voices in her head and threading itself into her existence. There were times when the sounds of Heloise scampering to meet Nick at the end of a long day morphed into the voices of the family in the story and reality seemed to shift aside like pieces of a stage set as the world of the book gusted in. Now and then, she would roam from room to room, unaware of her surroundings, wafted by the story's currents.

One afternoon when the house was quiet, Smudge found herself standing in a cream-carpeted room, facing a blond-wood dressing table with a wall of mirrored wardrobes off to her left. A large double bed occupied the centre of the room and there was a fluffy white rug lying in front of it. Behind her, a spiral staircase led down from the corner back to wherever she'd come from. Alarm ballooned through her as she realised she must have wandered into Nick and Hellie's room and she froze and listened for any

301

sound of Nick, Heloise or Eva, the new Lithuanian nanny, who always gave her disapproving looks when she crept down to the kitchen for a glass of water. But there was nothing.

Her head was quiet too. She probed cautiously at the recesses of her mind but no voices cawed or cackled. All was calm and still.

Light came in through the large sash windows, bringing sharpness and clarity. She ought to go back down the staircase and out, away to her part of the house. Why, then, did she stay here and walk slowly towards the wardrobes? Why did she draw aside one of the doors and stare in at Hellie's dresses?

She stretched out a trembling hand and fingered the fabrics — satins as smooth as oil, soft cashmere, petal-like silk. Hellie's clothes. Velvet, cotton, linen. As she moved along the row, a dress slipped loose of a hanger and slumped on to Smudge's arm. It was pink and made of fine chiffon with cloth roses attached in a swirl on the front — the sort of thing, Smudge supposed, you might wear to a summer garden party or for opening a summer fayre. It was a flamboyant dress, a look-at-me.

Before she knew it, she had shrugged off

the pyjamas they'd put her in and slipped the dress over her head. It dropped down easily over her bony frame, hanging slightly loosely over her ribcage and angular hips. She looked at herself in the mirror. Not bad, as a whole. Halfway Hellie. Only her hollowed face with its tell-tale tattoo to give her away, but perhaps there was a remedy for that.

She went to the dressing table and began to root through the make-up bags there. The pots and tubes flashed unintelligible names at her, but soon with her eye for colour and a little trial and error she found the raw materials to give her face Hellie's glossy glow. She spread a creamy, peach-coloured liquid over her skin and watched the MONSTER fade like a painted-out shop sign. Next she daubed her eyelids with pink powder, layering darker shades in the creases, as she'd seen on the models on posters in the bus shelters. She stood back to admire the effect: not bad, a little heavy-handed in the daylight, perhaps, but certainly far from shocking. A dusting of powder on the cheekbones and a sweep of mascara to make her lashes long and thick like spider's legs, and she was done: a Hellie-phant, a mademois-Hell. She whirled around to see the dress whisking and fluttering in the wardrobe mirrors and her foot struck a turquoise bag protruding from under the dressing table. She picked it up. Inside was a purse containing a fifty-pound note, and a set of house keys. She beamed at herself in the mirror as the next stage of the plan arrived, fully formed. It was brilliant, inspired. Incredible that she hadn't thought of it before. She skipped, laughing, down the spiral staircase. She would take back her life by force.

The world blared at her, the colours dancing, as she let herself out of the front door. She went down the drive and walked up the street, feeling the paving stones rough and hard under her soles. She looked left and right, searching for signs that people were noticing her being Helen Sallis, walking confidently along. But she had forgotten how loud it all was. On the high street she stopped, bewildered by the noise, the traffic, the people and the shops offering heaps and rows of stuff. A woman with a buggy barged into her and rolled her eyes. 'Don't stand in the way,' she huffed, bustling past.

Smudge staggered, shocked by the pain where the buggy had caught her ankle. Her eyes filled with tears. She felt the fragile vase of the moment shift and teeter on the high shelf of her mind. She screwed up her fists and swallowed, thinking of calmness, water, open fields where she could breathe.

An idea surfaced. She should get something. That would be the Hellie thing to do — some sort of treat that they could all enjoy this evening, a thank you for Nick. Yes, a treat. She clutched the bag and looked around hopefully for a shop that might sell such a thing. There was the butcher's (unlikely), the post office (hardly) and a Tesco Express (which somehow felt mean). Behind her was the greengrocer's, from which the woman with the buggy had emerged. But there — over by the postbox — she caught sight of something wrapped in cellophane and girded with a ribbon. It was part of a display in the window of a chocolate shop: a large white chocolate rabbit, surrounded by lots of small animals arranged in a woodland scene. She smiled, delight fluttering in her throat like a caged budgie. She'd cracked it. It was perfect. And it was exactly the sort of thing Hellie would choose.

She pushed through the glass door into the rich-smelling interior. The chocolate animals stared down at her from ranks of shelves that stretched up to the ceiling. There were birds and cats and sheep and horses. There were dragons and unicorns and strange mythical hybrids that she couldn't pinpoint. And in the midst of it all, behind the counter at the far end, sat the shopkeeper, watching her like a toad.

Anxiety crackled along her nerves and she felt the urge for a cigarette. Perhaps this was a bad idea. She brushed the thought aside and turned to the shelves. The ribbons flashed at her, as though transmitting messages in secret code. She took a deep breath. She could do this. She could do this. She just had to Hellie it up for all she was worth.

Behind her, the shopkeeper coughed. 'Yes!' she wanted to say. 'In a minute!' But she was aware that that was not how normal people talked. Normal people smiled and joked easily, small talk always to hand. She couldn't think of the words they'd say, but she knew the feel of them: smooth, effortless, refined. She clenched her fingers around the bag, biting her lip. The shelf loomed, the chocolate animals snickered. It was getting worse. In one of its leaps ahead, her mind showed her herself sitting hunched on the wooden floor of the shop, weeping amid fragments of chocolate and slivers of cellophane. She had to get out.

In a panic, she snatched up the nearest thing: a dark, bug-eyed sort of dog. She went to the counter and thrust it at the man, not daring to look at his face as she paid. He took the fifty-pound note in his with fat, hairy fingers. She imagined them trailing through vats of chocolate and the thought made her feel ill. She didn't want the dog any more, but she made herself go through the motions of the purchase, gritting her teeth against a scream. Like a pack of wolves gathering ready to savage her, the voices began to whisper their way back into her mind.

The man glanced at her face and his stern expression broke like clouds before the sun. A smile shone through.

'Well,' he said. 'It's good to see you out and about, Ms Sallis.'

Triumph scudded through her, whisking paranoia's screens and curtains aside. She pushed her shoulders back and looked him in the eye with a grin. 'Thanks,' she said.

'You gave us all a scare there for a while.'

'Yes, I did, didn't I?'

'But it looks as though you're well on the road to recovery now.'

'Yes, I am,' she said fervently, as confident as any Hellie could be. 'I really am.'

She held his gaze for a time, grinning. His smile wavered.

'Well, I won't keep you,' he said, glancing

down at his half-finished crossword on the counter. 'You take care now. Mind how you go.'

She burst from the shop wreathed in smiles. It couldn't have gone better. She couldn't have done better. Here she was at last taking control of her life, being her actual self, and the world was welcoming her with open arms. The universe was smiling upon her. The links between things shimmered, revealing reality as a web of gleaming connections. The film of her life was building to its inspiring climax. It all made complete sense.

She whirled round, the chiffon skirt flaring, the bag holding the chocolate dog bashing at people passing by.

'Whoa there,' said a woman's voice with a faint Australian twang. 'Are you OK?'

Smudge saw blonde dreadlocks, a nose ring, a bright, tie-dyed top, a hand clutching a sheaf of yellow flyers.

'Yes,' said Smudge, beaming.

Colours bloomed, splashing the shop fronts pink, purple, aquamarine — a special psychedelic light show just for her, a welcome back to the world.

'Are you sure?' said the woman, glancing down at Smudge's bare feet. 'You look a bit . . . hectic.'

'Sure I'm sure I'm sure,' said Smudge. 'It's such a brilliant day. It's such a brilliant life. And I've just seen how it all links up. I've seen the truth behind it all. And I'm just so grateful. I'm so amazingly grateful.'

She was gabbling, like a soundtrack played at double speed, but there was so much to say and each word carried such a tiny amount of significance on its own that she had to talk fast to get them out, to stand a chance of making it all heard.

'Seems like you're freaking out a bit,' said the woman. 'Here, why don't you come with me? My studio's just through that archway. You could sit down for a minute. We could get you some water.'

She took Smudge's arm and tried to steer her towards the side street. Smudge shook her head. Around her, time jumped and bucked like a scratched record. ('Lose her,' urged a voice, 'She's getting in the way. She's trying to take you off track from who you really are.') 'No!' shrieked Smudge, wrenching her arm free and jerking around, so that the woman's leaflets whirled up into the air. She set off up the pavement at a run, lurching in between the shoppers, one of the yellow flyers flattened to the front of the Hellie dress. At the corner, she pulled it off and stared down.

Patterson's Walk Artists' Collective's Open House, it read in bold type. **Artworks available to buy from £50.** She shook her head and dropped the slip of paper into the gutter. She'd had a lucky escape. The time for distractions was over.

32

They take you into the dining room and shut the door. Outside, you can hear Mother pacing, the rumble of Akela's voice. They start a video for Richard in the living room — the room Mother calls the lounge — and you hear its music playing through the walls: 'Teenage Mutant Hero Turtles. Heroes in a half shell. Turtle power!'

You look round at the furniture: the cabinet with the Sunday-best crockery — covered in primroses and rimmed with gold — the sideboard that houses Akela's whisky and the gin. Under other circumstances you might be tempted to have a gulp, but today everything feels sealed off and out of reach. The lace curtains on the French doors shrug disapprovingly in the breeze, the clock above the sideboard tuts with each second that passes. There is no place for you here.

You go away in your mind for a while to a blank sea shore and when you come back, you hear the wail of a siren and unfamiliar voices in the hall. You expect that they'll all stay outside in the street with Hellie and leave you alone, but after a while you hear footsteps approaching and the door cracks open.

'In there, Officer,' says Mother in a distant voice.

The policeman takes you by surprise. You seem to do the same to him, because he comes in, blinking, and sticks to the corner of the room by the door as though you are a wild animal that might at any moment pounce. His fear sets off fireworks in your brain.

'Nooo!' you scream, and you shove past him and out into the hall.

You're up the stairs before you know it and into the bedroom — your bedroom — gripping the bookcase for all you're worth. The books tremble and flutter at you like birds. Hands are on you, pulling you away, voices urging, soothing, cajoling. But you won't hear it and you won't listen. You hang on for all you're worth, your feet digging into the wood at the base, gouging a scar. A voice shouts over and over again: nonsense sounds, mad sounds. It might be Hellie's; it might be yours. Who gives a shit? It goes on. But in the end they're too much for you and they prise you away and bundle you down and out to the waiting car. Your breath rasps like an animal's. A hand presses down on your head and they slide you in. The postbox on the corner purses its lips.

As the car pulls away, you look back at the house. Mother is standing there on the doorstep her chin raised, staring out into the gathering dusk. You try to find her eyes, but the light from the hall behind makes it impossible, turning her into a flat, black silhouette.

33

The next night, she had another crack at Hellie. She waited until Nick finished clattering in the kitchen and the light went on in the garden office. Then she let herself out and teetered off to a small pub just off the high street. She sat in the corner staring up at a screen showing a football match, inhaling the sour smell of booze. After a while, a guy in a suit came over and stood in front of her, obscuring her view.

'Has anyone ever told you you look exactly like Helen Sallis?' he began.

She stared up at him and saw he was young and a little bit drunk, his eyes beginning to swim behind his glasses and his tightly knotted tie ever so slightly askew. Easily handled.

She yawned. 'Yeah, I get that all the time.'

('Smooth,' remarked a voice and she smiled.) She looked good today and she knew it, wearing a tight little top and ra-ra skirt she'd found tucked at the back of one of the wardrobes — outrageous, flamboyant, the sort of things you had to be famous to get away with. She'd remembered shoes this time too — a pair of Hellie's stilettos that she'd been practising wearing about the house this morning when no one else was in. She was quite confident in them now. Every hour, it seemed, she'd been adding another skill to her Hellie repertoire.

The young man nodded. 'Drink?'

'I —'

But he was already turning and making some improbable gesture to the barman.

'So,' he said, plonking himself down beside her on the padded bench. 'What's a pretty lady like you doing in a place like this?'

She twisted her mouth in an effort not to laugh. 'Oh, you know,' she said, shrugging.

He nodded. 'Myself, I'm a journalist,' he said, and then watched her face for the reaction.

'Oh,' she said, mustering some sort of grimace. 'That's —'

'Yes,' he said firmly. 'It is.'

A beat of silence. The football crowd roared. His eyes drifted towards the screen.

'So, um, what title do you work for?' she said in her best Hellie voice. It sounded so professional and polished in her head that she might as well be interviewing him for ITV.

He looked back at her as if surprised by her presence. 'Oh . . . ah, here are our drinks.'

'Two double vodka and tonics,' said the barman, setting a pair of brimming glasses down on the table.

She held up a hand. 'Actually, I'm on the lime and soda waters.'

Her companion looked at her. 'Why?' he said, with a worried glance at her abdomen. 'You're not pregnant, are you?'

She shook her head.

'Well, bollocks to that then. Cheers!' And so saying he gulped half his glass before setting it down with a pantomime 'Ah!'

Her drink sat in front of her on the table. She could smell its petrol fumes.

'So,' said the young man, turning back to her with renewed enthusiasm. 'Where were we?'

'Er,' she said quickly. 'You were telling me what newspaper you work for.'

He coughed. 'Oh yeah,' he said, and mumbled something.

'What?' she said.

'*Waste Management Monthly*,' he said. 'It's based in Croydon.'

'Oh,' she said. 'That must be —'

'Yeah, it is,' he said breezily. Then his face fell. 'Actually, who am I kidding? It's shit, all right? Like, literally. It's really boring and everybody hates me and now I've got this fucking two-hour commute just because I didn't know where anything was when I moved to London. But I can't leave because I only moved into my house share last month and besides, like, Mum and Dad have told everyone I'm this big-shot journalist in London, so basically I'm screwed.'

They looked at each other and burst out laughing so loudly that the people at the nearest table turned round to look. A reckless feeling came over her and she reached for her drink and knocked it back in one long draw. The alcohol seeped through her, stirring up velvet violence. When she put the glass down, he was staring at her.

'Wow, that was hardcore,' he said. He narrowed his eyes. 'You know, you really do look like Helen Sallis.'

She stared at him. Things were glittering on the edge of her vision. 'How do you know I'm not?' she said.

He blinked. 'Well, because . . . wasn't she in a car crash?'

Smudge touched the scar on her temple. 'Yeah, several months ago.'

'Blimey,' he said. 'In a bar drinking with Helen Sallis. Facebook status gold.'

On a whim, she leant over and kissed him full on the mouth, licking his lips with her tongue.

'In a bar snogging Helen Sallis,' she said.

'Bloody hell,' he said, adjusting his glasses. 'But hold on. Aren't you married?'

She shrugged. 'So what if I am? Does it make a difference?'

He took a deep breath and looked up at the ceiling as though calculating a hard sum. 'Not in the fucking slightest,' he said, looking back at her with flushed cheeks. 'Actually, I think it's hot.'

She seized his wrist. The need to act without thinking — to make Hellie do something extreme — was strong upon her. 'Come on then,' she said, dragging him up.

'But where are we — ?' he burbled as he stumbled after her across the pub. 'Oh,' he said as they got to the toilet door. And then with a blaze of pride: 'This really is London living, isn't it?'

She pushed him inside and into a cubicle. There was someone at one of the urinals, but she didn't care. All the better. Let it be shocking, in your face, something to put a stamp on the day. Let them call the police if they wanted, drag her off for a night in the cells. That would really smear Hellie, wouldn't it? That would bring her under her control. That would show her.

With the door pushed to behind her, she set about his belt in a business-like manner. He had other ideas, however, and launched himself at her face, slobbering on her mouth like an over-enthusiastic Labrador puppy. She endured his tongue probing her gums for a few moments, his teeth clinking against hers, then she pressed on, eager to get it over with before the wave of purposefulness left her.

The belt undone, she popped open the button at the top of his trousers, unpeeled the fly and stepped back. He stood before her, his erection nudging against the newly exposed fabric of his underwear, a half-excited, half-pained expression on his face. His shirt was tucked into his Y-fronts, revealing a teenage leanness to his body that it would take a year or two of sinking pints and kebabs to fill out. But it was the Y-fronts that made her pause: gleaming, soft and pressed even this late in the day, pristine beyond the capabilities of laundry mouldering on the radiators of a shared house. They spoke of washing taken home on the weekends, of a mother humming to herself over the ironing board, of Sunday lunches where the family gathered like in the Oxo ad, brimming with pride at the achievements of its young son: a journalist, in London, imagine! Faced with them, she felt grimy, unclean, more Smudge-like than ever. She was not equal to them and the vulnerability and strength they revealed. She was not worthy. A gust of sadness bellied up through her and before it rattled her to pieces, she turned to go.

'I'm sorry,' she said, fumbling open the cubicle door. 'I can't.'

Outside, the man at the urinal turned, a lewd comment dying on his lips as he caught sight of her face. She pushed past him and on, out, through the pub, elbowing her way until she reached the street. A car drew up and she saw her face reflected in the passenger window: haggard and lined beneath Hellie's foundation, the MONSTER beginning to loom through. In the orange streetlight the clothes made her look like a wizened teenybopper and gave her a pathetic, desperate air. Then the window wound down and Nick leant over to glare up at her.

'What the hell are you doing?' he shouted. 'Get in!'

34

There are interviews in a series of fluorescent-lit rooms with plastic chairs. They assign someone called an appropriate adult to you: a woman with straggly grey hair and a lumpy cardigan who looks as though she'd rather be in bed. She comes along and listens as they ask you things and you reply with whatever comes into your mind, watching their expressions to see what they'll do. There are forms and assessments and people talking in hushed voices in the corners of rooms. For a while it looks like you might have to go to juvenile court and maybe some detention centre. Then they decide you're too crazy for that. The talking continues, back and forth. The same questions over and over, as if they hope you'll morph into someone else and give different answers if they keep asking long enough.

When at last they get bored, they take you

to a grey, boxy building somewhere just inside the M25 and leave you there. There's a common room and a games room and something called a chill-out garden laid out in front of a thick hedge behind which the traffic whizzes by. Look at it one way and you'd think it was a sort of holiday camp, like the PGL place you and Hellie went to once in primary school. The thing that gives it away, though, is the bedrooms: blank cells with thick doors like on submarines and a little observation hatch that can be pulled open at any time. 'You are trapped,' these rooms whisper. 'You are here to be watched and scrutinised and talked about in low voices. They might even carry out experiments on you when you're asleep. And there's nothing you can do.'

That's what keeps you spouting crap whenever the staff ask you questions — wacky statements about aliens and monsters, things nicked from video games and films. If you keep shifting ground, you think, they won't be able to pin you down and no one will be able to touch you. There's a fat one called Ange who clearly fancies herself as some sort of counsellor, the way she keeps on at you, the way she doesn't give up. Sometimes you let her think she's winning. Sometimes you soften your face and make as if you're going to cry, but it's never real. You're always standing outside yourself, watching, laughing at how Ange gets taken in. It's always only a matter of time before you whirl off into some nonsense or other, leaving her spinning in your wake.

It's harsh but the only way to stay sane is to keep yourself to yourself. Stay behind the mental wall. Don't engage. Don't look at the other inmates. Don't get sucked into anyone else's lies or their shit smearing or their cutting or any of the fighting, kicking and thrashing that sets the alarm system shrieking. Don't become part of the crises that send the staff thundering up the corridor at night, voices raised with the bluff confidence mixed with adrenaline you grow to hate.

You spend a lot of time in your room, staring at the walls. You learn where the cracks are, the weaknesses — the places that might crumble and offer you an escape route in the event of a security breach or, say, a nuclear attack. You watch for signs of this or some other disaster. You make notes and tuck them under your mattress where no one else will see. Some days you listen to Radiohead's 'Creep' over and over again on your headphones, the sound turned up as loud as it will go, the lyrics drilling into your brain. It calms you. You prefer it to Kurt Cobain these days. It's more where you are.

Twice a day you line up with the rest to take your medication under supervision. It's a selection of pills — one large as a hockey puck — and a cup of brown liquid.

'You know what they're doing to us with these, right?' whispers the girl behind you in the line on the third day. 'Mind control. Pure and simple. All these drugs.' She prods you on the arm to emphasise the point. 'Lithium, right, is what they use to stop coyotes killing sheep. No word of a lie. One dose on a sheep carcass is enough to make a dog so sick he never touches the animals again. Seriously. That's what they think of us. That's the kind of shit they're trying to pull. You should do what I do — tuck it in your cheek and spit it out down the toilet. Don't let them win.'

But you're not interested in making friends and when you get to the drugs table you look her in the eye and down it all in two gulps. Even though you know it's going to screw with you. Even though you can already feel it shaving off your hard edges and turning the volume down on who you are.

You don't hear anything from home. The others get letters and phone calls sometimes, although visitors are rare (having relatives who are both mad and bad seems to be more than most people can take face to face), but there's never anything for you, not even on your birthday. Especially not then.

Christmas at the unit is particularly shit: balding tinsel and a plastic tree and value mince pies from the convenience store up the road. You wonder why they bother. All their efforts just make everything seem worse, like make-up over a black eye. It would be better to flip the calendar forward a month and do January twice.

You know you're not going to get any presents from outside, but here's the thing: it still hurts when they go round giving the parcels out on Christmas morning. Some little part of you clearly hasn't given up hoping it lives in a different world with a family that loves and understands you, despite all the rubbish you've been through, despite all the evidence to the contrary. That's the worst thing about that day — discovering again how fucking stupid you are, that you're really just a mug no matter how much you try not to care. And no amount of Accessorise crap wrapped up to look like more than it is by the staff can make that better.

After lunch, you escape to the art room. At least it's quiet in there. At least you can be alone. The easels stand and look at you, waiting. At first you think of scribbling something violent and spiky, of letting the black fury inside you score its way out through rips and smears on paper. You flip open the A3 sheet on the stand nearest the door with this in mind. But then, as a hush spreads over the unit — people shut away in their rooms trying out their presents or watching some Christmas rubbish in the common room — the kind of focus you remember from the art projects you did in Miss Hogan's class settles over you. You are filled with that old sense of absorption, that sense that everything is fair game for you to manipulate and present as you choose, powerful and strange. The thick, creamy paper beckons, offering itself to you, and you pick up a pencil in answer.

You start off by drawing a Christmas scene: a family sitting round in a living room watching TV, with a big decorated tree in the corner. The thing with the scene is, when you glance at it, you think it's all normal. It's only when you look closer that you see things aren't what they seem. Like, the Mother has AIDS, for example. You can't show this explicitly in the picture, but what you can show are her sunken cheeks and hollow eyes and the scars on her spindly arms from injecting. The unwrapped Christmas present on the table beside her turns out to be a needle and the food in the bowl in front of her is vomit. There are scars and bruises on the little boy: the daddy hits him when no one else is around. And as for the teenage girl, well, it doesn't take a rocket scientist to work out from her ripped clothes and haunted expression what he does to her.

You drape the Christmas decorations with cobwebs. The thing about this tree, you realise, is it's up all year. No one can be arsed to take it down. That means that what looks special at first sight is actually a bit like torture, all its specialness leached away to be replaced by boredom and shame — another thing the girl has to hide from her friends at school. In fact, if you look closely, you can see it's June in the world outside. The sun is shining even though it's after 21:30 on the VCR. It's the longest day.

Then there's the question of what's on TV. Instead of the usual schmaltz you'd expect — *Noel's Christmas Presents* or a repeat of *Morecambe and Wise* — there's something hardcore and nasty. Something utterly unsuitable for kids. Blood and guts and actual injuries, like one of those snuff films Hailey up the corridor is supposed to have escaped from, where they were going to rape and kill her live on camera (at least that's what she tells everyone — personally, you think it's more likely she just got felt up by a few perverts and is trying to make it more than it is). You work hard to get as much gore on to the small screen as possible. It's tricky to balance it so that it still makes sense to the eye, but you spend a lot of time focusing on the spurting stomach, getting the hand twisting the knife just right.

You're so absorbed that you don't notice Ange until she's next to you. She leans over to look at the screen, the fat around her middle pressing into your side.

'That's really good,' she says.

You shoot her a look, annoyed that someone's intruding on your private thing without being invited. She doesn't take the hint.

'I like the way you've caught the faces,' she says. 'And how all the details in the house are there. It's really smart.'

Her jaw churns, working a piece of gum as you watch her, wondering quite what sense her brain is making of the things in front of it on the sheet of paper. After a moment her expression clouds.

'It's quite dark, isn't it?' she says. 'Not your average Christmas. Still it's really good, Ellie. Really good.'

Looking back at the easel, you suddenly see what you've done through her eyes: not as a great, sprawling mess of pain, but as something complete and organised that you can stand outside and judge. A picture that can add something — even give pleasure — to the world. A realisation lands that stretches your brain like a piece of elastic: you see how a drawing can be both a private, coded thing and have something to say to the rest of the world. It's fucking mental and it could be dangerous, but it's also great.

After Ange goes, giving you a pat on the shoulder, you sit and stare at the page. A quiet feeling that you haven't experienced for ages — maybe ever — settles into you. It's weird to name it, sitting here in the scuzzy art room with snot smeared on the desks and swearwords scratched into the walls, but it feels a bit like peace.

35

In the days that followed, Smudge kept to the attic. There was nothing she could say to account for the shameful state in which Nick had found her. There were so many layers of stories that the explanation was unplayable, like multiple songs recorded one over the other on a worn-out mixer tape. She could only stay in the little room, inhabiting her silence, staring at the ceiling, pacing round and round. She tried not to think but when images from those escapades in Hellie's party clothes came at her, the smashed logic behind them made her shiver. The idea that she could muscle her way into Hellie's grown-up, fully fledged existence by sheer bluster was hideous. It frightened her to think that her brain — the very apparatus with which she was apprehending the stupidity of the whole thing now — had cooked up the wheeze and presented it in such glowing colours. It made everything she thought dubious, every idea a potential lie. There were hours when she lay on the bed, her hands pressed over her face, afraid to trust even her eyes.

When she passed the attic studio, the memory of the easel, paints, pencils and charcoals within jabbed at her. The outrage of the other evening came back with all its horrid force and made her ashamed to think of Nick buying those things and arranging them in the hope of tempting her into something productive and good, something worthwhile. His faith in her felt like a reproach. Mother had a point: she was broken, she was ruined, she was poisonous. She should leave now before she infected him and warped his way of seeing. She should let herself out of their lives for good.

But something about the cleanness of the paper on the easel would not let her go. Through the aimless hours of the afternoon, the possibility of the colours and textures it could hold tugged at her. She could not bear to leave the pad blank, so one night she let herself into the studio and made a tentative sketch. Then another. Before long, she was attacking the easel as though her life depended on it, working through sheet after sheet. The images came crowding into her brain, like passengers waiting to board a bus, and she worked urgently to deal with them one by one. She drew pictures of Ellie and herself as children, complete with plaits and bunches the right way round; she drew a bungalow with broken engine parts littering the lawn; she sketched Bill the budgie lying stiff at the bottom of the page; and she made a whimsical wash painting of three figures skipping along a pavement clutching bags of colourful clothes. Some of the pictures were of things the significance of which she didn't want to examine: a forest with a wolf-like figure peering through the trees, clutching a scrap of red cape; a woman staring out from the banks of a vast river as a boat pulled away; a smashed traffic light stuck on red.

Days and nights passed. She forgot about sleep. Her hand worked on, drawing the rest of her with it. Now and then food and drink appeared on the landing outside and when she noticed it she ate it. For the most part, though, she didn't know whether she was hungry or thirsty. The past and future ceased to exist. There were only the lines and the colours and the ridged texture of the pages. She had no history and nothing to plan for. It was all over for the time being. She just was.

36

The year unfolds. New people come to the unit, others leave. They move the drug-spitting girl out to somewhere else.

At some point, they make you sit exams. GCSEs. It's a joke. You don't even bother to read the papers — you just turn them over and stare at the wall. What do they expect you to do? How could anyone relate what's written on the paper to what's going on in here? Fools.

You refuse to think about Hellie, sitting at a little square desk in the Bridge Oak assembly hall, scribbling furiously, her rounded handwriting covering line after line.

Another Christmas. Another birthday. You don't pay much attention. Every moment you can, you spend in the art room, trying things out with charcoal and paint. After they realise you're not going to get anywhere with the exams, they encourage you to focus on that. Ange buys you a notebook that you can scribble ideas in as they come to you. You probably remember to say thank you — you're not sure.

You fall into a rhythm. Every morning, after breakfast, you go to the art room and start work. The pictures are what's real. Everything else is far away. That's probably partly the drugs they keep giving you — the pills that rinse you blank as though the tide has gone out on your emotions, leaving you high and dry. The pictures are the only way you feel these days.

Then one afternoon, Ange takes you aside. She's wearing this beaming, pleased look that makes you want to run to the art room and shut the door, but she grips your arm and won't let you. They've entered your work into a local art show at the town hall, she tells you. You've got a spot. The exhibition's next week and she's got special permission to take you.

You stand there, feelings fighting inside you. Part of you is pleased, part of you doesn't care and part of you is, well, like, a bit affronted if you're honest that they went behind your back and didn't ask. You can't decide which part to let win, so you just stand there and stare at a big zit on Ange's double chin.

'Isn't it great?' she says, grinning, giving your arm a squeeze.

You see that it's easier if you let it be great for now, so you nod and jerk a smile. By and large these days, you do your best not to be a bitch.

You go to the exhibition. It's in this big, olde-worlde hall — the sort of place Akela and Mother would visit for fun on the weekends — and all the pictures are hung round the walls like in a proper gallery. There's a bit of a mix-up on the door because of your tracksuit and baseball cap and the MONSTER tattoo. It's clear they think you're there to cause trouble, but Ange smoothes it out and then they're all smiles. Someone goes so far as to use the words 'star guest'.

The place is full of people. If you're honest, it's all a bit mental after the unit — too much going on at once and all in your face. Anxiety bubbles through you, but you keep a lid on it for Ange's sake and pretend to look at the other pictures.

What you enjoy most, however, is standing near your own paintings and hearing the crap that people say about them. There are two of your things in the show — both called 'Untitled' because you never gave them names. One is a big canvas showing a car that's been smashed up in an accident and the other one is a small line drawing of a teddy bear that's rotting and falling to pieces, with maggots crawling out of its eyes. You're secretly pleased they chose these ones because you had a good feeling about both of them when you did them — a sort of rightness that carried you through, not like some of the other things you've worked on, where you have to scrub things out and force your way.

It's amazing the rubbish these pictures bring out in other people, though. Like, there's this one couple who stand there for ages, looking at the teddy bear, saying how it's got all these connections to Paddington Bear and some shit like that. Then there's this pair of old ladies who huddle together making clucking noises about the car and saying how it's evidence of a disturbed mind and shouldn't be allowed. Someone else makes out it's got to do with the recession in the early-nineties and the economic crash. Then another says some nonsense about the Berlin Wall — apparently they think the car looks German.

These comments make you snigger to yourself because the truth is, nothing like that was on your mind when you did these pictures. For the most part you were too busy focusing on getting the ears right on the bear and trying to find the right colour combination for the car's mashed-up paint job to worry about anything as wanky as meaning. You just wanted them to fit, that's what concerned you, nothing grander than that.

Hearing all this makes you realise something too: what you put out there and what people take away are two totally separate things. People's minds process things in diverse ways. Everyone lives in different worlds, which is sort of sad but also has potential if you can work out how to turn it to your advantage.

After a while there's a speech: some bigwig from the council in a crumpled suit bores everyone for, like, twenty minutes with what a great occasion it all is and isn't everyone having fun? He has a crumb from a mini sausage roll on the lapel of his jacket and you focus on that, so you miss the moment when he says there's been some sort of competition and, well, the thing is, you've won. But suddenly they're all staring and you realise the way to play it is to look a mixture of pleased and sort of like you expected it all along.

After that, everyone wants to talk to you. Lots of people come and make intense eye contact, like they are trying to winkle your brain out from behind your face so they can inspect it at close range. Mostly, they are older women in colourful scarves, with posh, blustery voices. You catch a few of them staring at your tattoo, but for the most part everyone's nice. There's even someone from the local paper who asks to take your picture. He gets you standing between your two exhibits and tries a few poses — once with you pointing at the walls, once with you holding the little glass trophy, which it turns out is what you've won. If you're honest, you think the poses are cheesy, but you don't say anything, you just stand there and try and give him a smile.

Then, all of a sudden, the hall is emptying out and it's time to go back to the unit. Ange comes and takes your arm.

'Well,' she says, and she gives you a squeeze. You can feel the pride radiating off her like the heat from the old cast-iron radiators in the canteen that got so hot last winter some girl got her face scalded in a fight.

'Yeah,' you say.

'You see?' she says.

You don't know what she expects you to see, but you're not really up for a big discussion. It's been exhausting talking to all those people and being in a new place. You're not used to it. Your mind has shrunk to the limits of the unit and it's hard work stretching it to make room for the world beyond.

'Yeah,' you say again.

'Come on,' she says, and she takes you to the van they've let her borrow for the evening. 'You can sit in the front if you like. I won't tell anyone.'

You climb up into the cab and buckle the seat belt. You stare forward out of the windscreen. A thought blows into your mind: the last time you sat in the front of a vehicle was the day you knocked Ellie down. You suppose you should feel traumatised. If you were one of the other kids you'd be having a panic attack about now — wheezing and swearing and making to vomit. But you don't. Nothing touches you. You don't feel anything at all.

37

A knock at the door. Nick standing there.

'You've been busy,' he said, gesturing at the sheets of paintings laid out to dry around the walls and heaped in drifts in the corners.

Smudge shrugged, impatient at the interruption. Irritation sizzled along her nerves. She didn't know why he was here. Couldn't he fuck off and leave her alone?

He coughed and a sliver of a memory of the other night glinted in the surging waters of Smudge's thoughts. She ought to be civil. By rights, she ought to be ashamed. She crossed her arms to contain the energy crackling through her, pressed her lips together and tried to look receptive.

'So, I have a bit of news.' Nick nudged a study of a rotten bowl of fruit out of the way with his foot. (She hated the way he looked at everything as if he owned it. This might be his house, but this was the inside of her mind. It was private. He had no right.) 'The Hairpin has got the green light. It's all going ahead.'

Smudge blinked. Like a swimmer trying to surface from great depths, her brain struggled towards the light of his words.

'The Hairpin?' she said. She broke the surface and was in the world again. She remembered the tall, twisted towers. 'Oh, that's great. You must be —'

He nodded. 'Actually, it's a bit of an odd feeling.' He put his hands in his pockets and tapped his foot. 'Usually I get a bit down after these big projects. Before Heloise, Helen used to take me away when I finished them, to help me through the initial funk.' He looked at her, sidelong. 'Anyway, I was wondering if you wanted to have dinner tonight, to help me celebrate? Nothing fancy, just low-key. I'll cook. I thought maybe it could be a fresh start. A clean slate.'

The silence stretched. Smudge coughed.

'I don't know if that's a good idea,' she said. 'I mean, to be honest, I'm not sure I'm in a very dinner-companionable place right now.' She took a deep breath. 'I think I might be ill again.'

Nick nodded. 'I understand. But seriously, you'd be doing me a favour.'

Suddenly the atmosphere in the room was too intense.

She fidgeted, impatient to get rid of him. 'Sure,' she said. 'Whatever.'

As soon as the door closed after him, she knew she'd made a mistake.

She went down at about ten to seven, unable to sit in the little box room any longer, staring unseeingly at a book. The afternoon had been a washout: since she'd agreed to dinner all inspiration had deserted her, leaving her mind filled with fog. Twice she'd stood up determined to quit the house for good, but both times she'd stopped and returned to the bed, hemmed in by the image of herself as Hellie blundering about the streets. She could not trust her fluid, ill-defined, volatile being out in the world. Beside, after he'd put up with so much of her crap, she owed Nick the courtesy of eating a meal with him at least.

Coming down the stairs, she met Heloise.

'Oh, it's you,' said the little girl. 'Where have you been?'

Smudge put a hand up to her hair, which was brushed and felt strangely conspicuous as a result.

'Yeah, sorry about that,' she said. 'I've not been very well.'

'Liar!' exploded Heloise. 'I heard you moving about up there. You don't move about if you're not very well: you lie in bed and go "Oh, I'm not very well" and people bring you things.'

'This was a different sort of ill,' said Smudge.

Heloise narrowed her eyes and folded her arms, looking, for a moment, disconcertingly like Mother. 'A likely story,' she said.

From two floors below, Nick called up the stairs, 'I'll be up in a little while to kiss you goodnight!'

Smudge blinked, confused, before she realised who his words were intended for.

' 'K!' yelled Heloise. She turned back to Smudge. 'You look very nice.'

Smudge glanced down at the jeans and grey top she had fished out of the pile of clothes Nick had left for her. She had hoped for neutral, understated, nothing that could in any way be construed as trying to put her sister on.

'That top is one of Mummy's favourites for at-home days. But it looks almost just as nice on you,' said Heloise, glaring with the effort to be generous.

'Oh, is it?' said Smudge. She pulled the hem forwards and considered the top. It was ruched down one side and the fabric had a

343

soft, cashmere feel. Of course, it must be very expensive, she realised all of a sudden. She should have gone for one of the long-sleeved T-shirts from M&S.

'Thank you,' began Smudge. 'I didn't choose it on purpose. I —'

But Heloise was suddenly bored.

'Well, goodnight then,' she said, flapping a hand. She scampered up the stairs.

Nick was standing at the range when Smudge rounded the banister. He gave a start when he saw her. Then he collected himself.

'I'm sorry,' he said, walking towards her across the room. 'It's just that, for a minute, in the light . . .' He shook his head. 'You look very nice,' he said.

She blushed. 'Oh, sorry,' she said. 'I didn't realise the top was — is — one of Hellie's favourites. I can go and change. It won't take a minute.'

He held up a hand. 'Not at all,' he said. 'You look very nice. You look very . . . well, if you don't mind my saying, much better than you did the other night.'

She looked down at her shoes — nearly new grey Converses, apparently of no special significance.

'About that,' she began, and stopped. How to find the words to explain the squalls of illogic that blew in across the landscape of her mind?

'First things first,' said Nick. He turned and picked up an open bottle. 'Wine?'

'Oh, I shouldn't,' she said.

'Nobody should on the face of it,' he said. 'That's part of the point. Wine?'

She shrugged. 'Why not?' she said, and then laughed, surprised by the feeble pun.

He'd cooked a feast of asparagus wrapped in Parma ham with homemade Hollandaise sauce, accompanied by several generous glasses of crisp white wine, and coq au vin to follow.

'Wow,' she said when the casserole came brimming to the table. 'You've really gone to town. Anyone would think you were up to something.'

He caught her eye and looked away, embarrassed. Shadows from the garden crept over his face, hollowing out his cheekbones and putting circles round his eyes.

'It's been a tough time for you, hasn't it?' she said, and then flinched at the triteness of the words. She always hated it when people tried to wrap her experiences in everyday expressions and yet here she was doing exactly the same thing.

He kept his eyes on her glass as he poured from a fresh bottle of red wine. 'Tougher than you know.'

She served spoonfuls of the rich stew on to their plates. As she did so, she caught sight of a framed photograph hanging by the door to the utility room: Ellie and Nick raising glasses of champagne to the camera from a pod on the London Eye. Her sister's hair glimmered in the sunlight, arranged sleekly round her face. She was every inch the TV star.

Smudge swallowed and made a concerted effort. 'It must be so hard watching someone you love go through all this, not knowing how it's going to end,' she said. 'I guess you feel trapped. Like your life can't move forward until she's well.'

Nick accepted the plate with a sigh. 'I do feel trapped,' he said. 'But it's not entirely how you think.'

He looked over at her, as though sizing her up like one of his structural walls, deciding how much weight she could bear. Then he threw back his head and drained his glass.

'Oh sod it,' he said. 'The truth is, we didn't love each other. Not any more. Things hadn't been right for a long time. Two days before the accident we'd decided to get a divorce.' He puffed out his cheeks. 'There. Now you know.'

Smudge said nothing. She forked a piece of chicken into her mouth and sat chewing the tender flesh.

Nick picked up his cutlery. 'I suppose you hate me now.'

Smudge frowned. 'Hate you? Why would I hate you?'

'Well, it doesn't exactly look great, does it? Here I am supposed to be the devoted husband, waiting at the bedside, and all the while I'm itching to run for the hills. The media would have a field day if they knew.'

He poured himself some more wine and gulped it greedily.

'They can't blame you for how you feel,' said Smudge.

'Oh, can't they?' said Nick, talking to his glass. 'It's just the sort of thing they'd love, what with all the hoo-hah over the Hairpin. They'd have me down as a cold-hearted bastard as soon as look at me. And they'd be right.'

Smudge frowned, trying to keep focus as the wine lapped at the fringes of her field of vision, blurring boundaries. It was a while since she'd had this much to drink and already she could feel the fuzzy pull of oblivion.

'I think you're being too hard on yourself,' she said slowly. 'You've been very nice to me. Putting me up and . . . the studio and everything.'

Nick snorted. 'Oh yes, very nice of me, very altruistic,' he sneered. 'The truth is, I only did it because I hoped you'd go and see her and wake her up so I could finally get myself out of this mess, once and for all. Pathetic really, given the odds, but I'd got to the point where almost any way out seemed worth a shot.'

Smudge held her breath. The table slanted, then righted itself again.

Nick wasn't finished. He waved his hand over the plates, his sleeve grazing the rim of her glass and setting the liquid inside trembling. 'Even all this, tonight, was just going to be another attempt to butter you up. I had a little speech planned and every-thing. I was going to tell you how much I love her and how much she means to me and plead with you to go and talk to her. And all the while I'd just be thinking of myself, of getting my life back.'

Smudge coughed. 'I . . .' she began, her voice sounding faint and far away. 'I can understand how you could get to that point.'

But Nick wasn't listening. 'A cold-hearted bastard,' he said again. 'In fact, the only person I know I come second to in that respect is my "darling" wife Helen, the biggest fake of them all.'

He stopped and looked at her, his eyes taking a moment to focus, a dribble of red wine on his chin.

'What did you say?' said Smudge.

Off in the utility room, the dishwasher whooshed and sighed.

'Sorry,' said Nick. 'I shouldn't be saying all this. She's your sister after all, even with whatever happened in the past —'

'No,' said Smudge, urgently. 'It's fine. What did you mean when you said about Helen being a fake?'

He stared out into the garden. 'This'll sound weird — and maybe I'm making too much of it, maybe it's the wine — but I never felt like I really knew her. Even when things were good between us, it felt like she was holding something back.'

Smudge lowered her fork. The room seemed to shimmer. 'Go on,' she said.

Nick took a deep breath. 'Well, you know how she is on TV — all polished and word perfect? That's not an act: she's like that all the time. It's like, there's a person in there somewhere — a real person — but you never get to her because of all the layers in between.'

He shook his head. 'Even on our wedding day, standing at the altar in that little church near Margaret and Horace's place, watching her walk up the aisle, I remember thinking: Maybe now I can really get to know you. But it didn't happen. She was never truly there. Even in our best moments, I felt like we were just going through the motions until someone yelled "Cut" from across the room.'

He made an expansive gesture with his glass. 'I mean, don't get me wrong. When it was good, it was lovely. But there was always a distance there, you know? And then when Emily died, things went to shit. We tried couples counselling, but it was a disaster. She wouldn't open up — she just sat there looking perfect, as though any minute we'd be live on TV.'

He put his glass down and looked at Smudge, flushed. 'I'm sorry,' he said. 'I don't know why I'm telling you this. It feels good, I suppose, to have it out in the open. That's the thing about living with a celebrity — you feel you have to be so fucking careful all the time.'

'And meanwhile you've got her crackpot twin sister bombing around the clubs and bars dressed up as her,' said Smudge. 'Just what you didn't need.'

Nick looked at her oddly. 'Is that what you were doing?' he said. 'I just thought you were on some regaining-your-youth bender. Helen never dressed like that in all the time I knew her.'

'Oh,' said Smudge quietly.

She swirled her wine glass gently, watching how the light from the jagged lamp hanging above the table played across the liquid inside. The drunkenness that had been flooding into her brain had receded, leaving her thoughts clean and exposed. She looked at Nick, weighing things up.

'Do you know why Helen was always so reserved?' she said slowly. 'Why she never seemed to be quite herself?'

Nick shrugged, drained his glass and began pouring himself another. 'No idea,' he said. 'I always assumed it was to do with being on TV. But, looking back, I think she was always like that — long before she got famous. Of course I knew the official story of what had happened with you from the interviews she did before we met. But I've never set much store by media stuff. I've seen enough in my career to know things can get twisted. And with her there was always something locked inside you couldn't get to. At least, I couldn't. Maybe someone else would have had more luck. Maybe someone else will.'

The bottle tilted in his hand, sloshing wine

on to the table, staining its blond wood. Smudge reached for it.

'Here, give me that,' she said, and helped herself to a generous top-up. She sipped it and looked at him.

'The reason she never seemed to be herself was because she wasn't.'

Nick frowned and looked at her. He rolled his eyes as though struggling to focus.

'She wasn't herself, because she was me,' said Smudge, her voice raised with the effort to get it said. 'She was pretending to be me her whole life. You were married to Ellie, not Helen.'

A wary look passed over Nick's features. He glanced around the room, as though half expecting to find a camera crew and a gurning presenter lurking somewhere, poised to catch him out.

His hand went to his throat. 'I'm sorry, I don't —' he said.

But Smudge silenced him with a shake of her head. It was done now. It had to be finished. Taking a deep breath, she launched into the story of the game and the swap and everything that had come since.

At some point during the telling, Nick stumbled up and fetched another bottle of wine to the table. This he splashed into their glasses without saying a word.

When she was finished and it was all said — at least as much of it as she could manage in one sitting — she risked a glance at him. They were sitting closer together now, their chairs pushed back from the table. Nick was slumped slightly towards her. His eyes were closed and for a moment she worried he'd fallen asleep. Then he looked at her.

'Ssshhittt,' he said, his consonants sodden with the wine. 'You've been through a fuck of a time, haven't you?'

She nodded, her bottom lip trembling.

He scraped his chair closer to her and patted her arm. 'A fuck of a time,' he said again.

His hand dropped down onto her leg and rested there a moment. Their eyes met and then he was out of his chair and upon her, his mouth on hers, his hand kneading her breasts. And she was kissing him back, urgently, hungrily, her fingers sliding up and down his spine.

She was drunk, a voice in her head kept saying. They were both drunk. This was what happened when people got drunk. There was nothing anyone could do to help it.

It was convincing but not quite enough to drown out the other, sour knowledge, whispering away in the background, that this wasn't about the man above her, thrusting his knee, now, between her legs, but about an unconscious woman several miles away. That at last now she was getting what should have been hers.

After a few moments they broke apart, gasping. A resolute look came over Nick's face.

'Come on,' he said. And he took her by the wrist and began to lead her up the stairs.

38

They call you in for a meeting in the director's office. They've been doing this for a while now, getting you in rooms and talking at you. Mostly it goes over your head, but this time it's different, more formal-feeling. There's Ange, one of the doctors, the director and another woman you haven't seen before.

'Ellie, good to see you,' says the director, standing up and holding out his hand like the man in that terrible educational video they made you watch about job interviews. 'Have a seat.'

You sit down and they all smile at you. Uneasily, you reach up and tug at the neck of your T-shirt. Behind them, there's a picture of a night sky filled with swirls and balls of blazing light.

'Well,' says the director. 'As you know, Ellie, we've been talking for a while now about the next steps as you're going to be eighteen next month, officially an adult.'

Adult. It's an odd word. It disintegrates when you think about it. Adult. It sounds as though it should mean some sort of weird creature — a pond dweller with bulbous, short-sighted eyes. You think you'll have a go at sketching one next time you're in the art room.

You're so busy thinking about what the dult will look like that you don't hear the rest of what the director says. It's only when he stops talking and there's a sort of eager hush in the room that you realise there's something you've missed.

'I'm sorry,' you say cautiously. 'I don't understand.'

'Well,' says the director, steepling his hands and shifting in his chair so that the blazes of light in the picture wink at you above his head. The painting is beautiful and strange and you wish they hadn't put it there. It deserves to be celebrated and admired, not stuck behind a pot plant looking down on piles of forms. You wonder who the artist is.

'As we've been discussing with you over the last few weeks,' continues the director, 'we've all been very impressed with the progress you've made — with the way you've thrown yourself into your art and what have you — and so we see no reason why you shouldn't — with the right guidance and support — er, make the transition into society.'

You blink and try to make the words add up in your head, but it's like trying to input wine gums into a calculator: it doesn't compute.

'So, what are you saying?'

'It's what we've been talking about, Ellie,' says Ange excitedly. 'In a month, you're going to be back in the world. You'll be free.'

The unknown woman purses her lips. 'Free's not exactly a term we encourage around mental health,' she says.

But you don't care what she would or wouldn't encourage: you're too busy trying to absorb the ten-tonne weight of knowledge that has landed on your head. When did they tell you this? Where was your head while all of this was going on?

'Out?' you say. 'But where will I go?' Then something hardens inside you, like resin setting in a mould. 'I'm not going back there. I'm not going to Mother's house.'

They exchange looks.

'We were hoping you might say that,' says the director. He takes off his glasses and rubs a hand across his eyes. The starry-night whorls above his head seem to swirl towards you. 'As you might remember, your parents have also expressed a wish, er, not to have you back in their home.'

You grit your teeth. Akela is not your parent. Why can no one ever get it right about who people are?

'So what we're proposing is that you go from here to a halfway house while you wait for permanent accommodation,' continues the director. 'Angela is going to spend some time with you researching the options and taking you through the specifics of some of the things you'll need to know. She's also offered to get the ball rolling with applications for the various benefits you might be entitled to, although, of course, eventually we hope you'll want to get a job and pay your own way and contribute as a normal member of society.'

His language, you think, is like the sort of stonework you see on old churches and town halls: fussy, impenetrable and hard.

'Do you have any questions?' says the other woman.

You look at her. She's about five years younger than Mother, you reckon, with that sort of scraggy turkey neck that very thin women get above a certain age. There's a glint in her eye that speaks of barging past homeless people in the street and pushing in in the supermarket.

Oh yes, you've got questions. You want to know how it is that they're sitting on that side of the desk and you're sitting here. You want them to let you in on the secret of 'normal' and what it really means. You wonder how it's possible in a world of *Friends* and novelty ringbinders for people to be shackled to a radiator so tightly they bleed, like the girl up the corridor was by her stepfather, or punched in the face until their bones go like jelly and the doctors have to rebuild them piece by piece.

But you have learnt these are not the questions people like this answer. They want easy questions. Questions they can see round the edges of. Questions you could probably answer by yourself if you gave it any thought.

So you don't say anything. You shrug and shake your head, and let them dot the 'i's and cross the 't's of your future as they see fit. Let them bring it, all of it, as much as they can manage: whatever it is, it can't be worse than what you've already been through.

39

Morning. She woke up to the smell of bacon frying, a radio chattering somewhere below. She lay in the big white bed, eyes focusing, coming to, blinking in the sunlight streaming through the gauzy curtains.

The hangover tightened around her skull as she sat up and saw her creased face reflected in the dressing-table mirror. Fragments of the night before came back: she and Nick at the kitchen table; wine; hands groping; his face moving above her in the dark. Or perhaps she was imagining that last bit. She put a hand under the covers, but the slick tenderness of her body put paid to any doubt. She sank back among the pillows and closed her eyes in an effort to block it all out. If she could only go back to sleep, perhaps things would seem better when she looked at them again.

But her brain wouldn't let it go. There'd been something else, hadn't there? Another significant event. She screwed up her eyes to cancel the throbbing of her temples. Think. Think!

The knowledge descended on her: she'd told him about the swap, about everything.

Oh fuck. Well, that was that then. She might as well get dressed and leave right now. If he didn't already think she was a fucking basket case, a complete, psycho loony tune, he certainly would now. She'd blown it again, like she always did when someone showed her kindness, when there was a chance of something more. She was a monster. She was shit, a leech on other people's goodness. He'd probably only fucked her out of pity.

She swung her feet out of the bed on to the soft, snowy rug as the sun went behind the clouds, turning the room grey.

Wait, though. That wasn't quite how it played out, was it? She delved through the sludge of her memories. He'd been understanding, hadn't he? He'd seemed to get it. What was it he'd said? Oh yes: 'You've been through a fuck of a time.' An odd phrase. Maybe that was why she remembered it.

A vision of him standing in front of her in the bedroom, a tender, searching look in his eyes, came to her. He'd been emotional to the point of tears, she remembered, as she shrugged Hellie's top off and stepped out of her jeans. He had stared at her body with awe, as if half afraid to touch her. She had thought at the time that it had to do with the knowledge that Hellie was lying inert in her hospital bed only a few miles away. But maybe that wasn't it at all. Now she came to think about it, wasn't it possible that his tenderness — the way he'd trembled as he moved in to kiss her once more — pointed quite another way? She stroked the soft cotton of the bed sheet and a new idea surfaced. Wonderment. Wasn't that what she had seen in his face? Wasn't that the word that had echoed through the corridors of her brain as she watched him looking at her? A kind of reverence?

Yes, she was sure of it.

Perhaps she hadn't been certain of it at the time because it was a sentiment she had never witnessed taking hold of another human being before. It had never made its presence felt in the glances of any of the men she had jerked and sweated with in alleyways, hotel rooms and parks. It hadn't even been part of that magical, heartbreaking time in Amsterdam. It was new ground for her, uncharted territory. And, looking around the sterile, white room, she knew that it was new for Nick too; he could never have shared that vulnerability with Hellie. That sort of connection was beyond her, sealed as she was within the fiction of her perfect life. Their sex would have been polite and functional — dutiful even — conducted at a set time of the week and managed so as not to mess up Hellie's hair. There would have been no shuddering on waves of sensation strong enough to sunder the self from its moorings for them. There would have been no surrender. Poor, foolish, superficial Hellie. It made Smudge almost sad, sitting there wrapped in the luxury goose-down duvet, to think how hollow and safe her sister's life must have been. What a mean existence it must be to stay always in the shallows, bobbing on little eddies of feeling, and never weather the pitching and plunging of the open ocean and face the knowledge that events might overwhelm and wreck you.

By contrast, what had happened last night was so much deeper and more honest than anything Hellie could have known. Because of course — the realisation burst upon her like the sun emerging now again from the clouds — it had been a homecoming for both of them. After ten years of marriage, he had finally slept with the woman who was truly his wife. It was a consummation, a transformative act. Holy, even.

And who was to say it couldn't mark the start of a meaningful connection now that they had found each other? All right, it was unconventional. There were those who wouldn't approve, but that was life, wasn't it? People screwed up in all sorts of ways and went off the script all the time. Who said this had to be a bad thing? Perhaps she'd been on the right track with her clumsy attempts to step into Hellie's shoes after all. Perhaps the course of events was leading her inexorably back to her rightful place; to where she belonged.

A vision came to her of the two of them standing in Mother's living room, presenting the facts calmly as a unit. She pictured the parade of emotions across Mother's face as the truth about their lives was told, vindication at last, the story straight. Satisfaction glimmered in the depths of her being as she envisaged what would follow: the guilt, the heartfelt apologies. Would she stand there and listen? Would she forgive? Or would she turn on her heel and walk away? Would she never see Mother and Akela again or would she and Nick make space for them in their life together? Perhaps there would be Sunday lunches and Christmases and long walks in the park. Maybe they would go and see the rightful Ellie together and stand round the bed in the fluorescent hospital light, reminiscing about old times.

She laughed as she walked across the room with a new lightness in her step, shrugging on an outsize sweater from the back of a chair. Not since Manchester — not since the enchantment of Amsterdam — had she felt this good, this energised.

The spiral staircase sighed happily under her weight, the books in the room below beamed in the mid-morning sunshine. The levity of a thousand Saturdays flooded her heart.

He was sitting at the kitchen table, his head in his hands, when she came down the stairs. Around him lay the debris of Heloise's breakfast: one of her Beatrix Potter plates streaked with egg, a colourful beaker. The bottles from last night stood on the side. She counted five. Shit! No wonder he was hungover.

She regarded him for a moment: the neat curve of the crown of his head, the grey beginning to thread its way through his hair, his delicate artist's hands covering his eyes. She had the feeling of being a swimmer poised on the edge of a pool, preparing to jump in. Perhaps one day they would look back on this moment fondly together and laugh.

She shuffled, coughed. 'Good morning,' she said.

He looked up. His eyes were bloodshot. Strange, but he seemed to have aged overnight. She could see what he would look like at sixty.

'Bit of a crazy evening, wasn't it?' she said brightly. 'Have you been up long? You look like you could do with some coffee. I know I could. I —'

He shook his head and she stopped talking. She caught the timbre of her final words: shrill, jangling, scurrying to fill the silence.

'Sorry,' she said without quite knowing why. 'I —'

He held up a hand. A cold wind blew through the outer reaches of her brain, trembling the vision lodged there.

He ran a hand across his face. 'They warned me,' he said, as though speaking to some unseen audience, watching and judging silently in the room. 'Margaret and Horace warned me, but I wouldn't listen. I thought that I was clever enough not to fall for it. But I did. I'm a fool like everyone else.'

His voice was as she'd never heard it

before: hard and biting. There was a cruel set to his jaw. It was as though he were possessed — so much so that she caught herself wondering for a moment if this might in fact not be Nick but some deranged doppelgänger.

'But, last night, you said . . .'

'Last night I said a lot of things.' He spoke through clenched teeth. 'And none of them were really me. Understand? I don't do things like that. I don't sleep with my comatose wife's sister.' His voice broke. 'That's not who I am.'

She watched him sitting there, drumming his fingers on the blond-wood table, his face twitching in agitation, his eyes refusing to meet hers. At last he looked up.

'Go and see her,' he said. 'Just go and see her. You owe her that now. Whoever you are.'

40

The day arrives. You pack all your things into a Naf Naf bag they give you 'specially: clothes, sketchbooks, pencils, fifty pounds in cash, your National Insurance card, directions to the halfway house hostel place, the medication they don't know you've stopped taking, a card that everyone's signed, except for Blessings, the Nigerian woman in the third room along from yours, who's drawn a circle instead. They all stand around in the canteen looking uncomfortable. Someone's bought a cake from the Co-op, but it's the kind you don't like: coffee and walnut with the dry sponge that sticks to the roof of your mouth.

Then it's time to go. They take you to the entrance. The director shakes your hand and wishes you luck. Ange is going to drive you to the hostel, but there's a problem with starting the van and while she's on the phone to someone about it, you decide you'd rather pop off by yourself. Neater that way. No stringing it out. There's bound to be a bus stop or something. Whatever happens, you'll find your way.

You glance through the office window and when Ange's back is turned, her hand twisting the telephone cord around her fingers, you slip off down the road. You suck the morning air deep into your lungs. At last you can breathe.

You fully intend to go to the hostel, but when you get to the end of the road it seems a shame not to explore first. There's so much world out there you haven't had the chance to see for years. Besides, it's only lunchtime now. What are you going to do? Sit in the hostel all day? What's the point of that?

You saunter on down the busiest turning at the junction. There's a road lined with fried chicken shops and the post office and places you can go to exchange jewellery for cash, and you follow that. Pretty soon, you're in the town centre. There are chain stores and Spice Girls posters everywhere and people have harassed expressions, as though they're surprised to find anyone else out and wanting to go to the same shops as them in the middle of the day. Because you can, you stop at a coffee shop — one of

those new Starbucks that have been spring-
ing up everywhere and look like the café
from *Friends*. You don't even like coffee or
sugar much, but you order the gooiest thing
you can see on the menu, a white chocolate
mocha, just so you can tell yourself you're
having a treat. You walk through town, sipping it and staring at the shops, and that's
when it hits you: you're out. You're free.
This is the rest of your life. The thought is
so momentous that you have to step into a
little public garden and sit down on a bench
dedicated to Freddie — 'gone but not
forgotten' — to take it in. Maybe it's the
coffee or maybe it's the largeness of what's
happening, but you start to feel a bit scattered. It's like all your tomorrows have
bundled themselves up into one mass and
come barrelling at you like a giant bowling
ball, knocking you sideways and making
your mind shimmer. This is a great day!
What the fuck are you doing, sitting in some
park drinking a coffee? This is your future!
This is all the shit left behind! It's a fresh
start, and you should celebrate.

You walk down the high street buzzing,
your head DJ playing a vicious beat. Your
fingers clutch and unclutch the air, as you
search for something worthy of the focus of
all your hopes, delight and energy, some-

370

thing that will reflect how huge this moment is. You look at mobile phones in the window of the Carphone Warehouse. But who are you going to call? You peer at jewellery in the window of a pawn shop. But it seems too cold and finished. It's got nothing to say to you. Then, just as you turn into the little shopping centre leading off the high street, you see it, beaming at you from the window of C&A: a dress, glinting like fishscales, suspended above a pair of silver shoes. You don't really have to think about what happens next. It's like the dress lassoes you with an invisible rope and draws you in. Before you know it, you're in the store and walking to the checkout clutching it. It's £45, which is perfect — exactly the money you've got left in your pocket, barring a bit of change, which you'll use for the bus to the halfway hostel thing later. You don't even bother with trying it on. Clearly the universe meant this to be yours.

On your way out, you slip your fingers in the back straps of the silver shoes and take them with you. It isn't your intention to start your new life with a crime — you certainly don't plan on going back to the unit — but you're sure that if anyone could see inside your brain they'd realise these shoes just have to be in your story, that they have to go with that dress, that you simply have to have them as a seal on this momentous day.

The next challenge is to find a place worthy of the get-up. You scan the high street but the local Wetherspoons isn't cutting it. The same goes for the Pizza Hut and Wimpy. No: you need somewhere you can shine. Then you see it, set back a bit from the road up past Somerfield, like someone shy about being overdressed at a party: the Crown Hotel. It's got a glass front and one of those entrances with pot plants either side and a man in a penguin suit waiting to open the door. It's perfect. Just the place to spend an hour or so before you get that bus.

You hurry up the paved approach and push through the entrance without looking at the doorman, like you're important and in a hurry or maybe you're a new member of the bar staff and late for work. Whatever you make him think, it works because a minute later you're in a cubicle in the shiny lobby loos, wriggling into the dress and forcing your feet into the shoes. You've got a pot of tinted lip balm and some mascara and you dab that on and run a brush through your hair. You stand back to admire the effect in the mirror over the sinks. It's not half bad. If you turn your head to the side and squint, you could almost fool yourself you were someone else: a woman out for a business dinner or an actress on the way to a premiere. When you smile, there are even glimmers of Julia Roberts in *Pretty Woman* about you — not the street scenes in the wig but the stuff that comes later with Richard Gere. Oh yes, you're something all right.

You shove the Naf Naf bag back into the cubicle under the u-bend of the toilet. Then you head back out into the lobby and stand, surveying the scene. At the front of the hotel is a little café, where one or two couples sit forking mouthfuls of cake and pastry into their mouths and rasping their coffee cups against their saucers to stop the drips. But you're not hungry and your brain is already working fast enough as it is without more coffee to help it on its way. Straight ahead, there's a sort of lounge with brown-leather sofas arranged in rectangles and shelves of fake books lining the walls. You think about going and sitting in there for a while. But what are you going to do? Read the newspapers? Look at the rubbish art on the walls? It would feel like sitting in a nut doctor's waiting room. Right now that's the last thing you need.

A strain of saxophone and a clink of

glasses come to your ears. You turn round. Of course — the bar. Where else? You push through the glass doors and strut across the carpet, gritting your teeth against the biting of the shoe straps. The bartender eyes you warily over the glass he's polishing but you hold your nerve and look him in the eye.

'Hi,' you say. 'I'd really like a drink.'

The barman stares at you. 'Sure,' he says. 'What do you want?'

The bottles ranged on the bar shelves swim before your eyes. Back in the day you'd have gone for an Archer's and lemonade but it seems a bit childish now you actually are eighteen. You play for time.

'Umm. What cocktails do you have?'

He throws his napkin over his arm and begins to count them off on his fingers.

'Manhattan, White Russian, Sex on the Beach, Mojito —'

Mojito. You've heard of that. And even though it sounds like mosquito and you're not sure what you're going to get, you clutch on to it like a life raft.

'Mojito,' you say. 'Yes. I'll have one of those.'

The bartender nods and busies himself with some ice and leaves of mint. You hoist yourself up on to one of the stools at the bar, hooking the heels of the silver shoes over the rail below. At length, he turns round and presents you with something that looks like frogspawn in a glass.

'Do you want to pay now or put it on your room?'

You think of the £2.23 tucked into the pocket of the Naf Naf bag in the ladies' loo.

'Put it on the room,' you say.

He nods. 'What's the number?'

A prickly heat runs up your arms, but you keep your gameface on. '145?' you say.

He nods again and types it into the till.

You raise the glass, silently saluting your unknown benefactor in room 145, and take a sip. It's actually very nice. And strong. You're not used to drinking after more than two years in the unit and it gets you in a rush, sweeping through the channels of your brain in a sparkling flood. It's so nice that before you have a chance to realise it, you've drunk it all down and your straw is rasping among the ice at the bottom of the glass. You raise your eyes for another and the bartender complies with a bored expression. Just one more, you think, and then you'll hit the road.

The room starts to feel like a friendly place. Someone's turned some music on — the sort of easy-listening, Magic FM pap you'd have sneered at if Hellie tried to play it in your room at Mother's house, but you have to admit it's all right here.

You glance at the clock beside the bar. Half-past three. They'll be doing afternoon activities at the unit now — group therapy sessions and gardening. You get a pang as you think about hanging around in the kitchen for a cup of tea after an afternoon out in the cold, but you push it from you. The unit's finished. That's done. You're not going back. Now it's the rest of your life.

You take another sip of your mojito and your stomach grumbles. You realise that you're hungry and that you didn't have lunch. That was something you and Ange talked about — the importance of sticking to a routine and making sure you eat at sensible times. Only thing is you weren't hungry at lunchtime. At the unit, you didn't have to think about it. Meals just appeared and you ate them or you pushed them round the plate. There was none of this getting organised bollocks. Well, sod it. You want to eat now. You'll eat now.

You pick up the bar menu and see the words 'club sandwich'. They make you want to burst out laughing. What you're imagining is one of those chocolate join-our-Club biscuits — two of them actually — between pieces of buttered bread. You can barely contain yourself it's so hilarious. You catch the bartender's eye.

'A club sandwich, please,' you say, trying to keep a straight face.

He gives you a weird look but he turns round and bustles off through the swing doors into the kitchen all the same. A clash of pots and pans escapes into the bar, then it's calm again, with just the music piping on — Whitney Houston's 'I Will Always Love You', so tinny it sounds as though it's being played on a mouse's ghettoblaster. You swing your feet. You drum your fingers on the bar. You feel good. You feel good. You feel good.

A note of alarm sounds somewhere faintly at the back of your mind but you shrug it off. All right, so technically you know from the buzzy feeling in your fingers and the way you're still giggling to yourself over the club sandwich that you're having one of your slightly up times. You and Ange have talked about this — about what to do when they come, about the breathing exercises and focusing on slowing everything down and about how if they come more and more you should go and see a doctor because there's more medication that might help you keep it under control. The thing is, though, right now it doesn't really seem to matter.

You're actually quite enjoying it. You don't see why it's such a bad thing. All right, so you know you're speeded up and everything's a bit hectic in your head, but if you don't mind, you don't see why anyone else should. All it is, is like someone's pressed the fast-forward button on your life, that's all. Like someone's put your brain on a rollercoaster or set your mind to the spin cycle. Sure, you wouldn't want to be like this all the time, but for now, today, it's fun. You feel powerful. You feel capable of achieving anything. It's good. In fact, you suspect the reason why people like Ange are so down on it is because they're jealous, because they're scared. They can't have it so they don't want you to. They're frightened of your potential when you're in this state, like you have access to reserves of energy they can only dream of. Selfish, that's what they are. Stealers of fun. That's why you stopped taking the meds a few weeks back, flushing them down the toilet after breakfast: you didn't want to be controlled by other people's fear.

A man and woman walk into the bar and sit down at one of the tables across the other side of the room. You stare at them angrily, watching for signs that they are out to contain you, but they just talk between themselves and don't seem to notice you at all. Good.

The club sandwich comes and you wolf it down, even though it's crap. You even eat the garnish on the side — the dried-up cucumber and tomato cut to look like a flower. Then you order another drink on room 145. The alcohol streams through you, bearing up the bright boat of your mind on its oily sea. You look at the clock and find it's suddenly after five. Also, there are other people round about you now that you hadn't noticed before.

One of them, a middle-aged man in a suit, lumbers up on the stool next to you and gives you a fat grin.

'Here for the conference?' he says, inclining his head towards a board rigged up in front of a pair of glass-panelled doors that you hadn't previously clocked. 'Boundless possibilities: middle management and the information superhighway', it reads.

'Nah,' you say.

The man nods. 'Me neither,' he says. 'At least, the wife thinks I am, but I'm not if you know what I mean.'

You raise your eyebrows and try to look wise.

'Drink?' says the man.

You shrug. Sure, why not. Give poor old

145 a break.

He orders something sour and unpleasant, but you drink it all the same, feeling his gaze running up and down your body as you do. Something about him — the red-rimmed eyes, perhaps, or the way he fumbles with the swizzle stick — tells you that this isn't his first drink either.

When you put the glass down, he says, 'OK, cut to the chase. How much?'

For a moment, you think he's asking you to guess the price of the drink. But just as you open your mouth to answer, another possible interpretation swims up from the depths of your mind. You remember Hailey the girl in the unit; you remember what she used to do before she got caught up with that snuff film. You sit twisting your glass on the bar so that the wet ring at the bottom of it spreads across the wooden surface. An instinct to spit in his face streaks through you, but you rein it in: if you learned anything during your time at the unit it's that it pays to keep your cards close to your chest. An idea occurs to you.

'Fifteen hundred,' you say.

Even buzzed up as you are, you know it is an obscene amount. But he doesn't flinch. 'How about for one hour?' he says.

'Fifteen hundred,' you say again, scenting

an opportunity.

He gives a low whistle. 'Classy girl,' he says. 'Well, I hope I'll be getting something extra special for that.' He looks round. 'OK then,' he says. 'I've got a room upstairs — a suite actually — come on.'

In the lift, panic flushes through you briefly as you wonder what special services he has in mind. But you keep your face blank and don't give anything away. You shoot him a bored look as the doors slide open on the fifth floor, like you do this all the time, like in your mind you're already finished and on to the next gig.

It turns out you've got nothing to worry about: it's all over in a few puffs and he peels off the money from a wad of fifties in his jacket pocket and hands it over without you asking. He makes you feel a bit stupid actually with how honest he is — you realise you should have got the financials locked in before. Like a real pro. Like in *Pretty Woman.*

You think about hanging around and helping yourself to some more of the cash, but it seems a bit harsh, so as soon as he starts to snore you straighten your dress, stick the heels on and stalk back out to the lift. When you get to the entrance lobby there's an argument going on with someone at the front desk. A couple of staff members are staring blankly at a computer screen as a man with a cricket jumper slung over his shoulders gesticulates in rage.

'But I never ordered a club sandwich!' he says as you walk by.

You keep on going, out on to the marble steps. The doorman gives you a smile and suddenly you're in the street again and it's dark, but the lights are so bright that for a moment it seems like the sky has come down to meet the earth and you are walking among the stars. You stroll down the high street, looking that way and this: McDonald's, HMV, W. H. Smith, Mothercare, Radio Rentals. It's all here. So much life. So much possibility. In the face of it, the halfway house is just a speck; one dot among a hundred billion. A green glow appears up ahead, a big glass wall: the bus station. Coaches lined up with all sorts of promises written on them 'Glasgow', 'Plymouth', 'Southampton'. You wander in and stroll along their ranks. At random, you stop by one and look up. 'London' it proclaims. In a second you're inside and handing over a fifty to the driver. He raises his eyebrows and makes a show of grubbing around his cashbox for change, but the dress keeps him quiet and he doesn't say a word.

You go and sit down on one of the red-and-purple-patterned seats, drumming your fingers on the seal along the edge of the window to make the seconds pass. Other people get on and choose their places but you don't look at them. They're not in this story. You're writing it and you've decided the characters in advance. You have control. It feels good.

It's only when the coach rumbles into life and the backdrop of the bus station slides away that you remember you left the bag in the toilet cubicle at the hotel. The knowledge sinks into you like a rag in a dirty pond, leaving no impression. You shrug. You don't care: it already belongs to someone else.

41

The hinges groaned as she turned the key and pushed her way in. She walked through to the living room and stood in the middle of the space looking around: armchair, scarred table, battered gas fire. Its bareness was shocking. It seemed smaller too, as though without her it had shrunk, like the skin on the bones of the dead fox she'd discovered in the park as a child.

She put her hand in her coat pocket and felt the handful of notes there — the remains of the contents of Hellie's bag. The old impulse to go to the corner shop for vodka flamed briefly and guttered. It seemed threadbare, not enough to lose herself in any more, not enough to blot out the image of Nick's face as it had been that morning. She slumped, defeated, into the armchair. Something crackled beneath her. Reaching down the side of the cushion, she pulled out the envelope addressed to Helen Sallis in Hellie's rounded scrawl.

She stared at it. The blandness of the writing was maddening — people pleasing, crafted for top marks, contrived. It was the way Hellie had been from the beginning, or from the start of everything that mattered at least. It was her game plan spelled out. And yet Mother, Akela and now Nick thought Smudge was the one scheming and plotting. They thought that she, this mess, was the one setting out to do people harm.

In a gust of rage, Smudge snatched up the envelope and slit its guts. Scraps of paper slewed out on to the carpet. For a moment she stared down at them confused: receipts mingled with architectural plans and pages of TV scripts. She bent down and picked up an old shopping list. Milk, bread, nappies, aubergines.

Puzzled, she turned the paper over. A cold thrill passed through her. Written from edge to edge, the back of the list was covered in a jagged, savage little hand; a hand that had scrambled its way across sheet after sheet, stabbing holes and ripping slashes where 'i's had to be dotted and 't's crossed; a hand that had scrawled arrows and squiggled stars and contrived a baffling system of numbers and letters to show how the chunks of text were linked. It filled the back of every last scrap: urgent, surging, running on. It tripped over itself in its eagerness to express as biro after biro sputtered and gave out. It demanded to be read and defied decoding. It was as familiar as it was strange. It was as unmistakable as it was illegible. And its manic style had a meaning all of its own.

42

You take a room above a drycleaner's just off the Edgware Road. If anyone asks, you say your name is Veronica — you don't know why, you just like how improbable it is. It cracks you up seeing people struggle to fit such a knick-knacks and pot-pourri name to you, a hard-faced girl with MON-STER tattooed on her head. It makes you sound like that woman in the BBC sitcom, the one who's always answering the phone in a poncy voice and singing at the frightened neighbour.

Mostly, though, no one does ask. The people in the lodging house don't hang around. Almost every morning there's the sound of bags and boxes being dragged up or down the staircase, gouging the Anaglypta on the walls. Sometimes in the middle of the night too. Most of them are foreign, from what you can make out — people far from home, on the way to elsewhere. This place is just a stop on a long journey for them. Ask them about it next week and they won't remember a thing.

The furniture is like that too: battered and scratched with handles snapped off and broken drawers. It's crap chucked together any-old-how, all its goodness long since used up. Once, a child used to keep her toys in the little white cupboard in the corner with transfer stickers of fairies on its door. Now, the cabinet groans under the weight of clothes and bags that are too big for it. Tinkerbell is scuffed blind.

You go out when you want to, walk around the streets. You map London one footstep at a time: the Houses of Parliament, Oxford Street, Piccadilly Circus, Trafalgar Square. Sometimes you go into galleries and museums and spend afternoons in the reverent hush, drifting from one display to the next. You stare at paintings and follow the lines, unpicking the thinking of the maniacs who obsessed over putting them together centuries ago. You spot the flaws — the sea that looks like fixed resin rather than sloshing liquid, the hand fumbled. A lot of them, you realise, are rubbish. Confidence tricks thrown together to take people in, stuff any idiot could do. But now and then something leaps out and shocks you with the purity, the brilliance, of what it is. In particular, there's this painting in the National Gallery of just a table with some fruit on it in front of a window open to a landscape outside. Anyone else would have homed in on the landscape, but this artist doesn't do that. He leaves it there, suggested with a few rough brushstrokes, and instead focuses on the fruit and the crumby plate left by someone who has just pushed their chair back and gone out of the room. But even so the way the light glints on the grapes and the plum lets you know it's morning and makes you feel the breeze blowing in at the window, bringing with it birdsong and the whisper of the sea. You stand looking at that painting for hours, right until they put an announcement out on the Tannoy saying the gallery is closing in fifteen minutes. And when you have to be guided away, muttering, by a security guard, the image stays etched on your mind. It's the simplicity of it. That's what gets you — how obvious and yet how right the artist's technique is. By focusing on something off to the side of what really matters, he manages to bring out things he could never paint. He knows the truth is round the edges, in the things you never look straight in the face.

When you need money, you put the dress

on and go and hang around in hotel bars. You charge much less than you did that first, giddy time — you quickly get wise to your market value — but you still make plenty. You forget the men as soon as their room doors shut behind you. They blend into one faceless figure — interchangeable, unremarkable, all the same. No one is special, you learn. Not underneath it all. When you strip reality down to its boxer shorts, people are boring and predictable.

You don't trust the lodging house — the lock on your door gives under the slightest pressure — so you rip a hole in the lining of an anorak you find in a skip and stuff the proceeds in there. You reckon there's probably less chance of you leaving it somewhere in one of your times than there is of someone coming in and going through your room when you're out. Not that it matters much either way: if you need more cash you'll just go out and make some more.

Some days, you don't get out of bed. You lie under the frayed counterpane as the beam of light that comes through the gap in the curtains makes its way around the room, listening to traffic outside: the car horns, the farts of buses, the sirens that rake the air. You know once the noise reaches a certain pitch and the light hits the chest of drawers that the day is lost, that you'll stay there until the sounds ebb away and the city empties of life, and sleep creeps out of the orange shadows of the night to drag you away.

But there are times when energy prickles in your fingertips and you feel your brain gathering speed, picking up momentum like a bicycle barrelling down a hill. Those are the moments when your mind flits to pages of blank paper and you find yourself thinking of trips to the art shop you spotted in a side street a couple of streets away. Those are the occasions when images invade your brain and your hand fidgets with the urge to get them down. A couple of times you think about giving in, about letting yourself run riot with shapes and colours. It would feel, you think, like nicotine to a smoker or alcohol to someone addicted to booze. But you always stop yourself before it's too late. You draw the line at drawing a line. Because you are not here — that's the truth of it. None of this is real. You don't exist and so nothing can touch you — not the past, not the future, not any of the men who pay to arch and twist above you. You are out of it all — floating in a blind, white mist rolling in off a boundless sea. You are immune. And

you prove that to yourself every day by
refusing to leave a mark.

43

(2)I was thinking about that time in the park the time we were riding down the hill on the park ~~you were riding down I was riding down~~ was it you or was it me I get confused sometimes do you get that? **a** Dad was there. ~~Father.~~ **b** I'll call him Dad. **c** Father was telling us about free-wheeling, putting your foot on the pedals and just coasting with the hill but the way he was explaining it was so chaotic so full of other things that it was hard to follow. It made no sense to little-girl brains. ~~So you didn't get it I didn't get it~~ **d** So there we were you riding down me riding down one of us maybe both (except it couldn't be both because one was watching, I have the pictures from one watching head) little legs going faster and faster round and round grass the air squinting against the sun the hill tilting away and suddenly . . . airborne . . . flying like a kite . . . the trees . . . before the bump and scrape of the ground. And then the other one running — HERE'S WHAT I REMEMBER MOST, I JUST DON'T REMEMBER WHO — getting there before Father-Dad. Little arms going round shuddering sobs. All right. All right. It's going to be all right. Love. That's the point. Love. I should write a poem about it I could write a poem about it if the words didn't come so fast I would write a poem about it. All I can do is hold on to the handlebars and see where it will take me next. It's tiring but it's a fantastic ride like cycling among the stars like swinging by the moon. You understand, don't you? What was I saying?

a — I don't get confused. I know exactly who you are. I know who I am. It's just sometimes, looking back, the past gets blurred. Back when we were really young. Before everything.

b — Mother always called him Father but what did we call him we don't have a name for him just an empty space.

c — That time (this I remember, this I've got all straight) I told you Horace was our father was a lie. I knew what was real. I was just locked in the story. I couldn't let things be another way. You were never locked in the story. Not really. That was the thing about you.

d — This is where it gets weird again. I see it from my head and I see it from your head. Seeing it from both heads can't be right, but my brain uses them both as though both of them are part of me, as though both stories are mine. It makes me scared sometimes. It makes me sad. And sometimes I like it.

(x) I sat by his feet. His shoes were scuffed. One of the laces had broken and he had replaced it with string and that was nearly broken too. I sat there for hours.

(1) Hello. So I found you. You were in the newspaper — one of those local ones we use to research stories for the show sometimes. Human interest extreme makeovers near-death experiences. That sort of thing. There was some picture of a community garden and runner beans and there you were and it said a different name underneath, but I could see it was you. The M from your tattoo was poking out from under your hair. It was ~~lucky~~ lucky in a way (that's not the right word) because I'd been wanting to speak to you ever since . . . well, you know (well you don't that's kind of the point). We haven't heard from you since . . . well, you know (and this one you do know

and that's also kind of the point). After I saw you in the picture, it was easy. I just got one of the researchers on to it. Kids just out of university — paid to turn people up for us all the time. I don't know how they do it. Facebook or something, except I'm pretty sure you're not on that. Think she thought I was mad wanting some care-in-the-community case tracked down. Ha. Many a true word. Did it, though — phone number, address, the works. Turns out no one's hidden now not truly not any more. How am I? I am living a colossal bluff. There. They think I'm all surface. Like all of them. Sometimes I hate them for how stupid they are and sometimes it makes me glad. Sometimes I'm frightened that if I let them in on what's going on inside the galaxy in my head they will want to contain it and shrink it down make it manageable like they tried to do to you. You weren't afraid though were you you just went right ahead and hang the consequences (no pun intended) you were always braver I miss you every day and every day I'm glad you're not here. It's almost as much as I miss ~~the baby Emily~~ her. Except with her I never wish she wasn't here she was not old enough to develop a personality and get complicated. With her it's like a limb's gone like they've ripped something out and carried it away. With you it's like half the story's missing the colour the intrigue. It's safer that way I have control no one's there to answer back or contradict there is one version but the version is flat and sometimes I wish it would throb and twist and surprise sometimes I'm frightened my telling has sucked all the life out of it. Losing her has given me another half story and words not to tell. I am living a television existence all neat and edited fobbing people off with elevenses and clever storage solutions and the lunchtime news. I think how it would look through your mind, your eyes, if you were here. Do I seem arrogant to you? Sometimes I think I must be the most arrogant shit on the planet and then other times I think the world really is as small and boring as it seems. Other people just don't seem to have as many layers. Nick is so simple and I hate simple. They seem happier with less all except you and we know what happened there or at least we know my version. There's an empty space where yours should be. Write back. Will you. Do I want you to.

(4) Remember that trip to Thorpe Park. Horace bought us both elephants and you had a tantrum. I think it was before every-

thing. But Horace was there so it couldn't have been. Still, I think it was before I became me and you became you. One of us was sick. Do you remember? Which one?

P.S. None of this might be true tomorrow.

(5) We packed up the car. For once Mother was laughing. She was wearing a dress with big white flowers that fluttered when she whirled. There was a lot of whirling. She never wore it after that. Not that I remember — do you? **a** Driving, talking, laughing. Tea at Auntie Bessie's. Something stupid with T-shirts in a shop. Colours I never wanted. Here's what I remember: you and me and Father-Dad skipping along a street. Laughing and laughing, going faster and faster. And then it was too fast and there was too much laughing and suddenly we were whirling around on a roundabout, around and about, feeling sick, and he would not stop laughing. And we looked at each other, you and I, as he whooped and caterwauled and we knew something was broken. And that was when you started to cry. This time it was definitely you. I remember, because I let go of the roundabout with one hand and reached out to comfort you. I remember the feel of your cold arm and Father's laughter singing like the wind in our ears as

he kept on yanking us round, faster, faster, more, more. Too much fun I shouted this is too much there should be less fun than this! But he wouldn't stop and all we could do was grip each other and the metal bars and stare at the middle of the roundabout, the still point around which everything else whirled. Again. Again. Again! It's all right, I whispered. It's all right. I knew we just had to get through the fun. I don't know if you heard you were shaking so hard. But here's the funny thing: when I remember that day now there's a time my brain goes back to before the roundabout, a moment where the road was clear and the laughing was wild and free but still with normal in sight. The three of us skipping and the sky huge above us. I think there was a bird flying and there was a feeling of space. It comes to me sometimes in dreams. It catches me when the wind blows in the horse chestnut trees and a balloon floats over from the park, like it's doing now above the skylight, the red ribbon dragging across the glass so that maybe I could open it and catch it if I move fast. And I know I'm not imagining it. I know that was real. We did not make that up. And I think sometimes if I could freeze my life and pick out a moment in the procession of days to go back to and inhabit for all time, I might stop it there.

a — I saw a dress like it in a charity shop up on the high street and I nearly bought it. But then I thought, what was I going to do? Wear it and be Mother? That would be insane.

(3) What if it never really happened? Have you ever asked yourself that? Have you ever sat down, looked at yourself in the mirror and told yourself that maybe that really is who you are? ~~Maybe we never swapped and this is all in my head~~ I try that game all the time when they're fussing over me in the green room, the power brush going, the conversation droning on — where are you going on your holidays?

What are you up to on the weekend? a — For fuck's sake. Sometimes I fantasise about breaking things smearing lipstick over the mirror, exploding powder pots up the wall. I'd like to see their faces. But they don't have rock stars in daytime TV so instead I sit and smile and have another cup of tea. Sometimes I think everybody is sleepwalking, just sleepwalking. I want to stand up and scream. Am I making sense?

a — What you're dealing with here is a person caught up in a world where extreme artifice insinuates itself almost everywhere. Nothing is as it appears. I am not saying this to be arrogant or difficult. **b** — I am simply stating facts.

b — If you ask people about me they will tell you that I am one of the loveliest presenters to work with. I have made a point of being that. Always. I have studied what people like and made myself fit it. It is one of my special gifts. Again, I am not saying this to be arrogant or difficult. I just need you to know the reality of who you're dealing with — a person who is <u>extremely conscious</u> of everything.

(6) The puppet theatre. He bought it and put it in the garden. There were going to be shows and shows and shows. All summer it sat there, going mouldy under Mother's dirty looks. By the end, there was green stuff on the curtains and black spots up the walls. Eventually the rag and bone man came and threw it on the back of his truck with a thud and a crack.

(xx) What I can't write about is her hands. How delicate they were, how soft, with the little fingers you were afraid of cutting every time you clipped the nails. Her mouth too — always pouting. She had a birthmark on her left foot. They talked about removing it, but I said no. I wanted her to stay. I wanted to keep her just as she was. That was all I wanted.

44

On, on. An hour spent staring at a caterpillar in a park. Another hour watching your feet. Look up and it's dark. Whee! Look up and it's light again. So much to do, so powerful. You sit making plans, hunched over tables in cafes, slurping down coffees, teas, hot chocolates, whatever they'll bring — again, again. People try to talk to you at times. You smile indulgently at them, wondering how they can be happy with so inefficient a method as words for expressing the universe within, all those rampant colours. There must be so little of them. They need to see how far you can see in comparison. You must find a way of lending them your eyes. This is for the good of humanity.

You find a stall on Portobello Market selling postcards of the work of Van Gogh. Of course. Suddenly the message left for you in the starry picture in the director's office makes sense — even fuddled on drugs as you were at the time, before you kicked them in the run up to your release, you knew it couldn't be hanging there by chance. You peel off notes from the wodge of cash in the anorak and buy the lot. These you distribute willy-nilly to everyone passing in the street. Some of the people assume they're flyers and cast them aside. *Sunflowers* in the gutter. *Chair with Pipe* beneath a bicycle's wheels. No matter. There will be such casualties along the way. The truth is, no one is capable of apprehending the genius of Van Gogh's use of colour and lines the way you do. If they did they'd all kill themselves instantly because they'd know their lives could never be anywhere near as valuable. That's why they need you: the intermediary, the prophet. Someone who can stand as a filter between them and ultimate art, who can open their minds to the power of such skill and yet protect them from the despair of it all along. They're fragile, poor things: they can't see how little stands between them and self-destruction. Between *Cash in the Attic* and suicide there is only the thinnest wisp of self-delusion. Thank God you're here.

What next? What next? Ah yes, a busker. Expressive dance. You throw yourself into it. Your body becomes lithe, snake-like. A crowd gathers. At the end, they applaud, as well they might. What they don't realise, of course, is that they should be throwing themselves at your feet in adulation. Not because of you, you understand — you're clear-eyed about your marginal role in all this — but because of the power of the universe that has been channelling itself through you, transforming you into a cipher for the original life force. That's what they should be recognising. That's what they should break down, weeping, in awe of. But of course they don't see it, poor, dear, dull, blunt-minded things. And on balance perhaps it's better that they don't. Else how would the post get delivered? The dirty clothes washed?

Speaking of which, might a laundrette be . . . No! The Natural History Museum! Of course! It's all coming together now. Funny you didn't work it out sooner. But that's the nature of your brilliance, you see, it's always there, turning over beneath the bonnet, steering you in directions calculated to leave you breathless with delight. Excellent mind! And here of course there's so much richness, so many connections to forge. Great discoveries shimmering round every pillar — only the dexterity of a mind like yours needed to make the links that have eluded scientists for centuries. In, then.

Oh yes, this is the place. Lots of ideas ripe for linking up here. Wander among the bones. The giant Diplodocus skeleton, make for that. Ribs like roof rafters. The inspiration, probably, for building as we know it. We all think we're so original, but the truth of it is most of our inventions are right there in nature all along if we'd only deign to look. On then. Glass cabinets. Teeth. Stuffed birds. A school party behind one of them. Exercise books, worksheets. That smell they have: sandwiches, crisps and cheese. One of them staring up at you from the other side of the cabinet, open-mouthed.

An idea takes you. This'll learn him. Quick as a flash you're round the corner and staring down at the child face to face. Ha-ha!

But this is no anonymous boy. He's older, taller, darker-haired than when you saw him last, but unmistakable nonetheless.

'Richard,' you say.

The boy stares up at you.

'Come away, Pavel,' calls a teacher, looking at you over her glasses. 'Leave the lady in peace.'

But you're not fooled. 'Richard,' you say again.

Richard frowns up at you and shuffles from foot to foot. His eyes are closer together than they used to be and he has grown weasely and sallow. There is a new birthmark on his chin, but that doesn't throw you off. You'd know him anywhere. He coughs as if in confirmation. The teacher bustles over, takes his hand and pulls him away, and as she does so, panic — oily, inky and suffocating — begins to ooze in at the doors of the gallery, flooding up to your nose until you can't breathe. You see the dastardly, treacherous plot, all its sordid machinery laid bare. Mother, Akela, the unit working everything from behind the scenes. They are all in on it, you realise, all trying to lure you into a trap, with Richard as bait. They have sent him here to spy on you and report back.

Fear jabs you in the heart. You have to get out of here. You turn and run, swiping someone in the stomach as you pass. A yell. No time. The exit. Somewhere on the other side of this rabbit warren of rooms. Signs, always fucking signs. Why should you give a crap about early man? The polar regions? You just want to get the hell out. Ah, there it is, the door. Light outside. Thank fuck. You lunge through the barriers, setting off an alarm. 'Excuse me, ma'am,' a voice calls, but you are long gone. They can tidy up the fag ends of today, you're already on to tomorrow.

You don't stop until you're on the pavement. Then you put a hand to your head. Think, think: a plan is what you need. You look around. The coaches line up at the end of the road, sucking in tourists. Of course. Away again. You hurry down to the one at the end of the row. Manchester, it promises in red, lighted letters across the top of its windscreen. Manchester, then. Yes, why not? It's half full but you push your way in among a crowd of Americans keeping the driver so busy with their stories of Lysester Square that he doesn't see you squeezing past. You plump for an empty double seat near the back and mutter to yourself in an ominous way like a mad person whenever anyone comes near. It works: everyone leaves you alone. In a little while, the bus revs up and sighs its way out into the evening traffic. You watch as London slides past in the twilight, buildings dwindling as the suburbs roll past. Then it's the grey verges and litter of the motorway and headlights flashing from oncoming cars on the other carriageway.

45

What Smudge hadn't been prepared for were the movements. Coma, she'd thought, meant out of action: suspended animation like in one of those sci-fi films where bodies hang lifeless in capsules waiting for someone to flick the switch to bring them back to life. But Hellie was far from motionless. Every so often, her hands twitched the line plugged into her veins, her eyelids flickered, her lips churned above the plastic tube connected to her throat, carrying air from the machine hissing and sighing by her bed. Now and then she even wrinkled her nose, as if objecting to the strong scent drifting from the pots and vases of flowers on the locker on the far side of the room.

Smudge found the jerks and twitches unnerving. They made it seem that Hellie might emerge from unconsciousness at any minute, so that if you didn't keep watching her you'd find her eyes suddenly fixed on you. Expressions scudded across her face: irritated, baffled, frustrated, as though she were locked in a long argument with an official who may or may not deign to let her back into the world. Most of the expressions were adult — a medley from the tougher human-interest interviews and phone-ins Helen Sallis conducted sometimes on her morning show — but every so often something younger and more unguarded would creep in. The little-girl-lost look of the old Ellie hesitating on the edge of a dubious game surfaced from time to time. Now and then the trembling pout that promised tears wobbled to the fore, sending time ricocheting back and forth between the decades, shuffling emotions like a deck of cards.

'Hellie,' said Smudge.

The face winced.

'Hellie,' she said again, louder this time.

The face stayed still. Something between a grunt and burp escaped from the mouth.

Smudge put out a finger and traced the line of her sister's cheek: smooth and peachy even after four months in a hospital bed. She looked for the suffering of the letters: lines and shadows to reflect the anguish and grief, but all was smooth. Untrammelled. Beautiful. My face, she couldn't help think-

410

ing, if things had gone differently and life had flowed another way. A spark of the old longing flared, the nights staring down at Hellie in the bedroom at Mother's house. She thought for a second about jabbing her nail in and yanking it, feeling the skin tear. She thought about grasping a hand and pulling the fingers back until she heard a crack. She leant down, wanting to be cruel.

'I had sex with him, you know,' she hissed suddenly. 'I had sex with Nick. We both enjoyed it. What you took away from me, I'm taking from you. It's my time now.'

Ellie's face lolled unmoved on the pillow. Smudge wanted to slap it. She raised a hand and the pages of the letter rustled in the pocket of her coat. The thought of the scraps of skittish writing made her dizzy. She turned abruptly and left the room. She strode down the corridor, fighting nausea, squinting against the glare of the fluorescent lights which seemed to be trying to bore its way into her brain. On the desk of the vacant nurses' station around the corner five doors along, she discovered a ham sandwich wrapped in cling film. This she snatched up, unwrapped and stuffed into her mouth, gulping chunks of bread and meat down unchewed, determined to deaden the surge and twist of her insides.

When she got back to Hellie's room, she heard a voice and ducked behind the door-jamb, peering through the crack.

'Now this is an interesting case,' said the speaker, an olive-skinned, middle-aged man in a white coat. 'RTA. Comatose for four months.'

There was a group of youngsters clustered around the bed, clutching notepads. She saw one of them catch sight of Hellie's face, and mouth something to a girl with plaits. Indifferent to the frisson of excitement in the room, the doctor continued his account of Hellie's condition. Speaking in a soft voice, he gave a brisk rundown of her injuries, in which the word 'contusion' featured heavily, and summarised the readings on the monitor. Ms Sallis had been put on auxiliary ventilator support, he explained, because of a chest infection and they had inserted something called a peg. Then he turned his attention to the figure on the bed.

'Unlike the patient next door, you'll see that Ms Sallis exhibits signs of agitation — twitching, blinking, even involuntary groans on occasion,' he said. 'These are the sort of signs that often give visitors the impression that the patient could be about to wake up. In fact, the reality is rather different and in

Ms Sallis's case these are largely due to agitation caused by hypoxia from the pulmonary infection, which we are attempting to bring under control with intravenous antibiotics. Ms Sallis's Glasgow Coma Score is very low — no more than four — as you'll see if I administer a few of the key tests.'

The doctor leant in and rubbed his knuckles over Ellie's breastbone. Her arms jerked straight with the palms turned out. He then shone a light into her eyes and turned her head from side to side before pulling back the lower section of her blanket, tapping each of her knees and scratching the soles of her feet.

'Decerebrate extensor posturing in response to noxious stimuli,' intoned the doctor. 'Doll's eye reflexes preserved, which suggests some brain-stem function, but sluggish pupillary responses. Brisk reflexes with extensor plantar responses. All in all, a poor long-term prognosis.'

As if in response to the doctor's impertinence, Ellie frowned. A ripple of awkward laughter spread round the group.

'But,' said the girl with plaits after it had subsided, 'sorry, Dr Jalil — aren't there instances of people with this level of function waking up?'

'You're quite right,' said Dr Jalil, replacing the blanket. 'There are. That's why we don't turn off all the machines and walk away. That's why we give the drugs to treat the infections. But the truth is, in cases such as this, the chance of a return to consciousness is extremely low. Probably less than nought point one per cent. Particularly after the length of time we are talking about now. And that's not even taking into account the level of brain damage that may have occurred. The reality is that sooner or later you have to look at the probabilities and ask yourself how much longer it's worth sustaining this level of existence and combating infections rather than letting them take their course.'

There was an uncomfortable silence for a moment. The group stared at Hellie in the bed.

'Right, that's enough for today,' said Dr Jalil. 'You'll be needing to get to your next session. I'll see most of you in the lecture theatre on Thursday.'

The students shuffled out, whispering and then talking as they went up the corridor. A laugh drifted back as the double doors slid to. Dr Jalil emerged from the room fiddling with a Parker pen clipped to the pocket of his white coat.

'Thank you,' he said distractedly, seeming to mistake her for one of the students. Smudge pressed against the wall to let him past.

After he'd gone she went in and over to the bed once more. The blanket was wrinkled where Dr Jalil had lifted it and she smoothed it and tucked it under until it matched the other side. Beneath the covers, Hellie looked smaller than she had before, as though the consultant and his students had taken part of her away with them, and Smudge felt a blast of indignation on her behalf.

'Don't worry, they've gone, Hellie,' she said, stroking her sister's tubed and taped hand where it lay on the covers. 'It's just me now.'

For a second the hand jerked and gripped her fingers. Then it slid away.

46

As soon as you arrive in Manchester, you feel better. The air seems clearer, the pavements solid. Your brain stops spinning and rotates in time with the rest of the world. Everything is in sync. Only a vestige of the powerful feeling remains, spurring you on, making you optimistic, putting haloes of possibility around everything.

You love the feel of the city. The big Victorian buildings converted into nightclubs and funky bars. The Gothic churches with their tall spires, like fingers raised in warning. The large squares and grand terracotta facades. It feels grounded and real and sure about what it is: a place for a fresh start.

With most of what's left from the stash in the anorak, you take a room in a lodging house near the city centre. Unlike the dive in London, this is a proper place with rules and curfews and breakfast served between seven and nine. It's run by a woman called

Beryl, a former nurse. There are fresh flowers in a vase on the hall table and homemade biscuits in a jar in the kitchen and it smells of citrus.

It's touch and go whether Beryl will take you without references — it's not her normal policy, as she mentions several times. Even after you tell her that you, Elisabeth, have escaped from an abusive relationship, she still looks at you askance. Nevertheless, over the second cup of tea around the table with its blue-checked cloth, something in her relents and, glancing up at the small cross nailed above the back door, she agrees to let you stay on the strength of two weeks' rent paid up front in cash.

'There you are, Elisa,' she says, leading you upstairs and opening a door on to a room under the eaves. 'Will this be all right for you?'

It's big and airy, with views out to the edge of the city, and the bed is made with fresh, white linen — you can smell its cleanness from where you stand.

'Yes, thank you,' you say. 'This will do just fine.'

Beryl's routine rubs off on you. Before long, you're getting up at 6.30 a.m., having an early breakfast and heading out to explore the city as the rush-hour builds. You find an art shop in a back street not far from the imposing town hall and this time you treat yourself to a pad of thick, creamy paper and a fistful of pencils and charcoals. These you take out with you, spending hours here and there roughing out the things that you see: the moulding on the corner of a building; the face of a newspaper vendor in a kiosk near the station; an umbrella dropped in front of the elaborate fire station.

When it rains, you take yourself to a cafe in the new glazed, circular shopping centre called the Barnacle up near the train station. You sit at a table by one of the angular panes of glass on the top floor and go over what you've done, finessing and refining, doing things again. It's the first time you've worked in this way. Before, you always dashed sketches off in a blur, when the enthusiasm for it possessed you, barely looking at the results once the urge passed. Now, you start to realise, the looking back is everything. The process of sifting and realignment is what makes the work whole, what makes it live. And behind every broken, botched attempt there is usually something worth digging into and drawing out.

You enjoy the rhythm of these days. But as time goes by and the money dwindles, you find the thought of the long term nags at you. You know you wouldn't want to go back to how things were in London. There is something different and pure about where you are now that you wouldn't want to tarnish by bringing that other life in. It feels a very long time ago. You are not the person that you were back then, all those tens of hours before.

Knowing that, you set your mind to trying to find other ways of bringing money in. You ask in the cafe at the Barnacle and it turns out there's a vacancy on the cleaning team that scours the shopping centre after-hours. The money's rubbish and the guy who fixes it is clearly dodgy, taking a cut before giving you and the other women, who don't speak English, your pay in cash, but you don't argue — anything to get started on building life another way, on protecting this clear, precious space you've found.

Except it turns out cleaning doesn't suit you. You're much slower than the others and when the boss comes to inspect your work, he's not happy. You only last three shifts before he tells you not to come back.

Next, you try your hand at washing up for one of the curry houses two streets down from Beryl's, but it's the same story: your mind wanders as you stand with your hands in the suds and before you know it, the kitchen staff are gathered around you, glaring. You overhear two women talking in the newsagent's about a pub looking for someone to collect the empty glasses and occasionally lend a hand behind the bar. You think you might be quite good at this and when you pop in they like the fact that you've no issues with it being under the table and off the books. You're hired on the spot. But the first evening, something terrible happens: you're carrying a tray of glasses round to the dishwasher when you hear a couple arguing over in the far corner by the pinball machine.

'Just get the bloke who does the fake IDs to knock you one up,' says the man. 'I don't see what the problem is. Hell, go the full nine yards and get a passport. I've seen the ones he's done. They're really good.'

But the woman's not having it. 'Nah,' she says loudly, sweeping her hand out in a way that suggests she's had more than a few to drink. 'I don't trust him. Something about the eyes. He looks like a wolf.'

And that's it. Before you know it, you've dropped the glasses. There are shards all over the floor and your shoes and the whole pub has turned to look at you, but all you can see is the snarl of his face jerking furiously above you and all you can hear is his flat, dead voice in your ears. And you know it can't be him. You know it's paranoia, some vestige of the chaos you're trying to leave behind. You know your brain does this: conjuring up people where they have no right to be. But all the same you can't shake the trembling that grips you. When they come to tell you it's all right and everybody makes mistakes, you make a break for it and run out of the door even though it's half an hour 'til the end of your shift. Bollocks to the money. You know you won't be going back there again.

One day, walking past the art shop, you notice a small design studio next door with a gallery attached. The door is open and there's a sign in the window: receptionist wanted, enquire within. You think about it for a moment. Reception work. That's answering the phone, right? Maybe it's something you could do. You wander in, but it's the middle of the day and no one's around, so you spend some time staring at the pieces on the walls, a range of artworks with commercial twists: air fresheners nestled in the creepers of a sprawling vine; cows with cartons where their udders should be; a washing machine with a television set cracked and tossed in the drum. It's edgy and you like it: a sort of advertising-art mash-up.

Behind the gallery space, a large open-plan studio stretches away to the back of the building — all wooden floors and bare brickwork. There are vast tables and easels with works in progress clamped to them and huge angle-poise lamps positioned above, as though the whole room were some giant's desk. Curious, you wander off towards the tables and pick your way among them, looking at the pictures. Some of them are really good; some need a bit of work. At one particularly cluttered workbench, you stop and look at a sketch of a skeletal, ragged bird with a tube of toothpaste clutched in its beak. The bringing together of two such disparate things is pleasing, but the composition is all wrong. The bird, you realise, should be looking straight at you, its head cocked quizzically on one side in that way they do, not staring off somewhere to the right as it is now. Your fingers itch to pick up a pencil and fix it.

As you're looking, a door opens at the back of the room and footsteps approach.

'Oh, thank God,' says a voice. 'You're here.'

You turn to see a tall, blond man in an

open-necked shirt advancing towards you.

'Trudy, isn't it?' he says, holding out a hand.

'Um —'

'Anton,' says the man, indicating himself. 'The agency said you'd be here two hours ago.'

'Sorry,' you begin, gesturing vaguely towards the sign. 'I —'

'Never mind that now,' he says, passing a hand over his forehead. 'We're in a crisis. The senior designer's gone AWOL and there's been no one to answer the phones. Reception's this way.'

He ushers you over to a table by the door.

'Computer, phone, coffee machine,' he says, flicking a hand in the direction of each object. 'All the usual things. You'll be all right, won't you? Of course you will. Thanks so much. Lifesaver. I can't tell you.'

'I think —' you say. Then it hits you: this could be it, the chance you've been looking for. You decide not to blow it just yet. Instead, you close your mouth and smile.

'Lifesaver,' says Anton again. He strides back across the studio and into a room beyond. You catch a glimpse of a large window looking out over a yard full of bins. The door shuts.

You puff out your cheeks and sit down at

the desk. There's a calendar showing pictures of a young woman with pink hair posing at various landmarks with a dark, hairy guy in metaller T-shirts, and a paperweight containing a tiny model of the Eiffel Tower. 'Edgewise' proclaims a banner floating around the computer's screen. 'Artful concepts'. The phone rings and panic grips you. You think for a moment about running out and leaving it. But the memory of the empty streets and the fifteen pounds left in your pocket make you pause. The problem of tomorrow and the next day and the next throbs like a headache in your brain. You take a deep breath. You can do this. If London has taught you anything, it's the value of being what people expect.

You glance at the computer screen once more and pick up the receiver. 'Hello, Edgewise?' you say.

You pop out to get something to eat and when you get back, the studio is occupied. Two blokes stand behind easels. They stop what they're doing as you approach. One, with stubble and wearing an old Nirvana *Nevermind* T-shirt, scowls at you. The other, in an ink-stained denim shirt, with acne scars at his temples, chews a pencil.

'Um,' you say, swallowing, 'I'm Trudy.

Anton said I should start today.'

There's a silence. Ink-stained denim takes the pencil out of his mouth.

'Hi, Trudy, I'm G-Gareth,' he says, contorting his mouth slightly to get the word out. 'And this is the senior designer, Edmund.'

'Ed,' says Edmund.

'Hi,' you say. And then, anxious to please: 'Edmund's a good name.'

Edmund rolls his eyes.

'Don't m-mind him,' says Gareth. 'It's been a tough few days. Nice to have you a-with us.'

You walk to the reception desk and see with a start that the hairy bloke with the pink-haired woman in the photographs is Edmund. Doubt about the wisdom of sticking with the Trudy lie wells up in you once more but you counsel yourself silently to keep your nerve. Compared to what you've lived through, this is nothing. You may as well ride this rollercoaster as far as it takes you, squeeze as much advantage out of it as you can. It's not as though the world is offering you many other options. Baby steps, that's the secret. Dealing with each challenge as it arises. Playing the cards as and when. You look at the guys again.

'Sorry,' you say. 'Am I supposed to be doing anything apart from answering the phone?'

To the right, you catch sight of a bank of machines: computers, a scanner and something that looks like an electronic walk-in wardrobe. You hope they won't expect you to know how to operate that.

'For fuck's sake,' mutters Edmund. He stumps over. 'Hasn't Anton told you anything?'

You shrug. Trudy, you decide, is a woman of few words.

'Fucking typical,' says Edmund. He runs a hand through his hair. You catch a whiff of cigarette smoke.

'All right, where were you before?' he says.

'London,' you say cautiously.

'No, fuckwit. What company?'

'Edmund,' says Gareth from across the room.

'What agency?' Edmund says, drumming his fingers on the desk.

'Join the Dots,' you say. You could kick yourself as soon as you've said it, it's so lame.

'Never heard of it,' says Edmund. 'But wherever the fuck it was, I expect the designers worked by getting a brief, coming up with a concept with the copywriters, and then producing a piece in which the words and design worked together to sell some sort of project or idea. Am I right?'

You nod. You wish you could write this down.

'Well, you can forget all that shit here,' says Edmund. 'All that normal, logical crap counts for nothing. Here, we're in the dark. If we're lucky, Anton gives us a word and then we have to produce something — an artistic response, he calls it. A piss in the wind more like! And then he takes all our efforts to the client and more often than not they throw it out and he comes back with another word . . . and we have to go through the whole half-arsed charade again. Meanwhile, Anton tries to palm off our also-rans as art to footballers' wives and re-ality TV show winners, hence the gallery at the front. Battery artists, that's what we are here. And you're the poor sod who has to deal with the clients when they ring up to complain.'

'Oh come on, Edmund,' says Gareth. 'It's not that bad.'

'It fucking is that bad!' says Edmund, turning and swiping a can of pens off the reception desk on to the floor. 'We're the pawns of some rich twat who gets to order us around and make us jump through hoops just because his grandfather . . . I don't know, shot down a hundred Indians or something. It makes me sick.'

Gareth held up his hands. 'OK, firstly — sorry, Trudy — Anton's g-grandfather was an Admiral in the navy. He had nothing to do a-with any Indian m-massacre. Secondly: yeah, there's m-money in his family and his m-methods are a bit eccentric, but you can't deny he g-gets results.'

'He's been lucky,' says Edmund, folding his arms so that the baby on the front of his T-shirt seems to frown.

'He g-gets results,' says Gareth again, firmly.

'Yeah, by shafting people and firing the receptionist just because she messed up once.'

Gareth put his hands to his head. 'Gina was taking the piss,' he says. 'Everyone said so. Even you said so!'

'Fuck this, I'm going for a fag,' says Edmund. He turns and stomps out of the studio to huddle just beyond the entrance. You see the edge of his arm and the puff of smoke when the cigarette's lit.

'Trudy, I'm so sorry,' says Gareth, standing stiffly behind his easel. 'As you've probably g-gathered, things have been a bit up in the air lately. I just want you to know it's g-got nothing to do with you.'

You shrug, grin and then scale it back, trying not to look too relieved. It is cruel, you think, that Gareth's name should begin with one of the letters he finds most difficult to pronounce.

'It's OK,' you say. And then, because the occasion seems to demand it: 'I'm used to it. My old boss was a . . . bitch.'

Gareth nods, his hair flopping over the pock marks next to his eyes. 'All the same, you shouldn't have to put up with that on your first day. It's just, well, you know . . . Edmund and Gina . . . It's complicated.'

You smile and nod and he turns his attention back to his work. You pick up the pens and stick them back in the pot. A little while later Edmund comes back in. He shoots you a look and in that moment you understand two things: Edmund hates you, and everything's going to be all right.

47

She was there when visiting hours began and stayed until they ended. She sat and watched uniformed figures bustling past in the corridor, their shoes squeaking on the linoleum, and the buds swaying and shivering on the horse chestnut tree outside. When she got the chance, she helped herself to snacks from the nurses' station. She discovered a biscuit tin kept stocked with Hobnobs and chocolate digestives and a little fridge next to the fax machine that sometimes contained yoghurts and cheese and the odd piece of fruit. Once, when she was passing on her way to the toilet, she spotted an unattended wedge of chocolate cake next to a steaming cup of tea. She left the plate in the bathroom at the end of the corridor. If anyone noticed, they never said anything. The nurses just smiled at her distractedly when they came to administer their checks and change Hellie's bags, pads and sheets.

Sometimes she talked to Hellie — long, rambling things about the hospital with its imposing front entrance where carriages would have drawn up in a century gone by or stories about people she saw wandering in the manicured grounds outside the window. Sometimes she just sat and looked.

Once or twice she brought out the letter and read it aloud, rehearsing Hellie's memories that were almost — but not quite — her own, probing the grief of the passage about little Emily, and communing with the manic enthusiasm that tore through her sister's mind like wildfire, sending sentences skittering to the fibres at the far edges of each page. Only one bit eluded her: the description of sitting by the feet and the shoes with the string for laces. She stared at it as time ticked past on the clock, but could not unlock its significance.

'What did you mean here, Hellie?' she said, as if she might catch her sister unawares, and jerk her into consciousness with her own words, but the figure in the bed lay still.

On a whim one afternoon, she picked up a peach-coloured nail varnish in the chemist's up the road and spent a careful hour layering the polish on to Hellie's nails. It was years since she'd used any herself and putting it on someone else's hand was an added complication. She found she had to keep dabbing with a tissue to stop it pooling round the edges. Hellie's hand lay on the blanket in front of her: slender, yet dimpled on the knuckles like Smudge's own. There was a freckle, she noticed, on the right thumb: a mark all Hellie's own. Had it come in later years or had it always been there? A tell-tale speckle for anyone careful enough to read the signs. If it had always been there, then why had no one seen the truth, the reality of the swap and all that followed? Like dust beaten out of a cushion, a memory rose up around her: afternoons hidden behind curtains. Doorstep honey sandwiches hacked off mouldy loaves by arms stretching up to reach the breadboard. A bedroom door shut and a dressing gown and slippers looking thin and indecent in the middle of the day. Then, suddenly, bright smiles and Sunday best and Akela there, beaming like it had been happy families all along. She and Ellie standing shoulder to shoulder in the hallway with Mother and Akela looming above. Chocolate and the panicky feeling of needing the toilet. Summer blowing in from the garden and change hefting itself up the stairs. She stroked Hellie's poor, freckled hand. They had been so little. Sadness bloomed and she pushed it hurriedly away and turned to look at the clock. Easy to lose track of the hours in this perpetual, beeping twilight.

But when she looked again, she was not in the room any more. Another tide of memory engulfed her, toppling the hospital's walls: she was standing on a cliff in the swirling mist, looking up at a bird wheeling in the sky above, and laughing. A hand, Father's, was in the small of her back and there was a wild, giddy feeling as if at any moment anything could happen, as if magic could rain down from the sky. Dredged up by Hellie's presence, by her parallel eye and words, the memory began to spill the rest of its circumstances: a holiday cottage in Dorset. Father hiring bicycles. Mother muttering about the expense. The juggler forced to flee his pitch in the market square when Ellie kept demanding he showed them another trick. And then another. Laughter — even Mother, in spite of herself, joining in. Possibility. Sandwiches wrapped in tin foil. Father kissing Mother, whirling her round. She telling him not to be so stupid but smiling all the same. Searching for pixies in the trees at the bottom of the cottage garden. Father urging them on to look harder, working everybody up. The funny, fat little man on the Splat the Rat Stall at a local fete who worried about people trying to sneak extra goes. Ellie posed, wielding the mallet with solemn concentration, determined to give the rat what for.

Marvellous and strange to have the past fleshed out like this. Marvellous and strange to feel sensations buried under years of clipboards and fluorescent lights and rooms with carpet on the walls. She had forgotten.

'We were happy,' she said wonderingly, looking at her sister. 'Before everything, we were happy.'

Hellie winced, her face momentarily betraying the wavering, vulnerable look from when they were very young, the feeble expression that had made the original Helen want to pinch and slap and bite her. Smudge stared at her. Where had it come from, she wondered, that timidity of Ellie's, as though she were afraid of what the world might have to show her? That fear? The story went that her sluggishness and reserve were down to her difficult birth, the cord caught around her neck and choking her. But there had been a time when the discrepancy between the two of them didn't exist. The Ellie in those early recollections was sturdy and intrepid. What had sent that little girl retreating into herself and caused her, Helen, to try to compensate with cruelty, to winkle her sister back out by any means? What had skewed the balance?

Smudge pulled out the letter and spread its pages, dog-eared and creased, on the blanket in front of her. Perhaps it was in here somewhere, the key to all that had come since: her own unkindness, Ellie's intransigence after the swap, the misery and madness that gusted up, whirling them both into other lives.

But the sentences huddled together, opaque and closed.

'It doesn't make sense,' said Smudge out loud. 'What happened, Hellie? When did it change?'

But Ellie just gaped at the ceiling and didn't say a word.

48

On your first pay day, you feel great. You leave the office beaming, clutching the wad of cash you persuaded Anton to give you directly on the pretext of getting round the temping agency's fees — he didn't like the idea at first, but when you told him everyone did it, he shrugged and finally gave in. You have to frown to hide your relief and delight. For the first time ever, the universe seems to be letting you win; you are slotting yourself into this new wonderful life and everything is conspiring to help.

The money for the month is less than you might have made on a single weekend job at one of London's swanky hotels, but it feels like so much more. You decide to treat yourself to a new top from the Barnacle shopping centre on the way home and choose a ruched grey T-shirt with spatters of red across its front — nothing too extravagant, there's no way you're about to blow

Beryl's rent. Afterwards you stop by the Coach and Horses, a little pub with dried-up window boxes and a flaking sign, for a celebratory drink. It's quiet so you see him as soon as you step inside, through the glass of the inner door. He's older and lined about the face, and he has that hollow look that addicts get when the heroin suddenly stops keeping them young, but the wolfishness is still there about the eyes.

It's such a shock that, for a moment, you doubt yourself. You hover on the threshold, wondering if it's your brain switching back to the old frequencies again, raking trouble out of thin air. Even with everything you've been through, you struggle to believe that life could be such a bastard as to bring him here, now, crashing the party of your happiness. It seems too cruel a joke.

Then, as you watch, a guy in a suede jacket walks over and slides an envelope across the table — some sort of documents, by the look of it. You think you spot a driving licence blushing an unlikely shade of pink. Your mind flashes back to the fake IDs that used to litter the living-room floor and leave rectangular imprints on your arms and legs. You remember the flat vowels and the talk of Manchester — of an uncle living somewhere around here. You think of the conversation you overheard the other week. Certainty clobbers you. It's him all right, Mary's brother, sitting in the corner of the pub.

He looks up and you turn quickly so he can't see you. You hurry out of the door and down the street, heart pounding, a sour taste in your mouth. When you get back to Beryl's, you lock yourself in the bathroom and dash cold water on your face. You watch your spattered reflection, until the immediate danger of chaos snatching you up is past. When the shuddering subsides, you realise you dropped the bag with the grey and red top in the doorway of the pub. You resolve to let that be the last thing he costs you.

The weeks pass. You keep yourself to yourself in the office and let the others do the talking — Gareth, Edmund, the older designer called Matt whose wife has recently had a baby and the copywriter Gayle, who sits on her high stool in the far corner and complains if the music gets too loud. When you have to answer questions, you're careful. You don't fling out details willy-nilly as you've done before with all the Roses, Ruths and Veronicas. You take thought over Trudy's background, her schooling, her parents who sadly died when she was at university.

You craft a biography you can live with and work at making it real. Every detail bedded in and every day that passes without incident is a victory, another plank nailed on to the structure of Trudy's being, sheltering you from the cold blasts of used-to-be. The more solid she becomes, the more the wild ideas and sirens of panic recede. Sometimes you want to burst out laughing with how glad all this makes you — how giddy with luck you feel — but you know enough to sit quietly on your padded desk chair and bite your lip.

Back at the lodging house you do your bit to help out, wiping down the surfaces and taking out the rubbish. Beryl seems to appreciate it. Some evenings she even invites you into her sitting room and the pair of you pass a few hours in front of cookery programmes and home-improvement shows. You get addicted to a series where a group of amateur seamstresses go head to head to win a contract to design a day-time TV presenter's wedding dress, going through a series of challenges that whittles them down week by week. Your loyalties are split between a small Glaswegian with a flair for working feathers into her designs and a black woman from Dudley who likes gingham and has an infectious laugh. At odd moments throughout the day, you catch yourself thinking about the programme, wondering who will win. It feels luxurious to have the headspace to give to such things, to be able to get excited about something so wonderfully trivial. You hug it to yourself and look for opportunities to gossip about the show as you've heard other people do on buses and in the corner shop. When you do, a bit of you stands outside your head watching, marvelling at how normal you sound.

A month goes by and then another. Summer blazes gold and then begins to brown around the edges. Edgewise lands a big project and it's all hands on deck. Gareth and Edmund pull long days, roughing out a sheaf of ideas. But whatever they suggest, the client's not happy. The edges of Anton's smile start to twitch. One afternoon, when Edmund's out at the dentist's, you saunter over to Gareth's desk and ask him to show you the work. It's wide-ranging, with pictures of vehicles and country houses and statues sprayed with rainbow paint.

'So what is it?' you say. 'What's the concept?'

Gareth puts a hand to the acne scars on his temple. 'Anton's a-word is "estate",' he groans. 'Like the car, but it can also be

440

anything connected — and they a-want something that puts it in a new light. Something edgy and cool. A-We've been all over it and turned it inside out. It's d-driving us insane.'

You wander back to your desk. Something is beckoning to you on the edge of your thoughts, but when you try to look at it directly, it scurries away into the under-growth. That afternoon, in the lull between calls, you get a sketchpad and try to sum-mon the image forth, covering what you're doing whenever anyone walks past, but the shapes stay blurred and indistinct, the ideas confused. Once work has finished, you go to the cafe in the Barnacle and sit at your favourite table overlooking the doors and the atrium below. You rough out a few tenta-tive, blocky sketches: people with hard faces, litter blowing in the gutter. But something's missing. The pictures stay flat on the page.

All the same, when you wake up the next day, the word is still nagging at you. Estate, estate, estate. At your desk, you open the sketchpad to a blank page but the little rectangle of paper feels too cramped to contain your ideas. You need something more. At the end of the day, you linger in the studio. When everyone else has gone, you help yourself to one of the A3 pads of art paper and a handful of pencils and charcoals from Gareth's desk.

Back at Beryl's, you shut yourself up in your room. No television tonight: you've got work to do. You open the pad on the floor. The walk home has cleared your head and already you can see the idea looming through the grain of the pulp. It's a tower block and it leads off to a corridor of tower blocks cutting diagonally away to the right side of the paper. But this is no common-or-garden estate, you realise, as you start to rough it out, hunched over the page. It's grim as they come — blackened edges around smashed windows showing a recent fire, an overturned buggy frame with the seat fabric ripped away, the suggestion of a needle lying in the gutter at the front (you keep it a suggestion because you don't know how the client will feel about that, so you make it so it could be a bit of an old tin can).

You work on, absorbed in what's unfolding on the paper in front of you. Apart from getting up to turn the light on when it gets dark, you don't move. The rest of the world recedes.

Once you've got the outlines of the buildings and a bit of the detailing, you set about pulling together a figure in the foreground. You want her to be both vulnerable and defiant; young and soaked in experience. You want rich, comfortable people to look at her and think 'there but for the grace of God'. You draw on all your reserves, the patient hours spent sketching and re-sketching in the Barnacle's cafe, to get the slant of her eyes just right — the squint that could be a flinch or a precursor to a snarl — and create a vision of a moment that could go either way.

Some of the pencils you nicked from Gareth's desk are coloured and when you look at them you realise they're those water-soluble ones they used to have in the art room in the unit. 'Special needs paints' as you used to call them. You empty the toothbrushes out of the mug in the bathroom, fill it with water and get going with the pencils — streaking the walls of the tower blocks, blackening the window frames. You give the girl green eyes but smear her face with dirt — perhaps she's escaped from the fire or perhaps she's been on the streets several nights. That's not your call. And then, to offset the misery of the foreground, you start to do something about the sky. You put purple clouds overhead but in the far distance, where the line of blocks gives on to the horizon, you work in reds, pinks and a splash of gold, as though beauty could be dawning or receding from the scene: the start of better times or the prelude to something worse.

When you next look up, it's light. With a jolt, you see from the little clock on the bedside table that it's 8.40. Shit! If you don't get the pencils back before Gareth gets in, it's really not going to look good. You gather everything up and hurry downstairs, mumbling something about an urgent deadline on your way past as Beryl emerges from the kitchen.

When you get to the studio, you see with relief that you're the first to arrive. You fumble in your bag for the keys, but as you're reaching for the handle something slips and the pencils, charcoals and pad tumble all over the pavement. You look down to see your tower-block picture staring at the sky. Then a shadow moves over it.

'Hullo,' says Anton. 'Been having a bit of a scribble?'

He bends down and picks up your picture, a frown spreading over his face.

'It's a council estate,' you say, feeling foolish. 'You know, urban deprivation and things.'

Anton taps his fingers on his lips.

444

'Yes, I see that,' he says. 'And who's this?' He points to the woman on the page.

'Just some girl,' you say, feeling stupid. 'It's up to the viewer to decide. Like it's up to them to say whether things in the picture are getting better or getting worse: is the sun —'

'Going up or going down. Yes, I see.'

He turns back to you and his frown cracks into a smile.

'It's brilliant,' he says. 'Utterly unexpected. Inspired. When can you finish it?'

You look back at the paper, shrug. The original focus has gone, leaving only a residual buzz and the muffled sensation of not having slept. To be honest, you're not sure what else you'd do to it.

'Half an hour?'

Anton claps a hand to his forehead. 'Half an hour!' he says. 'Brilliant! I'll put it to David this afternoon. Excellent, excellent work!'

And so saying, he strides into the studio ahead of you, sending a gust of air rolling across the room, flapping papers.

Twenty minutes later, Edmund arrives to find you standing at the spare easel by Gareth's desk.

'Did I miss something?' he says.

■ ■ ■ ■

You stop by the Morrisons on the way home to pick up a bottle of wine. You're feeling exuberant after the success of the day and the admiration that they all — even Edmund — showed for your piece. Besides, it's a special night — the final of the sewing show — and you and Beryl have agreed to watch it together.

The smell of hotpot hits you as you enter the house: wholesome and warming. Just the thing to combat the first hints of the autumn chill starting to rise in the evening air. Soon you're both in the sitting room, sipping wine and tucking into steaming plates of dumplings and rich, meaty sauce.

'Does you good,' says Beryl with a contented sigh. 'Cheers.'

The programme comes on. The final challenge is for the last three contestants — the Dudley woman, the Glaswegian and a camp hairdresser from Hull — to create their wedding dresses for the daytime celebrity, whose measurements they have but whose identity will only be revealed at the end when she arrives to pick the winner. It's a close-run thing. Dudley's design looks promising but the Glaswegian shoots herself in the foot by venturing away from her tried and tested feathers formula and making a rat's nest out of strings of fake pearls. You can't see how she's going to rescue it. It looks as though the hairdresser might edge it with a chic, boxy design he calls 'Fifties Futuristic', but in the final ten minutes Dudley pulls out the stops with a lovely empire-line *Pride and Prejudice* number and the Glaswegian's rat's nest resolves itself into an elegant piece of lattice-work netting dropped over a satin shift.

'It's a tough one to call,' confides the presenter to the camera. 'They've done all they can. Now it comes down to our celebrity's personal taste. Which design will she pick for her special day?'

You're leaning over to top up the glasses when the celebrity first appears on the screen.

'Oh, it's her,' says Beryl, clicking her fingers. 'What's her name from, you know . . . thing.'

You look up and suddenly the room around the set goes dark. On the screen, going into raptures over Dudley's period references, is Hellie. But not Hellie as you remember her, a scrawny teenager covered in glitter dust and cherry lipgloss. This Hellie is sleek and self-assured, filled out and cinched in, in just the right places.

'What's her name?' says Beryl again. 'She won that competition for a new young presenter for that mid-morning show on ITV. The one that used to have the big floating weather map. I catch it sometimes when I'm doing the ironing.'

'I don't know,' you say dully. Everything seems to have withdrawn from you so that it is as though you are looking at the world down the wrong end of a long, dark telescope. The voices from the television sound very far away.

'Helen Sallis,' says Beryl, clapping her hands together and turning in her armchair for your approval. 'Come to think of it, you look a lot like her. Has anyone ever told you that?'

For a moment, the world seems to teeter on the edge of a cliff. It's almost as if you can see the room and everything in it — Beryl's Royal Doulton ladies, the carriage clock on the mantelpiece, the rack of *Reader's Digest* magazines by the fire — tilting and sliding into the abyss. The street outside the bay window seems to yawn, ready to suck you in.

Then something in you hardens. You grit your teeth. You will not let her take everything from you again. You will not let Hellie rob you this time.

You meet Beryl's gaze and shrug. 'Not really,' you say, keeping your tone as light as the ruffles on Dudley's sleeves. 'Just a co-incidence. One of those things.'

'Suppose it must be,' said Beryl. 'Funny though, in't it?'

She turns back to the television. 'Some people think I look like Victoria Wood,' she remarks.

You breathe a sigh of relief. The sensations of the evening creep back in. You can taste the wine again. You hear cars passing in the road outside. But through it all a strange sensation swills around the pit of your stomach. It's part gladness at having kept your nerve, but there's more to it than that: something tender and vulnerable, a sore spot you didn't know was there before. It takes you a while to make sense of it. Then, as the credits roll over scenes of Hellie and the Glaswegian toasting each other and accepting congratulations from members of the studio audience, you realise what it means: for the first time almost since you can remember, you've got something to lose.

49

On her fifth day in the hospital, Nick arrived. He walked in through the door carrying a stack of books. It wasn't until he reached the locker and dropped them noisily into a gap among the flowers that he realised there was anyone else in the room. She saw him freeze as soon as he clocked it was her.

'Oh,' he said. 'You're here.'

'I'll go,' Smudge said, making as if to get up.

'No, no,' he said stiffly. He shifted from foot to foot and glanced at the machines. 'It's my first trip in for a while actually. Work has been . . .' He caught her eye and looked away.

A trolley clattered along the corridor. Nick coughed. 'Has there been any — ?'

She shook her head. 'Just agitation from the chest infection. She's been calmer these last few days. The antibiotics seem to be doing the trick.'

For a moment neither of them said anything. Nick drummed his fingers on the back of the cabinet on the far side of the bed. He looked around the room: at the ceiling, out of the window, at the sign on the back of the door prohibiting smoking. His gaze fell on the pile of books.

'Thought I might read to her,' he said.

Smudge nodded. The ventilator heaved a series of sighs. A flush spread over Nick's face.

'I should go,' he said. He took a step towards the door and turned back, passing a hand over his forehead. 'Oh, by the way, I spoke to the benefits people. Explained there'd been some mistake. With your money, you know. They said they'd be in touch. Some sort of date for a meeting, I think. Sounds like it can all be sorted out. Nothing to worry about. So, all's well that end's well.'

He wouldn't meet her eye and resentment gathered in the pit of her stomach. She wasn't about to let him pass off his cowardice, his desire to be rid of the mess of the last few weeks, as a generous thing. She wasn't going to be grateful to him for trying to erase her from his life.

'Oh, yes,' she said in a hard voice. 'How

convenient. Nothing for you to worry about any more.'

Nick frowned, his hand on the doorframe. 'I thought you'd be pleased.'

She didn't reply. He coughed again and dug in his pockets.

'In the meantime, this should tide you over,' he said, holding out some notes.

Fury erupted through her. 'I don't want your money!'

'Suit yourself,' he said, recoiling. He made as if to stuff the money back in his pocket, then seemed to think better of it and went over to put it on the locker. 'I'll just leave it here,' he said.

His voice had an affronted, peevish tone: a school boy aggrieved at getting C+ for his homework when he'd expected an A. She saw there was weakness about his chin she hadn't noticed before, as though whoever had modelled him had run out of clay. All of a sudden she felt indignant for her sister that this was who everyone lumped her together with, that this was the person with whom Hellie was supposed to share her life.

'What's this?' said Nick, picking up a scrap of paper from the locker.

Peering over, Smudge saw with horror that it was a piece of the letter. She must have left it on the side after the last time she read it to Hellie.

'Oh, it's nothing,' she said, holding out her hand for it. 'Rubbish.'

But Nick wasn't listening. 'Is that Helen's writing?' He frowned at the jagged scrawl. 'Oh no,' he said. 'It's not like hers . . . except . . . that is the way she does her "t"s. And the "y"s are the same.'

He shot Smudge a look, suspicion marshalling its forces behind his eyes.

'Where did you get this?' he said. 'Did this come from the house? Did you take this from her room?'

'For fuck's sake! No. All right?' She rolled her eyes. 'If you must know, she wrote to me. Before she drove to see me that day, she sent me a letter.'

Nick frowned. 'How come I'm only hearing about this now?'

'I've only recently got round to reading it myself.' And then, because he didn't look convinced: 'I wasn't very . . . on top of my mail for quite a while. And when I did find it, I didn't feel . . . equal to opening it. If that makes sense.'

She gestured for the page again. 'Anyway, it's nothing really,' she said. 'Just odds and ends, you know.'

But Nick was still peering at the writing. 'It's a bit . . . manic, isn't it?'

She looked up sharply, but there was no significance in his eyes. The word didn't have the same cavernous resonances for him — shouts, guffaws and screams echoing up into the great dome of the sky. It was just another adjective. He might as easily have chosen 'frenetic', 'chaotic', 'odd'.

'I suppose it is,' she said, being careful to keep her voice light. She looked at the piece of paper he held in his hand, fighting the urge to lunge up and snatch it from him. She didn't like the thought of his eyes on it, his brain processing Hellie's private words.

He was staring at it, rubbing a hand back and forth across his mouth. The silence lengthened.

'Are they all about this?' he said. 'About your father's suicide?'

Smudge narrowed her eyes. 'How do you mean?'

'The shoes. The string for laces. Sitting by the feet. It's your father. It's the day he died.'

Smudge shook her head. 'It can't be,' she said, studying the sentences. 'Why would she torture herself by imagining that?'

'But she didn't have to imagine it, did she?' said Nick. 'She was there. When they found him hanging from the banister, she was sitting by his feet.'

454

Smudge gaped at him.

'Sorry,' he said blankly. 'I thought you knew.'

'No. She never told me.'

He nodded. 'If it makes you feel any better, I only found out last year. It all came out after Emily. Something about the experience, the way she died, brought it all back. Therapy got her to reveal that much, at least.'

'Where was I? When it happened. How come I wasn't there?'

Nick pulled a face and stared at the ceiling. 'I think you'd been out with your mother. Shopping. Something like that. They said he'd been dead for a good hour when you got home. And she'd just sat there, staring up. Watching. She was talking to him apparently. Asking him to get down.'

He shuddered.

'I can't imagine what that does to a person,' he said. 'I can't imagine how on earth you begin to get past something like that.'

He looked at her for a moment, as though the answer might be written in her face. Then he recollected himself and the coldness dropped back over his features.

'Anyway,' he mumbled. He laid the sheet of paper on the end of the bed and walked out of the room.

Smudge stared at her sister's face, its contours so familiar yet so sleekly different from her own. The same material, the same DNA, the same genetic plans tilted quite another way. The realisation came in a rush: while Helen might have ceased to be herself on the day Akela moved in, Ellie had started to disappear on a dark afternoon a whole two years before.

She turned her head and looked out of the window at the blank clouds, blinking back a surge of tears.

50

One day Anton calls you into the back office. You leave the easel where you've been roughing out ideas for a series of modern landscapes for Visit Britain and go in to find him sitting at his desk, a dark silhouette against the yard outside, where, for once, the afternoon sun is shining, glinting off the silver bins.

'Sit down,' he says, and coughs.

You sit in one of the armchairs facing the desk. It makes you much lower than Anton, like a child. There's a pause. You look up at a ship's barometer hanging on the wall: changeable, it reads.

'The thing is, er, Trudy, I've had a phone call and, to be honest, it puts me in a rather awkward position,' begins Anton. He stops and runs a hand over his blond hair. It is starting to thin on top, you notice, the pink scalp showing through. It makes you think unpleasantly of streaky bacon.

'Look, I'll come out with it,' he says. 'No use beating about the bush. The call was from Office Elves apologising that Trudy, the temp worker they were supposed to send us three months ago, didn't show up and asking if we still needed someone. Apparently there was some glitch in their system which means a load of messages are only coming through now — all of which is rather strange because, well, you're here.'

He drums his fingers on the desk and looks at you sidelong. 'Anything you can say to clear this up?'

You flash a smile and summon up the confidence that has seen you through this far.

'I am Trudy,' you say brightly. 'The office must have made a mistake —'

Anton holds up a hand. 'Sorry to be difficult, but I'm afraid you're quite clearly not. Not *that* Trudy, at any rate. *That* Trudy went into premature labour and had to be hospitalised the night before she was due to start covering reception here. Her partner emailed the agency to explain, but, er, as I said, the message didn't come through.'

A weight plunges through you, hollowing you out. The room starts to swirl and your thoughts flit like birds, looking for something — anything — you could salvage from

458

the situation. You open your mouth and close it again. You feel tired and sad.

'The thing is,' says Anton, watching you warily, 'I like your work. You fit into the team well and since you've started on the art side the clients certainly have no complaints. Truth be told, I've never seen so many private commissions come in in all my ten years of doing this. It's just . . . well, I have to trust the people I employ and this . . . rather puts that in the shade.'

He tugs at the collar of his shirt. 'If you could just explain, perhaps it wouldn't be an issue,' he suggests.

The silence seems to go on and on. You look around the room at the shelves of books and trophies next to the barometer, the black-and-white photograph of a bearded man in a naval uniform staring proudly at the camera, and back at Anton. Anger flares and dies. He's being more than reasonable, you see that. Most people would have chucked you out, no questions asked, in the face of such an abuse of trust, such fraud. For all he knows, you could be anyone.

A door creaks open in the back of your mind. What if you did come clean? What if you told him about the accident and the institutions and having to start again? You consider it for a moment, but the thought of slipping back into the harness of Ellie, of squashing yourself into those constricting bindings and shouldering the burdens of sadness and shame once again, is more than you can bear. You like Trudy and all she's come to mean. You like the neatness of her life, her can-do approach and the way she sticks to healthy routines. Ellie would taint that. Simply by speaking about her with Trudy's mouth, you would bring her chaos tumbling into this room. It would be like opening a cupboard door that could never be shut and there would always be more rubbish spilling from it, faster than you could clear it, so that you would have to spend the whole time shovelling shit out of the way when all you really wanted to do was get on with leading a completely different, unfettered life.

You shake your head. 'I'm afraid I can't explain it,' you say. 'I'm sorry.'

Anton knits his brows and looks at you solemnly. In this instant you feel you can trace in him the figure of his grandfather, the Admiral; you can see the same expression on the figure in the photograph. If you were Trudy pure and simple at this moment you would be roughing out plans to draw Anton this way in your mind. But you can't focus because Ellie is out there, prowling round the edges of your consciousness, rattling the cages of your thoughts, and you have to find a way to drive her back into the scrub of No Man's Land.

Anton drums his fingers on the desk. 'You're making this rather difficult for me,' he says. 'At least tell me why you can't explain.'

You open your mouth to try to frame the reasons, but the words won't come. You find yourself surrounded by blankness, the margin round the edge of the page where the writing gives way to space.

'I'm sorry,' you say again. 'I'm just not able to be myself. I haven't been for a long time.' The shadows in the corners flex and pulse, ready to rush in and steal all this away. You can't bear it. 'But you should know, I've never been so happy,' you say in a rush. 'I love this life. I love what I'm doing here. I might not be Trudy, but I am really, truly me.'

You sit back and stare at the floor. Your voice echoes in your ears: pleading, needy. You know you've blown it now. First rule you learnt in the unit: never show your weakness to anyone, never reveal what you really care about. People will only ever use it to fuck you up. You sit and wait for it all to come tumbling down like a pack of cards.

The silence lengthens. You look up. A light glimmers in Anton's eyes. 'Hmmn. By rights I should sack you on the spot,' he says. He glances up at the ship's barometer. He takes a deep breath. 'But perhaps we all have our reasons for not doing what's expected of us from time to time.'

He coughs again. 'Just tell me one thing,' he says. 'You're not in trouble with the law, are you?'

You look at him steadily. 'Not any more,' you say.

He nods. 'I see.' He lifts one hand and taps his fingers on his top lip. 'And I'm not going to have the police pitching up? Or anything nicked?'

'Nothing like that,' you say.

'You're not a murderer, are you?'

The abruptness of it — the look of unease on his usually complacent face — almost makes you want to laugh. You rein it in. Now would not be the time.

'No,' you say.

Anton looks at you, some sort of calculation going on behind his eyes. Behind him, in the square of sky above the yard, a plane glides into view and seems to disappear into his left ear. You picture it soaring down the canal, getting lodged in the passages of his brain.

'OK,' says Anton with a sigh. 'I hope I'm not going to regret this . . . You can stay.'

You blink. You look around. The walls are still standing. Outside, your desk is still waiting for you, the easel poised for your next idea. The world has not collapsed.

A flood of feeling engulfs you — all your emotions switched on and blaring. You stand up in your excitement.

'Thank you,' you say. You want to run and embrace him, but something holds you back. You've never done that before. Perhaps he wouldn't welcome it.

Anton recognises your impulse and looks pleased and embarrassed.

'That's all right,' he says, holding up his hands. 'But we keep all this between us. As far as the rest of the team are concerned, you're still Trudy who came to temp. The first hint of any kind of . . . dodgy shenanigans and you're out. Understand?'

You nod energetically and make for the door.

'Hold on,' says Anton. 'There's something else.' He gestures to the armchair again.

You sit back down, pulse racing, gladness and anxiety fizzing in your blood. He fiddles with a stack of papers on his desk.

'An opportunity's come up: three months' work for a client in Amsterdam. They want two artists. Big, ambitious project — creating twists on Old Masters to launch a new tablet. I was thinking of sending Edmund and, er, you. If you'd like to go . . .'

You shrug. 'Love to,' you say.

'Well, that's a relief anyhow. At least you're not a convicted drug mule,' he guffaws, and looks at you. 'Sorry. Bad taste. They'll want you to send some preliminary ideas over and then be out there solidly from about four weeks' time, but you'll have to do quite a lot of preparation in between and some wrapping up afterwards. We're probably looking at roughly six months' work all told. Perhaps under the circumstances a bit of time away wouldn't be a bad thing. Sound like something you'd be interested in?'

You nod again. 'Absolutely,' you say.

When you get out of the office, everyone's looking at you.

'You were in there a long time,' says Edmund. He's wearing a Pearl Jam T-shirt today and his jawline is dark with stubble.

You shrug and try to appear nonchalant through the maelstrom of excitement swirling round your head, the euphoria at finding everything still here unchanged. Trudy's life — your life — exactly as you left it. You

464

think it must be like coming back to your house after you've been told it's been burgled and finding that the thieves have left everything just as it was. Untouched.

'So what did he want then, old Tim-Nice-But-Dim?' continues Edmund.

The others are trying to pretend they're not listening, fiddling with things on their desks. Gayle the copywriter is tapping away at her keyboard, but you know she's probably just typing random letters the way she does when she wants to eavesdrop on Matt's fights with his wife.

You shrug again. 'Oh, you know. This and that. Just seeing how I was doing.'

Edmund sneers. 'Half an hour's a long time to be seeing how you're doing,' he says. 'What else did he say?'

Something in you warns against it, but you're happy and so relieved that you just blurt it out. 'Amsterdam,' you say. 'He told me about you and me going to Amsterdam for this big client job.'

The others abandon the pretence of busyness and straighten up like meerkats. Edmund frowns.

'Amsterdam,' he says. 'What the fuck . . . ?'

'Yeah,' you say. 'He's sending you and me for this big tablet campaign. New twists on Old Masters or something.'

465

Edmund nods. 'And of course he decides to tell the fucking newbie, the fucking receptionist-who-draws-a-bit, before he runs it past the senior fucking designer who's only been in the job five fucking years!'

'Ed—' cautions Gareth, peering round the side of his easel.

'No, I'm sorry, this is fucking bullshit. First he promotes her without asking me, and now this. I'm not having it!' storms Edmund, and he strides across the studio and bursts into Anton's office, slamming the door behind him. Muffled voices come through the wall.

You go to your easel as the others shift uneasily on their stools. You pick up a pencil and think about roughing out your image of plane brain, but something in the room feels blocked as though all the doors and windows have been stopped up with cotton wool and no one can really breathe.

Five minutes later, Edmund is back.

'Right. I'm out of here,' he says. He goes to his desk and starts shunting paper aggressively into stacks which he crams into his bag.

'You m-mean, you're off for the rest of the day?' ventures Gareth.

'No, fuckface,' says Edmund. 'I'm done.

I'm gone. Yesterday's paper telling yesterday's news. Or some shit.'

'Now hang on,' says Gareth, holding up his hands. 'Surely there's some a-way to sort this out.'

'No,' says Edmund, ripping a half-finished sketch showing a monkey eating a Mars Bar off his easel, screwing it up and hurling it at the bin. 'I've had it with this place. The whole thing's a joke. I didn't spend three years working in McDonald's to pay my way through art school so that I could sit around taking orders from some clueless public-school boy with a chip on his shoulder about not getting into the navy. I'm telling you, I'm done.'

'What about Amsterdam?' you say.

'Don't worry,' says Edmund, rounding on you with a bitter smile. 'Your jolly's still on. I told the boss to send Mahatma Gandhi here with you instead. Better get on with packing your knickers and passport. Just don't count on this place still being here when you get back.'

The conversation continues, jerking back and forth between Edmund and Gareth with Matt and Gayle interjecting now and then, but you don't hear it. With Edmund's words, that airy, buoyant feeling you've carried since your meeting with Anton disperses like so much hot air. Another obstacle looms on the horizon, blotting out the light: a passport.

All afternoon, the issue preys on your mind. Long after Edmund has packed up and stormed out and Anton has shuffled through, muttering something about all pulling together and a lunch meeting in town, it lingers. When the others crowd round Matt's laptop to watch a YouTube video of a surprise proposal at a mud-wrestling tournament, you sneak away to one of the Macs in the far corner and spend an anxious few minutes tapping questions about passports into Google. It frustrates you how slow you are with things like this: the years in the unit just as everyone else was discovering the internet have made you clueless and clumsy. Your fingers fumble over the keyboard. Nevertheless, what you do find isn't good news. A passport will require a birth certificate and fuck knows where you're going to get one of those.

Come hometime, you slip out without saying goodbye to anyone. The heat of the day radiates off the pavement, making your face hot. You walk through street after street: past the old police station, the park, the parcel depot, and up under the railway line. Before you know it, you're walking blindly, choosing turnings at random. Stretch upon stretch of terraced red-brick housing with front doors opening straight on to the street. Smells of dinner drifting out of windows, the stern tones of the six o'clock news. You don't know where you are, but then a familiar landmark looms on a corner: a pub with dried-up window boxes and a flaking sign. The Coach and Horses. It seems unavoidable, just as if it has been drawing you here all along. Before you know it, you're at the door and going in.

You look over at the corner, but there's really no need: he's there, just as you've known he would be. He's almost the only person in the place. The bartender is slumped at the bar, gawping up at a home-improvement show playing silently on the screen above the fruit machine. There's a glossy couple sitting by the window with a guidebook open on the table between them: tourists lost while searching for the real Manchester. Other than them, there's no one else.

You walk over to him. You cough. He looks up.

'I need a passport,' you mutter. 'How much?'

He takes out a cigarette and taps it on the table. Recognition drops into place on his features like a line of cherries on the fruit machine.

'Oh, hello,' he says. 'Been a while.'

'How much?' you say again.

He sits back in his chair, head framed by the wall and a Save the Children collection box on the shelf beside him.

'I often think about you, you know,' he says with a smirk. 'Even now. I think about you long and hard. Sometimes very hard.'

You set your jaw. 'Fuck you,' you say quietly.

'Yeah,' he says, nodding and weaving the cigarette through his fingers. 'That's one of the things I think about. That attitude of yours — that little bit of spark that no one could ever get to. You were a special girl, Ellie. My special girl.'

A wave of feeling surges through you, threatening to fill your eyes with tears. You bite it back and think of hard, cold things: doors clanging shut, clipboards, plastic chairs in bare rooms. After what you've survived today, you are not going to let him get in your way.

'Look, are you going to help me or not?' you say.

He sniffs. 'Oh yeah, I'll help you,' he says. 'For a price.'

You shift impatiently. 'That's what I said,'

you say. 'How much?'

He looks you up and down, taking in your coat from Marks and Spencer, the bag you picked up in an Oxfam shop.

'A grand,' he says. Then his gaze shifts to your crotch. 'Unless you can suggest another way to pay.'

You think of the money mounting up steadily in the account Beryl helped you set up. You'd hoped for something better for it than this.

'Fine,' you say. 'A grand.'

Surprise flashes in his eyes. He scrambles to cover it. 'Two.'

You shake your head. 'You said a grand.'

He shrugs. 'Inflation. Guess you'd better get creative.'

You narrow your eyes at him. Over by the window, the tourists stand up to leave.

'By the way,' you say, 'I've been meaning to ask: how's Mary?'

The shutters come down over his eyes. 'Dead.'

'Oh, I'm sorry to hear that,' you say. 'Overdose, was it? Slash her wrists? Or did your bastard father fuck her to death the same way he tried to do to you?'

He fidgets and drops the cigarette. 'All right, fuck it,' he says. 'I'll do it for a grand.'

He pulls a curled bit of paper out of a

pocket inside his leather jacket. 'Write down what you want on there,' he says. 'Name, date of birth, all that shit.'

You write Trudy's name and that she was born in Camden. Then you put that she was born in 1984 and for her birthday you give today's date.

51

She spent every hour she could with Hellie. Sometimes she read to her from the letter or the pile of books that Nick had brought (although she avoided *Frankenstein* with its tortured margin notes). She agonised for a while over the eighty pounds he'd left, itching to stuff it into the Syria relief fund collection box at the nurses' station and have done. Then she decided to keep it — she had no idea how long she might be here and it was probably a good idea to have something to keep her going other than filching from the nurses, especially as one of them had started narrowing her eyes when she passed her in the corridor. As Nick could barely be bothered to visit and Mother and Akela hadn't appeared once in the time she'd been there, Smudge would treat the money as a contribution to Hellie's welfare, enabling her to stay and watch over her. She tucked the notes under the big tub of hyacinths sent by the *Room for Improvement* producers. When she wasn't reading the scraps of the letter, she kept them there too. It seemed safer than carting it all around in her coat pocket, with its corner that was starting to tear.

She did what she could to keep Hellie comfortable and thought about ways to draw her out. One day, in a charity shop along the South Circular, she happened upon an old cassette player and a selection of tapes with music from the nineties — Blur, the Spice Girls, No Doubt. Exactly the sort of saccharine stuff Hellie used to love. She snapped them up and took them to the ward. A nurse gave her an approving glance as she fumbled to plug it in.

'Music and the radio is good,' she said in a Trinidadian lilt. 'We've seen so many people improve because of it.'

'Really?' said Smudge, straightening up, her face flushed. 'I thought we were past any chance of that now.'

The nurse leaned in conspiratorially. 'The doctors won't tell you this, but don't give up,' she said. 'While there's life, there's hope.'

Smudge put on the Spice Girls. Synthesised gusts of sound enveloped the room, filling it with faintly robotic voices. She closed her eyes, shocked at the vividness of the images that crowded her head: Hellie dabbing on lip gloss on a Saturday evening, while she, Smudge, sat hunched on the bed against the wall. The giggles of the popular girls from school as they sat around Hellie on the bus, sharing headphones, chewing gum and poring over *More* and *Just 17.* The strains of 'Two Become One' drifting down the staircase as she let herself out of the front door and made for the park and the dark oblivion of the trees.

When she wasn't reading or playing music to Hellie, she'd talk. As the days went by, she found herself dredging up more memories and bringing events out into the light that she hadn't thought about in years. Her mind was full of the past. The more she said, the more there was to say. Pictures and incidents thronged her brain, clamouring to be taken up, considered, expressed. She remembered the time they first met Mary loitering by the swings and the games in the park and a birthday party — had it really happened? — where Father donned a red nose and pretended to be a clown. It was as though they were rebuilding the past between them, piecing it together, her speaking and Hellie listening, and thereby making it real. Sometimes she almost felt that

Hellie was speaking too, so sudden and unexpected were the images that crowded into her head, as though they had been suggested not by her own mind but by someone else who had also been there.

Some days she lost track of time. Morning bled into afternoon, which merged with evening, as though someone were blurring the day with water and a thick brush. Visiting hours ceased to mean much. She popped out when it occurred to her to do so; otherwise she sat in the chair by the window and talked to Hellie. When June, the Trinidadian nurse, was on duty, she turned a blind eye and let Smudge stay on long after the sun had sunk below the skyline, plunging the city into an orange gloom. Sometimes she even brought her sandwiches, slipping them on to the locker with a wink.

Slumped in the humming dusk as the monitors winked and the machines sighed, Smudge found time surged and receded. Now the beeping was coming from the machines around Hellie's bed, now it was the lorry reversing outside their house that summer afternoon, bringing Akela's clutter to their lives, and sometimes it was from contraptions in an amusement arcade. Next it was the beeping from the supermarket checkout as Mother stuffed items absently into bags, staring over their heads out into the car park. Smudge was five, fifteen, her own age; she was Helen, Ellie, Trudy then Smudge again. Pictures flowered. Real images sprinkled with the taunts of Neverland. Never was.

She sat in the pink leatherette chair by the window and watched Hellie's chest rise and fall, the shifting of her eyelids. She matched her breathing to her twin's, pulling the air in and out in unison with her until she had the impression that if she stopped, they might both of them founder and die, floating to the surface of the room like fish in a freak-show aquarium on some ghastly pier. Those were the times when she felt — so keenly it was painful — how much she wanted her sister to live. Those were the moments when her desire to hear Hellie speak was so strong that it cancelled all other thoughts and sensations, shunting the paraphernalia of her disordered brain to the far reaches of her consciousness and crowding out the whispers and mutterings of her mind, so that all the while she was in the hospital the voices that usually picked over her thoughts like vultures did not say a word.

52

You and Gareth spend the afternoons in the lead up to the trip playing with classic paintings like children experimenting with Lego, taking the constituent parts and arranging them into outlandish shapes. You introduce Picasso's angular women to Gainsborough's aristocratic beauties. You set Hockney-style sailboats afloat on Constable seas.

The best times are the early evenings, after everyone else has gone, when the two of you push on into the heart of the project and the rest of the world tiptoes away. It reminds you of the sort of laser focus you used to have in the art room at the unit, except there's a difference here: there are two of you in it together and it makes the whole thing calmer. With Gareth there, the experience feels more solid: a tanker ploughing the waters the skiff of your imagination used to skim. It slows things down, but it makes them deeper, more substantial — less liable to capsize.

'I like this,' you tell him one evening, looking across from your easel to see his fair head bent over an A2 sheet of paper, intent on the urban landscape taking shape beneath his hand.

He looks up blinking, disorientated for a second. Then he risks a smile. You will yourself to hold his gaze for more than a second.

The hardest thing about the trip will be leaving Beryl's house. Things have got so comfortable between you that you don't even need to say much any more. You sit mute, balancing your trays on your laps, watching whatever the programmers at the BBC or ITV decide to serve up to you. It's not a hostile silence like you used to have at the table with Mother and Akela or a dead silence such as you'd get with most people in the unit where you felt like there was a wall between you; it's an active, friendly silence. Companionable, that's the word. You feel like you could break it any moment, only you don't need to. It's like what you imagine family — real family — to be. If it didn't sound so weird, you'd tell her so. Only you know she'd purse her lips and think you were coming over all unnecessary.

She's not that sold on you going to Amsterdam.

'Lots of drugs there,' she observes when you first mention it. 'Fallen women. Prostitutes, I should say.'

You nod, shrug. Don't say a word. You know she doesn't mean it how it sounds. You know very well that if one of those fallen women should knock on Beryl's door in a crisis, she'd take her in without a second thought. Hell, you realise with a shock, she already has.

On the last evening, Beryl cooks one of her specialities: toad in the hole with onion gravy. The two of you sit and eat it in front of *Coronation Street.*

'Thanks for everything,' you say, and the words catch in your throat. She flaps them away, bustles out to the kitchen with the empty plates.

'You'll be wanting these, I expect,' she says when she returns, holding out a cool bag packed with sandwiches and slices of home-made banana loaf wrapped up in foil. 'For the ferry,' she adds.

'I'll be in touch, Beryl,' you say. 'I'll call.'

'No,' she says, settling back into her chair. 'You won't. I've seen it a million times. It's as it should be. Now get off upstairs with you and don't forget to strip that bed first thing.'

Then it's morning. You step, blinking, off the bus you caught in what felt like the middle of the night. The white railings of the ferry are tinged blue in the half-light. As the boat pulls out from Hull and into the open waters of the North Sea, you stand at the stern, looking back at the shrinking strip of land, chewing one of Beryl's sandwiches. Mother and Akela are there, you think. Hellie and Richard and the staff at the unit. All at once the past seems very small.

53

She didn't go to the Walworth flat for several days, preferring to wander the leafy streets near the hospital at night and sip cups of tea in a greasy spoon on the South Circular. A couple of afternoons she dozed in the chair beside Hellie's bed, but mostly she was buzzing too much to think about sleep.

When at last she did go back to change her clothes, she found someone had scrawled FUUUUCK! on the wall by the bins and there were fag ends and bits of broken glass around the back door. The clothes in her room smelled sour but she put them on anyway, closing her eyes to zone out the panic that reverberated at her from the ceiling and the walls — all the jagged energy absorbed into the woodchip and crumbling plaster over the preceding years.

Back at the hospital, she popped into the canteen to pick up a Mars Bar. She was queuing to pay when she felt a hand on her shoulder. Turning round, she saw a familiar man with wavy blond hair and a slightly dominant chin looking down at her.

'Trudy,' said the man. 'Well, not Trudy, but . . .'

'Yes,' she said, gaping with surprise as the pieces fell into place. 'Anton. Fuck!'

She saw him look around anxiously.

'Sorry,' she mumbled. 'Knee-jerk reaction.'

He shook his head. 'Quite all right.'

He was holding a banana and a carton of Um Bongo.

'Oh, it's not for me,' he said quickly. 'It's for my sister's son. My nephew. He's eight. We're here visiting my father.'

He nodded over to a group of well-dressed people at a table by the window.

'Oh,' she said. 'Sorry to hear that. What . . . ?'

'Stroke,' said Anton briskly. 'Nothing to be done about it. Not long now, I suspect. Still, they keep trying to see if they can get some sort of response out of him.'

She nodded awkwardly, feeling the chocolate bar starting to go soft in her hand through its wrapper. What must he think of her after the way she left things? After she ran out like that? She glanced at his face, trying to read the answer there, but his expression was contained and cordial.

'And you?' he said.

'I'm here visiting my . . . friend. She had an accident. A car accident. She's in a coma.'

Anton shook his head. 'Rotten luck.'

There was a pause. He fiddled with the straw stuck on the back of the Um Bongo carton. Then they both tried to talk at once.

'How have you been?' he ventured, but she waved the words away.

'Best not go into it,' she said. Her voice was different, talking to him. Lighter, posher. The old Trudy confidence seeping through in spite of everything.

Anton nodded. 'Right-oh.' He tapped his foot on the floor. 'Listen, I'm glad I ran into you — even in these circumstances. There's something I've been wanting to tell you.'

She held up her hands, alarmed suddenly that he was going to do something to bring it all back: what happened up in Manchester, the beautiful, bright things ruined.

'Please, really,' she said. 'It's all in the past. I can't do anything about that now. I'm sorry, I should have handled things better. I should have been more open with you from day one, but I —'

'No,' he said, putting his hand on her arm, commandeering the conversation once again. It must be something they taught them at public school, she reflected — that cast-iron ability to insist, to impose your will on others. 'No,' he said again. 'It's nothing to do with what happened.'

He glanced over at the table by the window. The people there were getting up, putting on their coats. Amongst them, next to a glamorous girl in a trouser suit, she saw someone who must be Anton's mother: the chin was the same and there was something familiar about the eyes. She was a sturdy woman, Smudge saw, resolute. The sort who would think it poor form to cry.

When she looked back at Anton, she noticed a change had come over him, his assurance sunk beneath a boyish nervousness. He was scuffing his shoe on the linoleum.

'Look, I've got to go,' he said, fumbling in his trouser pocket. 'But here, take my card. Call me and let's arrange a time to meet up. I promise, you won't regret it.'

'Anton,' came a voice from across the room.

'Yes,' he said. 'Coming.'

He pressed the card into her hand. 'You won't forget, will you?'

She shrugged. 'Sure,' she said, not meeting his eye.

He gave her a brilliant smile and hurried away to join his relatives. She slipped the card into her coat pocket to join the empty chewing-gum wrappers and receipts and the other bits of yesterday's rubbish.

54

The office is in a side street, just off one of the canals, above a shop selling shoes made from car tyres. You have to climb a narrow wooden staircase to reach it, but once you're up the place opens into a huge, light-filled loft with large, long windows looking down on to the pedestrians and cyclists passing in the street below. The room is sparsely furnished, but everything you might need is there: easels, Macs, a large drawing board, a kettle, microwave and selection of tea and coffee, a sofa. You turn to Gareth with a grin. Your expressions both say the same thing: you've lucked out.

'We hope you like it,' says the small man in spectacles who shows you round. 'We hope it is —' his fingers pluck the air for the word — 'conducive to artistic work. We are business people. What do we know? We have done our best but if there is anything you want, just call. No one will disturb you here.

You come and go as you please.'

He is so self-effacing that it's not until you ask him to repeat his name when he's leaving that you realise he is Jan Heijn, director of Air Bubble, the company you'll be working for, and heir to a sizeable chunk of the Ahold millions.

After the door closes behind him, cutting off the street noise, Gareth turns to you with a laugh. 'Fuck me,' he says. 'Just . . . fuck m-me!'

You laugh with him. It's the first time you've ever heard him swear.

That first day, you don't do much. You get out the sketches and line them up along the walls. There is a neat clip system that lets you hang them against the bare brickwork so you can consider them all together. Some of the ideas are good, others are dead in the water.

'The Mona Lisa's rubbish,' observes Gareth, looking at the rough of the famous figure cradling an outsize mobile phone. You have to agree.

You have lunch in a small cafe across the way. Somehow, that turns into an afternoon outing and soon you're both strolling through the streets, drinking in the sights and sounds of the new city. You wander in and out of shops, picking up things just to feel the weight of them.

'Is it me or is design just so much better here?' says Gareth, staring at a desk lamp created out of a single curve of wood.

'Everything's better,' you say. 'All of it.'

You mean it. This place gives you a feeling of life expanding, possibility unfurling its red carpet in every direction you look. You are different here. More.

Towards the middle of the afternoon, you come upon a long line of people snaking from a crossroads in the direction of one of the main canals.

'Queue for a gig?' speculates Gareth.

'Unlikely,' you say, looking at a grey-haired American couple squinting at a map.

It turns out the people are waiting to go into the Anne Frank House.

'Shall we?' says Gareth.

You shrug.

Within half an hour, you're clambering up the steep staircase behind the bookshelf and into the cramped rooms beyond. You're shocked to find Anne's pin-ups on one of the walls: pictures of a young Princess Elizabeth, Greta Garbo and Ginger Rogers. It seems an intrusion somehow that these things should be opened up for the scrutiny of so many eyes: ephemera made permanent by virtue of any untimely death. Had Anne lived another six months, you think, she might have decided that Elizabeth was too heavy about the jaw to be beautiful and taken the picture down, just as she might have gone off that dork of a boy she mooned about the attic space with, but instead, here she was, for ever chalked up as a fan of the future Queen of England, with a teenage crush because of factors beyond her control. A frozen version of an unfinished self.

You're both subdued when you get out. There's nothing appropriate to say. Gareth keeps blinking and shaking his head, whistling through his teeth.

You stroll silently through the streets for a while. Then an idea strikes you.

'Come on,' you say, taking Gareth's hand. 'I know what we need.'

You've heard about them from people in the unit: the coffee shops that sell weed. In your mind you picture them as genteel places, with cookies on the counter and an espresso machine bubbling against the back wall. But it turns out they're nothing like that. The first one you come to is packed with English guys in tracksuits — some sort of stag do or birthday jaunt. There's a grim, aggressive feeling in the air, a menace that seems to suggest that someone or something is going to get punched or fucked before very long.

You lead the way on through the back streets, becoming adept at spotting the cannabis leaf symbol on plastic signs jutting out over doorways. The next couple of places are equally unpromising, but at last you find yourself in a quiet alleyway, facing a doorway that seems less intimidating. You push through hanging strands of coloured tape into what looks like a sweetshop run by teenagers. The whole place is painted black, with scuffmarks up the walls. There is a foosball table in the middle and a television playing an episode of Dutch *X Factor*. The glass counter is stacked with chocolate bars and packets of crisps. A scruffy guy leans on it, chewing the end of his ponytail.

Fear throbs in your chest for a moment. There is something familiar about the place that you do not like — a recklessness hiding in the corners that might rush in and wrest you into giddy spirals once more. You swallow it back and head for the counter.

'Pre-rolled, please,' you say.

'Hash or grass?' says the guy.

You plump for grass. He yawns and reaches one down from a box on the shelf behind him without looking back.

You pay and settle yourselves at a table by

the window, an ashtray between you. Gareth stares about him, wide-eyed.

'It's surreal, isn't it?' he says. 'That you can just do this here. That no one bats an eyelid.'

You shrug and spark up. Cloudiness floods down your throat and into your lungs: a breath of herbal peace. Yep, this is going to be a good thing after all. You take another toke and pass it over.

Gareth puts the joint gingerly to his lips. You squint; think about asking him if he's ever done it before; dismiss the idea.

You smoke in silence for a bit, passing the joint back and forth between you. Gareth draws at it with urgent little gasps. After a while, he gets this loose look about his face. His hair starts to stick out at odd angles and it's as though someone has unlatched his features, expanding his expressions by half a centimetre. The craters at his temples stand out dark against his skin.

'I like this place,' he says, nodding. 'I . . . I like this place.'

You reach for the joint, take a few more puffs. A sense of well-being floods through you. Life's owed you this, you think. All the shit you've been through and now here you are, working as an artist in Amsterdam. It's like, the crap that a normal person would go through in a lifetime has been concentrated just in your first two and a bit decades. But now you're through it and what's left is years and years of good times. You smile to yourself, hum something, a half-remembered tune . . . something about celebration and good times. Cheesy, but it has a kind of truth to it, you realise. Everything does, if only you know where to look.

Gareth's eyes go wider still. He studies your face as though seeing it for the first time.

'I have a confession to make,' he says. 'Don't laugh.'

He scrubs his hands over his head, making his hair even tuftier. He leans in.

'I fancy you,' he says.

You narrow your eyes at him. 'Fuck off,' you say.

'Seriously,' he says. 'I'm not joking.'

You roll your eyes.

'Seriously,' he says again. 'I fancy you hard. Literally. The first time you came in, your first day, I got, like, this m-massive boner. Edmund was g-getting all aggro and there was me, stuck behind the easel, trying to hide my m-massive boner.'

You look at him for a second. Then a gust of laughter blows through you, exploding out of your mouth, spattering him with spray.

'Hey!' he says, wiping his face. 'I said, don't laugh.'

But he is laughing too. You're both laughing. It's so fucking funny. You laugh so much that three guys playing dominoes in the corner turn around to stare. You laugh until the table shakes and you think you might fall off your chair.

'Oh, blow it, that's really unprofessional, isn't it?' says Gareth when the shuddering subsides. 'Why did I say that? You're going to hate me now, aren't you?'

You pick up the joint, respark it, take a toke.

'Let me get one thing straight,' you say. 'When you say "massive boner" . . .'

'Oh, get lost,' says Gareth. 'All right. M-Medium-sized boner. M-Massive for me, anyway.'

There's a pause. 'Not that I'm —' he begins, and sags in his seat, unable to carry the sentence through. 'Anyway, a-we shouldn't be talking about this. A-We're colleagues. Professionals.'

You grin. 'Yes, we are,' you say.

You stay in the coffee shop for a while, eating crisps and drinking Coke. You'll be the first to admit it: you're quite stoned.

That joint packed more of a punch than you were expecting. You realise it when the two of you start to analyse Dutch *X Factor* and seem to hit upon a recipe that would cancel out all the problems of the European Union and, ultimately, resolve conflicts around the world. You can't keep hold of the precise details, but it has something to do with establishing a massive global judging panel and the music of ABBA.

The sun is starting to set when at last you shuffle out. It shines along the street, turning the windows golden.

'Wow,' says Gareth. 'A-What a day.'

You look up at him, seeing how the light gilds him, turning the tips of his hair orange. With a shock, you see that he is beautiful. His eyes, you realise, are glittering stars.

You reach up and place a kiss upon his lips. His body jolts, then softens, folding you into an embrace. You kiss for a while, standing there in the street with bikes zipping past. Then he pulls away.

'Come on,' he says, taking your hand. This time he leads the way.

55

Just gone three, according to the clock above the door, and outside it was dark. The lights were low, the humming and sighing of the machines muffled. Night lay like a blanket over everything deadening sound. If she popped her head out of the room now, the corridor would look like something from a horror film: deserted, jaundiced, grim. Smudge sat blinking in the chair by the window. What had happened? Had she fallen asleep? How come they hadn't kicked her out?

The room shrank and expanded with each sigh of the ventilator. Other rooms tried to crowd in and take its place: Nick and Hellie's attic. The bedroom in the maisonette in Walworth. The one at the unit. The room at Beryl's place. The one back at Mother's house where two girls lay side by side all those years ago. Single beds, all of them, with only one exception: that apartment room in Amsterdam. None of them truly hers.

She screwed up her eyes against the memories and shook her head. When she opened them, she saw Hellie was watching her.

'Hello,' said Hellie.

'Hello,' said Smudge. Shock sent ripples through her, making her arms and legs numb.

Hellie wrinkled her nose. 'Well, this is a turn up for the books,' she said.

Smudge said nothing. The moment stretched. She had the sense that everything had turned to porcelain and if she made a false move the world might smash.

'You must hate me,' said Hellie at length, wincing as though the words were painful.

Smudge shifted in her chair. The plastic cover grunted under her, farted. She thought of the letter with its manic scrawl.

'No,' she said. 'I did, but not any more.'

Hellie nodded. Seemed to understand.

'I had to do what I did,' she said, her voice rasping and faint.

'Because of Father,' anticipated Smudge. 'Because of what you saw.'

Hellie inclined her head.

'I didn't have the strength to be her as she was,' she said. 'To be Ellie. I couldn't live to

497

that script.'

She paused. The tube in her throat glistened. It occurred to Smudge that she should call someone, alert the staff to Hellie's consciousness. But she was frightened of what might happen if she looked away. The seconds passed and she did not.

'Neither could I,' said Smudge. 'I just smashed on. Screwed things up. I went to prison, for fuck's sake. Well, not prison, but as good as. Worse.'

'Exactly,' said Hellie. 'You escaped.'

Smudge closed her eyes.

'And we had fun, didn't we?' Hellie's voice continued. 'Before it all happened, we did have fun sometimes. The trip to Dorset . . . cycling in the park. That day on the cliffs with him before he went. He used to bring us so many things. You remember the time he bought up every T-shirt in that shop?'

'Because he liked the colours,' Smudge said.

'And the day we came home to find the living room full of cuddly toys —'

'Because he thought they'd be lonely if he left any of them behind.' Smudge saw it now: every surface covered with stuffed animals with plastic eyes and goofy grins, and Mother with her head in her hands in the midst of their whoops of delight.

'He was like one of those characters on children's television,' said Hellie. 'Magical. Larger than life. I always thought of him when I watched those programmes with the girls . . . with Heloise. Reality wasn't colourful enough for him. He should have been in a story, but instead someone's imagination got cracked and he ended up in the real world.'

Smudge nodded. It was true, that was Father, an escapee from a daydream. Mr Majeika.

Hellie took a rattling breath and put a hand to her throat where the tube dug in. 'I saved one of his pictures,' she said. 'That day Mother cleared out the box room and burned his paintings in the garden. It's a little one of an exploding firework, glittering like him. I hid it behind the wardrobe in our room at Mother's house. It's in the attic at my place now. I thought I should tell you about it so you can have it, in case . . . you know.'

Smudge bent forward and took her sister's hand. It was cool to the touch, soft.

'I'm sorry,' she said.

Hellie blinked. 'What for?'

'For the things we did. Me. Mary. Mother too, I suppose. Father — for what we made Ellie become.'

Hellie shook her head, the tube shimmering.

'You were just being yourself,' she said in a distant voice. 'That's all any of us can do. Most of the time.'

Smudge looked at Hellie and saw how small she was: how the bones stuck out through her cheeks and sinews quivered in her throat. Suffering, she saw, was written there. A pang of compassion ricocheted through her and she wanted to lean in and gather her sister up, take her back to the little bed by the wall in the small house and make everything cheery and joyful, screw up the past like a child's drawing and do it all over again.

'I'm sorry about Emily,' she said and it came out with a sob. 'Losing a baby . . . I . . .'

Hellie shook her head again. She opened her mouth to reply and emitted a high-pitched beep. Smudge stared at her for a moment, uncomprehending, her sister's face sparkling through the lens of her tears. Then she glanced up at the monitor above the bed and saw its flat green line. When she looked back at the bed Hellie's eyes were closed and she was lying as she always had done, facing the ceiling.

Daylight was streaming through the window. There was the sound of feet running in the corridor. Then bodies pushed in between Smudge and the bed. She was left sitting in the corner, the cool sensation of Hellie's fingers fading against her palm.

56

You move into Gareth's room in the rented apartment. It has a large window looking out over the trees that run down the centre of the road towards the train station that will one day take you to the airport and home. You like to stand naked at the window and look out across the city. Any pedestrian or cyclist who glances up going by could see you, but you don't care. You're happy and you know it and you really want to show it. Sometimes you clap your hands.

When the two of you are feeling reckless, you go back to the coffee shop and sit squinting up at *Lotto Weekend Miljonairs* and *Holland's Got Talent* through plumes of smoke. You don't venture there often, however. You don't feel you need to. As the weeks pass, you prefer to spend your time walking around the lake in Vondelpark and visiting the art galleries, the Rijksmuseum and the Van Gogh Museum, where you sit on the floor, often for hours at a time, sketching out elements for ideas. What's interesting is how, even when you're drawing from the same painting — Van Gogh's chair, for example, or Rembrandt's self-portrait (you have an idea for a while of redoing it to show the artist clutching an MP3 player) — the pair of you come up with quite different results. They always relate and they're always recognisable, but whereas you home in on minute aspects, capturing the veins on the back of a hand, the sweep of an ear, Gareth draws down the essence of the picture on to the page. His lines are bold and strong, sure. Yours are little scuffmarks stitched together to form a whole.

'You have an amazing eye for detail,' he says one day, looking over your shoulder. 'You could be a good forger.'

You wonder for a moment if he's on to you — if he knows Trudy is a fake — but you paste a smile over your alarm and when he starts to talk about a new idea for the campaign, you realise he meant nothing by it. All the same, you're relieved that the museum doesn't have *The Starry Night.* You don't know what you'd do if you had to sit here, with him sketching the swirls of the painting that framed the director's face that day they told you you were leaving the unit.

Your favourite times are when you're both in the studio, working on ideas. There are moments when you'll lose yourself in a picture and look up to find him there. The joy of it startles you: a bolt of feeling enlivening your senses. It is as though someone has plunged you into another reality; as if the channel has been changed on the TV set of your existence and now you are in another life.

The feeling deepens on the rare occasions you meet the clients. Jan Heijn's staff members from Air Bubble are every bit as respectful and kind as he is, expressing wonder and admiration at even the most mediocre of your efforts and venturing gentle jokes in their quirkily modulated English. They take you out for meals at tastefully expensive restaurants and, once, for an afternoon going up and down the canals on Jan's private launch.

It seems unreal a lot of the time. As the weeks go by, you learn to trust it more, but there are still nights when you lie awake next to Gareth, staring up at the dark blue sky and the silhouette of the trees outside the window. One night he shocks you by reaching for you and murmuring something when you thought he was asleep.

'Tell me something,' he says, his voice thick and sleepy.

'Like what?' you say after a pause.

'Tell me about the tattoo,' he says. 'The "MONSTER" written on your forehead. Tell me about that.'

You touch your fingers to the edge of your eyebrow. You'd forgotten the word was there. It's been so long since you've thought about it. You've grown used to wearing your fringe long, screening the letters from view. You blink in the darkness.

'Why?' you say.

He runs his palm over your belly.

'Because I want to know you. Because I want to have something that g-gives me the key to all of what you are.'

You open your mouth and it comes out in a rush. 'I had mental health issues as a teenager. I wasn't well. This was one of the things I did then.'

You feel his body stiffen. Outside the window, the trees shake their heads. You shouldn't have said that.

He takes a deep breath. 'What sort of mental health issues?' he says. And then, hopefully: 'Depression?'

You lie still. 'Bipolar disorder,' you say. 'What they used to call manic depression. At least, that's what they decided it was.'

505

'How does that . . . ?' he ventures in a small voice.

'Highs and lows,' you say. 'Ups and downs. Proper mental.' And then, because you've done it now and you might as well finish the job while it's still in your control: 'My family didn't understand it. They basically threw me out. I had to go into a secure unit.'

Time freezes. The night yawns. Reality, cold-eyed and slimy, sits in the black depths, licking its lips like a toad. 'I knew it,' it whispers. 'You couldn't keep it up, could you? You were only ever going to screw this up. That was the way this story was always going to end. We both know happiness isn't meant for the likes of you.'

The world sags and begins to slip away. Gareth gives a long, low whistle. Then he turns to you and takes you in his arms.

'My poor baby,' he says, rocking you against him. 'What fucking, hideous bad luck.'

His gentleness shocks you and the tears come in a rush, dissolving you into sobs. Because it was bad luck. It was. It was fucking, hideous bad luck. It was. It was. And why didn't anyone ever see that — say that — before? You cry for the little girl in the garden, the teenager in one beige room after another, the child standing in the hallway staring up at Mother and Akela as a man lugs luggage up the stairs.

He holds you until at last you fall quiet, stroking his fingers through your hair. Suddenly you're afraid his tenderness might suffocate you. You push him away, wriggle back.

'Now you,' you say.

'Me?' he says.

'You,' you say again, pointedly, urgently — shocked by how vulnerable you are all of a sudden, by how much he knows. 'Tell me something about you. The key to you. Something that gives me the same power.'

He puts a hand to his face. In the dim light, his eyes are pools of darkness. The pockmarks on his temples harbour shadows.

'Something that g-gives you the same power?' he says wonderingly. 'It's not a competition, you know. I'm not trying to control you. That's not a-what this is about.'

You nod. But secretly you know it is. That's the thing. It is.

'All the same,' you say.

He coughs. 'A-Well, all right.' He takes a deep breath. 'I've only slept with one person.'

The words sound tight, as though he has buttoned up his throat.

'You've only slept with one person before

me?' you say.

'No. I've only slept with one person.'

The truth assembles itself in the silence.

'Oh,' you say. 'I —'

'I knew it!' he said. 'I knew it would ruin everything if I told you that. I wasn't g-going to say anything. Just forget it, please. Try to forget.'

The little boy in his voice clutches at your heart.

'No, it's OK,' you say. 'It's just a surprise, that's all.'

You draw him to you, breathing in his newness, his innocence. You want to take it and wrap it round you like a cloak. Perhaps it will be enough for both of you. Gladness bobs to the surface. You were wrong: this isn't about control. You stroke his smooth skin. Its softness makes you want to climb inside him, put on what he is, and begin the world again.

57

A pulmonary embolism. A blood clot travelling up from the legs until it blocks the artery from the heart to the lungs. That was the most likely explanation. That's what they would write on Hellie's death certificate, subject to the findings of the coroner's post mortem. Dr Jalil didn't seem all that surprised. They were quite common in people who had been immobile for long periods, he said — his voice assuming a weary tone as he explained, as though he'd seen it coming all along. They took precautions — stockings, blood thinners in some cases — but nothing was a hundred per cent. It made Smudge want to shake him. Wake up, Doctor, she wanted to say. This was someone's life. This was my sister's — my — life.

But she didn't. She sat still and nodded while he talked, a sad, respectful smile on her face. She didn't mention the middle-of-the-night conversation. She didn't trust herself to put it into words. As far as she could see, there was no box for it on any of Dr Jalil's forms.

When Nick arrived — rumpled, bewildered, not meeting her eye — she kept it from him too. Within an hour it was unsayable.

They were in the canteen when Mother and Horace appeared, striding across the linoleum clutching overnight bags. The chairs shrieked as they pulled them out.

'Oh Nick,' sighed Mother, pecking her son-in-law on the cheek. She had had time to style her hair with curling tongs.

She didn't glance at Smudge.

They sat in silence for a minute or two while Nick went to get everyone coffee. Mother looked everywhere but at Smudge. Horace drummed his fingers on the table top. There was a flake of superglue stuck to one of his nails. He'd been working at the model planes again.

Smudge took a deep breath.

'It was all very sudden,' she said. 'But they say it's one of those things that can happen with coma patients. It's all the lying down, you see. It makes people vulnerable to clots.'

Behind the counter, the coffee machine hissed disapprovingly.

Mother pursed her lips and looked out of the window.

'They did everything they could,' said Smudge. 'The response was very quick. There were three or four people in the room within seconds.'

Mother jerked a nod. Said nothing. The make-up was slathered over her wrinkles like paint on cracked plaster.

'I'm just trying to tell you how it was,' said Smudge. 'I thought you'd want to know.'

Mother turned from the window, fire flashing in her eyes.

'I'll tell you how it was,' she said. 'You sat and waited for this. You've been wanting this to happen for years. You *prayed* for this — if you even believe in God, which I very much doubt. And now you're sitting there triumphant. You've got what you wanted. Things are finally ruined beyond repair.'

Horace put a hand on her arm but she brushed it away.

'No, Horace, I won't be quiet,' she said. 'I don't know what she's doing here. Or rather, I do know. Yes, I do. She's come to gloat. To glory in our misery. Well, she can take a good look because this is all she's getting.'

Mother clamped her mouth shut, but the

words kept coming and she had to spit them out like bitter coffee grounds.

'I wouldn't be surprised if she didn't have a hand in it somewhere along the line,' she continued, not to Horace or to Smudge but to the air, to some jury she seemed to feel was sitting in judgement on proceedings. 'Flicking a button on a machine or some such. A fit young woman dying of a blood clot — whoever heard of such a thing? She must take us all for fools. Well, she might find she's miscalculated. She might find that when we look into it, when we get a proper investigation, when the coroner does his post mortem, the story doesn't hang together. She might find it's only a matter of time before things come crashing down around her again and we gather the evidence to put her back inside, back in the criminal loony bin where she should have stayed all along to protect decent people from her bile and poison. She might find —'

Smudge stood up.

'You're wrong,' she said. 'You're wrong about how things were between us.'

Mother offered a sour smile. 'Am I?' she said. 'Am I really?'

'She wrote to me,' said Smudge. 'You didn't know that, did you? She wrote to me — all sorts of thoughts about her life, about

Emily, about Father, about us growing up. She admitted the swap had happened. She called me Helen. It was on the envelope. "Helen Sallis" it said. She knew the truth. And she was ill too, Mother. Mentally ill. Like Father. Like me.'

Mother gave a jolt. Her expression faltered for a moment. She blinked rapidly. Then she glanced at Horace and folded her arms.

'Oh, really,' she said, her disdain sharper than ever. 'Helen said that, did she? And why should I believe that?'

'Because I've got the letter,' said Smudge. 'You only have to look at it to see. She wasn't well.'

She delved into her coat pocket but her fingers met wrappers and scraps. Apart from that her pockets were empty. Then she remembered the hyacinth tub on the locker.

'It's in the room,' she said. 'Wait here.'

She didn't hang around for the lift but took the stairs two at a time up to the second floor. She ran down the corridors, erupting through swing doors, barging past trolleys, impatient with anything standing in her way. Soon it would be out. Soon it would all be out. And Mother would be forced to acknowledge the truth.

But when she got to Hellie's room, the bed was bare, the mattress stripped. She

513

turned to the locker and saw only the scuffed plastic of its surface. She ran to it in panic and pulled open its doors. She wrenched it away from the wall and peered down at the balls of dust behind it. Everything was gone. There was nothing left.

She heard footsteps and looked round.

'Poor child,' said June, coming up to pat her arm. 'I'm so sorry about your sister. It's cruel how it can happen like that, totally out of the blue.'

But she couldn't focus on June's kindness.

'June,' she said. 'Where would they have put things when they cleaned out the room?'

'What, the flowers and such? I expect most of them went into the bin. They were getting a bit past it.'

'There was a tub of hyacinths . . .'

'Oh, yes,' said June, smiling. 'We've got that at the nurses' station. I'll put it in a bag for you to take home.'

'It had some paper under it. Pages with writing on it. Money too. I don't suppose —'

June sucked her teeth and frowned. She leant closer.

'There's been trouble since we've had these new cleaning contractors in. We've had food go missing — biscuits and people's lunch. If there was money, I'm afraid you're unlikely to see it again. If people will take the food out of other people's mouths, they'll surely stop at nothing.'

Smudge waved the words away. 'The money's not important,' she said. 'It's the papers. They were letters from my sister, you see, and . . . I mean, they didn't look like much. The cleaner probably thought they were rubbish. But if there's a recycling bin, perhaps —'

June squeezed her shoulder. 'Let me go and check,' she said and bustled out.

Smudge looked around the room as she waited, trying to remember it as it had been when Hellie was there. Already she was struggling to recall the colours and scents of the flowers, the sounds of the machines. It was as though, with the chlorine bleach and swipes of the mop, the cleaner had not only disinfected the space but neutralised it too. It was faceless now: an insipid backdrop ready to form the setting for someone else's drama.

She turned as June came back into the room and saw sorrow in the nurse's eyes.

'Oh, sweetness, I'm so sorry,' she said gently. 'The collection's already been done. They emptied the bins an hour ago. There's no way you'll get things back now.'

Smudge said goodbye and left, carrying

the bag with the hyacinths. When she got to the ground floor, she glanced across at the canteen. Through the glass doors, she could see them sitting at the table, Mother holding forth on something to Nick while Horace jabbed at a Bakewell slice. She would not go in and tell them what had happened. There was nothing she could bring herself to say. Let them stay there with the possibility of the truth for a little while longer. They would draw their own conclusions soon enough.

She left the hospital for the last time and stepped into the dull daylight. A bus sighed as it pulled away from the stop outside. Somewhere, a siren wailed.

58

You don't know precisely when you become aware of it. The knowledge comes upon you gradually, like a photograph developing, becoming more and more distinct every time you look at it until you feel the truth: your body, which has been filling out over the past weeks, has begun a new project. Deep within you a little knot of life is forming: a hard, condensed nubbin of all the happiness you've taken in since you've been here. Of all the love.

At first, you don't believe it. You'd never have thought that was possible for you. Not after all the years, the risks. You'd always assumed that part of you was broken, and that it was probably for the best.

But your body keeps insisting on a different account, until, one Saturday morning, you stand in front of the crooked little mirror in the Amsterdam apartment's bathroom with a hand on your belly. As you let the realisation in, your stomach takes a roller-coaster plunge. Seconds pass. Minutes. But the giddy whirling doesn't stop. You probe the feeling cautiously. It's unfamiliar to you, this fluttering, tingling sensation. It's so unknown that it takes you some time to decode it. At first you think it's fear, plain and simple. Then you realise, wonderingly, that it's joy. You're joyful. You.

You carry the feeling carefully from the bathroom, vigilant in case it spills or cracks. You get dressed with the fluttering going on inside you, shocked into smiles by the pinch of your jeans about your waist as you try to do them up.

When you and Gareth go out to a bar a bit later, you hum to yourself as you stroll past the ponds in Vondelpark.

'Happy?' he says, catching hold of your hand.

You nod and smile, give him a kiss. But you don't say anything. It's too early yet, too unformed. It's like the flash of an image you have when you first get an idea for a drawing. You need to give it time to become solid and three-dimensional before you can let him in to walk round it, appreciate it for what it is. 'Beer?' he says when you sit down at a little table at the bar.

You open your mouth to say yes, before

you remember. 'Yes,' you say. 'I mean, no. Apple juice, please.'

He shrugs OK and lopes off to the bar.

You watch him standing there talking to the bartender in the halting Dutch he's somehow picked up, despite everyone here speaking English. And that's when it hits you in a warm, glad flood: you are going to have this baby. You are going to be a family. You are going to choose this life.

59

The sun was sinking towards the tip of the Shard, and the space on the skyline where Nick's Hairpin would eventually stand, when she arrived in Walworth. She drifted to the flat. In the absence of a better plan, she thought dully, she would spend the night there. Time enough to face the rest of her life in the morning. Hours — years probably — to sit in the battered armchair in the living room, staring at the slant of sun making its way across the ripped lino and bare concrete, and take it all in. She sniffed and blinked away the memory of Hellie lying in her hospital bed, holding her hand. One thing was certain: no one would bother her now.

But when she walked round the side of the maisonette, she found the back door smashed open. A rotten, charred smell emanated from the interior. Gingerly, she pushed her way in, trainers crunching broken glass.

'Hello?' she called. 'Hello?'

The only reply her calls met with was the reproachful glare of the kitchen cabinets, which had been smashed and splintered and sprayed with red paint. There were cans and bottles strewn over the floors, graffiti tags and scribbles on every surface, and in the living room, she saw, someone had tried to start a fire. There was a blackened circle on the space where the coffee table once stood. She didn't bother to go into the bedroom.

Back on the street, she stood and stared at the bay window of the front room. She could just make out the slashes of paint across the dirty glass and remains of the tie-dyed sarong. From here, they looked like large red crosses banning her, cancelling her out.

'Disgusting, isn't it?' said a voice.

Smudge turned to see the woman from next door emerging from her flat, the Rottweiler straining at its lead.

'Estate kids got in,' said the woman, squinting against the afternoon sun. 'Trashed the place.'

'Oh,' said Smudge.

'Not that it was much better before,' said the woman with a shrug. 'Some scrubber lived there. Drug addict most likely. Real piece of scum. The sort you didn't want to be around your kids, you know?'

She shifted and wrapped another loop of the lead around her hand. She looked at Smudge and unease flashed on her face.

'Sorry. You don't know her, do you? She wasn't a friend of yours?'

Smudge shook her head. 'No,' she said. 'She used to be. But that was a long time ago.'

The woman exhaled noisily. 'Well, that's a relief,' she said with a guffaw. 'Thought I'd gone and put my foot in it there. Me and my big mouth.'

She turned and headed off up the road in the direction of the high street, the dog surging and strutting. Smudge watched them go. A cold wind blew through her. Well, that was it then. She was finished. There was nowhere left to go. She felt blank — emptied out like the little hospital room — and tired. Even her mind seemed to have abandoned her body, floating off into the ether so that she seemed to be looking down on herself from a cloud. Dully, she wondered what would happen if she just stood here for ever. Whether anyone would do anything.

She dug her hands into her pockets against the beginnings of the evening chill. Amid the wrappers and shreds of receipts, her fingers met a small, smooth rectangle tucked into the seam. She pulled it out. *Anton Cartwright,* it read.

60

The end of your time in Amsterdam seems a long way off and then all of a sudden it's next week. The autumn has faded and blown away, stripping the trees in Vondelpark. Christmas has come and gone — a quiet one that you spend together in the little apartment, wrapped in a duvet on the sofa, eating Kerststol and chocolate. By the middle of January, the ideas you and Gareth have been playing with and kicking around have crystallised into six sharp canvases. There's a reworking of *The Windmill at Wijk bij Duurstede* with a big water-cooling tower where the original building stands, and one of Van Gogh's sunflower paintings with some of the blooms creased and crumpled around the base of the vase, showing that they are, in fact, paper imitations. There's also — you're particularly proud of this one — a rendering of the *Girl with a Pearl Earring* with headphones where the jewellery should be.

The client can't get enough of them.

'We love how they're so subtle,' says Jan. 'You have to look twice. That's what we want. That's what the product is all about. You shouldn't notice anything is different at a first glance. Only later should you see that there has been a modification. In fact, an upgrade.'

The company is going to launch the campaign at a grand reception in an exclusive restaurant in town: a place serving tasting menus on tiny plates, with flights of wine to match. It's in a carefully restored seventeenth-century building. You've walked past it a few times but never dared to go in. Now you're set to be guests of honour, schmoozing the local glitterati.

'We want them to feel they can talk to you about the process,' says Heike, Jan's assistant, toying with a lettuce leaf over lunch at their pristine head office one day in the final week. 'We hope you don't mind. We know artists are particular about that sort of thing, but you see it's so interesting for those of us who are not talented in such a way to hear how it all comes together. And, of course, for us it adds something to the campaign.'

You bite back your smile and try to look

grudging, feeling that it would be unprofessional to seem too keen. If your eighteen-year-old self, setting out from the unit that grubby day, had known that you would be here now, preparing to do this, she'd scarcely have believed it.

The final few days are so filled with last-minute alterations and decisions about the best way to display the works that you and Gareth barely get a chance to talk. You fall into bed exhausted, your feet throbbing, your head pounding. For you, it's extra tiring. The little knot of being in your belly has started to exert its influence over you, whipping up squalls of nausea from the flat calm of a bright morning and sending your thoughts straying into sleepy backwaters when you should be focusing on the problems at hand. There are times when Gareth has to repeat things to you, hammering sentences out slowly and deliberately to make the meaning plain. He looks at you strangely now and then but he never asks what's going on and you haven't said a word.

On the afternoon before the launch, you treat yourselves to lunch in a cafe by one of the canals. Everything's done. The paintings are up and the room in the restaurant is in the capable hands of the client's PR firm.

There is nothing for you to do but while away the time between now and six o'clock when you must present yourselves at the launch looking artistic and approachable.

You take a sip of your orange juice and set the glass down on the table. You clear your throat.

'It's been great, hasn't it?' you say.

'Mmmn?' says Gareth. He looks distracted, his mind on the show.

For a moment, your resolve falters. Then you remember that tomorrow the pair of you will be on a plane back to Manchester. This time won't come again.

'All this,' you say. 'Being here.'

'Oh God, yeah,' he says. 'It's been a dream.'

You relax, smile. It's going to be all right.

'What's been your favourite part of it?'

He puffs out his cheeks, looks around. 'The work, I'd say,' he says. 'Getting to do that sort of work. Having that freedom. It's incredible.'

Something curls up inside you. You strive to keep your smile from slipping. The bright future you've imagined starts to tarnish. A voice whispers that you have been a fool, that life is a game you have never understood, at which you will only ever fail.

'And us?' you say, running your finger

around the rim of your glass.

He looks at you. Blinks. 'God, yeah,' he says, reaching across the table and taking your hand. 'That's a given. You know how I feel about you. This is amazing. You don't need me to tell you that.'

Your insides begin to untwist.

'So you want to continue,' you say. 'When we get back, I mean. You're not all, like, "what happens in Amsterdam stays in Amsterdam".'

This last bit you say in a brash American accent with your hands doing the quote marks and your face zany. It's the only way you can dare to bring it out. And that scares you again. The thickening layers nestled inside your pelvis seem to throb.

Gareth frowns. 'What's got into you?' he says. 'Is something wrong?'

You shrug and sniff back the embarrassing urge to cry. Hormones, you tell yourself. Fucking hormones.

'Nothing,' you say, your mouth trembling. 'I guess it's just this coming to an end. Everything.'

He nods. 'I know,' he says. 'But you don't have to worry about me. I'm not going anywhere. You know that, right?'

You incline your head to look like you do. You don't know anything. All you know is that out of nowhere you have something precious and it makes you scared.

'This is fixed,' he says, taking your hand and pulling it to somewhere above his heart. 'This is solid. This is going nowhere.'

You nod. You take a deep breath. Now is the time to say it. You open your mouth. But his eyes are following a pleasure boat ploughing along the canal outside.

'You know what I'm really looking forward to?' he says.

'What?' you say.

'Just the two of us, back in Manchester, building our life together.'

You nod and open your mouth to speak again, but he isn't finished.

'I mean, a-we wouldn't even necessarily have to stay working for Anton — or in Manchester,' he says. 'I've been thinking it might be nice to go travelling. See the world, you know. Experience life. A-We've neither of us g-got ties or responsibilities. There's nothing to stop us taking the leap. It's something I've always dreamt of doing and I can't imagine anyone I'd rather have adventures with than you.'

He leans in and kisses you. You taste the sweet, slightly biscuity savour of his lips.

'Right,' he says, pushing back his chair. 'I need to pee.'

You watch him walk between the tables to the toilets. Then you turn to stare out at the canal, at a couple huddled together posing for a picture by the lock. It's fine, you tell yourself. Life is good. Unbidden, Gareth's words float back into your mind — 'This is going nowhere' — and you realise with a catch of fear how they can also be understood. But he didn't mean it like that. He meant it as a statement of commitment, you rush to reassure yourself. It was just an unfortunate turn of phrase.

61

The cafe in Shoreditch was called The Bathroom. It was tricked out in avocado plastic and orange tiles from the seventies, and there was a big mirror just inside the door which showed her to herself as she walked in. She started at the sight of the scraggy woman in an anorak, with lined eyes and greyed skin from all those days under the hospital's fluorescent lights, not to mention the last few nights spent hunched in an all-night caff on the Old Kent Road.

'Excuse me,' said a man with a beard and glasses, pushing past her as she stood there undecided.

She stumbled on into the main room. There were chandeliers constructed out of scraps of bathroom fittings, and two toilets suspended from the walls and filled with giant spider plants. She stood bewildered for a moment, blinking at the space.

It wasn't until Anton raised a hand that

she saw him. He was sitting at a table made out of a giant mirrored cabinet. He was wearing a leather jacket. His hair was cut in a sharp, angular way and when she got closer she saw that there was a stud glinting in the lobe of his right ear.

'Hullo,' she said, staring down at him. 'I didn't recognise you.'

Anton smiled. 'There've been one or two changes.'

Then he seemed to recollect himself. He stood up and pecked her on the cheek. The chairs scraped loudly on the tiled floor as they sat back down.

'How is your friend?' he said.

She frowned for a moment before the question made sense. 'Oh,' she said. 'Actually she was my sister. My twin sister, Helen Sallis. Sorry, it seemed easier to say friend when I saw you. She died earlier this week. A blood clot. The post mortem's just confirmed it. You might have seen it in the papers. One of those things.'

Anton nodded, understanding dawning in his eyes.

'Of course.' He coughed. 'When is the funeral?'

'I —' She frowned. 'I don't know. I'm not sure I'll go. I'm not sure I'm invited.'

Anton narrowed his eyes. 'Not sure you're

invited?'

'Yes. It's complicated, you know. Families.' Her face started to twist out of her control so she forced it into a bright smile. 'But anyway, what about you? What about your dad?'

Anton sighed. 'He died three weeks ago,' he said. 'The day I saw you, in fact. It's been an odd time. Horrible obviously, but it has been something of a release as well.'

On the cabinet table between them, Anton's phone flashed into life. 'Michael', read the screen.

'Excuse me,' said Anton, putting the phone to his ear and turning his head away from the table. 'Hello,' he said quietly. 'Mmn. Mmn. I'm just with her now . . .' He glanced back at her. 'Not long. About five minutes, I reckon . . . Mmn . . . I don't know. How about Thai? . . . All right, sweetness. *Ciao ciao.*'

He slid the phone into his jacket pocket. 'Sorry about that,' he said. 'That was . . . Actually it was my boyfriend.' He cracked a smile that showed the gap between his top teeth, giving him a slightly goofy air.

The waitress came to their table: a young girl with red lipstick and a Victory roll in her hair, wearing a flannel dressing gown.

'Specials are Eggnog with Lavender, and

Cherry Brandy Surprise,' she said sullenly. 'We're out of the Crème de Menthe Sundaes.'

They ordered a Diet Coke and an orange juice.

'So where are you living now?' said Smudge as the waitress slouched away in her slippers.

'Round the corner, actually,' said Anton. 'This lovely little loft apartment. Former blacking factory or something. The money from Dad, you see. Not that it's through yet, but, well it opened up a lot of possibilities.'

He winced ruefully.

She sat and watched him, wondering what it must be like to have the sort of life where you felt constantly obliged to apologise for your own good fortune.

'And you?' he said as the waitress plonked their glasses down on the table. 'Where are you now?'

Smudge thought of the trashed shell of the Walworth flat, the Formica tables of the all-night caff.

'I'm still making plans,' she said. 'It's been a difficult time.'

Anton nodded. 'Well, look, the reason I wanted to see you was because I've got something to give you.' He slid a folded bit of paper out of the inside pocket of his jacket and put it on the table. 'You remember that painting you did? The tower block? Well, it sold. Not long after you . . . left Edgewise. I felt bad about how all that worked out. The police and everything. All that stuff in the media with your sister. It must have been hell. I've been hoping I'd run into you and when I saw you at the hospital, well, it seemed only right that you should get your share.' He gestured to the paper. 'That's not all of it,' he said. 'Some of it got used when the business wound up. But when I get the money through from my father, there'll be another instalment. Anyway, in the meantime, I thought it might be enough to get you started on something else. Sort you out with a studio or something. Paints, materials. Whatever you need.'

Smudge held up her hands. 'Really, it's kind of you, Anton,' she said. 'But I don't need anything. I can look after myself.' She sipped her orange juice. It was sour and made her pucker her lips. 'Besides, right now I think I just need a break from the past,' she said. 'I need to start somewhere new with a clean slate.'

Anton leant forward. 'This isn't charity,' he said. 'This is money you made. Look, even if you take it and just give it away to someone or whatever, that's your right. But take it at least. I wouldn't feel right if you didn't.'

He slid the cheque towards her and she sat back, panic in her eyes. She didn't want to go back there. She didn't want any of that to come with her. She wanted finally, fully, at last, to be free.

'I'm sorry,' she said, standing up. 'But I think I'd better go. I shouldn't have come. Thanks for the drink.'

She turned and made for the exit, colliding with a waitress in a housecoat and headscarf carrying a tray of Cherry Brandy Surprises. The girl sucked her teeth as the glasses trembled, shivering drops on to the floor.

Outside, the blankness of the day greeted her: a white sky, people hurrying here and there. She had no idea where to go.

Then she felt a hand on her arm. Anton was standing next to her.

'I'm sorry,' he said. 'I know it's difficult. Believe me, I know what it's like to want to make a clean break. But the thing is, you see, the past doesn't always have to be a bad thing. Sometimes good things come from it as well.'

He handed her the cheque. 'Take it at least. Burn it. Use it in a Satanic ritual.

Whatever you like. Just think about it.'

He patted her arm. 'You going to be all right?'

She nodded.

'Good,' he said. 'Well, take care.'

He started to walk away towards the high street. When he got to the first lamp post he turned.

'And go to your sister's funeral,' he called.

She watched him head up the road. The cheque waited between her fingers. Smooth and crisp. She turned it over and unfolded it. The name space was left blank, but there was a lot of writing underneath. It was for sixty thousand pounds.

62

The PR firm has gone to town. There are arrangements of dark lilies up the stairs into the function room, and smiling staff waiting with trays of martinis and champagne cocktails. Inside, young men in black mill about with boards of vol au vents: little parcels of smoked salmon, mousse on chicory leaves, blinis topped with caviar glittering under the spotlights.

The paintings hang behind curtains on the walls, ready for the unveiling. Distinguished guests stroll around between them, stopping now and then to sip, laugh, air kiss or tap a colleague on the arm. There are some faces you recognise. Over there by the cloakroom is the woman who presents the TV breakfast show you and Gareth often stick on before heading out to the studio. The tall man with round glasses is an art critic for *De Telegraaf* and next to him is the discussion-show host who always crops up on late-night TV, hauling politicians over the coals. There are lots of other people you feel you should know too, but their identities escape you for the moment. Luckily the PR firm has assigned a member of staff to mind you and she whispers information in your ear as people approach. You find yourself talking to a local councillor, the head of a big drinks firm, a producer from NOS and a curator from the Rijksmuseum.

About twenty minutes after you arrive, Jan Heijn clatters a spoon against his glass and makes a short speech, introducing the concept of the campaign and explaining the rationale behind hiring Edgewise to bring the vision to life. When he's finished speaking he makes a gesture and the servers in black, who have migrated to stand next to the paintings during his speech, tug the strings to reveal the artworks.

After Jan's speech, the crowds thicken and more and more distinguished visitors press in to share their praise and shake your hand. When the art critic comes over to quiz you about your technique in achieving the brushstrokes in *Girl with a Pearl Earphone,* you talk authoritatively about the thought you gave to the layering of colour and the use of light. You even correct one of his observations about Vermeer's deployment of glaze. You sound like an expert — someone who has spent hours, days and weeks thinking about this particular issue, turning it round and round in her mind until she comprehends it from many angles. And, you realise with a catch of joy, that that is precisely because it is what you are. There is no artifice here. There is no need to dissemble, talk around the issues or pretend. You have done the work. You have lived the life. This is who you are.

The conversations continue in a flurry. Now and then you are caught in a camera's flash. People press business cards into your hands. Grand statements get made about future projects. You receive invitations to tour the rest of the Netherlands, the promise of commissions further down the line. Afterwards they will tell you that you met the mayor, and one of the runners up of the Dutch *Big Brother,* and an art collector known for spending millions of euros on new, obscure works (she wanted to buy your reworking of Constable, you later hear, but Heike told her it wasn't for sale).

It's only when the crowd begins to thin out that you realise your feet hurt and your head's aching. You and Gareth take your leave of Jan and his team who are beaming, delighted with how well things have gone and the promise of coverage in tomorrow's papers. You stroll back through the streets, skirting the red-light district, and over the canal towards the bare trees of Vondelpark.

'You were on fire tonight,' says Gareth as you turn into your street for the last time.

As a thank you for your hard work, Jan Heijn has arranged business-class flights back to Manchester for you so you don't have to brave the ferry and the choppy January squalls on the North Sea. You're both half asleep when you get to the airport. You doze during the flight. The announcements from the captain and chief steward come to you from the end of a long tunnel. They are barely enough to make you stir. In the queue for Immigration you giggle at Gareth's passport photo — a spotty, student shot from when he'd just turned eighteen.

'To be fair, you don't really look that different,' you joke, and he slaps you affectionately on the arm.

Weird to think that when you left on the ferry three months ago you were practically strangers. You can't imagine not being close now.

There's a bit of an issue when you try to come through passport control. The border guard takes a long time, glancing between your face and the photograph. You're on such a wave of euphoria after last night that you forget that the passport is a fake. When you remember you flush and feel your pulse quicken, but by that time the danger has passed. He hands it over and waves you through.

You find Gareth standing staring up at a TV screen showing a breakfast news show. There's a ribbon of text running along the bottom of the screen: 'Two dead in Staffordshire shooting. Police to question minister over fresh expenses allegations. Daytime star reveals childhood trauma.'

Gareth turns to you. 'Back to real life with a bump,' he says.

'Shit, isn't it?' you say.

Gareth breaks into a grin. 'Nah,' he says, reaching for you. 'The best ever.' He kisses the top of your head. 'Come on,' he says. 'Let's g-go home.'

Perhaps it's because you're still spaced out from yesterday, but in baggage reclaim you start to notice something strange: people seem to be looking at you. You see a couple of women whisper to each other, their eyes glued to your face. A little boy zipping between the conveyor belts on a scooter stops to point and stare.

The illogic of this makes you worry. You're

afraid paranoia is readying itself to over-whelm your mind once more and hurl you into chaos. Not now, you whisper to your brain, as you pull your second suitcase off the conveyor belt. Stay with the programme. Everything's going to be OK.

At the taxi rank, the first driver glances up at you when Gareth asks for Manchester. Then he shakes his head and drives off.

'That's a-weird,' says Gareth. 'M-must've been my stammer. Ignorant sod.'

You shrug and try to look indignant. It's all normal, it's all normal, you tell yourself, resolutely blocking out the staring faces your mind seems set on manufacturing on the edges of your vision. Nobody's looking at you.

The moment's quickly forgotten in the next taxi. You snuggle up together on the back seat and watch the motorway verges skim past and then the unspooling of Man-chester's outer suburbs as Friday evening settles over the streets.

Gareth's flat is in a new development beside the Bridgewater Canal. There's a keypad by the door to buzz you into the building and a lift that can only be operated with an electronic fob. A new-carpet smell wafts along the corridors.

'It's a bit plasticky,' he says apologetically.

'I would have preferred something older and more scuffed about. Still, needs m-must and all that.'

But you like the newness of the place, the fact that no one has lived in it before Gareth. There has not been time for sadness to seep into the walls and insinuate itself into the soft furnishings. Anger has not stamped its way up the stairs. The block is a blank page ready for a new drawing, a fresh start.

Gareth's flat is small but light, with windows looking out over the canal. He hurries into the bedroom to tidy up before you see it and you stand in the living room, looking around. There's a brown corduroy sofa, a little folding table with two chairs, and some psychedelic prints on the walls. Over by the window is an old vinyl turntable, surrounded by cardboard boxes of records. Turning, you see these take up most of the shelving space on the far wall behind the door too. You walk over and run your fingers along their edges. From what you can make out, there are old classics and rare survivals alongside limited-edition vinyl versions of more modern releases. You pull out *Use Your Illusion II* and gaze at it, thinking how strange it is to see the design you remember from a cassette sleeve blown up to ten times its size.

'They're my secret vice,' says Gareth, coming into the room. 'I spend hours searching for them online. I like the sleeves as much as anything — the artwork.' He pauses, coughs. 'But of course we can always put them in storage to make space for your stuff. That is, if you want to, of course.' He shakes his head. 'I m-mean, if you think . . . if . . .'

He's blushing furiously, his mouth opening and closing. You go over and stop it with a kiss. Of course you want to. Why on earth wouldn't you? There's nothing you've ever wanted more.

You order in a Chinese takeaway. You'd planned to tell him about the pregnancy over dinner but as soon as you take your first mouthful, you realise how exhausted you are, so instead you give in to Gareth's suggestion of watching *Star Wars* and doze on the sofa as Luke Skywalker goes off in search of Obi-Wan Kenobi. You go to bed early, leaving the suitcases standing in the hall.

The next morning, Gareth gets up and goes out to buy milk and croissants for breakfast. You wander to the kitchen and spoon some coffee into a cafetiere. While the kettle boils, you wash up the plates from the takeaway, staring out of the window as a boat chugs its way along the canal. The woman at the tiller is muffled up against the morning drizzle and the sight of her makes you glad to be in the warm kitchen with the kettle bubbling away on the side and Gareth set to return with breakfast any minute. You smile and your mind jumps ahead to the rest of the day. You'll tell him when you're having breakfast, you think, sitting at the little table in the living room. It'll seem sudden and he'll be surprised at first, but pretty soon you know he'll be pleased. Your brain fetches up a vision of his shy face breaking into a radiant smile. Then, after you've talked it over and finished eating and — maybe — had sex again, you'll suggest going out for a walk. You might find a local park to stroll through, like you did in Amsterdam, or visit an exhibition. Perhaps you'll go to a cafe. You might even — although this could be pushing it — stop by Mothercare in the Barnacle to look at baby clothes. You'll have a quiet dinner and tomorrow there'll be more of the same — more companionship, more love, more plans. And then on Monday there'll be the return to the office and the happy resumption of the old routine, except this time so much more solid, more real.

You can see it all and it thrills you — so

much so that when you hear Gareth come in the front door, you know you can't wait until breakfast. You want the future now. As he walks into the kitchen, you take one last look at the woman chugging along the canal in the cold and wet, and a deep breath. Then you turn.

His face is pale and drawn. Shadows have crept into the hollows around his eyes. He slaps a newspaper bearing a picture of what appears to be your face on the counter. You're so caught up in your bright visions that for a moment you think it's you, that there must have been a news crew that you missed at the campaign launch the other night and that the whole thing is now being reported around the world. You start to laugh excitedly. Then you notice that your hair is shaped perfectly under your chin and there is no scar across your forehead, no MONSTER peeping out from under the fringe. Underneath the picture, the caption reads, *Presenter Helen Sallis: the day my twin tried to kill me.*

Gareth stares at you. 'A-What the fuck is this?' he says.

63

She sat in the Costa across the road from the church and watched people arriving: chat-show hosts, TV weather men, the faces off auction challenges, gardening programmes and home-improvement shows. They were the sort of everyday celebrities you might wave at in the street before realising you didn't actually know them in real life, the people they'd used to watch in Beryl's living room most nights. They circulated, studiously ignoring the photographers on the pavement, as she observed them through her sunglasses, fingers raking through her newly peroxided hair. Her cappuccino had gone cold, but still she sat there, unable to make up her mind to move.

At five to twelve a bell started tolling and the crowd on the pavement began to thin out as people made their way inside. A hearse pulled up, followed by two black Bentleys, and she saw Nick get out, leading

Heloise, who was wearing a little pink dress with a black cardigan. Behind them came Horace and Mother, getting out of the second car with a young man in military uniform who must be Richard. She got a shock for a moment when Mother seemed to look towards her and catch her eye, but her gaze swept on past the man tapping at his laptop and away up the street.

Shortly after they went in, the bell stopped tolling. Smudge pushed back her stool and stood up. Her shoes were new and she wasn't sure about them. They were very high — unlike anything she'd worn for years — but when she'd seen them in a charity shop window earlier in the week she'd felt that they would be the right choice for Hellie's funeral. Their brashness would help her to blend in.

The church door creaked as she let herself in. Heads turned but no one seemed to register who she was. A man in a dark suit handed her an order of service bearing a picture of Hellie's face — the same shot that had graced the front pages in the days after the crash. *Helen Sallis,* it said on the cover. *15.04.80 — 03.09.13.*

Smudge slid into a pew near the back. The church yawned in front of her, its arched ceiling ridged like a throat. There was a man

549

standing at the lectern, which was hard to make out from where she sat. He was reading a poem but she couldn't concentrate on it. She kept scouring the rows in front of her for Mother's waved helmet of hair, all the while tugging her own blonde strands forward over her own face, lest anyone should catch a glimpse of her profile and start to wonder.

They stood up to sing and sat down to listen to the words of a bearded priest, but none of it reached her. It all seemed to be coming down a long, echoing tunnel from very far away. There was nothing here of the Hellie from later and that last night. Smudge shouldn't have listened to Anton. It was a mistake to have come.

Afterwards, following the instructions of the priest, the guests began to make their way to a hotel a couple of streets away for a reception while a private cremation took place in Ealing. The family, apparently, had particularly requested that everyone come and there would be a collection for a road-safety awareness charity. Smudge edged her way towards the church's side door, avoiding the throng of people heading out of the main entrance to the street. She was just about to slip away when —

'There you are,' said a familiar voice. 'You

big naughty. Where have you been?'

Smudge looked round to find Heloise standing behind her, arms folded, a scowl stamped on her face.

'You went away and you didn't say good-bye to me,' said Heloise. 'That was rude.'

'I . . . I'm sorry,' said Smudge, glancing around warily. 'I didn't mean to be rude. I just had to go.'

'No, you didn't,' said Heloise, picking a service sheet off the pile on the stand next to the door. 'You just did what you wanted to. Like all the grown ups. You are big, self-ish poos. And by the way your hair looks silly.'

('She's right, you know,' said someone. 'Look at you, you big idiot. Mutton dressed as lamb. No one wants you here.')

Smudge looked around, but there was no one behind her, only the heavy wooden door standing ajar. With a sinking feeling she re-alised they were back: the voices circling her thoughts like sharks once again. She felt the old panic start to bubble through her veins.

'Why did you do that?' said Heloise.

'What?'

'Look around like there was someone there.'

('Charlatan. You big, fat fake.')

Smudge ran a hand through her hair, blinking. 'I — I thought someone said something, that's all. It must have been my imagination.'

Heloise nodded solemnly. 'I get that sometimes,' she said. 'I get a boy shouting "knickers" and a man called Mr Tomlinson who tries to do "The Owl and the Pussy Cat" with different words. Sometimes he makes me giggle.'

Smudge stared at her. Then there was the sound of clattering heels.

'Heloise?' called Mother's voice. 'Heloise? Oh, there you are. You mustn't walk off like that!'

She glanced at Smudge and gave a start of recognition

'Hello, Mother,' said Smudge.

('Hello, Marmaduke.')

Mother blinked, then drew herself up. 'Eleanor,' she said, her voice cold as the marble memorial plaque on the wall above her head. 'Come to show me that miraculous letter, have you?'

Smudge opened her mouth but no words came out.

'I thought not,' said Mother, pursing her lips. 'Two hours we sat in that canteen. I knew it was pointless but Horace would wait.'

There was a muffled thud as someone dropped a hymn book on the far side of the church. Mother looked round then back at Smudge, taking in her dyed hair and stilettos.

'I'm surprised you've got the nerve to come here at all,' she said.

Indignation sparked in Smudge's stomach. 'Why?' It came out louder than she'd expected and a huddle of people over by the main door turned to stare.

('There you go again, letting the side down.')

Mother folded her arms. 'Well,' she said, 'it's not as though there's anything for you here. It's not as though you had any connection with Helen any more. You haven't for years, for all you might have hung about the hospital at the bitter end.' She narrowed her eyes. 'You're not going to get anything, you know. You're not mentioned in the will.'

Smudge held up her service sheet, bearing the picture of Hellie's face.

'I came because of this!' she said, pointing to the photograph and the name. 'Because she was my twin sister. And because once upon a time . . . I was her and she was me.'

('Ooh, hark at you.')

Mother rolled her eyes and shifted so that the light from the stained-glass window above Smudge's head fell on her, daubing her face with pinks and blues. 'Still on this, are we? Still on this . . . this obsession. I told Horace it was foolish to believe you. I knew — I *knew* — all that nonsense about a letter couldn't possibly be true. As if Helen would ever be so stupid as to write something like that. He's too trusting for his own good sometimes.'

'Maybe Horace wants to get to the bottom of things,' said Smudge, haltingly. 'Maybe he's tired of sweeping things under the carpet.'

'Sweeping what under the carpet?' retorted Mother, slipping her service sheet into her handbag and snapping it shut. 'There are no secrets between Horace and me.'

'I think we both know that's not true,' said Smudge.

'Bollocks,' said Mother.

The word exploded in the quiet of the church. In the nave on the far side a verger tidying up halted what he was doing.

'Everything all right?' he called across.

'Yes, quite all right, thank you,' answered Mother, slipping on her polite-company voice. She glanced down and caught sight of Heloise, staring up at her saucer-eyed.

'Heloise dear, go and find Daddy and

Peeps,' she said, tapping her granddaughter on the arm. 'Quickly!

'Now you listen to me,' she said, her voice becoming a vicious hiss as Heloise scuttled off. 'I won't have any more of your lies. I won't have any more of your poison. This stops now.'

Looking closely, Smudge noticed that her mother was trembling beneath the flawless helmet of her hair. Every sinew in her neck was taut. She saw what she had never seen before: Mother was terrified. The woman who had once shrieked with laughter as they all whirled round on the beach, and stood expressionless on the doorstep as the police drove her daughter away, was desperately afraid. 'Oh, Mother,' she said quietly. 'What are you so frightened of?'

Mother blinked at her, uncertainty in her eyes. Deep within her gaze, something of the old Ellie look was lodged: vulnerable, lost. A wave of pity engulfed Smudge.

'What happened to you, Mother?' she said, reaching out and taking her hand. It felt smaller than she'd expected, the fingers thin and fragile inside their black leather glove. 'Was it Father? Or something further back than that?'

Something flashed inside her thoughts, a bulb flaring in the far reaches of her brain.

Hadn't there been something? If only she could think clearly. If only she could recall. But all her mind would offer was the image of a little pink glass holding a row of false teeth.

'You don't have to keep it all buttoned up,' said Smudge. 'If something happened you can talk about these things. Perhaps it might help.'

('Who are you kidding?' carped a voice. 'Call the fire brigade, I say. Douse her in foam!')

Mother stared at her, moisture gathering in her eyes. The ribbed throat of the church's roof seemed to expand, as though the building were taking a deep breath. Then she pursed her lips and gave a harsh laugh.

'Ha!' she said. 'You're talking to me about getting help? That's a joke. Well, I have news for you. Some of us don't need help. We don't expect it. We're not weak in that way. We don't go in for that self-regarding support-group therapy rubbish. Because at the end of it, what do you come back to? That you're on your own and you've got to put one foot in front of the other and keep going. Well, some of us have known that all along.'

A man in a fawn-coloured coat stopped

next to them and Mother assumed a wan smile to accept his murmured condolences. When he moved on, she looked at Smudge and her face settled back into its old, hard lines.

'Oh, yes,' she said. 'Some of us have been managing just fine, thank you very much, with self-discipline. With routine. Structure, that's the thing. People like you might do well to remember that.'

('And people like you might do well to stick it up your arse and dance the fandango.')

Smudge screwed up her eyes against the voices, fighting the urge to turn and hurry away out of the great, gloomy space. She tried to think. Beneath all Mother's fire and indignation, something wasn't making sense. She goaded her brain to trace the threads of the conversation, to find the hole in its weave.

Mother smiled triumphantly and shifted her handbag on to her shoulder. She looked round to see Nick, Heloise, Horace and Richard approaching along the aisle. In the dappled light from the windows, Richard was revealed to be tall with a round head like his father and a weak chin.

'Now, if you'll excuse me —' Mother began in a voice she might have used to round off a complaining phone call to her bank.

'No. Wait,' said Smudge. With a massive effort, she brought it forth: 'It hasn't always worked for you, has it?'

Mother frowned. 'I beg your pardon?' she said.

'Before,' said Smudge. 'After Father's death. There was no routine then. No structure. You were a wreck. You stayed in bed with the curtains closed. We had to fend for ourselves.' A vision floated before her eyes of an empty bread bin, little hands sawing precariously at the heel of a mouldy loaf. 'You were struggling then, Mother. You needed help.'

She folded her arms. 'So that's the tale you've been spinning, is it? A pitiful childhood of neglect. The Little Match Girl. Well, I'm sure it's very effective in many quarters but I don't have time for it. Today I am burying my daughter. That is the end of the story.'

'Burying two daughters,' said Smudge, pointing out through the church doors to the waiting hearse. 'There are two people in that coffin.'

Mother shot her a look. 'Oh, I buried you a long time ago.'

Smudge swallowed. 'That's right,' she

said. 'You did. You buried me the day you failed to notice we'd swapped places — that she'd become me and I'd become her. And you buried her too. You gave us both up for dead when we were six years old.'

Mother glanced quickly over her shoulder, but the others were muttering between themselves, peering at something on Nick's iPhone while Heloise wandered a little apart, gawping up at the ornate memorial plaques on the wall.

Mother took a deep breath. 'All right, you want the truth?'

('It's a trap! Don't listen to her! She'll kill us all!')

'Yes,' said Smudge. 'Yes, I do.'

Mother hesitated. She looked round once more.

'Not here,' she said. 'Come with me.'

64

Blur and crash. Emotions wash in and out. You are hot, then you are cold, then you are burning up again.

At first you cling to the buoyant fiction of Trudy, to the simplicity of her life. Without that, you are afraid you will sink into the mire and drown. So you try to pass the story off as a coincidence, a bit of celebrity nonsense. Someone who happens to look like you. Someone else. It's not impossible, you argue, in a world of nearly seven billion people, that there should be someone who looks so similar to you. In fact you saw something about it — didn't you? — on one of the Dutch cable channels, a chat show with people and their doppelgängers brought face to face.

You take a tea towel from the rail on the oven door and start to dry one of the plates. If you can just keep performing the Saturday morning you planned, you think, perhaps the rest of the world will follow your lead. Maybe you can wrench reality back on to the right track simply by refusing to live it any other way.

But Gareth is not playing along. He stands there, stony-faced, a muscle pulsing in his jaw. After a moment, he reaches out and taps the newspaper print. You lean in to read the line next to his finger. The bitch has only gone and mentioned your MONSTER tattoo.

You open your mouth to try to brazen that one away too, but the words stick in your throat. You can hear how it will sound in advance: flimsy, thin, false. He doesn't deserve that.

You set the plate and tea towel down on the side. You turn to look at him. There is a thrumming in your head and your vision keeps blurring and sharpening as though someone is twiddling the focus knob in your brain, but you do your best to hold his gaze.

'All right,' you say. 'She is talking about me. Sorry I lied, I just —'

But he doesn't wait to hear any more. He turns and strides out of the kitchen. You hurry after him.

'Gareth, please,' you say. You put a hand on his shoulder but he shrugs it off. You follow him into the living room.

'Please,' you say again. 'I can explain all this. Just give me a chance. Please.'

He turns to you, the light from the window behind him throwing his face into shadow. He once told you that he never says much when he's angry, that his stammer gets worse when his feelings run high so he prefers to keep quiet. At the time, you joked that this would make arguments easy, but now you find his silence stifling. Fear pinches your heart.

You open your mouth and bring it out quickly, hurrying over the details. Yes, it's true, you tell him. That was you. You did that — what she said. Or at least, that was how other people saw it. But it was years ago. You were a very different person. You'd been through hell. You spent a long time lost and — as you told him — ill, but you're past that now. It's ancient history. You've started a new life. He's got to believe you.

He stares at you as the canal oozes its way along behind him in the rain. Heat prickles at your temples. The little knot of being lodged deep within you seems to throb.

He blinks. 'You told m-me you were ill,' he says slowly. 'You told m-me your family didn't understand you. You said they threw you out. And all the time . . .' He narrows his eyes. 'I bet your name's not even really

Trudy, is it?'

'It is now,' you say urgently. 'That's my name now. Trudy. That's who I am.'

But he shakes his head and will not look at you.

'How can I believe you?' he says. 'How can I trust anything you say?'

You swallow and close your eyes, delving within yourself for something hard and solid enough to shatter his incredulity.

'Things weren't easy, growing up,' you say at length. 'It was a screwed-up family. My dad killed himself when we were four. My mum had . . . well, her own demons.'

'So what?' says Gareth. 'M-My dad had cancer. You don't see m-me running around trying to kill people.'

'It wasn't like that,' you say. 'I wasn't running around trying to kill people. What happened was an accident. And because I was ill, because they didn't know how to deal with me, they chose to see the worst. There was something that happened, you see, back when we were very young. If you'd just let me explain —'

But Gareth swipes your words away and hurries from the room. For a panicked second you think he's making for the front door, but instead he turns towards the bedroom. You trot after him, stars exploding wherever you look.

'Please, Gareth,' you say. 'You've got to believe me.'

Your voice sounds so weak and pathetic, it makes your stomach churn. Passing the bathroom, you catch sight of yourself in the mirror above the sink: your face blotched and stricken.

In the bedroom, in front of the rumpled bed in which only an hour ago he moved above you, sighing, he turns to face you. There's a coldness about him you've not seen before, a wall rising up between you. It scares you. Panic bubbles up, sending the truth spilling everywhere. You put a hand to your belly.

'There's another thing I've got to tell you,' you say urgently as he opens his mouth to say something that might cement the wall in place for good. 'I'm pregnant.'

He stares at you with the eyes of a stranger you have bumped into in the street.

'What do you m-mean you're pregnant?' he says. 'A-Weren't you taking the pill?'

'It was an accident,' you say. 'I didn't think it could happen to me. I've never had anything like this happen before.'

His face is blank.

'You have to believe me,' you say again, like a child saying a made-up incantation,

564

hoping that wishing can make it true.

But the spell is broken. Gareth shakes his head. He holds up his hands. And this time he does stride down the hallway to the front door.

'Gareth, wait!' you shout. No matter: your words are empty and powerless now. The door closes behind him, answering you with a tut.

You stay in the flat, wandering from room to room. You stare at yourself in the bathroom mirror. You slump on the sofa. You stretch out on the bed. You go over what happened. You go over it. Again. Again. What you said. What you could have said differently. What you should have said.

You talk to the empty air. At first your tone is pleading, then it's hurt, then it's angry — indignant that after everything he can't grant you more credence, that he isn't here, expressing sorrow for all you've gone through. He owes you that. Someone owes you that. Why the fuck isn't someone giving you that? You rage for some time in a voice fit to shake the windows. Cruel bastard world, you admonish the sofa, the turntable, why the fuck should you be saddled with this? Why the fuck can't he just put it all aside and love you? Why does no one ever give you a fucking, cunting break? The furniture surveys your unloveliness unmoved. You subside into mumbles and whimpers: pitiful, animal noise.

Still he doesn't come. You put the television on and turn it off, unable to stand its gabbling. You stare for what feels like hours at Hellie's face in the newspaper. Tracing her difference from you — the sleek roundedness of her cheeks, the subtle slant in the angling of her eyes.

Time gallops and stands still. You seem to spend years stuck at 15:23 on the oven clock then suddenly it's an hour later and the sickly winter light is starting to fade. It is as though the flat itself has been cut from its moorings and sent drifting off down the canal, bobbing and swaying on the currents of Gareth's absence. Your head throbs. When you touch a hand to your forehead, it's clammy and cold. The walls seem to rush towards you and retreat, doing the hokey-cokey on the fringes of your field of view.

Oh, where is he?

When it gets dark, you sit at the table in the living room and stare out at the evening coming on. Your thoughts are sluggish and murky now, the bulb illuminating them fused. All you know is you can't leave; you

can't let yourself out of this reality. The being knitting itself together inside you won't
let you. And something else — a raw, liquid
feeling in your chest — demands that you
stay here too. This life has got its claws into
you and unlike all the other times since you
left the unit, you can't shrug it off.

You must fall asleep at the table because
the next thing you know is the sound of a
key in the lock and the light flicking on.

'Hello,' says Gareth, coming into the
room. 'I didn't know if you'd still be here.'

You open your mouth and find no words
waiting. So you close it again and stare up
at him. He seems to loom towards you and
then swoop away.

He indicates the plastic bag he's carrying.

'I've got some food if you're hungry,' he
says. 'Stuff to m-make an omelette. Enough
for two.'

You shrug. He goes to the kitchen and
prepares the meal. You're still sitting at the
table when he carries the plates through.

You eat in silence, glancing at him between
mouthfuls, wary. Finally, you both speak at
the same time.

'About earlier,' he says when you nod that
he should talk. 'I'm sorry if . . . It was a lot
to take in. I'm not used to dealing a-with
other people's stuff, you see. It's always just

been m-me.'

'That stuff in the papers,' you say. 'It's not the whole story. There is another side. Things got twisted and —'

'Yes,' says Gareth. 'That's something that occurred to me when I was walking around. That's something I'll have to hear properly from you.'

You nod. 'Where did you go?'

'Around,' he says. Then he scratches his head. 'A-Weirdly, I spent quite a bit of time in Pizza Hut. I don't know why. M-Maybe it was the free refills of Coke.'

The bathos of it makes you both smile.

'I had to think, you see,' he continues. 'I had to make sense of things for m-myself.'

'So what does that mean?' you say. You wince and add: 'For us?'

Gareth sighs. He looks round the room then back at you. 'It m-means I don't know,' he says. 'It m-means let's see. But we'll have to take things slowly. I think living together is probably not a g-good idea for now. I need time to get used to things, to adjust.'

Relief pours into you. You nod. Of course. You completely understand. Whatever he needs. You'll start looking for a place tomorrow. You'll leave tonight if he wants.

He waves the suggestion away. There's no need for you to do that. Of course you can stay until you have somewhere to go. He cares about you. He wants to look after you — and the baby if that is what you want too. He just needs a bit of space for now. It'll take him a little while to trust everything again, to feel ready to mix your lives up together full-time.

Oh, and there's one more thing.

'No m-more secrets,' he says. 'No m-more revelations. I couldn't take it again.'

You nod and smile. You take his hand.

'Absolutely,' you say, staring deep into his eyes. 'I promise. No more secrets.'

He returns the nod and stands up to collect the plates.

'I love you,' you say, and in this moment you know you'll do anything to hold on to this, to take this chance of happiness and make it count.

'I know,' he says quietly. 'That I do believe.'

65

Smudge climbed into the funeral car and settled herself against the leather upholstery. There was a click and the roar of the high street rushed in as Mother got in the other side.

'The others will follow in the third car,' she said.

Smudge nodded and stared straight ahead at the back of Hellie's coffin in the hearse parked in front. She swallowed and clutched at her bag. The fire and bluster that had gripped her only moments before in the church had blazed themselves out in the walk down the path, leaving her cold and empty. Even though the sun had warmed the car, her fingers felt like ice. At the back of her mind, the voices whispered and bickered, getting ready to strike.

'All ready?' said the driver, climbing in and flicking his coat tails back with a practised gesture.

Mother nodded and the car pulled away behind the hearse, into the lunchtime traffic.

Smudge sat and waited for her to speak, but for several moments nothing came. They drove silently through the streets of west London. Outside the car, shoppers barged past one another, stretched their arms up to snap selfies, thrust sandwich packets into overflowing bins. Ahead, the exotic blooms on Hellie's coffin shuddered and nodded as the hearse took one turning, then the next, making for the A4.

('My old man said "follow the van and don't dilly dally on the way",' warbled a voice.)

Smudge bit her lip against a hideous urge to laugh and forced her mind back to the matter in hand. A sideways glance at Mother showed that she seemed to be deliberating over something, her lips forming silent words. She was fidgeting too. She took her gloves off and put them in her bag. Then she opened her bag again, got out a powder compact and spent several minutes peering at her face from different angles, patting at the skin under her eyes. Finally, as the cortege eased its way on to the dual carriageway, Mother took a deep breath.

'What I'm about to say . . .' she began,

and stopped. She leant forward to the driver.

'Would you mind putting the radio on?'

'Certainly, Madam,' he said. 'Talk radio or music?'

'Whichever you prefer,' said Mother.

The driver pressed a button and the strains of LBC Radio filled the car. A man was complaining at length about parking restrictions in Lambeth.

'What I am about to tell you will not be repeated,' said Mother in a tight voice, speaking below the outraged tones coming from the speaker. 'If you try to tell anyone else — Richard, Nick, Heloise, anyone at all — I will deny it utterly. If you go to the media, I will pursue you through the courts. You understand?'

('I'll canoo you through the quartz, you dirty hand.') Smudge shook her head, battling to stay listening to Mother's voice.

'Do you understand?' she pressed, as the Bentley came to a halt behind the hearse at the Hogarth roundabout.

Smudge nodded distractedly to show she had heard. Against the barrage from the radio, on which a woman was now reporting on a spike in class sizes, and the whispers and snickering inside her own head ('Elasticated knickers . . . Loose in the crotch . . . Come here and give these melons a squeeze . . .'), she was struggling to hold on to the thread of what she was supposed to understand.

'The truth is, I did know,' continued Mother, looking in the compact mirror once more so that she seemed to be talking to her reflection, performing herself to herself. 'I did know about the swap. There. I knew you had become Ellie and she had changed to Helen. Maybe not instantly, but soon. I started to suspect not long after Horace moved in and pretty soon it was obvious. Your little mannerisms. The shape of your faces. You forget how well I know you. You forget I was the one who washed and fed and kept you from the very first. Of course I know who you are.'

Smudge stared at the back of the driver's head with its neat line of greying hair. The voices in her mind fell silent. Even the radio seemed to inch its volume down a notch. But still the words wouldn't compute. She turned and looked at Mother, open-mouthed. A moment passed. Then the lights changed on the roundabout and they pulled forward into the traffic, the flowers in the hearse ahead shivering.

'You're saying you knew about the swap?' she said slowly.

'I knew,' said Mother, closing the compact

with a smug click.

('You are the Queen of Sheba and I claim my five pounds.')

Smudge screwed up her face and looked again, but the world was still there just as she had last seen it. Outrage began to beat a distant drum.

'If you knew about it, then why didn't you say anything?' she said. 'Why didn't you make it stop?'

Mother blinked. 'Because I . . . by the time I was certain, it was too late. There was no way to correct it without ruining everything. Ellie would have acted up — she was always far more of a prima donna than you were about things like that — and Horace would have found out and I . . . couldn't have that.'

Mother looked across and out of Smudge's window as they turned off the main road into a tree-lined residential street. Close up, her eyes seemed cold and unreadable as a lizard's.

'So you sacrificed me for the sake of keeping up appearances?' said Smudge, her voice rising. 'Because you didn't want to admit you were wrong?'

'Shhh,' said Mother, with a glance at the driver. 'Keep your voice down. It wasn't like that.' She swallowed and looked up at the beige-upholstered ceiling of the car. 'Look, you don't know what it was like. Things had been awful for so long. Since your father's death — even before. He wasn't an easy man, you know. Highs and lows, madcap schemes, always running after the next thing, then long black spells. You don't know what it's like dealing with someone who has that kind of . . . condition.'

'Don't I?' said Smudge quietly. ('How d'you like them onions?')

But Mother wasn't listening. 'What you said earlier, in the church . . . about me struggling,' she told the ceiling. 'Well, it was true. I'm not proud of it. But, yes, I was . . . unhappy for a while and I suppose I let things slip.' She fumbled suddenly at the clasp of her bag and snatched out a hand-kerchief with which she dabbed at the corners of her eyes with an odd, furtive little gesture. Her hands — strangely naked without the gloves — still sported the hallmark red nails Smudge remembered from the early Akela days. Only now their skin was almost translucent, revealing the veins and tendons underneath, exposing her workings to the world. The thought struck her: Mother was getting old.

'Then Horace came along and he was so kind and uncomplicated, so steady,' Mother was saying. 'And I started to see another way. I saw someone who'd look after things for a change and I wanted that. I wanted to give it a chance. Is that so very wrong?'

She gave a sniff and looked at Smudge as the radio blurted out a jingle for cheaper car insurance and the Bentley followed the hearse in between a pair of redbrick pillars. Smudge sat still.

'So, you see, how could I possibly take the risk of Horace finding out that I'd confused my own children?' she continued. 'What sort of a mother would that make me? How could he be expected to stay around after that?' She folded the handkerchief and tucked it back into her bag. 'So, yes. Perhaps it was selfish, perhaps it was wrong, but at the time I couldn't bring myself to do otherwise. I would have done anything to snatch at that chance of happiness. I just wanted things to be simple for a while, after everything. And the truth is, I would do the same again. Yes, I would.'

Mother folded her arms and regarded Smudge, thrusting her chin forward as though defying her to disapprove. The pose had the opposite effect, however. In the dappled light from the trees shading the crematorium drive, Mother looked oddly frail and vulnerable, a player pitted against loaded dice. The helplessness Smudge had glimpsed in her in the church was back. It was sobering to think that underneath all the severity — the rigidly pressed jacket, the lipstick applied just so — there might be another little girl trapped by other people's choices.

('Oh, spare me the violins,' scoffed a voice.)

Moved by a wave of pity, Smudge reached out to put her hand on Mother's shoulder. Mother bowed her head and tolerated the touch for a moment. Then she looked up, flinching Smudge's hand away.

'Anyway, I never understood what all the fuss was about,' she said briskly as the car pulled to a halt outside the chapel.

Smudge frowned. 'How do you mean?'

'You carrying on the way you did for so long,' said Mother, getting her gloves out of her bag and sliding them back on. 'It was hardly a drastic change, after all. You were still living the same life. You were still in the same family. I expected you'd forget it happened soon enough.'

The radio fell silent as the driver switched the engine off and opened his door. The sounds of birdsong and the distant hum of the main road filtered into the car.

'Did you really believe that?' said Smudge.

'Of course,' said Mother, snapping her bag shut. 'After all, it wasn't as though changing your name was really going to alter who you were underneath. You would still have been you, and Helen — Ellie — would still have been Ellie, no matter what we called you. No amount of swapping back and forth was going to change that. Really, I couldn't see it would make all that much difference in the long run, which of you was which.'

Smudge gaped at the woman she had put out a hand to comfort only a moment before. Only now did she see that she could not reach her. 'Oh Mother,' she said quietly. 'You never knew us at all.'

Mother looked back. Her gaze wavered for a second. Then one of the undertakers came forward to open her door and Mother stepped out of the car, leaving Smudge staring at empty space.

When she got out a moment later, she saw Horace, Richard and Nick emerging from the car behind. Mother was standing talking to the priest, inclining her head and wearing a pinched smile. She looked like a stranger standing there — they all did — and Smudge knew then, coldly, that that was what they would become. Already a door was swinging closed in her mind, shutting all this, finally, in the past.

She glanced one last time at Hellie's coffin. The flowers were still now, serene. 'Goodbye, Hellie,' she whispered.

Turning, she set off walking away, up the drive, between the trees.

Behind her came the clatter of footsteps.

'Are you going then?' said Heloise, hurtling round to block her path.

'Yes,' said Smudge. 'I think it's time.'

Heloise nodded solemnly. 'The wind's changed, hasn't it?' she said. 'Like in *Mary Poppins.*'

'Something like that,' said Smudge.

She regarded the little girl and something occurred to her. 'Listen, Heloise. There's a secret your mummy told me. Up in your attic there's supposed to be a painting by Mummy's daddy.'

'Peeps?'

'No, not Peeps. Another daddy before Peeps. It's a picture of fireworks. You can't tell anyone about it just yet, but maybe one day, when things are happier, you could see if you can find it and get your daddy to take it out and put it somewhere you can see it. Do you think you'll remember that?'

Heloise nodded again. 'Yes, I will.'

A cassocked figure approached.

'Are you staying for the committal?' asked the chaplain, offering a smile.

'No,' said Smudge. 'I think I'd better not.'

He gave his head a prayerful tilt. 'I quite understand,' he said. 'I'm sure Mrs Sallis appreciated you accompanying her in the car. A terrible thing to lose a child.'

('Pompous arse.')

'Yes,' said Smudge. She looked back at the chapel. Horace was standing next to Margaret now, his pudgy fingers on her shoulder. Nick and Richard were hovering by the hearse. Later, they would attend the reception at the chic hotel in town, accepting people's condolences with rueful smiles, behaving appropriately. She was glad she would not be there to see it.

'Goodbye, Heloise,' she said to the little girl who was standing a little way off now, sucking her fingers thoughtfully. 'Don't forget.'

'I won't,' mumbled Heloise, waggling her free hand. ' 'Bye.'

Smudge turned and went on up the drive. The voices rushed in to set up a triumphal roar inside her head. ('Good riddance!' 'Simon and Garfunkel!' 'See you next Tuesday!' 'Darling, you were marvellous!' 'As God is my witness, I'm never going to be hungry again!') This time she did not try to block them out.

She walked to the corner. The R68 bus

was just passing and it was starting to rain. She put a hand in her pocket to feel for an umbrella and pulled out a slip of paper: Anton's cheque. Creased and wrinkled now, but still good, the name space blank. A song started to play softly through the speakers of her brain. She set off up the road.

66

It's mid-morning by the time you leave for the office the following Monday. After the freedom of Amsterdam, it comes as a shock to have to fit back into the old routine. Besides, neither of you is eager to get there. You're both nervy and fragile after the weekend — a Sunday spent tiptoeing round each other, hours of talking about Hellie, two nights lying sleepless side by side in Gareth's bed. When you couldn't take it any more, you got up and went to the living room, flicking the TV on with the sound turned low. You switched it off soon after the screen showed a picture of Hellie's face and the presenter began to recount how the new host of *Coffee Break* had had an emotional outburst during a phone-in about domestic violence and revealed that her identical twin sister had tried to kill her when they were teenagers. The general consensus seemed to be that the twin sister

582

must have been a monster. In the darkened room after the screen went black, the old voice started to whisper once more that you're broken beyond repair, that you will never be any good.

To cap it all, the morning sickness that gave you a wide berth in Amsterdam has hit with a vengeance. You spent long stretches of Sunday hunched over the toilet bowl in Gareth's bathroom, retching until your stomach burned.

He gives you an apologetic smile when you emerge for the third time this morning.

'A-What's it like being pregnant?' he says, handing you a cup of tea, the sight of which makes you gag. 'Is it horrible all the time?'

'Nah,' you say, gripping the kitchen door-frame to keep you from swaying. 'It's mostly fine. I think I'm lucky.'

But the truth is the last forty-eight hours haven't been fine. Along with the nausea, you've found yourself blowing hot and cold. Waves of heat travel up and down your body, bringing shivers in their wake, and you feel faint, febrile. You know it's just the emotional strain you're under, the worry that everything might be about to shatter, that Gareth could, at any moment, tell you to go. Still, you can't help thinking that the pregnancy is making this much harder on you than it is on him. You never used to suffer your emotions so physically as this.

You've agreed to keep your relationship secret for now, so when you get to the studio, you hang around outside for a few minutes and let Gareth go in first so no one gets suspicious that you've arrived together. While you wait, you catch sight of yourself in the window of a police car parked in the street: your hair is knotted, your eyes are rimmed with red and ringed with dark circles. God, it's a wonder Gareth doesn't dump you right now, you're so gross.

When you go in, everyone turns to look. You don't see Gareth, but there are two new members of staff: a young, eager-looking guy with a ponytail and a girl with feathery hair. They all have the same expression on their faces — fear mixed with contempt, as though you're a dangerous dog that has just pissed on the rug. You wonder which news reports they've seen.

For the sake of having somewhere to go, you walk over to Anton's office. You open the door and go in without knocking — you can't stand to wait out there for a second more than you have to, feeling the weight of their stares.

Anton is in there with two policemen and Gareth stands awkwardly against the far wall, a hectic flush on his cheeks. They turn to look at you.

'Ah, Trudy,' says Anton. 'We were hoping you might arrive. These gentlemen are investigating a passport fraud network and wanted to ask you a few questions.'

You try to meet Gareth's eyes, but he looks away. And in that instant, you know: it's no good. This has destroyed it. Whatever existed between you is dead.

After that, you don't think. You turn and run. Before you know it, you're out on the street, feet pounding the pavement, doorways and lamp posts flashing by. Behind you, you hear voices, but you don't look back, you just keep going: one turning, then the next, then the next. Your lungs burn and your head swims but you keep on, running for freedom, running for sanity, running to escape the trap of your former life. They won't catch you this time. They won't drag you back into what you were.

The narrow streets give way to wide thoroughfares and squares. You're in the centre of town, barging past shoppers and tourists, slamming past street signs and litter bins. You hear shouts of indignation and gasps but you don't stop. That is nothing. This is nothing compared to what you have to escape. You have made yourself a future and you will not give it up now. It will not be taken from you. They can all go to hell. They can all fuck themselves. But they will not get you. Hellie will not get you. You are making your own story now. You are living your own life. Even without Gareth, even without work, you have something to live for. You have something to protect.

You don't know how long you run for, but finally your strength gives out and you lean over a bin, retching. You look up fearfully but no one is following you. There are no men in dark blue uniforms hot on your heels, no *Carry On* cries of: 'Stop! Thief!' You are alone in a side street, flanked by tall glass buildings that seem to sway in and out with each gasp of air you take. Stars crackle in your field of view. As they fade, you look about you and start to think again. A plan. You need a plan. Somewhere you can go to gather yourself together and work out what's next. A safe place. A lightbulb flicks on in your brain. Of course: Beryl's. You'll go there.

You walk to the end of the street and sigh with relief as you make out the grand terra-cotta facade of the old fire station a few blocks up. You know where you are. You turn left. It won't take more than fifteen minutes to get to Beryl's. And once you're there she'll sit you down at the kitchen table and you can tell her all about it. And even though you'll be frightened and in pain and still feeling sick — and even though you know that what happened with Gareth has been bundled into a vault of suffering that will very soon burst open — at least you won't be on your own. Beryl will listen in that calm way of hers as you tell her all about Gareth and the pregnancy and what happened with Hellie and the TV show —

You stop abruptly and a woman carrying shopping bangs into your back.

'Careful!' she says. She narrows her eyes when you turn round. 'Hey, aren't you . . . ?'

'Fuck off!' you say, and stride viciously away. Because of course you've realised you can't go to Beryl's. You can never go back there and sit at the table and drink tea. Settled in front of her TV night after night, Beryl will have seen the news and heard the gossip. She'll know Trudy — or Elisa as she thought you were — wasn't real. She'll see you for the would-be murderer everyone thinks you are and the thought of her face hardening against you is more than you can take. You can never go back there.

Somewhere else then, quickly, because you are starting to reel. If you don't sit down in a minute, you're afraid you might

587

faint. You turn a corner and the glass entrance of the Barnacle rears up in front of you, revealing afternoon shoppers milling about its atrium inside. Yes, of course: the cafe where you used to sit and draw. You'll go up and get something to drink — you've still got money, you've still got your bank card, assuming the bastards haven't stopped your account. You'll go to the cafe and maybe up there, in that old, familiar space where inspiration has struck you so often in the past, looking down on the atrium, something will occur to you. Perhaps then you'll know what to do next.

You hurry through the clear doors. You pause for a second to look about you for the escalator, ducking the stares of passers by, but at that moment a pain rips through you, tearing your belly apart. You double over and feel moisture flooding out of you and seeping down your legs. The agony continues as people cluster round you, clucking like hens. Voices call in your ear but you don't listen. There is only the shredding inside you, grinding up the future, emptying you out, pouring all the possibilities away on to the Barnacle's fake marble floor until all your lines are blurred, until you are voided: a shell, a carcass, a mess. Until you are nothing but a smudge.

67

The estate agent let her in and stood whistling to himself, his shiny suit glinting in the
light coming from the cobwebbed window.
She looked around. It was exactly as she'd
hoped: a large industrial space with bare
brick walls, an old carpenter's workshop.
You could still see the wood shavings on the
floor. There was a sink in the main room
and a basic bathroom set into one corner.
The whole place needed a clean and some
furniture but she could see how it would
work. She could see where she would set up
the easel, next to the window looking down
on to the cobbled street.

'It's not pretty,' said the agent. 'But at
least you get a lot of space. Certainly more
than anything you'd find north of the river.
And there's a big Sainsbury's round the
corner, which you can't argue with.'

'It's perfect,' she said. 'I'll take it.'

The agent stared at her.

'What? Now this minute?' he said.

'Now this minute,' she said. 'Six months, a year. Whatever you can give me. If you've got a contract, I'll sign it right away.'

'Well, fuck me,' he said. 'That's the quickest one ever. You haven't even seen the bit up on the roof yet. Just wait here and I'll go out to the car and call the office so they can get the paperwork together.'

He scurried to the head of the staircase.

'You are sure?' he said, turning back.

She nodded.

'Right you are.'

She stayed and walked around the space, running her fingers over the rough brickwork. A cracked mirror hung on a nail by the sink, and when she saw her face in it, she knew what her first painting in the studio would be. The old tingle ran through her, the sense of where to start. ('Ripe for the picking,' enthused a voice.) She chuckled in agreement.

A moment or so later, she headed down the staircase and out of the street door. The agent was sitting in his car, talking excitedly into his phone. He gave her a series of complicated eye-rollings and winks through the window. Across the street, a van had pulled up and a man and a woman were unloading parts of what looked like a giant papier-mâché parrot from the back.

One of them caught her eye.

'Here to see the place, are you?' he said.

'Moving in, I think.'

The man set down the head of the bird, which regarded her with a solemn marble eye, and walked towards her, holding out his hand.

'Amos,' he said. 'And that's my partner Dale.'

'Hi,' she said, shaking his hand.

'Oh, and the bird's Roger. He's appearing in a show down in Brighton next weekend.'

She laughed. 'I see.'

Amos jammed his hands into his pockets.

'So are you an artist too?'

'Sort of.' She shrugged. 'I mean, yeah.'

Amos smiled, revealing wonky teeth.

'I thought so,' he said. 'Good to see another one moving in. Dale and I were the first in this street, but they've been trickling in over the last couple of years. We want to make it another Patterson's Walk, like they've got up in Islington, before prices in the area go through the roof.'

She nodded. 'Oh, right.'

'Don't you know Patterson's Walk?' said Amos. 'Oh, we'll have to take you next time they have an open house weekend. We've got a couple of friends with studios there.'

'Great,' she said. 'I'd like that.'

'Amos!' called Dale, staggering under the weight of a large feathered wing.

'Better go,' said Amos, pulling a face. 'Nice to meet you — er . . .'

'Ellie,' she said. 'Ellie Sallis.'

'Nice to meet you, Ellie,' he said, and bounded back across the street.

She watched them manoeuvre the wing into their studio. She put a hand on the doorframe of the carpenter's workshop, feeling the splinters catch on her skin. A cold breeze was blowing. Overhead, a plane drew a smile in the sky. Yes, she thought, nice to meet you at last.

ACKNOWLEDGEMENTS

This book only has my name on the cover, but it is the product of many people's energy and vision. My wonderful agent, Caroline Hardman, believed in this project from the start and put an enormous amount of work into finding the right home for it with Bloomsbury. I am also very grateful to her partner, Jo Swainson, and co-agents and colleagues at the Marsh Agency and dotted around the globe for their support.

My editors, Helen Garnons-Williams, Lea Beresford and Alexa von Hirschberg, have been excellent champions for the novel, and sources of great encouragement and insight. In particular, *Beside Myself* would not be the book it is today without Helen's care and expertise. And I have been blown away by the enthusiasm, industry and creativity of Bloomsbury's other editorial and production staff, and its marketing and design teams around the world.

I owe much gratitude to the readers of the early drafts — Steve, Emily, Ol and Diane — each of whom provided valuable input. The novel would be much poorer without you.

Then there are the people who helped with research. My mum and dad, Pat and Richard, were great sources of advice on a number of medical points. Similarly, numerous friends and acquaintances responded generously to my often rather random questions about anything from police procedure and the benefits system to the experience of living with bipolar disorder. To have such a network of experts on hand was a huge help. Any errors are my own.

As ever, I am grateful to my friends and family for indulging my desire to spend my time making things up long before Helen and Ellie were a kilobyte on my laptop's hard drive. And to Steve, who has been there through it all and has just brought me a cup of tea as I sit here writing this, thank you.

ABOUT THE AUTHOR

Ann Morgan is a freelance writer and editor based in London. Ann's writing has appeared in the *Guardian,* the *Independent,* the *Financial Times,* the *Australian* and the *New Internationalist,* and she was a finalist in the *Guardian*'s International Development Journalism Competition 2010. She has also sub-edited for publications including *Tatler* and *Vanity Fair.* Following the success of her project to read a book from every country in 2012, Ann continues to blog about international literature at ayearofreadingtheworld.com. Her first book, *Reading the World: Confessions of a Literary Explorer,* was published to great critical acclaim in 2015. *Beside Myself* is her first novel.